DAMNATION: QUEST FOR GLORY PART 1

QUINCY HARKER, DEMON HUNTER YEAR 3

JOHN G. HARTNESS

WHAT CAME BEFORE

In *The Cambion Cycle,* Quincy Harker and The Shadow Council defeated the demon Barachiel and saved the Earth from certain destruction. In the battle, Harker's guardian angel, Glory, had her wings severed by the demon's sword. Only God Himself can grant an angel's wings, and He's been missing in action since shortly after the Great Flood.

Now Harker and the Shadow Council must locate the eight Archangels to call the Almighty back to His throne and restore Glory's wings.

I

CALLING ALL ANGELS

Jo shook her head to clear the cobwebs, spat a mouthful of blood onto the stained canvas, and made a "come at me" gesture to her opponent.

The other woman obliged, taking two quick steps forward and throwing a low kick in a feint before stepping into a roundhouse designed to catch Jo on the side of the head and end the bout in decisive fashion. And it would have done exactly that, if it had connected.

But there was no head there to kick because Jo dropped to her hands and swept her opponent's legs out from under her. The blonde woman went down flat on her back, and Jo was on her in a flash. Less than ten seconds later, she had her opponent trapped in a fully extended arm bar, and she felt the slap of a glove on her shin as the other woman tapped out.

Jo rolled to her feet, both hands raised in triumph. She took a quick victory lap around the ring—really an eight-foot high cage made of chain link and steel posts wrapped in thick padding. The referee motioned both women to the center of the ring and raised Jo's fist over his head, announcing her victory to the crowd.

Jo turned to her opponent and held out her hand. The other woman leaned in, they shook, and then leaned in for a brief hug.

"I almost had you," the woman said.

"Horseshoes and hand grenades, like my grandma always said," Jo replied. They both laughed, any animosity left lying on the ring with more than one new bloodstain. Jo stepped out of the cage first, high-fiving the crowd on the way back to her locker room with her corner man.

The athletic black woman stripped off her gloves as soon as she was through the door, tossing them into the general vicinity of a basket on the floor. "Holy crap, she kicked like a mule!" Jo said as she sat on a bench and rubbed her inner thigh. "My quads are all kinds of knotted up."

"She landed some pretty good ones," Jake, her corner man, said. Jake picked up her gloves and the shoes she kicked off and shoved them in a big duffel. "You gonna shower before you leave?"

"God yes," Jo said. "I don't want to bleed all over the car on the way home. You keep Shelton the heck out of here while I get the funk washed off?"

"Yeah, no problem. He'll probably run right over to Marla's locker room anyway, to offer her a shoulder to cry on."

"Or whatever," Jo said, her mouth twisting into a grimace at the thought of the sleazy promoter going after the younger woman while she was down from losing the bout. "You wanna stick your head in over there, see if she wants to go get some breakfast?"

"Yeah, I can do that. IHOP or Waffle House?"

Jo laughed. "Let's go big-time tonight. We'll take the winner's purse and spring for Denny's."

Jake chuckled as he made for the door. "I'll be back in a sec. Try not to break anybody for five minutes."

"Okay, but no promises if you run late." Jo leaned back on the bench, her arms folded over her face. She replayed the bout in her mind, going over all three rounds looking for things she could have done better, things she missed, or places she could have ended the match sooner. This one almost went to time, and that put the fight in the hands of the judges. Jo was pretty sure she'd outpunched her opponent, but she'd rather have control of the decision herself.

She opened her eyes and stared up at the bare fluorescent tubes hanging on thin chain from the water-stained ceiling. This wasn't the worst place she'd ever thrown a punch, but fighting the underground scene wasn't anything like the clean, brightly lit gyms she trained in most of the time.

This whole world was new to her—fighting for money in unsanctioned bouts, advertised through word of mouth, ducking the cops and anything that even looked like an athletic commission. But the money was pretty good, which was more than she could say for any other assignment she'd ever had for the Shadow Council. And so far, everyone she'd fought had been one hundred percent human, another improvement over her last scrap, which featured at least three different types of demon trying to open the Gates of Hell into downtown Atlanta.

The door to her dressing room opened after just a couple minutes, and Jo sat up. Jake shouldn't have been back so quickly, but there he was. And he wasn't alone. Right behind him was a fuming Marla Jonas, a scowl on her face and fire in her eyes.

Marla stalked over to her and stood right in front of Jo. "What?" she demanded.

"What do you mean, what?" Jo asked, working to keep her tone mild. She didn't like strangers in her personal space, and this woman was definitely there.

"Your guy said you needed to talk to me. Said it was urgent. Shel was about to tell me about the big fight he's putting me in next month."

Jo looked past the angry fighter at Jake, who shrugged. "Sorry, Jo. It's all I could think of."

Jo sighed, then stood up. She started toward the shower. "Go get her stuff, Jake. We'll be in the shower. The dressing room key is in the side pocket of my bag. Keep Shelton *out* of here when you come back." Jake nodded, then turned to go.

"Wait a minute, what the fuck is going on here? I'm not showering with you. I'm not into that. I mean, it's cool if you are, whatever, but it's not my thing."

"Get over here," Jo said. "I'm not into you, either. But Shelton obviously is, and the next thing he was going to say was how he *wants* to put you in that big fight, but since you lost tonight, he couldn't really do it, so he'd need some kind of...convincing to give you that kind of opportunity." Jo peeled off her top and shorts and turned on the water, adjusting the knobs to get the water as hot as she could stand it. She stood under the spray, letting the heat relax her sore arms and shoulders, wincing now and then as the water pounded on a particularly tender spot.

"Oh, bullshit," Marla called from outside the shower. "Shelton knows better than to try that shit with me."

"Yeah?" Jo said. "You're that special? So special he wouldn't try the same crap he's tried on every single chick that's thrown a punch in his cage? Dang, girl, you must be really amazing. Oh wait, you're not. 'Cause I just tapped you out. Just like I tapped out the last five women I stepped in the cage with. And Shelton's tried that crap on me three times in the past six weeks. So if you really do think you're so special that little weasel won't try to con you into blowing him for a bigger payday, go on back to your locker room and have a great night. But if you think you're probably just like everybody else scrapping on this circuit, then come grab a shower, and we can all go to Denny's and get something to eat."

Jo squirted a healthy amount of the body wash she liked into her scrunchie and started to lather up. It didn't matter if the other woman joined her for a shower or not. Just taking her out of Shelton's line of sight for a few minutes meant she was probably fine. He still had four more fights on the card to run and payouts to handle to fighters, security, and referees. That was before he dealt with paying out the guys running the betting on the fights, the payoffs to the cops who patrolled this neighborhood, and the janitor and principal of the high school where they were holding their unlicensed mixed martial arts event.

The sound of water turning on from a nearby station was Jo's only notice that Marla had entered the shower. "Why do you give a shit?"

It was always either a thank you or that same question. Which one

Jo got told her a lot about the woman asking. The broken ones asked why she cared. They didn't understand that some people just wanted to do good in the world, just wanted to make it a little bit better place to live.

"Because we've got to look out for each other," she said.

"All us fighters?"

"All us *people*," Jo corrected. "We stopped being fighters the second the ref raised one of our hands. Now we're just people again. And people gotta look out for people. It's what keeps us from being...I don't know what."

"What world you live in, girl?" Marla asked. "Ain't nobody gonna look out for you but you."

"I've got Jake," Jo said. "And now, I've got you."

"Me? Why you think I'm gonna look out for you?"

"Because you owe me one," Jo said with a grin. She reached over and turned off the water. "Help yourself to the body wash, but I didn't bring any shampoo with me." She pointed to the tight cornrows running the length of her scalp with a smile. Jo wrapped one towel around her head and another around her body, then walked out into the locker room.

Jake stood there, his back to the shower and arms folded across his chest. Another duffel sat on the bench beside Jo's, with Marla's blue silk ring robe lying across it. "I got all her stuff, but Shelly says you both gotta go see him for payout. Said he couldn't give it to anybody but the fighter."

Jo read from the set of his shoulders that there was more to it. She pulled on a pair of fresh panties and a sports bra, then slipped into a pair of loose sweatpants. "He said he wouldn't give my money to a Mexican, didn't he?"

"He said the only way I was getting any cash out of him was to do his lawn." Jake shook his head. "That fucking piece of trash is a disgrace to illegal fights. He should be running cock fights in the backwoods of Alabama, not the biggest underground fight club in Arizona."

"He shouldn't be running anything, but you get more with money than with honor these days," Jo said.

"Hey, did your corner man get back with my bag?" Marla called from the shower.

"Yeah, what do you need?" Jo called back.

"Can you bring me my shampoo?"

"No problem." Jo grabbed a bottle of Head & Shoulders from the bag and carried it into the shower. "Holy crap, girl, did I do that?" she said, pointing to a softball-sized bruise on Marla's upper ribcage.

"Oh, that...um, no, that wasn't you. That was from...sparring a couple days ago."

Jo looked in her eyes, but the other woman wouldn't meet her gaze. She held out the shampoo bottle, then let out a sigh. "I've got some Tiger Balm in my bag. I'll leave it out for you. You should maybe find a new sparring partner. Looks like that one doesn't know how to pull her punches."

Jo walked out of the shower and finished dressing. She pulled out her phone and sent a text to a contact that only said "Sparkles." "Need you to find out everything there is about a fighter named Marla Jonas."

"Problem?" the reply came instantly.

"Not for me. She's got a couple bruises that don't look like they came from fighting legit opponents."

"You're not fighting legitimately," Sparkles replied.

"Yeah, but this looks like somebody hit her in the ribs with a base-ball bat."

"Shit. You think husband?"

"Maybe boyfriend. Either way, I think he needs to be persuaded not to do it again."

"I'll get back to you in a flash. Don't do anything stupid until I find out the details."

"Would I ever do anything stupid?" Jo typed back.

"Between you, Harker, and Gabby, if I still had a body, you'd give me a stroke," Sparkles replied.

Jo pulled on a tattered Randy Savage t-shirt and sat down to slip into socks and shoes. "I think we might have a situation," she whispered to Jake's back.

"Hammer time?" he asked.

"You know I hate it when you say that."

"Why do you think I do it?" His shoulders shook with quiet laughter. "What's the problem?"

"I think somebody's hitting Marla outside of the ring."

"You gonna stop it?" It was only nominally a question.

"I can't just let it go," she said.

"I guess you can't, can you?"

"Never have, never will."

Their muted conversation was cut short when Marla stepped out of the shower. "Wow, he actually keeps his back turned while you dress?" She gestured at Jake.

"I told him I'm not that modest, but he insists."

"I've got three daughters, girl. I've seen everything you got, but everybody deserves the respect to not have people staring at them while they're naked," Jake said, his face locked straight ahead.

"Well, thank you, Jake. I appreciate it," Marla said. She quickly slipped into a pair of shorts and a sweatshirt, then slipped some sneakers on and hefted her bag to her shoulder.

"Come on, then. Let's go get paid and head over to someplace that will fill us full of bacon grease and runny eggs," Jo said, motioning for the other two to follow as she headed out the door to argue with Shelton about her cut of the betting and get some much-needed dinner.

2

The sun was just peeking over the horizon when Jo walked through the door of her three-bedroom house. She dropped her duffel bag on the sofa and walked into the kitchen, giving a rueful smile to the white-haired woman leaning on the stove with a scowl on her face. Cassandra Harrison was a slender woman in her seventies, but she still stood ramrod straight, the steel in her spine no different from the spikes Jo's legendary great-grandfather had driven into the railroad ties so many years before.

"Good morning, Mama," Jo said, reaching into the refrigerator for a carton of orange juice. She didn't bother with a glass, just turned the carton up, and took a long swig. She put the OJ back in the fridge and closed the door.

"You want to yell at me now or wait until I've had some sleep?" she asked her mother.

"I don't want to yell at you at all, baby, but you been out all night. A mother worries, you know."

"I know, Mama. I know." Jo pulled out a battered ladder-back wooden chair and sat down at the table in what most houses would call a breakfast nook. At the Harrison household, they just called it the kitchen table. It was the centerpiece of the house, no matter how far from the middle of the structure it sat. The family ate as many meals together around that wooden oval as possible, but lately Jo's work with the Shadow Council had kept her away from too many dinners and break-fasts, and her freelance editing had her eating far too many lunches at her desk while answering emails or proofreading manuscripts.

"I'm sorry I was out all night. It was around three when I got done at the gym, and then I wanted to get a bite to eat with the girl I fought tonight," Jo said, leaning her head back and working it side to side to stretch out the knots building in her muscles. Another hot shower might be in order before she finally saw her bed.

"You beat this girl up, then you went out to dinner with her? I don't understand that, Joanna. I really don't."

"It wasn't anything personal, Mama. We didn't fight because we hate each other; we fought for money. Oh, by the way, here, put this in the kitty." She reached into the pocket of her hoodie and tossed a roll of bills to her mother. Shelton was a pervert and a shady fight promoter, but he kept his word about payout. Jo got a guaranteed two hundred per fight, five hundred if she won, plus twenty percent of the house cut of any bets on her fights, and five percent of the door. Tonight that all added up to a little under a thousand dollars. Not bad for a night that she didn't even bleed. Much.

"I don't need your money, child. You my daughter, I'm gonna take care of you," her mother said. But Jo noticed that the money disap-peared into a pocket on the front of the flowered apron she wore over her clothes.

"I know, Mama, but I can pull my own weight around here. I'm not living on the streets."

"And you never will be, as long as I've got anything to say about it," Cassandra replied.

Jo let it pass. No point in arguing with her this late. Or early, depending on whether or not you'd slept yet. "How was Ginny?" Jo asked.

"Oh, she's fine," Cassandra said. "Missed having her mama around this past couple months. When you gonna be done with all this nonsense, anyhow?"

"I don't know," Jo said. "I've been winning, and that means I get to fight more, but I still haven't been there late enough in the show to meet the man I'm there to find."

"What's this man done, anyhow, that you got to stay up all night getting your face messed up to find him? Is he a bad man? Is this dangerous, baby?"

"Well, I am working in an illegal club fighting inside a steel cage where there are no rules except to make your opponent tap out or knock them unconscious. But other than that, I don't think it's that dangerous." After her last trip to Atlanta with Quincy Harker and the rest of the Shadow Council, Jo's bar for "dangerous" was significantly higher than it used to be. After all, once you defuse a bomb under a basketball arena and fight off a demonic invasion, getting decked in a fight just isn't quite as scary anymore.

"You don't have to be smart, Joanna. I worry is all." Her mother's voice was quiet, and Jo knew she'd hurt the other woman's feelings.

"I know, Mama. I'm sorry. I like that you worry about me." She stood up and hugged her mother, giving the shorter woman a kiss on the top of her head. "Now I'm going to grab a quick shower and get some sleep. I've got a self-help book to work on today before I go back tonight." Jo made her living most weeks as a freelance copy editor, and fighting in a cage at night meant that her clients weren't getting the attention they deserved. She had to spend at least a little time on her "day job" or she wouldn't have any clients left to ignore.

"You gonna stay up to kiss Ginny goodbye?" Her mother didn't put anything extra into her tone: the recrimination was all there without any help.

Jo nodded as she turned to walk to the bathroom. "I'll stay up 'til she gets on the bus, then I'm crashing for a few hours." She pulled her hoodie over her head as she walked down the hall to the bathroom. She opened the door to the "master" bedroom, more a name than anything designating extra size in the compact little home. She stripped and slipped on a robe before padding back down two doors to the bathroom.

She turned the water on until steam poured from the shower, then stepped under the near-scalding spray. The heat immediately started to soak into her abused shoulders and arms, making her eyelids heavy. She snapped awake as the door to the bathroom opened, but she relaxed as she made out the form of her ten-year-old daughter Ginny through the gauzy shower curtain.

"Morning, Mama," the little girl said as she sat on the toilet.

"Good morning, Ginny-girl." Jo forced her voice into a chipper, high-pitched thing that Shelton and the girls at the gym would never recognize.

"Did you win?" Ginny asked, flushing the toilet.

"Yes, I did," Jo said, raising her arms over her head and letting the water beat down along her ribcage. She felt the knots slowly ease on her sides, soothing the tense muscles that Marla had pounded earlier.

"Did you hurt the other lady?"

"Not very much, sweetie. I put her in an arm bar and she tapped out. She was a smart lady, and she knew she was beat." Jo saw no point in hiding what she did from her daughter. It was a lot easier to explain to her that she was doing MMA at night than trying to make up some lie about why she came home with split lips and bruises all the time. Plus, doing what Ronda Rousey did on TV got Jo some "cool mommy" points, and Ginny was fast approaching the age where those would be in short supply.

"That's good. You shouldn't hurt people," Ginny said with the conviction of a child who knows everything in the world is black and white.

Jo smiled at her daughter's voice. "That's right, sweetie. You shouldn't hurt people. Now you go get ready for school and let Mommy get some clothes on."

"Okay," Ginny said. Jo watched through the curtain as the door opened, then closed after the girl. She pulled the shower curtain aside and looked at herself in the mirror. *Looking a little rough, Joanna. Gotta stop pulling these all-nighters for no pay. Might be time to hit up Luke about*

Council members drawing a salary. Or at least get a group insurance plan. God knows I go through enough painkillers working for those fools.

She got out of the shower and toweled off, slipping into clean underwear and sweatpants with a tattered Arizona Cardinals t-shirt. She walked barefoot down the hall to the table, then took a seat next to Ginny.

"What are you doing in school this week, honey?" Jo asked.

"Fractions in math, and in drama we're doing a scene from *Alice in Wonderland*. I'm the Mad Hatter." Ginny grinned up at her mother, a little dribble of milk running down her chin. "Ms. Holman says I'm the maddest hatter she's ever seen."

"I bet you are, baby. I bet you are," Jo said.

"Will you be home tonight, Mommy? I can show you my part." The girl's enthusiasm jabbed a dagger into Jo's gut and twisted.

"I can't, sweetie. I have to work again."

Disappointment flashed across the girl's face, but it fell away as Cassandra sat down at the table with half a grapefruit and two pieces of toast on a plate. "I'll be here, honey-bear. We can make a video on my phone and your mama can see it when she gets home."

Jo shot her mother a grateful look, then stood at the sound of a car pulling up outside. "There's Katie's mom," she said to Ginny. "Get your backpack and lunch."

The girl did as she was told, then kissed her mother and grandmother, and dashed out into the sunny morning. Jo locked the door behind her, then sat down at the table across from her mother.

"Thank you for that," Jo said.

"I know what you're doing is important, honey..."

"I know, but she's important, too. It's just...what I'm doing, with the Council? It could literally change the world. The stuff we did in Atlanta saved lives, maybe everybody's lives. It's...surreal, you know?"

"Oh honey, I know. Your daddy wasn't even in the Council when we got married. That damn Luke came to him just a few weeks after our first anniversary. If I'd known who he was, I never would have invited that fool into my home." Cassandra took a sip of her coffee, then smiled at Jo. "You know that ain't true, neither. Your daddy never would tell me any of the stuff he got up to with Luke and those people, but sometimes he would come home all battered and beaten, but smiling. He had that same smile you got on your face right now, thinking about what y'all did in Atlanta. I knew that he was helping people, just like you are. And I know that my way of helping those people is to let you go do what you do."

The women sat at the table for another few minutes, then Jo stood up. "I've got to go get some sleep, Mama. Will you make sure I'm awake by two? If I get up then, I'll have time to get some work done before I have to go to the club tonight."

"You fighting two nights in a row?"

"Yeah," Jo said. "I'm moving up the card. Maybe tonight is the night I finally get to meet him."

"I hope so, honey. But you never did explain it to me. What in the world is the Archangel Michael doing beating up people in an illegal fight club in Phoenix?"

"I have no idea, Mama. I don't even know if he knows who he is. But that's why I'm there—to find him, to make him remember his duty, and get him back in Heaven where he belongs."

"And what you gonna do if he don't want to go?" Cassandra asked.

Joanna grinned at her mother, then cracked her knuckles. "Well, Mama. I'm a fighter. If he don't want to do what's got to be done, I reckon I'm gonna have to kick an angel's ass."

3

I *might have spoken too soon about kicking anybody's ass, much less Michael's,* Jo thought as she shook her head to clear the cobwebs. It was the beginning of the third round, and she was pretty sure she was behind on points. Not that things were very scientific in Shelton's club—if the match went to time, he decided who won. And that, more often than not, had as much to do with where the money was laying than with number of punches thrown.

Her opponent was a thick-bodied woman who looked like the poster child for the 1980 Soviet women's shot put team. She had boulders for shoulders and biceps the size of Jo's thighs. And her fists felt like blocks of cement crashing into Jo's upraised forearms.

A kick slammed into Jo's thigh, and she took a step back, anticipating the other woman's next move. She was right, the blonde behemoth shot in, trying for a single-leg takedown, but Jo met her with a stiff left that landed behind her ear and rocked the big woman for the first time in their match. Jo followed up with a flurry of strikes, raining punches to the sides of the other woman's head. She knew a knockout wasn't coming, but if she could create just enough frustration to make to giantess drop her guard, she might have a chance.

In a flash, the opening she was looking for appeared. After a stinging left to the other woman's ear, Jo saw her guard slip for just a fraction of a second. But it was enough. She darted forward and jammed her flat belly up against the woman's shoulder, sliding her right arm around her opponent's head and neck, then cinching the front choke tight before the big woman could block the hold.

I've got you now...oh shit! Jo smacked hard into the cage with her back as the larger woman picked her up and bull-rushed her across the octagon. Her spine met the support beam with a jarring crash, but she kept the choke applied as though her life depended on it. Which, judging by how pissed off the woman struggling in her grip seemed, it just might be.

"Off!" Jo grunted as she was slammed into the cage again, this time on the opposite side of the ring. There might have been slightly less force in this charge than the one before, but if so, Jo couldn't tell.

Jo hung on doggedly as her opponent picked her up again, using her body as a battering ram against the steel. Jo's head snapped back against the beam, and she saw stars. The beam was padded, but there was still steel under there. Jo held on, though, knowing the only way she was winning this fight was by choking out her opponent. The bigger woman straightened up, taking Jo off her feet once again, and charged across the ring. She stumbled before she made it all the way to the other side and fell forward. Jo locked her feet around the other woman's waist, adding pressure to the choke. She squeezed, feeling the veins pop out in her forehead from the effort, then finally felt the welcome tap on her shoulder.

The referee called for the bell, and Jo released the hold. The exhausted women slumped to the ground, Jo rolling to her feet as the referee walked over to check on both combatants.

"You okay?" he asked.

"Yeah," Jo panted. "I'm good."

"What about you?" he asked her opponent.

"I'm okay," the larger woman gasped. Both women scrambled to their feet and stood by the referee awaiting his announcement. He raised Jo's hand in victory, and she turned to her opponent, hand out.

"I'm Jo," she said.

"Gladys," the other woman said, taking her hand. "Good fight." Without another word, she turned and walked out of the cage, leaving Jo to celebrate for a moment before the ref cleared her out. Jake walked her back to the dressing room, slapping her on the shoulder and hugging her the whole way.

They burst into the empty room, smiles plastered on their faces. Jo peeled off her clothes as Jake resolutely faced the wall. "You know you don't have to do that, right?" she said over her shoulder. "I'm a fighter, just like everybody else you work with. You don't have to not look at me."

"You ain't like everybody else I work with, Jo," he corrected. "You're a lady, and I was raised to respect that. Besides, if my Daniella found out I was looking at some beautiful naked woman, she'd choke me out a lot faster than you tapped that Russian chick."

Jo laughed as she headed to the shower. "You didn't think I could beat her, did you?" She fiddled with the water until steam billowed around her.

"No," Jake said. His honesty didn't surprise Jo. It was one of the reasons she had hired him. That and his reputation as one of the best corner men on the scene. It was only a falling out with his last client that left him available when she started fighting three months ago.

"I didn't either. Probably wouldn't have, if she hadn't dropped her guard finally." Three months. A long three months of getting her ass kicked almost every night. Even the fights she won left their marks on her skin, and she wasn't sure what left deeper bruises on her soul: losing, or what she sometimes had to do to win. But she was close, she could feel it. Maybe tonight, maybe tomorrow, but she was going to end up close enough to Michael to put his sword in his hand, and hopefully that would wake the Archangel from his slumber and get him back to Heaven where he belonged.

"I'm sorry, Shel. You can't go in right now. She's taking her shower." Jo heard Jake say from the locker room.

"Jake, baby, you know the deal. It's my club, and I go where I want, when I want." This wasn't the first time Shelton had tried to walk in while Jo or other female fighters were showering or dressing. It was the main reason she liked having Jake around outside of his corner man duties. She didn't mind fighting for Shelton, didn't even mind him getting the lion's cut of the betting take on her work, but letting him see her naked wasn't one of the perks he got out of the deal. Besides, she didn't trust the little sleaze not to hide a tiny video camera in the locker room and broadcast "naked fight girls" on the internet for extra cash.

An enchanted stone in the bottom of her duffel bag took care of that, thanks to Harker and his magical mojo. Any video recording within a ten-yard radius of the stone turned to static.

"I know that's your rule, Shel. And you know my rule: you want to look at naked women, go to the strip club. You want to talk to my fighter, you wait until she's dressed. I'll send her to your office when she's cleaned up."

Jo wished she could see the look on Shelton's face as the implacable Jake stood in front of him, arms crossed and feet planted. Shel wouldn't toss Jake. He was too good a corner man, and too many of his fighters would walk with him. And Jake wouldn't budge on his morals for Shelton, no matter how much the promoter argued, threatened, or cajoled.

Jo turned off the water and dried off, then wrapped a towel around herself and stepped out into the locker room. "You need me, Shel?"

The promoter looked up, hope blossoming on his face, then wilting like a daisy in the July sun when he saw her completely covered by the huge towel she carried in every night. "Yeah, come to my office when you're dressed. I'll settle up with you and talk about Saturday night. You're off tomorrow to rest up. You're headlining Saturday with Mitchell."

Finally. Mitchell Carson was the name Michael fought under, and apparently lived under these days. Fighting right before him on Saturday would put them in close contact, and hopefully give her a chance to get the Archangel's sword back to its owner and get her back to her normal life where nobody tried to knock her unconscious on a daily basis.

"Sweet," she said, trying to keep the excitement out of her voice.

"I'll come to your office in a few minutes. Just let me throw some clothes on and get my gear together."

"Okay," Shelton said, then turned to go. He stopped at the door. "Good fight tonight. I thought she was going to kick your ass." He walked out into the hall, the metal locker room door slamming behind him.

Jo dropped the towel and started to pull her clothes on. "Yeah. You, me, and everybody else in the world," she said, pulling on her jeans and sitting down to lace up her boots. "You can turn around now, Jake."

He did, then sat next to her. "How bad you hurt?"

"I've got a couple of bruises from last night that didn't get any better for the pounding, and I'll probably have a shiner in the morning, but I don't think she did any real damage."

"Good thing," Jake said. "I've seen some of the people Gladys has fought. She's a killer."

"I guess I'm faster, or luckier, than they were."

"Yeah, one of those," Jake said. His voice was low, like he was thinking about something.

"What's bugging you, Jakey?"

"Something doesn't smell right."

"What do you mean?"

"Look, don't take this the wrong way. You're a good fighter. You've got natural instincts, and have obviously had some training. And you've come further in no time than anybody I've ever seen. But there's no way you should have been able to beat Gladys tonight. Most of the girls you've fought are just that—girls. They've been at this maybe six months, maybe a year. They haven't been hit in the face a lot. You've taken some licks, and it lets you compete with people at your level."

"Yeah, that all makes sense," Jo said. She knew enough to let Jake get to his point in his own time. He didn't often say a lot, but Jo had learned to value the man's opinions when he gave them.

"But Gladys has been around for years. She had a couple of UFC and Strikeforce tryouts, and got close to fighting in the big time more than once. But something always fell apart at the last minute. Either there was a drug thing, or a visa thing, or something sketchy. So she ended up back here."

Realization dawned on Jo, and she nodded. "You think she threw the fight." She wasn't offended—everything Jake said made perfect sense. She should have been more banged up after going three rounds with a musclebound monster like Gladys. And an experienced fighter like that should never drop her guard and get caught in a submission so easily.

"Yeah, I do. I'm sorry, Jo—"

"Don't be," Jo interrupted. "You're right. But who? And why?"

"I got no idea, girl. But I know one thing. You be careful dealing with Shelton. He's more than just a pervert running a fight club. He's connected to some bad people, and I've seen some bad things go on in some of his clubs before."

"Like what?" Jo asked, but Jake just shook his head.

"Nah, I ain't telling no tales. That's a good way for somebody who don't bring in no fans and don't get no bets laid on the table to find himself sitting outside looking in real fast."

Jo nodded. "I can respect that. I guess there's nothing for it but to go get my money from Shel and see what he's got planned for Saturday night. My luck he'll have me fighting a grizzly bear."

"Some of the women I've seen come through this place, I think a grizzly bear would be an easier scrap."

4

I *should have just fought the damn grizzly,* Jo thought as she stared across the ring at her opponent. She was not looking forward to five rounds against the woman they called La Machina, or The Machine. She fought under a mask, like the Mexican *luchadores,* and because Shel thought it added drama to the matches, he allowed it. But the black mask covering her face was a layer of protection from strikes and cuts and made life a lot harder on her opponents.

Not that Rochelle, as La Machina was known outside the octagon, needed any advantage. She was a tall, solidly built woman with a strong background in Muy Thai and boxing. Her combination of strikes and kicks made her a tough opponent for anyone, and her grappling ability made her even more dangerous.

Jo moved around the ring, circling her opponent with a wary eye. She knew Rochelle was quicker than her size led most people to expect, and her long legs made for some vicious head kicks to the unsuspecting. Rochelle strode in with her hands up, confidence oozing in her every step and blood in her eyes, but just before the women closed on each other, Jake flung open the door of the cage and stuck his head in.

"Raid coming, ladies. Time to book!" Both women turned to see him gesturing frantically for them to come to him. Jo followed without hesitation, Rochelle snapping into action a half-second later. They fled the cage just as the sound of splintering wood told the truth of Jake's words—someone had screwed up. The cops had joined the party.

Guess I'm not getting paid even the loser's purse tonight. Jo ran behind Jake, then stopped cold. "My bag!"

Jake turned to her. "Girl, forget your shoes and underwear. We gotta go!"

"I can't leave my bag," Jo insisted. She couldn't tell Jake that her hammer, her great-grandfather's legendary hammer, was in the bag. That would lead to all sorts of explanations about why she was carrying a nine-pound hammer in her gym bag.

Jo spun to the right and dashed off down a deserted hallway, away from the shouting and the stampeding footsteps behind her, toward the locker room where her stuff was stashed. She flung open the door and skidded to a halt, her bare feet slipping on the tile.

"Shit, sorry, man," she said to the back of the man in the room. The naked man in the room. The tall, blond, very chiseled man in the room. The man with two long scars on his back making a "V" along the lines of his heavily muscled torso. *Well, I guess that's what they mean when they say "heavenly body." Da-yum, with extra yum.* Jo got her first good look at Mitchell, the current persona of the Archangel Michael, and decided it was pretty angelic indeed.

The man turned, his blue eyes piercing, and a curl of that impossible blond hair falling just perfectly across one of them to make him even more irresistible. *Eyes up top, Joanna. Eyes up—oh my goodness.*

"I told Shel I didn't want a girl before the fight," the beautiful man said, a little smile playing across his chiseled jaw. "Come back after I beat this mook, and we can play."

"Wait, what?" *Oh no, he didn't. Oh yes, he did.* "I'm not one of Shel's girls. I'm a fighter. And you want to get some pants on and get the hell out of here with me, right now."

His smile grew. "I wouldn't mind leaving with you, sweetheart, but I've got a fight in a few minutes. As soon as the girls are done with the warm-up act, I'll take out tonight's jamoke and we can go get better acquainted."

Great. Not only is he beautiful, and an angel, but he's a chauvinist douche, too. "I'm still not here for that," Jo said. "I'm here for that." She pointed at her bag, which she picked up and slung over one shoulder. "We take turns in the locker room, remember? I was dressing here before you got in tonight. Now it's time to go. You need to come with me. Right now. The cops are raiding the place, and I don't think you want to take that pretty face to jail, no matter how good a fighter you are."

The grin fell from his face like a boulder. "You're not wrong there, toots. Let's skedaddle."

Toots? What is this guy, eighty? More like eight million, Jo mentally corrected. *I guess he's allowed to be a walking anachronism.* She turned to the door, then back to Mitchell. "You should probably put on some clothes before we run out into the alley."

He jumped into a pair of jeans and slipped on a pair of shoes, then followed her out of the locker room. Jake stood at the end of the hall, peering down a long corridor to the gym where the fights were held. "Come on, girl. We got to roll."

"I'm coming, Jakey. I'm coming." She made good on her promise, running to her corner man and looking up at him. "Which way?"

He pointed back toward the gym. "Looks like all the po-po are down that way, so if we go this way, we should be okay." He jerked a thumb behind him. "He coming with?" Jake gave a nod to Mitchell, who ran up just then.

"Yeah, he's with us. Let's go." She started off at a brisk walk in the direction Jake indicated, keeping an ear out for shouts of police behind them. Hearing nothing, they took a left turn at the first hallway, heading in the general direction of the parking lot where their cars awaited them. They stopped short at a pair of chained fire doors, looking at each other as if for new ideas.

"I guess we look for another way out," Jake said.

"I doubt you'll find anything," came a new voice from behind them. They turned to see a lone police officer standing in the hallway about ten yards from them. He was almost completely in shadow, but looked...off somehow, like his muscles and joints didn't fit together quite right, or like he wasn't used to walking in this form.

"Get behind me, Jake," Jo said, pulling open the zipper from her bag and dropping to one knee to reach inside.

"What's wrong, Jo-Jo? Nervous? Scared about what happens to pretty girls in jail?" the "cop" asked.

"Might be more scared of what happens when people dress up like police," Jo said. She stood up, a nine-pound rectangular maul head in one hand and a twelve-inch handle in the other.

"Looks like Grandpappy's hammer needs a little repair work," the man said, stepping closer. He made no move to draw a weapon, but his posture was full of menace. Jo drew in a sharp breath as the man's eyes began to glow crimson in the gloom of the darkened hallway. Jake took a step back, muttering *"Dios mio"* under his breath.

"No, Jacob," the "man" corrected, bat-like wings stretching out from his shoulders to fill the width of the hallway. "Not God. Never God. That lazy fuck hasn't cared about you worthless meat sacks for millennia, no sense praying to him now. You'd be better off throwing up a tweet to Superman. You've got a better chance of getting an answer."

He turned his attention back to Jo. "Now, where was I? Oh yes, I was going to rip your guts out and paint the ceiling with your blood." He stretched out his arms, and Jo watched in horror as his fingers lengthened and narrowed, coming to razor-sharp points.

Jo pressed a button on the handle in her hand and flicked her wrist. The titanium handle extended to two-and-a-half feet, and she jammed the maul head onto it. The handle and head snapped together with a twist of her wrist and the click of a pair of heavy-duty magnets. She swung the assembled hammer in a lazy circle in front of her.

"Come get some, monster. It's been a couple weeks since I splattered demon brains all over something," Jo said with a grimace.

Jake gaped at her, then turned and started jerking at the chain on the doors. The demon just laughed and stepped closer, swiping his hands through the air with a terrible *snick-whoosh* sound as he flicked his claws together.

Mitchell stepped in front of Jo, shielding her with his body. "Get back, whatever-the-fuck-you-are. Leave this girl alone."

Girl? Oh, I am definitely gonna have to have a talk with this dude if we survive this. Jo pushed past the man and gave him a dark look. The demon leapt at her, but Jo was ready. Weeks in the cage had her reflexes honed to a razor's edge, so she easily side-stepped the creature's charge and brought the hammer around to smash into the back of its knee.

The monster went down with an ear-splitting shriek, and Jo slammed the hammer down at its head. The demon was fast, though, and sprang to its feet and lashed out at her with its talons. Jo ducked under the first slash and brought the hammer up to block the second, kicking out at the thing's midsection with her right foot.

Pain raced up her leg as her toes crashed into the demon's chitinous exterior. The dim light revealed more of the monster in all its unnatural glory. It looked like a two-legged insect of some sort, with a glistening exoskeleton and razor-sharp mandibles protruding from what passed for a face.

"What the fuck is that thing?" Mitchell asked, his voice hushed with fear.

"It looks like the world's ugliest ant," Jake said.

"It's a demon," Jo replied. "And right now, it's a demon that wants to kill us all, so could we please have a little less chit-chat and a little more kicking demon behind?" She swung the hammer in wide figure-eights in front of her, slowly forcing the demon back but doing no damage. The beast appeared content to bide its time, waiting for a hole in Jo's defenses.

So she manufactured one. On the next spin of her hammer, she wobbled just a little, just enough to give a tiny opening. The monster took the bait, charging forward with claws darting in for the woman's throat. Jo spun to the left and put everything she had into a massive swing at the back of the creature's head.

The silvered side of the hammer smacked into the demon's skull with a sound like an egg hitting the kitchen floor. The hammer buried itself up to the haft in the creature's brainpan, and the force of Jo's swing carried it and the weapon around to smack into a wall of lockers with a resounding *clang*. Yellow-grey brain matter and blood splattered along the wall and coated Jo, Mitchell, and Jake with a healthy splattering of demon goo.

Jo planted her foot in the monster's back, grimacing at the feel of the slimy carapace under her bare foot, and yanked her hammer out of the crushed skull. The weapon came loose with a wet sucking sound, and Jo staggered back, almost slipping but pinwheeling her arms to catch her balance at the last moment. *That's all I need, to land flat on my ass in demon guts in the middle of a deserted high school that I'm already trespassing in.*

The trio stood in the darkened hallway staring at each other for a long moment before Jake finally broke the silence. "That was damn gross, Jo-Jo. What the hell was that thing?"

"If I had to hazard a guess, I'd say it was a demon."

"You say that like it ain't the first time you've seen this kind of thing," he continued. Mitchell just stared at her like she was from another planet.

"I wish it was, Jakey, I wish it was," Jo said. "But we still need to be somewhere else, and pretty soon. I can't hear anything from the other end of the building, but that doesn't mean all the cops are gone."

"Well, you can't get in a car with all that goop all over you, and I know I can't go home looking like this," Jake said. "My Daniella is an understanding woman, but if I start dripping demon-snot all over her rugs, I better look for someplace else to sleep at night."

"Yeah, let's go find a bathroom, get cleaned up as best we can, and get out of here," Jo agreed. She turned to Mitchell. "You okay, big guy? You haven't said a word since that thing came at us."

He looked at her, a haunted expression on his face. "I knew that thing. I knew it was a demon, and I knew it the second it opened its mouth."

"Okay..." Jo said.

"How did I know that?" Mitchell asked. "I've never seen a demon before. I don't know anything about demons. Shit, lady, I don't even go to church!"

Jo sighed. "We're gonna need to go ahead and deal with this, aren't we? Okay, let's get the worst of the muck wiped off and get somewhere better lit. With coffee."

"How about someplace with whiskey?" Jake asked. "I got a feeling we're gonna need something stronger than coffee."

"Whiskey it is. But first, a bathroom. I think I've got demon brains between my toes, and I really need to pee."

5

"So, Mitch, what else do you know?" Jo asked. The three of them were seated around her small kitchen table, with the warm yellow glow of the bulb overhead holding most thoughts of demons and monsters at bay for the moment. The steady *drip-drip* of the coffee maker in the background and shuffle of Cassandra's slippers on the worn linoleum were the only sounds in the house.

Mitch looked at Jo over folded hands. "I don't know what I know. And I don't know how I know it." The big man looked confused, with a healthy dash of frightened. "Why was there a demon in the schoolhouse, and what did it want with us?"

"I think that's probably more of a 'you' than an 'us,' pal," Jo said, accepting the mug her mother brought to the table. Jo took a long sip from the "World's Greatest Grandma" mug and let out a sigh. Cassandra knew how she took her coffee—two heaping spoonfuls of sugar with a dash of Kahlua for good measure.

"Why do you think the thing was after me?" Mitch asked. "It seemed like it wanted to kill you pretty bad, too."

"Yeah, but I was just a bonus," Jo said. She looked over at her mother, who gave her a little nod. "Mitchell, I think there are some things you might not understand about yourself, and it might be better if I showed you rather than tried to tell you."

Jake and Mitch exchanged perplexed looks and shrugs as Jo got up from the table. She walked to the small living room, got down on her hands and knees, and reached under the sofa. She fished around under the couch for a moment, then pulled her arm back with a cloth-wrapped bundle in hand. She stood and walked back to the table, unwrapping her prize as she did.

Jo laid the sword on the table, hilt toward Mitch. "Do you recognize this?" she asked.

"It's a sword," Mitch replied.

"That's right, but is there anything familiar about the sword?"

"No, I've never seen it before in my life."

"I don't think that's correct," Jo said. "Why don't you pick it up and take a closer look?"

Mitchell shrugged and reached out his hand for the weapon. The second his fingers wrapped around the hilt, the blade of the sword burst into flames, and a sound like choirs of angels rang through the minds of everyone in the room.

Jo felt like a grenade of sunlight had gone off in her chest, and light and goodness and *right* filled her almost to overflowing. Then, in an instant, the flames winked out, the light vanished, and Mitchell toppled out of his chair with an unceremonious *thump*.

"Holy shit!" Jo said, springing to her feet and hurrying to where Mitch lay curled up in a ball on the floor. "Mitch, are you okay? What happened? I mean, I know what happened, but what happened to you?"

Mitch shook his head, then snapped to full awareness and shoved Jo back. "Get away from me! What the fuck did you do to me? Jesus fucking Christ, what was that?"

Jo sat back on her heels, stunned, but Cassandra leaned over and slapped Mitch right across the face. "You keep a civil tongue in your mouth when you speak the Lord's name in my house, son."

Mitch rolled to his feet, glaring at the seemingly frail older woman, but she didn't flinch. After a few seconds of silent confrontation, Mitch turned, righted his chair, and sat. "My apologies, ma'am. I'll try to contain myself."

"I appreciate that," Cassandra said, a tight smile playing across her lips. "Now," she looked around the table, "why don't you tell us what happened, and what you *thought* was gonna happen, sweetheart, because they are obviously two very different things."

Jo nodded. "You're not wrong there, Mama. I expected something to happen when Mitch touched the sword, but I didn't expect it to knock him on his butt, and I sure didn't expect to almost burn down my kitchen."

"Sorry about that," Mitch said.

"Not your fault," Jo replied. "There's no real good way to say this, so I'll just throw it out there. You're an angel. You're actually kinda *the* angel. You're the Archangel Michael, the warrior of Heaven, and this is your sword."

"Huh?" Mitch looked at Jo like she had grown a second head.

"Jo-Jo, did that girl crack you across the face one time too many last night?" Jake asked.

"I don't know, Jake. Did we get attacked by a giant bug-demon in the halls of a high school tonight?" Jo shot back.

"Good point. Stranger things on heaven and earth and all that, I guess," Jake said.

Cassandra raised an eyebrow. "*Hamlet?*"

"Hey, I read!" Jake protested. "Plus, it was in that movie with Ethan Hawke and Bill Murray."

"Anyway," Jo said. "There's a whole thing going on where a bunch of the archangels are kinda on vacation and neglecting their duty, and a friend of mine really needs their help. So, me and a bunch of other friends are hunting them down, and we're supposed to be able to use their implements to wake them up and get them back to acting like angels."

"Implements?" Mitch asked.

"Apparently each of the archangels has an iconic item associated with them. Michael's is his sword. It's the flaming blade he wielded in the War on Heaven when Lucifer was cast out and the rebellion of the angels was put down. We thought that when you touched it, you'd remember who you are, and that would be all we needed to do. But apparently that's not how it works. At least not with you."

"How has it worked with the other angels you've found?" Jake asked.

Jo didn't answer right away, just took a long sip of her coffee and wished for much more liquor in the drink. "Well, that's the thing..."

"I'm the first one you've found," Mitch supplied.

"Yup," Jo agreed.

"Why me?"

"Well, we already had the sword, so we were halfway there. And when the spell led us to Phoenix, it made sense to start with you, since I already live here. So, I started looking for warriors, and that led me to this undefeated fighter kicking tail all over the underground fight scene."

"But how do you know I'm really your guy?" Mitch asked.

"Remember the whole sword bursting into flames thing?" Jo asked with a smile.

"But maybe that's just some kind of switch or trigger that I couldn't see," Mitch said.

"Jake, pick up the sword," Jo said.

"Why do I got to pick up the fiery angel sword?" Jake protested.

"Because you don't know where the mystery switch is, so if it's there, you're as likely to hit it as Mitch."

"That makes sense, I guess," he said, reaching for the hilt. He picked up the sword. Nothing happened. He stood up and waved it around a little. Nothing happened. He slashed through the air, and Cassandra ducked.

"Sorry," Jake said, sitting back down. He turned to Mitch and held out the sword. "You wanna try again?"

"Not really, but I guess I—" His words abruptly cut off as he touched the hilt and a line of flame erupted around the blade. Mitch jerked his hand back, and the sword tumbled to the kitchen floor. The flames winked out as soon as he broke contact, but the blade clattered on the tile with a loud *clang*. "Oh, shit!" he exclaimed.

"Mommy? Gramma?" a small voice called from the back of the house. "Who's out there?"

"Now you've done it." Cassandra glared at Mitch as she stood. "She'll never get back to sleep if there are new people to meet." The older Harrison woman hustled to the hallway and disappeared, making reassuring noises as she went.

Jo looked at the men. "My daughter, Ginny. She's ten."

"Her dad?" Mitch asked.

"Your business?" Jo shot back. "Sorry," she said, raising her hands to Mitch. "I'm sorry. He died four years ago. Stroke. I just get defensive, you know. Black woman, single mom, living with her mother, that whole thing. But we were the perfect suburban couple. Two incomes, minivan, the whole thing. Then Darren...got hurt at work and was on life support for two weeks. Even with insurance, the part we had to pay was back-breaking. So I moved in with Mama so I'd have some help with Gin."

"I'm sorry," Mitch said. "For asking, and for what happened. It's none of my business. You don't owe me anything."

I certainly don't owe you the truth, Jo thought. *So if you'll buy the stroke story, that's the story you'll get.* Angel or not, Mitch didn't need to know the real story of her husband's death, and the demon that killed him. That was Council business, and her business.

Cassandra came back to the table, a small smile on her face. "I promised her you'd read to her tonight before bed if she stayed in her room and tried to go back to sleep." She handed Jo a battered copy of *Darwen Arkwright and the Peregrine Pact.*

"She loves these books," Jo said. She turned to Mitch. "So, do you believe us now?"

"Believe that there's something about that sword? Yeah. Believe that I'm an archangel? Not by a long shot." He held up a hand to Jo. "I know, you think this is some kind of proof. Well, maybe it is. But maybe there's something else. But something is going on with this sword, and there was a demon in the high school last night, so if this thing helps us kill them, then I guess I'd better learn how to swing it." He picked the sword up from the floor, and it burst into flames right on cue. Mitch held on to the blade this time, standing up and taking an experimental swing through the air.

His jaw was tight, and the crinkling around his eyes told of the strain he was under. After a minute, he set the blade carefully on the table. The flames winked out the second he let go. Cassandra reached out with a fingertip to push the blade aside, but there wasn't even a hint of burn or scarring on the table's surface.

"Good boy," she said. "You'da been in for a world of hurt if you'd messed up my table. And I don't care if you an angel or not, I'da whooped your butt good."

Mitch chuckled. "I believe it." He turned to Jo. "What's next? For now, I'll go along with something being all...messed up." He nodded to Cassandra as he censored his language. She gave him a sly smile. "But I don't know what to do about it."

"Neither do I, but I know where to start looking. We need to go back to the school tonight and see what we can find. I'll touch base with some of my sources today and meet you over there tonight around eleven."

"Let's meet at my gym instead," Jake said. "That way we park and only take one car on our felony field trip."

"Good idea," Jo agreed. The three exchanged cell phone numbers, then Jo said, "We'll meet you at your place at eleven and drive over to the school. We find out where the demons are coming from and what they're after, and then maybe we can find some more clues to waking Michael up."

"You make it sound like he's taking a nap in my head," Mitch said.

"That's probably pretty close," Jo said. "I have a couple ideas I want to run past some folks, then we can go demon-hunting."

"You gonna bring that big hammer?" Jake asked. "Or do you have something better?"

"I like my hammer," Jo said. "And it did alright last night, didn't it?"

"Can't argue with that," Mitch said. "But why a hammer?"

"It's a family tradition," Cassandra said. "People in this family been swingin' a nine-pound hammer at the bad things for a long, long time."

"Well, let's hope we don't have to fight anything tomorrow night," Jake said.

"Optimism," Jo said with a smile. "I'd forgotten what that looked like. It's kinda cute. Now get out of my kitchen. I'm going to go cuddle up with my little girl before I turn around and it's her senior prom. I'll see y'all tomorrow night."

Jake and Mitch walked to the door. Mitch stopped, his hand on the knob, and turned back to Jo. "This is pretty weird, right? I mean, how crazy is this whole thing?"

Jo laughed, a bright, sincere, melodic thing that brightened the room. "Mitch, you think this is weird, remind me to tell you about my last trip to Georgia."

6

J o sat on the floor of her den, laptop on the coffee table in front of her with half a dozen browser tabs open, four leather-bound books arranged carefully in a leaning tower of research on the carpet to her left, and a giant sports bottle full of Mountain Dew sitting on the end table behind her to the right. Her mother sat in a rocking chair in the corner of the room, occasionally looking up from the scarf she was knitting to cluck at Jo and her "organization."

Jo glared at the smiling unicorn head on the screen. Sparkles was resplendent with his rainbow mane and glittering diamond teeth, but he was ultimately useless. "I'm sorry, Jo," the horse-headed tech genius said. "There's nothing on the net anywhere that would explain Michael's memory loss. Everything I can find that would destroy a celestial being's memory would destroy the angel's mind as well, and you said he's not crazy." If it was on the net, Sparkles would find it. Even before he got turned into pure energy and had his soul transferred into the internet, Dennis Bolton was an amazing programmer and hacker. Since becoming a latter-day Tron, there was nothing connected to the internet that he couldn't access, hack, or take over.

"Well, I don't think I actually said he wasn't *crazy*, I just said his brain seemed to be in working order. Could it have anything to do with his fighting? Like maybe post-concussion syndrome or something?"

"I thought about that, but I checked in with Glory, and she says it's pretty much impossible for an angel to get a concussion. Since they're pure energy, when they manifest, it's not like they have real bodies," Sparkles replied.

"If you think that, you've never seen him without a shirt on," Jo muttered under her breath.

"What's that? Oh, you're a giant horndog? That's what I thought you said," Bolton teased.

Jo heard her mother chuckle in the corner and shook her head. "I'm sitting in the floor of my den in sweatpants with my hair up talking to an imaginary man who chooses to present as a unicorn instead of going out and actually *meeting* a human being. Yeah, I'm the tail-chaser."

Cassandra chuckled from her chair, and Jo turned to her. "You stay out of it, Mother," Jo said. Her face grew serious as she turned back to the screen. "So there's nothing?"

"There's not a whole lot of information out there on angels hiding their light under the proverbial bushel," Bolton replied. "Pretty much everything I've found has a lot more to do with Michael swinging that giant flaming toothpick of his around than it does with his mental state. I think you might be dealing with the first recorded case of angelic amnesia in history."

"Yay," Jo replied, leaning back against the couch. "So what next?"

"Are you asking me?" Sparkles asked.

"Well, yeah."

"Oh," he said. "I was kinda hoping you were talking to your mother again. Because I have absolutely no idea."

"What about Harker?" Jo asked.

"He knows less about angels than you do," Bolton said. "His studies have all been on the other end of the celestial spectrum, as it were. So, no help coming from that quarter. Are there any friends of your dad that could help?"

Jo turned to her mother. "Ma, do you know anything about that?"

"Hmmm?" Cassandra looked up from her knitting.

"Oh, don't even try to play me, old woman," Jo said, her voice warm. "I know you've heard every word we've said for the past thirty minutes."

"Well, I reckon that's true enough," the older woman agreed.

"So, did Daddy have any friends that might be useful?" Jo asked.

"I don't think so, honey. Most everybody he worked with on the Council was either Luke, Harker, or more interested in shooting monsters than learning about the good creatures out there. There was one man, though...what was his name?" She thought for a moment, then held up a finger as it came to her. "That's it! Robert Blinn. He teaches religion and philosophy at Gateway."

"The community college?" Jo asked.

"That's the one. He said he liked teaching at a smaller school. But he was a sharp one. Did a lot of research into angels. He always said if you're going to understand demons, you needed to know where they came from."

"That makes sense," Jo said. "Dennis, you got a number—"

"Way ahead of you, sunshine," the disembodied unicorn head replied. "I sent it to your phone already. According to his class schedule, he's got office hours tomorrow from ten to noon, and he's in class today until like six p.m."

"Do I want to know how you got that little tidbit?" Jo asked.

"I hacked the college's computer system," Bolton said.

"So, no, I don't want to know," Jo said, shaking her head. "You are so going to get me thrown in jail."

"Nah, it's fine. I left just enough footprints in their system to make them think the Russians did it."

"Great," Jo said. "When I get sent to Gitmo, just make sure Luke can get a night flight into Cuba to save me."

"Oh relax," Dennis said, tossing his mane. "It was on his public Facebook page. I didn't even have to pretend to be a student to friend him."

Jo's reply was on the tip of her tongue when her cell rang. She picked up the phone and looked at the screen, but didn't recognize the number. She swiped her finger across the screen and held the phone to her ear. "Hello?"

"Jo?" The voice on the other end was soft, tentative, like the speaker was afraid they'd dialed a wrong number, or maybe afraid they hadn't.

"This is she," Jo replied. "Can I help you?" She kept her tone light, but motioned to Sparkles then pointed to the phone. The horse head nodded, then vanished, a map of Phoenix popping up on the screen with a large circle blinking around the city. As the call went on and Dennis was able to trace the call through more towers, the circle grew smaller and smaller until finally it was a blinking dot immunizing the caller's location.

"I'm sorry, it's nothing. Never mind..." Jo had a brief moment of recognition. That voice...

"Marla?" Jo asked.

"Yeah," the woman's voice was quiet, as though she was afraid of being overheard. "I'm sorry, I shouldn't have called you. But I found your number from when we went out to breakfast the other night, and..."

"Do you need someplace safe to be?" Jo asked.

Cassandra's head snapped up, and she mouthed, "Is that her?"

Jo nodded. Cassandra nodded back, and that settled that. Now Jo just needed to talk the frightened woman into coming to her house.

After long seconds, Marla said, "Yes." Her voice was heavy with resignation and regret, like it took serious effort to agree.

"Do you have a car? Or can you get here if I text you the address?"

"No," the other woman said. "Our car's broke down, and if I take an Uber or something..." Her words trailed off.

"It'll be too easy to track it," Jo supplied.

LET ME HANDLE THAT. The words appeared on Jo's computer screen. *NOBODY TRACES ME UNLESS I LET THEM.*

Jo smiled. "I've got a guy that can send someone. Nobody will be able to follow. I promise."

"I don't know," Marla said. "Brian's pretty good about finding stuff out."

"Not as good as my guy is at hiding stuff. Trust me. Now where are you? I'll have a car there in fifteen minutes."

I t was nearly an hour later when Jo heard a car door slam in her driveway. She was up like a shot, moving toward the front door and pulling it open before Marla even had a chance to knock. The blonde woman had a giant bruise on her cheek and a haunted look in her eye. She ducked inside, looking around like she expected pursuit any second, then stopped a few feet into the small but neat living room.

"Um...thanks," she began, then stopped awkwardly.

"Don't mention it," Jo said, reaching out to take the duffel from the woman's hand. "This all you brought?"

"I don't have much."

I bet you don't. Bet that jerk doesn't let you have much, no matter how much money you bring in. "Well, we don't have a guest room, but the couch is comfy, there's plenty of food, and—"

"And you can stay as long as you like," Cassandra said, coming around the corner from the kitchen carrying a plate piled high with sandwiches. "But it's almost lunchtime." To Joanna, "Why don't you set the table while our guest washes her hands? It's the second door on the right, honey." Cassandra waved her hand down the hall, and Marla nodded at her.

After she was gone, her mother turned to Jo. "That one needs your help."

"That's what I'm doing, Mama."

"I know, baby. But be careful. A man that lays hands on a woman is worse than a dog."

"That's alright, Mama. I know how to take care of a rabid dog." Jo's voice was cold, the set of her jaw as hard as the hammer she frequently carried. The women bustled in the kitchen and dining nook, setting out three plates for a light lunch of sandwiches and fruit.

Marla came back from the bathroom and clapped her hands together. "What can I do to help? I might be a freeloader, but I can at least set a table." Her eyes were bright and her shoulders back, once more exuding some of the confidence Jo saw in the cage a few nights before.

The table was set in short order, and the women tucked into their meal. They ate in a companionable silence for a few minutes before Cassandra looked at Marla and spoke. "So Marla, what do you do besides fight? Jo tells me you're pretty good, but I don't expect nobody much is making the rent beating people up in cages for nasty men like that Shelton."

"You're not wrong there," Marla agreed. "But I don't have another job right now. I worked in a hospital for a while, but they cut back on their maintenance staff and let me go."

"What were you doing there?" Jo asked.

"General facilities stuff. You know, change lightbulbs, fix toilets, fix doorknobs, that kind of thing. I've been trying to get on with an apartment complex as a super or site manager job, because a lot of times those come with a place to stay, and then..." Her voice trailed off, and she looked down at her plate.

"Then you could get away from the son of a bitch who gave you that shiner?" Cassandra asked.

"Mother!" Jo exclaimed.

Marla just laughed. "It's fine. She's right. He is a son of a bitch. I would have left him months ago, but I didn't have any place to go. We used to work together, and then we started seeing each other. Then, when I lost my job, he let me move in, and we got serious for a while, but he started getting real jealous, and then..."

"Then he started using you for a punching bag," Cassandra finished for her.

"Pretty much," Marla said.

"But you're a fighter," Jo said. "Why not fight back?"

"'Cause he's a fighter, too, and he's been fighting longer than me, and he's bigger—"

"And stronger, and faster." Jo nodded. "It doesn't matter how tough Ronda Rousey is, she ain't never taking down Brock Lesnar."

"Yeah. He's no Brock, but I ain't no Ronda, neither. So I'm broke, unemployed, and beat up," Marla said.

"But now you're here, sweetheart," Cassandra said, reaching out to pat the other woman's hand. "And that asshole won't find you here. And if he does, he'll have to deal with me."

"Mother, language," Jo said, but her tone was mild. She looked at the steel in her mother's jaw and knew she'd defend this new charge against all threats if need be. Jo nodded slightly, planning to go out that evening and do a little defending of her very own. Pre-emptive defending, if you will.

7

"**Y**ou know this isn't really what the Council does, don't you?" The cultured British voice coming across her car's Bluetooth speaker was mild, but there was a hint of disapproval apparent. Or maybe he was just British. Jo could never tell if the condescension was real or a by-product of the accent.

"I know, Jack, but if our job is to protect innocents, this certainly falls under that umbrella." Jo backed her car out into the street and turned the headlights on, piercing the darkness between the pools of streetlight.

"Our mandate is to protect innocents from *demons* and supernatural beings, love. Not jealous boyfriends with heavy fists and substance abuse issues."

"Not all demons are summoned," Jo said. "And not every hell has lakes of fire."

"I know that all too well," the voice of Jack Watson, great-grandson of the legendary doctor and detective sidekick, replied. "But what exactly are you planning, Joanna?"

"Are you sure you want to know? Wouldn't want to mess up your plausible deniability." She grinned into the darkness, her face illuminated by the amber lights of the dash and the flickering white of oncoming headlights. Jo put on her blinker and slowed as she exited off I-17 and turned left back under the highway, headed toward the Prosperity Park neighborhood.

"I think being two thousand miles away gives me an excuse for not stopping you. Besides, if you end up in jail, I'll need to fabricate a plan for your extrication, and having all the information will give me what I need to make that happen." Jack sounded tired, Jo thought. Of course, New York made her tired just thinking about it, much less being there hunting angels. The Londoner was probably fighting subways as often as he was fighting demons or magical impediments to his search.

"I really just want to talk to the guy," Jo said. "I want to let him know that it's not cool to hit people, and he really shouldn't be using his girlfriend for a punching bag."

"You can appreciate the irony in that statement, given your current nocturnal employment, can't you?"

"Piss off, Watson. Don't you have back episodes of *Sherlock* to catch up on?"

"Not since I realized Moffat was involved," Jack replied. "I hated what that prat did to *Doctor Who*."

"God forbid I get into a conversation on *Doctor Who* with a Brit," Jo said with a laugh. She turned left down a side street where "Prosperity" was certainly nothing more than a name, any decent jobs or concept of home maintenance having left these run-down houses years ago.

"That seems somehow racist, or at the very least, nationalist, Joanna," Jack said, chuckling. "How goes the battle on your other front? You know, the one the Council actually assigned?"

Jo sighed. "I found him. But he doesn't know I found him. Or rather, he doesn't know who he is."

"Well, just—"

"I gave him the sword. It burst into holy fire and everything."

"What happened then?"

"He dropped it. Scared the crap out of the dude. He has no idea he's an angel, and I have no idea how to unlock that part of him. And there are demons in Phoenix, chasing us both. Because of course there are. I think I'm here." She saw the rusted-out Pontiac Fiero sitting in front of the small tract home, painted black with Bondo highlights. Sparkles had given her the make and model of Marla's boyfriend's car, and her address. Looked like Captain Butthead was home.

"Good luck," Jack said. "Try not to get arrested."

"If I do, I know exactly who to call."

"Yes," he agreed. "Someone else." He laughed and disconnected the call.

"Jerk," Jo muttered at the phone. She turned right at the next street and parked her car. Jo got out and slipped on her black biker jacket. It wasn't cold, but the thick leather provided a little padding in case things did get heated with her target.

She stepped onto the sidewalk, and a young white man immediately stood up from the steps of a nearby house. "Hey baby, you looking for me?" he catcalled.

Jo ignored him, walking without turning around. She heard footsteps get closer as the man, more a boy than anything, jogged up to her.

"Hey baby, I'm talking to you," the kid repeated.

Jo ignored him again, not speeding up, not slowing down. She just kept her eyes front, kept walking. She didn't know how many of his friends might be watching, and she didn't need to cause a ruckus before she got to Marla's place.

Then he grabbed her elbow. Jo stopped, and the man pulled her arm to turn her back to him. He was tall, maybe twenty years old, with a cursive neck tattoo and acne spilling across his narrow features. His red hair was close-cropped, barely peeking out from under the brim of a San Jose Sharks cap.

"Bitch, I'm talking to you!" he snarled at her.

"You must not be because I don't see any bitch here," Jo said. She looked the boy right in the eye, refusing to show fear. She'd stared down demons—one little suburban shithead wasn't going to scare her. As long as it wasn't half a dozen suburban shitheads, she was probably okay.

"Now why don't you go back to your porch and sit there like a good dog until your master gets home because I don't feel like playing tonight." Jo's words were soft, her voice even, but the look on her face was hard.

"I see a bitch, alright. I see one big stuck-up black bitch walking through my 'hood all alone. I reckon you goin' to meet a trick, ho?" He pushed up on her, walking her backward by pressing his chest against her. Jo steered herself away from the chain link fence behind her, then spun to the right. She put on hand on the boy's left shoulder and stepped on the back of his left knee, pushing him forward. He staggered forward into a parked Toyota, catching himself on the front fender of the car with his hands.

"Oh, you done done it now, bitch. I was just gonna fuck with you a little bit. Now I'm gonna fuck you up." He pulled a butterfly knife from his back pocket and flipped it open.

"What is this, 1987?" Jo asked. She shook her head at the boy, then stepped forward and kicked him between the legs. The toe of her hiking boot impacted his testicles, and the force of her kick stood the young man up on his tiptoes. He dropped to his knees as Jo pulled her foot back, then she put her hands on the side of his head and rammed her knee into his face. His nose broke with a wet *crack*, and blood poured out, covering his mouth and chin.

Jo took a step back, then leveled her would-be attacker with a snap kick to his temple that spun him around and slammed his face into the Toyota's tire before he bounced face-first to the sidewalk. He lay there motionless as Jo turned to see if he had any friends looking to join the fight.

Nobody approached, or even seemed to have taken notice of the fight. Jo left him lying on the concrete, blood seeping from his broken nose to pool under the car tire by his head. She turned and walked back to the address Sparkles had given her, taking note of the flickering light in the front room. Marla's boy-thing must be watching television.

Jo stepped up on the porch and knocked on the door.

"Fuck off!" came from inside, accompanied by the muffled sounds of gunfire and explosions.

Jo knocked again, louder and longer this time.

"I said, fuck off!" The sound of the TV got louder as the man inside turned the volume up to drown out her knocking.

Jo shook her head, then knocked again. She wasn't against kicking the door in on principle, but getting shot as a burglar was not part of the evening's plans.

"Goddammit, what does a man have to do—Well, hello there, what can I do for you?" The man almost tripped over himself changing gears as he answered the door and saw an attractive woman standing on his porch.

Jo could definitely see the attraction for Marla. Brian Krill was a good-looking man of about thirty. Tall, blond, with a strong jaw and patrician nose, he definitely had the body of a man who spent a lot of time in the gym. And Jo could see most of that body in front of her, since he answered the door in nothing but a pair of boxer briefs and a black tank top. His heavily muscled arms ended in a pair of thick hands with scarred up knuckles that spoke of many fights survived and many punches thrown.

"Are you Brian?" Jo asked.

"Who wants to know, pretty lady?" He pasted on a smile that made the hair on Jo's arms stand up, and not in a good way.

"I'm a friend of Marla's. I'm here to pick up a few of her things." The smile fell from his face like a stone.

"Is she with you? Where is she? I need to talk to her." He seemed nervous, like he was afraid of something. He peered around Joanna, looking up and down the street. Jo felt good about her decision to park a couple of blocks away. At least he wouldn't see her car and show up at her house when nobody was home but Ginny and Cassandra.

"She's not with me. I'm just here to pick up the rest of her things and to tell you she won't be coming back. Now where are her clothes?" She stepped forward, trying to get into the house, but Brian blocked her path.

"She doesn't have anything here. Everything in this house is mine. You tell that bitch that I don't want her back. No, tell you what, I'll tell her myself. Where is she?" His face got redder with every sentence, and Jo started to see the veins bulging on the side of his neck.

Jo stepped back onto the porch, but Brian grabbed her arm. "No, come on in." He pulled her into the living room and kicked the door shut behind her. "Who are you? Are you the bitch that told her to leave me? Is this all your fault? Are you a dyke? Is that it? You want to fuck my girl, so you stole her from me? That makes sense, you ni—"

Jo slapped him across the face. "Stop right there. You don't call me that word. Nobody calls me that word. As a matter of fact, you don't call me anything. You don't think about me. You don't think about me, and you don't think about Marla, either. She's out of your life, and she doesn't ever have to put up with your mouth or your abuse ever again. Now get out of my way. I'm leaving."

"The fuck you say, you dyke cunt. I'll beat you so black and blue my girl won't even look at you when I'm done." Brian threw a punch, a big, lazy right that had about as much chance of connecting as John Belushi running a marathon.

Jo ducked under the punch and stuck out three quick left jabs, tagging the larger man right in the mouth and nose with her fist. She drew back a bloody hand, her knuckle laid open on his front teeth. Brian staggered back, then lowered his head and charged her. He caught Jo right around the middle and slammed her into a far wall. Her back cracked the drywall, and she felt dust fall into her hair as his shoulder drove the air from her.

Jo lashed out, nailing Brian with three sharp elbow strikes to the back of the neck. He quickly retreated, then kicked at her head. Jo dropped down and wrapped her hands around his other ankle. She stood up sharply, pulling Brian down to flop on his back with a *whoof!* She held his ankle, then stepped forward to drive her heel into his lower abdomen. He covered up the best he could with his hands, but Jo had the advantage of position and holding his leg.

She stomped his stomach and chest mercilessly, hearing at least two ribs crack under her foot. After six or seven vicious stomps, she let his foot drop and knelt on the floor beside his head. Brian curled up in a fetal position on his side as Jo said to him in a low voice, "You will not come after Marla. You will forget you ever knew her. If I ever hear of you laying a finger on her again, I will be back. And that night I won't go so easy on you."

Then she drove her fist into the side of his skull, sandwiching his head between her strike and the floor. His eyes rolled back in his head, and Brian passed out cold. Jo thought for about half a second about the permanent brain injury she may have caused, then chalked it up to just desserts and stood up. She looked around the living room, saw a framed photo of Marla and a smiling older woman on the mantle. Jo took the picture, slipped it into her jacket pocket, and walked out the door, whistling into the night.

She got back to her car and pressed the speed dial for Sparkles. "One monster down, at least one to go. Anything new?"

Dennis's human face appeared on her phone's screen, his unicorn head uncharacteristically absent. "Jo, you need to get home. Now. There's a police escort waiting for you at the on-ramp to the 17. There's been an attack at your place. Get home now."

8

J o burst through her front door, then drew up short as the burly police officer took hold of her arms and steered her to the kitchen table. "You don't need to go in there," he said, motioning with his head to the hallway. "Just come here and sit down. Let's talk for a minute, and we'll tell you what we know."

"Who's hurt? Where's Ginny? Where's Mama? What about Marla? Who was here? What happened?" The words tumbled from her pell-mell, almost on top of each other in her panic. She looked up, noticed that she knew the cop, and her shoulders released a fraction of the tension there.

Randall Currence was a beat cop who patrolled the neighborhood. His partner this year was another rookie; Jo thought she remembered his name was Freddy or something like that. Randall got a lot of rookies to be their first partner out of the Academy. He'd been on the Phoenix PD for almost twenty years, and he was a calming influence in a tense situation. Freddy was nowhere to be seen tonight. *Maybe got sent home for puking at a crime scene. Again.* Jo thought.

His good looks and easy smile made the women trust him, and his broad shoulders and strong jaw made the men respect him. Randall was a big man, over six foot and a bit over two hundred pounds, but his uniform shirt had no bulge in the middle, and he moved like a man much younger than the thirty-nine years he'd only admit to if pushed.

Jo looked in his face. His normally sparkling blue eyes were somber. She took a deep breath. "Randall, I need you to tell me what happened here."

Her eyes scanned the living room from the seat where she's eaten just a few hours earlier. One of Ginny's socks peeked out from under the sofa, the pink one with blue trolls that she couldn't find when she did laundry on Saturday. Cassandra had left her sewing needles sticking in the arm of the rocker/recliner again, just waiting for Jo to put her hand down there all unsuspecting.

Those little Norman Rockwell snapshots felt so incongruous with the red and blue flashing lights strobing across the wall, the coppery scent of blood laying over a deeper, harsher smell of pain and death coming from somewhere. The smiling snapshots hanging on the refrigerator door with magnets cast in sharp relief by the snap of crime scene photographer flashes.

Joanna turned her attention back to Randall, to the policeman sitting in front of her. She tuned in halfway through his sentence. "...we don't know everything yet, Jo. It seems there was a home invasion. There was a young woman here..."

Jo shook off her shock and stupor enough to reply. "That's Marla, we met at work."

"Work?" Randall knew Jo usually made her living as a freelance editor, working from home.

"I've been picking up some side gigs here and there. I met Marla at one of those. She was having boyfriend problems, so I let her crash here."

"What do you know about her boyfriend? Is he the type to hold a grudge?" Randall pulled a small cop's notepad from the chest pocket of his uniform and flipped it open.

"It wasn't the boyfriend," Jo said with a shake of her head.

"How do you know?"

"Because I was just at his place beating the crap out of him and letting him know he wasn't ever to contact Marla again. Whoever broke into my place did it while I was there, so it wasn't him." Her words were flat, lifeless, like she was recounting something that happened to someone else, not something she'd done. That's how it felt, like her life was happening to someone else, like it wasn't real. It had felt like this the first time she saw a monster, the night she learned there were more wicked things in the world than even the stories could explain. The night she lost Darren. She shook her head, trying to focus on the policeman—Randall—staring at her.

"You know you just confessed to assault, right?" Randall asked, his brows knit.

"I also know you'll never find a jury without at least two women on it, and no woman will ever convict me for kicking that abusive jerk's behind. Now what happened here? Where is my mother? Where is Ginny?"

Randall didn't answer for a long moment. When he looked up at Jo again, his eyes told a deeper story. "We don't know. They aren't here."

"Then whose blood is splattered all over my...oh no." Jo stood, knocking Randall's hands aside as he tried to push her gently back into the chair. Jo walked past him, following the trail of blood down the hall. It arced along the walls like the start of a demented Jackson Pollack painting, the splatter going high then low as it traced the path of a fight. A fight that one player was destined to lose, and badly.

Jo stopped at the doorway to her bedroom, where the trail of blood on the walls ended and ran down to become a pool on the floor. Too much blood to soak into the carpet, it stood in a puddle running from under the door out into the hall.

"Randall, is my daughter in there?" Jo reached out, but couldn't bring herself to touch the door.

"We haven't seen any sign of Ginny. We don't know where she is, but she's not in there."

Jo pushed the door open. The lake of blood ran from just past the doorway all the way to her bed, where it seeped into the carpet and ran under the furniture out of sight. There was a void of lighter blood, an amorphous outline where a body had lain. Jo saw a few strands of blonde hair stuck in the blood, along with chips of bone, and other organic bits that marked the spot where Marla had died.

"Where is she?" Jo asked. She didn't turn around. She didn't need to, she could feel Randall right behind her.

"She's in the ambulance. They're going to take her to the morgue where the ME can do a more thorough exam."

"Who did this? Did anyone see anything?"

"We're canvassing neighbors now, but so far we've come up empty. Do you have any idea who would do something like this?"

Jo did, but she couldn't tell the police about it. Not only would that put her mother and daughter in more danger, but it would almost certainly get Randall killed, along with anyone else who tried to bring the demon into custody.

Her phone buzzed in her pocket. Jo ignored it, but it buzzed again.

"You should get that," Randall said. "It might be important." Jo knew that was code for "it might be ransom," but she hoped it wasn't. She didn't want the police to know anything about all this, but it seemed a little late for that now.

Jo pulled her phone out and looked at the screen. She had one new text message. She opened the text and saw an image of her mother's face. Cassandra had a bruise on her cheek and a split lip, but a defiant look on her face. Below her image was a caption that said *Midnight. School. Bring the Sword. Bring the Angel.*

Jo swiped a finger across the screen to delete the image, then looked up at Randall. "Nothing. It's just a client. Can I see Marla?"

Randall gave her a long look, but nodded. He led her from the house to the ambulance. Jo climbed in and unzipped the body bag. Marla's faced was battered, bloodied, and several bones in her jaw and cheeks were obviously broken. It was obvious to Jo that she didn't go down easily.

"I'm so sorry, sweetie," Jo said in a whisper. "I am so, so sorry. I was out trying to protect you, and you give your life protecting my family? Oh, you were a real fighter, girl, and I am so sorry for this." She looked to the heavens, then said, "Lord, please protect this child of yours and see her to your side, Amen."

A little part of her felt like a hypocrite, praying after everything she found out recently—that God had left Heaven centuries ago and his angels were all scattered across Earth completely ignorant of their true nature. But another part of her felt comforted in the prayer, like somebody heard her and would look after Marla in the next life. Jo wiped her eyes, then zipped the bag closed and stepped out of the ambulance.

"What's the plan, Jo?" Randall asked as he walked up to her. "I know that look. There's something going on more than you're telling me, and I want in on it. I owe you."

"You don't owe me nothing, Randall. I was just doing my job."

"Doing *my* job, more like it," the cop replied. He was talking about an incident a year before when Jo had put down a necromancer with a zombie fetish. The necromancer had raised a bunch of people all across the city, including a cousin of Randall's, and he got way more involved in the supernatural scene than he ever wanted to before she was laid to rest again.

"Either way, I can't have you involved in this," Jo said.

"Does it have anything to do with that text you got? Because you know the feds will subpoena your phone and read all your texts."

"I know they will, but I hope this will all be settled before they can find a judge, get the data from the phone company, and figure out what anything means. Until then, I need you to cover for me." Jo started back toward her car.

Randall followed close behind. "Cover for you? With who? What am I covering for?"

"This is some more of that stuff you don't like to know about," Jo said.

"Yeah, but if I'm going to lose my job, I think I'd better know what's going on," Randall said to her back.

Jo stopped. She turned back to Randall, who spread his hands in front of him. She sighed. "There's a lot more going on here than your job, Randall. There's a lot more going on than my mom and kid, not that I care much about that right now. But this is not anything you want to be involved in. Trust me."

"I can't, Jo. It doesn't matter how much I don't want to be involved, I *am* involved. I got involved the second you told me you were beating up this dead woman's boyfriend while somebody was at your house turning her insides into her outsides. You can't unring that bell. There's a dead woman here, and you're the alibi for our best suspect. That makes you our best suspect. Add to that the fact that your mother and daughter are missing, and you're not freaking out over that, and I am not letting you out of my sight."

Jo hung her head. "Fine. Then get in the car." She opened the driver's door and slid in behind the wheel. A pair of plainclothes police waved and started heading in her direction. She gave Randall a sharp look, and he opened the passenger door and got in.

"This is so gonna cost me my job," he said, clicking on his seat belt.

"Well, look at it this way, Randall. At least now you'll be able to get in all that deep-sea fishing you've been missing."

"We live in Phoenix, Jo. We're like three hundred miles from the ocean."

"Good thing you've got plenty of time to make the trip, then." She jammed the car in reverse and backed out of her driveway, narrowly missing the front of the ambulance as it turned around and headed to the hospital. Jo noted soberly that it wasn't running any lights or siren. It didn't need to, there was no need to hurry.

The same couldn't be said for them. With three hours until midnight, she had to wrangle an angel and devise a plan to get her mother and daughter back safely. And try to keep a nosy cop alive. And maybe kill a demon or three. *Well girl, nobody said this superhero life would be easy.*

"Why are we at a gym? You need to get a little workout in before we go find your daughter?" Randall asked as Jo put the car in park.

"I'm supposed to meet some people here," Jo said as she opened the door and slid out of the car. She walked to the side door of the squat cinderblock building. A large mural depicting champions of boxing and MMA from Muhammad Ali and Joe Frazier to Royce Gracie and Anderson Silva ranged across the wall, with graffiti-styled lettering two feet high proclaiming it "Dempsey's Gym & Fight Club—the best place nobody talks about."

Jo reached out to knock on the door, but her hand froze as she saw the twisted hunk of metal where the doorknob used to be. She reached under her jacket and unclipped the hammer head from her belt, then drew the handle from the other side, snapped the expandable titanium handle to its full length, and twisted it into place with a *click*.

"Nice toy," Randall said, drawing his sidearm and flashlight.

"I don't like to shoot things," Jo replied.

"I don't either," the stocky cop replied. "But some things really need to get shot."

Jo pulled the door open, and the pair entered the building. Randall played his flashlight around the room for a few seconds, then reached over and flipped on the light switch. Fluorescent tubes flickered to life through the cavernous room, illuminating heavy bags, speed bags, and weight benches arrayed around a central elevated boxing ring. A rough wooden desk sat in one corner of the room in a makeshift "office" consisting of the desk, two chairs, and one battered four-drawer file cabinet with a dead fern on top of it.

Along the back wall was a row of lockers with low wooden benches in front of them and a door marked "SHOWERS" nestled into the far corner. The room was empty, but signs of a struggle were everywhere. Weight benches lay scattered like pieces of a demented Erector Set, a dumbbell rack was overturned in front of a shattered mirror, and the water cooler lay gurgling on its side, its contents pouring out onto the floor.

"Looks like somebody put up a hell of a fight. Who were you supposed to be meeting here?" Randall asked, moving farther into the room.

"My corner man, Jake. He runs this place."

"He a fighter?"

"Not anymore. Says he used to fight some back in the day, but not for years."

"Yeah, looks like he remembered how to throw a punch," the cop said. Randall stepped close to the ring, then holstered his gun. "Jo?" he called.

"Yeah?"

"Your Jake a Hispanic guy?"

"Yeah, he's Latino." Jo stepped forward, then brought her hand to her mouth. "Oh no, Jake." She started forward but froze as Randall raised a hand to her.

"No," he said, all cop. "This is now a crime scene. And you can't be here. Hell, I shouldn't be here either, and I'm probably going to end up an ex-cop before this whole mess is said and done. But there's obviously something going on here that's more than I know, and I'm guessing you have to sort it out on your own."

Jo looked at him, then looked back into the ring, where she could just make out Jake's still form laying spread-eagled on the mat. She could tell even from a distance that his body had the stillness of death about him, and that was before the coppery scent of blood registered above the ever-present gym smell of leather and sweat.

"Give me a minute before you call it in," Jo said, moving toward the ring. "Please?"

Randall looked at her, then nodded. "Seriously, though. One minute."

Jo nodded, swallowing past the lump in her throat. She walked up the cinderblocks that served as de facto ring steps and ducked through the ropes. She pulled out her cell phone and started shooting video as she walked around the body.

"Dennis, video coming your way," she said quietly.

"Got it," the disembodied hacker replied. "That writing looks Enochian."

"I don't know anything about that, but have you seen this kind of...ritual before?" Jo asked.

"Yeah, I have. Unfortunately, I was a part of one. This is a summoning." Jo closed her eyes, but the image before her was seared into her mind's eye.

Jake was staked to the mat, spread-eagled like some demented Da Vinci sketch. He was stripped naked, but it was hard to tell because his body looked almost like it was wearing a red suit, it was covered in so much blood. His hands and feet were nailed to the mat with long spikes, and his body had been split down the middle, the skin peeled back in the center. His organs were set aside in neat piles around the circle, and words in some strange script were scrawled all around the canvas mat in blood and bodily fluids. The dead man's eyes were clenched shut, but his open mouth told the tale of the terrible suffering he had endured.

"Summoning?" Jo asked.

"Yeah, someone has called a demon and used your buddy as the portal. Judging by the amount of blood, it wasn't a very large demon. That's the good news."

"The bad news is that it's still a demon, and it's here."

"And in the company of someone with the knowledge and power to call it forth," Dennis agreed.

"There was already one demon here," Jo said. "We ran into it last night. I sent it home with my hammer."

"Good girl, but that one obviously wasn't the boss."

"How do you know?" Jo asked.

"You aren't dead," Dennis replied. "A boss demon, something like an Archduke, or even a Duke of Hell, would have just ripped your head off and sucked out your soul like eating a crawdad."

"That's an image that will spoil jambalaya for me forever," Jo said. "But yeah, I took that one out pretty easily."

"You're out of your weight class, Jo," Dennis said. "I'll put in a call to Luke. He can get a flight out of Charlotte and be there in four hours, tops. With a little luck, we can have this all settled by sunrise."

"That would be great, if I had that long," Jo replied. "But I have a midnight deadline or this monster kills my mother and my little girl. So you can put Luke on a light-tight private plane if you like, but I can't wait around for the cavalry. I have to take the fight to the monsters, and to do that, I need to wake up an archangel. Any ideas?"

"Yeah, but you aren't going to like it," came the voice from her phone.

"Is it any worse than having a demon murder my whole family?"

"Probably not, but it might be a close second," Dennis said.

A sinking feeling came over Jo as she realized what he was going to suggest. "Oh, come on. There has got to be someone else."

"I've been scouring the web, Dark and light, the whole time we've been on the phone. Phoenix isn't exactly a hot-spot of magical activity, you know. That's probably why Michael hid out there in the first place."

"I know there aren't many high-level practitioners, but this guy? Come on, there's not *anybody* else in the city who can help?" Jo wracked her brain through every Shadow Council contact, every seedy supernatural creature, and every undead or half-alive magic wielder she had ever come into contact with. Every road led back to the same place.

"Fine, call Dr. Evil and tell him I'm coming," she said with a sigh. She turned back to Randall. "You coming with me, or are you going to stay here and try to cover up my mess again?"

"I'm with you," the cop said. "Who's Dr. Evil? Is that his nickname or something?"

"Or something," Jo said, shaking her head as she turned toward the door. *This is gonna suck so bad. Why couldn't I just fight another demon?*

J o pulled up in front of Dr. Evil's Magical Emporium and Internet Cafe thirty minutes later. Despite the late hour, the front of the shop was brightly lit, and she had to park at the far end of the lot, jockeying for space between a cavalcade of Prius hybrids and Tesla electric cars. One battered pick truck stood out like a sore thumb, the exact opposite of the normal automotive distribution of Arizona.

"What the hell is this place?" Randall asked as they got out of the car. He gaped at the garish display of color-chasing LED signs screeching words like "GAMING" and "FREE WI-FI" into the desert night. "And doesn't the owner know we have ordinances on signage in this town?"

"I don't think he cares," Jo said, and I'm pretty sure he's located on the correct side of that for a reason." She jerked a thumb at the Phoenix City Limits sign that sat just at the edge of the Emporium parking lot. "As to what this place is, I like to call it heaven for nerds. Also the lair of one of the most powerful magicians in the Southwest, and the one most likely to help me with a case, provided the right incentive."

"Incentive? Are you going to bribe somebody?" Randall asked.

"Oh God, I wish," Jo said. By now she stood at the door, waiting for him. The entrance to the store was covered in window decals proclaiming the store a dueling center for Magic: the Gathering, Yo-Gi-Oh, Cardfight Vanguard, Bushiroad, Pokémon, and half a dozen other games with brightly colored stylized lettering.

The two stepped into the room, and Jo's ears were assailed with shouts of joy and fury as energetic gamers cajoled, cawed, and cackled at their vanquished opponents. A twelve-year-old white kid with faded green hair and freckles slumped in his chair, vanquished by a laughing Asian boy with a Justin Bieber haircut and a smattering of acne across his cheeks. Two overweight men with goatees and black t-shirts pored over a scattering of cards on a table, each pointing to one or another and making suggestions or snide comments while a wide-eyed college kid looked on, apparently soaking in the knowledge of older gamers. A trio of high school girls sat around a board game with a husky African-American man reading from a rulebook.

Everywhere Jo turned, people were playing one game or another, laughing, joking, and generally enjoying themselves. Until they noticed her companion. As soon as they took in Randall's uniform, a hush fell over the room.

Jo looked at the man. "You must be a real killer at parties."

"My wife always wonders why I never get invited," he said with an easy smile. "You wanna let them know I'm not here looking for illegal Adderall and an ounce of weed, or should I let them sweat?"

"Let's scare 'em a little. A little healthy fear of incarceration will do the youth of the world some good." She turned to the room. "I'm looking for Doctor E. Where is he?"

The green-haired boy pointed behind her. "He's in the Gundam Room."

Randall looked at her. "Do I even want to know what a Gundam Room is?"

Jo laughed at her friend's discomfort. "You're gonna get your nerd card revoked, Randall. A Gundam is a scale model of a Japanese battle mech from a cartoon. Don't you know anything?"

Randall just looked around the room, his eyes wide at the multitude of nerddoms on display. "Apparently not."

"Follow me. Let's go see Dr. Evil." Joanna turned around and walked through dozens of folding tables and matches of various collectible card games toward a small doorway. Through the door, she saw a desk with a big man in a lime-green dress shirt seated behind three brightly colored boxes. She stopped at the door and knocked. "Doc? Got a minute?"

The big man looked up from the boxes and motioned to the teenager sitting across from him. "Take these up front to David. Tell him to give you ten percent off whichever one you decide on. Fifteen percent if you buy all three." The kid nodded, scooped up the model boxes, and headed for the door.

Jo stepped in with Randall and closed the door behind her. "Good sale?" she asked.

"Not bad. Two fifty if he buys them all, about ninety for each one if he buys them separately," Dr. Evil replied.

"Does that math work?" Jo asked. She sat in one of the metal chairs across from the desk. Randall leaned against the door frame.

"Eh, rounding," the big man replied. "Now, what can I do for you, Joanna? I'm sure you aren't here just to help me maximize profits on model sales."

"I need your help," Jo said. Her voice was tight, clipped, and it was pretty obvious from the set of her shoulders that those were the last words she ever wanted to come from her lips.

Dr. Evil leaned forward, a grin splitting his face as he rubbed his hands together. "Absolutely, Jo. What can I do for you? You interested in getting back into the game? I'd be happy to sponsor The Iron Maiden in any tournaments you wanted to play. I'll get you cards, sleeves, supplies, teammates, anything you want. Hoodies, t-shirts...you name it, I'll have it made."

"Not that kind of help. The other kind. Magic."

"That's what I was talking about. Magic. I didn't think you were going to step down into Yu-Gi-Oh after playing in the big...oh." His face fell, and he leaned back in his chair. "You mean the real stuff."

"What else would she mean?" Randall asked. "What is this Iron Maiden stuff?"

"There's a card game called Magic: the Gathering," Jo began.

"Yeah, I saw signs and stuff out front. Looks interesting."

"Don't," Jo said with a sharp wave of her hand. "It's more addictive than crack, and at least as expensive. Anyway, I used to play. A lot. And I was good. Really good."

"One of the best," Dr. Evil agreed. He wore a solemn look, like he mourned something lost. "She was one of the best I'd ever seen. Until she quit. The world lost a great Magic player when you retired, Joanna."

"I grew up, Leon," Jo replied. "Sometimes we have to do things like that."

"I disagree. Growing older is mandatory; growing up is optional." Dr. Evil shook his head.

"Anyway," Jo went on. "I played a lot of Magic, and Leon...excuse me, Dr. Evil always wanted me to play on his team."

"I wanted you to anchor my team," Leon added. "I wanted to build the whole team around you. A different kind of Magic team. Not just a bunch of nerdy misfits, but a team with something dramatically different."

"A girl," Jo said.

"Women are dramatically underrepresented on professional teams and at competitive events, and you could have helped change that. But you quit." Leon's forehead wrinkled. "But I understand. You got married, had a kid, then..."

"Yeah, then," Jo said, her tone making it clear she didn't want to discuss "then." "But now I'm here, about magic, and not the card game. There's trouble, and I need your help."

"The demon?" the big man asked.

"You know about the demon?" Randall's eyes went wide. "Did you—"

"No," Leon waved a hand sharply. "I don't mess with the dark stuff. I don't even let the dabblers run their LARPs out of here."

Randall looked from Leon to Jo. "I don't..."

"Live Action Role Play," Jo supplied. "It's the stuff that even nerds think is nerdy. Look, Leon, I need your help. This demon, he's bad news. I don't know what he's up to, but he's after somebody I know. He...killed a friend of mine tonight, and he took my mom and..." Her words trailed off. Jo took a deep breath and squared her shoulders. "He's got my kid, Leon. He took Ginny, and I have to take my friend to him or he'll hurt her."

Leon looked at her for a long minute. "Ginny? I never even knew her name, Jo. Of course I'll help. What do you need? What's so special about your friend here?"

Jo looked confused for a second, then let out a sharp laugh. "Oh no, it's not Randall. He's just a cop. He's helping. The friend I have to take...well, he's an angel."

Dr. Evil's head snapped up. "What? What do you mean, an angel?"

"I mean an angel like wings, Heaven, harps, all that crap. You know, an angel. A big one."

The big man's eyes widened. "Is he here?"

"No, I have to go find him next. We were supposed to meet up tonight, but things have changed since we made our plans. So I'm going to him, then I have to convince him that he's really an angel and has to help me rescue my little girl."

"So he's asleep?" Leon asked.

"He doesn't know what he is, if that's what you mean by asleep," Jo agreed.

"Do angels sleep?" Randall asked. "I mean, the normal way."

"I have no idea, and I don't care right now. All I care about is getting Mitch to grab hold of that sword in my trunk and take the fight to this demon so I can get my mama and baby girl back home safe. Now, what do you have that can bring this angel to his senses, Leon?" Jo asked.

Leon leaned back in his chair, the metal protesting at the abuse. He clasped his hands on his expansive chest and looked up at the ceiling as though the answer was written in the fluorescent fixture. After almost a full minute, he looked at Joanna and Randall. "I don't know, but I have a couple of ideas. Can you go get him and bring him back here? I need to make a few preparations, and I'll have to clear out space in the back room. It's been a while since I did any major rituals. I've got some overstock in the middle of my circle."

Jo nodded. "Yeah, I can do that. We'll go get Mitch and bring him back here. But Leon, we have to hurry. I've got to meet this demon at midnight or he'll hurt Ginny."

"It's ten now, so don't screw around. Where does your guy live?" Leon asked.

"I'm not sure, but I can find him," Jo said. She stood up and turned to Randall. "Let's go."

"I need him," Dr. Evil said, pulling himself to his feet. He was even bigger standing, almost six-and-a-half feet tall, with his neon green shirt glaring in the hideous fluorescent light. "There's a lot of crap to move in the back."

"Fine," Jo said. "I'll be back as soon as I can." She opened the door and headed to the front of the store, pulling out her cell phone as she went. She swiped her finger across the screen and typed in her security code. "Dennis, I need you."

"What's up?" the unicorn head on her screen asked.

"I need you to trace Mitch's cell phone for me."

"Do you have the number?" the unicorn asked.

"Yeah, it's in my contacts."

"I've got him. But Jo?" The unicorn head was gone, replaced by Dennis's human face.

"Yeah, what's wrong?"

"He's moving."

"Okay, I guess he's headed over to the gym early. I can meet him there before he gets in and finds—"

"He's not going to the gym. He's driving east, toward the airport. I just checked the flights. He's booked on a redeye to New York leaving in ninety minutes."

"Son of a gun," Jo muttered. She jerked open her car door and slid behind the wheel. She stuck the phone in a cradle and activated the Bluetooth, then jammed the car in reverse and squealed out of the parking lot. "Get me on him, Dennis. We've got to catch that angel before he gets the heck out of Dodge."

———————

M itch was standing in the clear Plexiglas shelter marked with a blue "Z" when Jo pulled her red Kia Soul to a stop in front of him. The undercover angel's head snapped up and his eyes went wide as she walked around the front of the car, opened the passenger door, and gestured to him.

"Get in," she said. A thin blonde girl in sweatpants with pink headphones pressed to her ears looked up and pulled her headphones down around her neck. "Put the 'phones back on, Princess. This is grown-up business."

The girl opened her mouth to speak, but Jo held up one finger at her. "Didn't anybody ever tell you not to mess with a pissed-off black woman when she's fussin' at her man? Now sit your lily-white behind down and stay out of my business." The girl's eyes widened, but she put her headphones on and sat down. She pulled a cell phone out of her pocket and started typing furiously on the screen.

Jo looked back at Mitch. "Now get your butt in the car before Princess Barbie's tweet goes viral and I end up starring in the remake of *Diary of a Mad Black Woman*."

Mitch took the green duffel bag off his shoulder and let it drop to the ground by his feet. "I'm not going with you, Jo. I don't know how you did that trick with the sword, and I don't know what you want out of me, but I'm no angel, and I'm not going to go fight no monster."

"You are, and you are," Jo said. "I don't have time to play games with you, Mitch. You are the Archangel Michael, you are going with me to deal with this demon, and you are getting in my car right now."

"Is there a problem, sir?" Jo turned to see the airport shuttle idling behind her car with the door open. The blonde girl stepped up into the bus and leaned down to the driver's ear. He nodded, then said, "You folks take care of your personal business at home. I've got runs to make. You getting on or not?"

Mitch picked up his bag and stepped forward, but Jo put a hand on his chest. "He's got my daughter, Mitch. He came into my house, murdered Marla, and kidnapped my mother and my baby girl. I need you to help me get them back. I can't do it without you." Her voice was low, her words urgent. She looked up into the big man's blue eyes, saw his resistance start to waver.

"Please, Mitch. You're the only one that can help me." Her voice cracked, and she hated herself a little bit for it, but she couldn't hold everything inside. Not this time.

Mitch stepped back, then waved to the bus driver. "Go ahead. I'll catch the next one."

"Your funeral, dude. You gotta look out for the crazy ones." The driver closed the door and pulled around Jo's car, belching black diesel smoke all over the two of them.

Mitch looked down at Jo. "You fucking with me?"

"I don't do that," Jo said. "And watch your mouth."

"Did somebody really take your mother and kid?"

"Yeah. Slaughtered Marla in my living room. She must have put up some kind of a fight. Tore down a couple bookshelves and wrecked my TV. But apparently that wasn't a clear enough message. Got Jake, too. Left him lying in the middle of the gym in a pool of his own blood."

"Shit," Mitch said. He glanced at Jo, who frowned at him. "Sorry, slipped out. What are we going to do?"

"I've got a guy working on that right now. We need to go meet up with him, then get to the school by midnight or they'll hurt Mama and Ginny."

"Do you know how many there are?" Mitch asked.

"I don't know anything," Jo said. "I know where to be and when to be there. I don't know what we're going up against, or how many. I don't care. They've got my baby, and I'm going to get her back." She stood there, fists clenched and jaw set, looking up at Mitch.

"And I'm going to help you," Mitch said. He put a hand on her shoulder. "But we need to get as much information as we can. We can't just go in there half-cocked. We need to do some surveillance, get the lay of the land before we go charging in there guns blazing."

"Sword," Jo corrected.

"Huh?"

"We're going in there sword blazing, not guns blazing. Now where did you learn all that military talk? I thought you were just a dumb jock."

"I've been some places," Mitch said. "Seen some things."

"Yeah," Jo agreed. "More than you even remember. Now get in the car. We've got to go save my baby girl."

The parking lot was empty when they pulled back into Dr. Evil's game shop twenty minutes later. Jo opened the door, and Mitch turned to her. "This is the place? Your guy works here?"

"Something like that. Now come on. We've got to be at the school in an hour, and I don't know how long whatever Leon is planning will take."

Jo got a long duffel bag out of her trunk, and they walked into the deserted game shop. Half the overhead lights were off, and the green-haired boy was sitting at a long table playing something on a handheld game. He looked up when Mitch closed the door behind them.

"Go ahead and lock the deadbolt," the kid said. "I'll take you back to the Doc."

"You really call him that?" Jo asked.

The kid shot her a crooked grin. "Depends on whether I want to yank his chain or not. But yeah, sometimes I call him Doc. He says there used to be a chick that called him that, and we're the only two people who could ever get away with it. That you?"

Jo smiled, memories of a simpler life playing across her mind as they followed the kid through the darkened store. "Guilty as charged. I'm Jo."

"Spencer," the kid replied.

"You involved in the other business?" Jo asked.

"I'm learning. Leon thinks I've got some talent, so he's been teaching me a few things."

"Be careful. There's some bad things in the world."

"That's why I want to learn magic. I want to stop the bad things from hurting people. That's what you do, right? That's why you're here?" The kid stopped in front of a door with two deadbolts.

"Yeah, that's why I'm here. And sometimes it's what I do," Jo said. She reached out for the knob, then looked at the kid. "But you think hard before you go down this road, kid. There are doors that can't be closed again and things that can't be unseen. Once you start messing with the ugly stuff in the world, it has a bad habit of messing with you right back. That's why we're here. Something nasty has my mother and my daughter, and we've got to fight it to get them back and keep this thing from hurting anybody else."

Spencer looked up at her, his round face pale in the dim light. "I've already seen plenty of ugly. This isn't the best neighborhood, you know. And I live two blocks from here."

Jo knew the area. There were flop houses, whorehouses, and at least one meth lab within a quarter mile. Leon set up his shop there not just because the rent was cheap, but in hopes that he could give the kids in that part of town a safe place to go. It never hurt to have a wizard hanging out in a tough neighborhood, either.

She nodded to the kid. "Okay, just be careful."

He looked at her, then opened the door for her. "You too."

Jo and Mitch stepped through the door into the shop's storeroom, and Spencer closed and locked the door behind them. Mitch spun around, but Jo put a hand on his arm.

"It's okay. The deadbolts will open from either side, but if something mean and stupid gets loose, it gives the kid at least a chance of getting away." She pointed to the door, and there were indeed latches to throw the deadbolts on both sides. Mitch relaxed, then turned back to the room. His eyes grew wide as he took in the room.

What was probably a normal warehouse room less than an hour before now looked like something out of a bad horror movie. A large circle was drawn in the floor with a five-pointed star touching the circle with all the points. Strange symbols Jo recognized and wards in various ancient languages ringed the perimeter, Celtic runes alternating with Enochian script and hand-scrawled Latin. White pillar candles burned at each point of the star. Incense burned in several holders around the room, filling the air with the mixed scents of sandalwood, vanilla, lavender, and clove. A smudge stick lay smoldering in the upper segment of the circle, its smoke wafting up behind of Leon, who was seated in the center with his legs crossed and his hands extended, palm out.

The big man wore loose black pants that looked like they were homespun cotton, with a formless grey shirt on top. It looked like nothing more than a pair of cheap sweat pants, or maybe long-sleeved hospital scrubs, with blobs of colored wax and other odd stains dotting the shirt and pants. He was barefoot, and bareheaded, sweat beading on his expansive forehead, but there was a tranquility about him that made Jo smile. If she had to guess, she would say that he was happier than he'd been in quite some time.

She knew, from long conversations years ago, that he wanted nothing more than to do good in the world, but had stepped away from actively practicing magic when his son was born. He didn't want to attract the wrong kind of attention to his family, a concern that Jo felt all too acutely just then.

Leon looked up at her and smiled. "You're back. Good. Everything is in place, we can begin."

"It better all be in place," panted Randall from a folding chair in the corner of the room. "I can't even count how many boxes of crap I had to move. You'd think stock in a toy store would be easy, but no, that crap is heavy!"

Jo laughed. "Let me guess, Leon had to work on his very important preparations, so you did all the heavy lifting?"

"Girl, you ain't wrong," Randall said, wiping a bead of sweat from his chin. "I can't even pronounce most of the crap I moved, but I know I don't ever want to lay hands on it again!" He waved a hand at boxes of anime action figures, collectible card games, and stacks and stacks of Gundam models.

"What are we doing here, Jo? I thought we were going to get your daughter," Mitch said.

"Mitch, this is Leon. I hope he can wake you up." Jo gestured to the man seated in the circle, who nodded.

"Hello, Mitch. I would get up, but let's face it, I'm a big old man, and it's not easy to get up from the floor at my age. Now come sit down across from me in the circle, and we'll see what we can see. Jo, did you bring the sword?"

"Right here," she said, pulling the duffel from her shoulder. She set the bag on the floor, unzipped it, and drew out the sword. It was a plain weapon, nothing outwardly special about it. But she'd watched it burst into flames when Mitch touched it, and she'd seen demons tear through ruins to get it. She knew the unadorned weapon was actually one of the most holy objects on Earth, in the right hands.

She held it out to Mitch, who stepped back, his hands up. "No thank you," he said. "I remember the headache that thing gave me last night."

"You're going to have to touch it, Mitch. This whole thing hinges on you taking up the sword," Jo said. She stepped forward, hilt extended to the fighter, but Mitch just kept backing up.

"You guys do your hocus-pocus, then we'll talk about me putting my hands back on that thing," Mitch said.

Jo took a deep breath and turned to Leon. "It's okay," he said. "Give me the sword."

She handed him the sword, and Leon looked up at Mitch. "Sit." All hints of the jovial game shop owner were gone. His voice had steel behind it, and Mitch stepped into the circle and sat down in the center, his knees almost touching Leon's.

Leon laid the blade across his lap and stretched out his hands, palms up. "Put your hands on mine."

Mitch did as instructed.

Leon closed his eyes and began to mutter under his breath. Jo took a step back, making sure that her toes were nowhere near the edge of the circle, and closed her eyes as a bright flash of blue filled the room. When she opened her eyes and blinked away the dazzle-spots, a dome of blue-white energy crackled over the circle, completely enclosing Leon and Mitch. She could see the big man's mouth moving, but no sound penetrated the protective barrier of the circle.

Randall stepped to her side. "What the ever-loving shit is going on here?"

"You didn't buy any of it until right now, did you?" Jo asked.

"Not really," the stunned cop admitted. "I mean, I hoped you weren't crazy because I like you. I really hoped you weren't stupid *and* crazy because after what I saw at your house and your friend's gym, that was probably going to get me killed. But never in a million years did I think you were just telling me the truth. Like, the real truth. I figured you weren't lying because I've been a cop long enough to know when somebody's just lying to my face, but I thought you were probably..."

"Crazy or stupid?" Jo finished for him.

"Or both," he agreed.

"Yeah, a lot of times I think I probably am both, for ever getting mixed up in this mess."

"Then why?" Randall asked.

"Why what?"

"Why get mixed up in this stuff? It's not safe, and it can't pay much."

Jo laughed quietly. "Try nothing at all. This is a volunteer position, my friend."

"So why do it?"

Jo looked at him. "Why are you a cop? I know that ain't for the money."

Randall didn't hesitate for a second. "People need help. I can help. I'm supposed to do that." He nodded at her. "Okay. I get it."

"Yep," she said. "It's the exact same thing. There are bad people in the world. We have people like you to take care of that. There are bad things in this world, too. Things that might not have started in this world and might not be the kind of things that police can deal with. For those things, for the monsters in the closet, the creatures under the bed, the things that go bump in the night? For those things, you have me. Me and people like me. The Shadow Council. We fight against the dark, so the people we love can live in the light."

Randall nodded. "I get it. Kinda. I'm still trying to process the whole 'magic is real' thing. But I get why you mess with it."

"Because somebody's got to," Jo said. Just then, the light surrounding the circle winked out, and Leon looked up at them.

"I'm sorry," he said. "I can't reach him. I mean, there's something blocking him off from the divine part of himself, and I can't break through it. I'm just not strong enough, or don't know the right spells, or something. I don't even know what I don't know." The big man heaved himself to one knee, then stood as he spoke. His voice was tight with frustration, his forehead furrowed. "I don't get it, Joanna. I looked at him for mystical influences, and there was nothing. I dove into his consciousness looking for tampering, and there was nothing. It's like whatever makes him...I don't even know how to explain it, but the angel part of him is just missing. I'm sorry. I can't help you."

He kicked over one of the candles, and it flickered out, spilling wax on the floor. "Spencer!" he bellowed. "Come on back here and help clean up." Leon turned back to Jo and handed her the sword. "I could feel the power in this weapon. It *wants* to come to life. It wants to fight. Maybe that will be enough."

"It'll have to be," Jo said. She took the sword from him and turned to Mitch. "Let's go. We've got less than an hour before we have to meet up with whoever has my baby."

Mitch stood up, flowing to his feet in an easy motion. Even without the sword burning in his hand, he looked dangerous. "Okay," he said. "Let's do this."

Jo looked at him, her eyebrows raised. "You're not going to argue with me?"

"They've got your kid, right?"

"Yeah."

"Then we'll get her back. I was a dick before. I'm sorry. I won't let a little kid get hurt just because I don't want to play magic angel or whatever. I'll help."

"Me too," Randall said. "Besides, if I stay here, I have to help put all this crap back where it was." They all laughed but turned somber as they walked to the door.

Joanna put her hand on the door and turned back to Leon, who was gathering up candles and blowing them out. "Thank you, Doc."

"You're welcome," he said. "And don't call me Doc," he said with a smile.

She gave him a little smile back and stepped out into the dark store. "Come on boys, let's go fight a monster."

J o stepped out of her Kia and walked around to the back of the car. Randall and Mitch joined her as she lifted the door and pulled out her hammer and a long brown leather duster. She clipped a ring to her belt and threaded the handle through it, then slipped on the heavy coat.

"Are we in a blacksploitation remake of *Tombstone*, Jo?" Randall asked.

"No, and I'm too short to be Pam Grier," she replied. "This thing is heavy, hot as hell, and makes me look stupid, but the leather is thick and tough enough to stop a knife or claw, and I wish I'd had it last night when we ran into that thing in the hall."

She reached in and picked up the sword wrapped in a blue tarp. She held the bundle out to Mitch.

He stepped back, holding up both hands. "I'm not touching that thing, Jo."

"You're probably going to have to," she said. "It might be the only thing that can kill whatever is waiting for us in there."

Mitch shook his head and held up the shotgun Randall had given him. "Anything I can't kill with a twelve-gauge is something I shouldn't be trying to kill in the first place."

"I'll take it," Randall said, holding out his hand.

"Do you know how to use a sword, Randall?" Jo asked.

"I've seen *Braveheart* twice and every *Lord of the Rings* movie. That oughta count for something, right? Besides, I have my Sig for backup if I can't remember which end to put in the bad guys."

Jo shook her head and handed him the sword. He stripped the tarp off the blade and tested the weight, then slashed at the air a few times, getting the feel of the weapon.

"Let's go," Jo said. She closed the hatchback and passed a flashlight to Mitch. "I need both hands free," she said, gesturing with the hammer.

Randall pulled a flashlight from his belt and clicked it on. He led the way, with Jo behind him and Mitch bringing up the rear as they walked across the deserted parking lot. There was only one car on the premises besides Jo's little Kia, and it was parked on the opposite side of the building, pulled all the way up the sidewalk right to the door. Randall led the trio toward the back of the school, traversing a basketball court and an expansive lawn before coming to a closed double door.

Jo reached out and tried the handle, finding it unlocked. She looked at her companions. "You think they unlocked all the doors, or did they plan on us coming in this way?"

"This is the only door on this side of the building, so they probably parked where they did on purpose, assuming we'd use the door farthest from their car. So yeah, I guess they planned on us coming this way," Randall said.

"Should we look for another way in?" Jo asked.

"Why bother?" Mitch asked. The others turned to him. "You said these guys have your daughter and your mom, right?"

Jo nodded.

"Then it doesn't matter where we come in. All they have to do is sit in one place with the hostages, and we'll go to them. They know where we'll be, and they know roughly when we'll be there because you've only got about twenty minutes to get there before your midnight deadline now. Makes way more tactical sense for them to just let us in and wait for us."

"So that's we do, huh? We just do exactly what they want and go in there?" Randall asked.

"Yep," Jo said. "We go in there, kick some ass, and walk out with my daughter and my mother. Any questions?"

"Yeah," Randall said. "What are we waiting for?" He pulled open the door and stepped through, his flashlight cutting a narrow blue-white beam through the darkened hall. Jo followed, with Mitch again bringing up the rear. They walked down the long hallway, then turned right at the first intersection, heading toward the gym.

"He's probably got Mama and Ginny in one of the locker rooms. Randall, why don't you go see if you can find them while me and Mitch look for the demon?"

"We should stick together," Randall said. The others looked at him as if demanding a reason. "Oh come on, haven't you two ever seen a horror movie? You split up, and the one who goes off by himself dies. Especially if it's the black dude. Just in case you missed it, this doesn't rub off." He held up the back of his hand and rubbed the skin with a finger. His dark brown skin didn't change.

"So the black dude is not going off by himself in this movie," Randall said.

"One problem with that whole thing, Randall," Jo said. "I'm black, too."

"Doesn't matter. You're the hero. They won't kill you first. This isn't some M. Night Shamalamadingdong movie, just going for the cheap plot twist. This is real life, and I ain't getting killed tonight."

"Okay, we stay together. Then we need to go this way," Jo said, pointing down the hall. The men followed her lead, and they began to see a sliver of light under the double doors at the end of the hall.

"Is that the gym?" Randall asked.

"Yeah," Mitch said. "Keep an eye out up here. There are two locker rooms. If anybody's going to jump us, that's where they'll be."

They crossed to the far side of the hall to avoid passing directly in front of the locker room doors, but no one leapt out at them. Moments later, they stood at the entrance to the gym. Jo shifted her hammer to her left hand, reached out with her right, and yanked the door open.

They gym was lit by about a third of the overhead lights, casting deep shadows around the walls but illuminating the empty cage in the center of the basketball court. Jo's eyes scanned the room until she found her mother and daughter sitting on the one extended section of bleachers. Both Harrison women had their hands tied behind them and silver duct tape over their mouths, but even at a distance, Jo could see a fierce determination in their eyes. They may have been captured, but their spirits were unbowed.

Shelton stepped into the light, his hands clasped in front of him and a broad smile on his face. "Joanna, thank you so much for coming. I am thrilled that you could make our little soiree, and so pleased that you brought guests. I know Mitchell, of course, but who is your little blue friend?"

"Phoenix PD," Randall announced in a booming voice. "Get on your knees and put your hands on your head." He holstered his flashlight and drew his pistol, leveling the weapon at Shelton.

"Shel?" Jo said, bewildered. "You're part of this?"

"Part of this?" Shelton repeated. "Oh sweetie, I'm not part of this at all. I *am* this. This is all my operation. The whole fight club has been a plan to get my hands on your divine little friend here." He gestured to Mitch.

Mitch glared at the promoter and pointed the shotgun at him. "I think the officer gave you an order, Shel. I think you should do what he said."

"I think you should shut up when your betters are speaking, angel," Shel snapped, waving a hand at the group. A wave of force struck them, carrying away the shotgun and Randall's pistol. Jo held onto her hammer, drawing a raised eyebrow from Shelton. "Really? That's interesting."

Shelton walked forward, his eyes glowing red in the gloom. His appearance began to change as he approached, growing larger, his clothes vanishing as he grew to six, then seven feet tall. Black bat wings extended from his shoulders, and his skin took on a deep crimson tone. A long, spiked tail waved sinuously behind him, and his heavily muscled arms ended in black inch-long claws.

He shook his head, long black braids flowing down his back. "Ah, that's better. You have no idea how cramped my wings get after being folded up in that stupid human suit. But this is better, isn't it? No need for subterfuge, no need to hide anything. Just good, old-fashioned, honest murder."

Jo stepped forward, swinging her hammer in a looping blow. Shel raised an arm and wrapped his hand around the head of the weapon, enclosing it in his huge fist. Smoke billowed from his fingers, and he snatched his hand back. "Ouch! That hurt, Jo. What did you do, have this thing blessed?"

"First thing I did when I got home from Atlanta. I went to church, prayed about what I'd seen, and asked Father Timothy to bless my hammer. He was a little confused, but he did it."

"Well, that hurt, and that means I'm going to have to kill you, too. I was just going to kill the angel and let you go, but now...well, everybody into the cage!"

"Screw you, demon," Jo said, raising the hammer again. "I'm not getting into that cage again, especially with you."

Demon-Shel smiled at her. "Of course you are. Or I'll kill your family."

Jo took a menacing step forward, but stopped at the demon's upraised hand. "You don't want me to prove it, do you?" he asked. Shel pointed his hand at the opposite bleachers, and his eyes glowed red. Seconds later, a tendril of smoke curled up from behind the bleachers. The fire broke free and climbed the stacked wall of closed wooden seats, engulfing the entire wall in flame. Shel waved his hand, and the fire vanished, leaving soot and cinders behind.

"I don't have to be near them to kill them, Jo. I just have to want to make it happen. Now get your ass in the cage, or I will cook them from the inside out!" He bellowed the last, and Jo saw the pair of wicked fangs jutting up from his lower jaw.

Jo glared at him. "If I do this, if I fight you, you let them go?"

"You have my word. If you get into the cage and fight me, your mother and daughter will leave this place unharmed. I will even return your grandfather's hammer to them after I finish gutting you."

Jo recognized this for the generosity the demon thought it was and nodded. "Fine, I'll fight. Come on, Mitch." She started toward the cage, Mitch beside her.

"Well, I'm not going in no cage. And you aren't going to hurt them, asshole." Randall punctuated his words with five shots from the small revolver he held in his hand.

Jo shouted, "Randall, no!" then watched in horror as Shel took all five rounds right to the chest, staggering but not falling down.

The demon looked at Randall, then looked down at the cluster of five small holes in his torso. "Ouch," he said. "That wasn't very nice, Randall. Or very smart." He snarled at the stunned police officer, then took three big strides forward and ripped Randall's throat out with his right hand.

Shel looked at the trachea in his hand, licked the blood pouring from it, then spat on Randall's dying body. "Too many trans fats, Randall. Your cholesterol was awful. Makes the blood too thick, messes with the texture." He dropped the bloody hunk of flesh on the floor, then leaned down and wiped his hand on Randall's pants leg.

Shel straightened up and waved to the cage. "Let's go, children. We have a fight to get to, and your daughter has years of therapy to earn." He walked past Jo and Mitch, straight into the cage. Jo handed her hammer to Mitch and went to kneel at Randall's side. She closed his eyes, folded his hands on his chest, and picked up the sword from where it lay by his body.

Mitch and Jo went into the cage together but split as soon as they entered the octagon, spreading out to attack from two angles. As they readied for a charge, Shel held up his hand.

"Wait for it, my dears. You don't think this is a private event, do you?" He snapped his fingers, and the rest of the lights in the gym flashed to life. Jo blinked from the sudden brightness, bringing one hand up to shield her eyes.

"Welcome, my friends, to the show that never ends," Shel said in a sing-song voice. "Tonight we have your inimitable host—me, facing two challengers at once. Please welcome Iron Jo Henry and the Archangel Michael!" Canned applause echoed through the deserted room as Shel twirled in place and pumped his arms over his head.

He sighed and looked at Jo. "Aren't you two even going to *pretend* to be excited? I mean it's not every day you get to battle a demon, is it?"

"You'd be surprised," Jo replied.

"Okay," Shel said. "But how often do you get it streamed live direct to Hell!" He waved his hand around the ring, and Jo looked up. Mounted above the cage were half a dozen GoPro miniature video cameras, no doubt doing exactly what Shel said—streaming the match to whatever and whoever wanted to see it.

"Great, I get to die on live TV, and I forgot to wear makeup," Jo growled.

"Don't worry," Shel said. "When you're dead, I'll paint your face in angel blood. I hear it does wonders for the skin. Now let's ring the bell!"

Shel waved his hand again, and a bell rang from somewhere. He grinned across the ring at Jo and Mitch, then said, "Who wants to die first?"

Mitch and Jo spread out farther, working to make life as difficult for their opponent as possible. Jo tossed the sword in Mitch's direction, but he just scowled at her and shook his head. She hefted her hammer and charged the demon, hoping Mitch would at least take a couple of shots at its head while she distracted it.

She swung, but Shel ducked the blow easily. He came up with a slash at her stomach, his claws flashing out just an inch or two in front of her as she hopped back out of range. She ducked a slash at her face, then rolled to one side as she heard the bark of a gun at close range.

"Ow, dammit!" Shel said, his hand going to the back of his head. He turned around, and Jo saw Mitch standing there, a smoking pistol in his hand.

"Where the hell did you get that?" she asked.

"I swiped it out of Randall's trunk," he replied, squeezing off three more rounds. The bullets smacked into the demon's head and neck, tearing chunks of flesh from his face. Shel didn't go down, though, just waved his hand at Mitch and grinned as the gun flew from his hand over the top of the cage.

Jo took advantage of the momentary distraction and laid a shot on

Shel's knee that landed with a sickening *crunch*. The big demon dropped, a howl of pain piercing the night. He spun on one knee, then sprang at Jo, who dove to the left in a frantic attempt to avoid getting ripped to shreds by an angry demon.

"Bitch, I will eat your entrails for that," Shel snarled.

Jo stood and squared her shoulders. "Don't call me that."

"I will call you anything I want, bitch," the demon said, moving forward at a limp. Its right leg dragged, nearly useless, but in a cage barely thirty feet across, Shel didn't have to get far. One good lunge and Jo had to duck under outstretch claws and lash out with her hammer again to keep from being crushed.

The hammer landed a glancing blow on the demon's hip, just enough to spin the monster around and give Jo a little breathing room. Mitch darted in, his gun forgotten, and launched a series of kicks at Shel, alternating between head and knee shots. Nothing significant landed, though, and when the demon planted its good leg and sprang away from Mitch's assault, it caught Jo around the middle and tumbled her to the floor.

Before she could react, Shel was on her. He straddled her middle and wrapped his hands around her neck. Even without using his claws, the demon's hands enveloped her throat. Jo thrashed and struggled the best she could, but the beast was too big, and she couldn't get any leverage to hit it with her hammer.

She lay there, struggling, as the world started to shift to grey, and black dots closed in on her vision. She turned her face to the side, and just before everything went away, she caught one last glimpse of her mother and daughter in the stands, looking on in terror. Ginny's eyes were huge, and Cassandra's face was streaked with tears, but the old woman didn't look away, just like she hadn't looked away when Jo's father died, all those years ago. Jo saw one last loving look in her mother's eyes, then her vision faded to nothing.

Suddenly a shriek like a thousand tormented bats filled the air, and the pressure vanished from Jo's throat. The weight on her chest gone, she rolled to her side and coughed, sucking in huge gasps of sweet, welcome air.

After long seconds of coughing and trying to breathe, Jo looked up and saw Mitch standing over her, flaming sword in his hand. His face was a rictus of pain, and his knuckles were white on the hilt of the sword, but he held it. He held it upright, the flames dancing along the edge of the blade and casting yellow-orange light across the ring.

"Come at me, motherfucker," Mitch said in a low growl.

Shel leaned against the far wall of the cage, a mixture of fear and elation on his face. "It really is you. I didn't know, but now...the sword...I see it. You really are Michael."

"Apparently so," Mitch said.

"I have to leave," Shelton said. "There are people who will be very interested in this news."

"You're not going anywhere, demon. Not even to Hell." Jo levered herself up from the floor with her hammer, then hefted it into both hands as she caught her balance. She looked over to Mitch, who nodded. "Let's finish this."

Mitch and Jo advanced on the demon, who now had a black-rimmed wound in its shoulder to match its pulped knee. Shel waved his clawed hands in front of his body, holding them at bay with his razor-sharp talons. He steered their fight around the perimeter of the octagon, turning slightly to his left with every step, working to position himself with his back to the cage door for a quick exit.

Jo took in his plan in an instant and took a deep breath. "There's no way this doesn't suck," she said, holding her hammer straight out in front of her and letting out a guttural yell. "Aaaahhhh!"

Jo charged the demon, lowering her shoulder into Shel's abdomen and slamming his spine into the cage, right on one of the lightly padded uprights. She knew from experience just how thin the padding was and just how solid the four-inch metal tubing that made up the corners of the homemade ring was.

Shel's head snapped back and impacted the ringpost with a hollow *gong* sound, and Jo heard a rib or two snap under her shoulder. She backed up a few inches, then drove her shoulder into the demon's gut again, letting a grim smile play across her lips at the *whoosh* of air escaping the monster's lungs.

She felt the claws scrabbling across the leather coat on her back, tearing the thick material but unable to get to her flesh. She jammed the hammer into Shel's lower abdomen, pressing the blessed silver-coated head into the demon's body for a little more damage. The beast howled and tried to pull back, but there was nowhere to go. Jo felt the hammer blow of an elbow crash into her spine, and she fell to her knees.

On the ground, she bobbed her head side to side avoiding knee strikes from the demon, then slammed the hammer down onto one of Shel's unprotected feet. A shriek filled the room, and Jo found herself rolling to the side as he thrust her off and dove for the middle of the ring.

Only to run right into a flaming sword held by a pissed-off angel in disguise. Mitch jabbed the blade at the demon's middle, forcing Shel to backpedal and pinwheel his arms to keep balance. Jo stood up and swung her hammer at the demon's head, connecting with a resounding *crack*.

The monster fell to the canvas, unmoving. Jo stayed back, rolling her shoulders and checking for wounds. Her coat was much the worse for wear, but the leather did its job in protecting her from the demon's claws. She looked at Mitch, who stood with the sword in hand, a grimace of pain fixed on his face.

"Still nothing?" she asked.

"I still don't feel like picking up a harp and dancing on clouds, if that's what you mean," he replied, his voice tight.

"That still hurt?" She nodded at the flaming blade.

"Like somebody jabbing needles into my palms," he said with a nod.

"Let's trade." Jo walked over to him and held out a hand. He passed her the sword and took her hammer with a relieved sigh. The flames winked out the instant the sword left his grasp, and the room dimmed considerably. Jo looked up at the bleachers. "Y'all okay up there?"

Her mother and daughter nodded vigorously, and Jo called out, "I'll be up there in just a second. Mama, you cover Ginny's eyes." She looked back at the demon sprawled in the center of the ring.

"I don't know if this will work, or if you have to do it," she said, walking to Shel's lifeless body. "But there is no way I'm leaving this son of a gun in one piece."

"Do you ever just say son of a bitch like a normal person?" Mitch said, stepping up next to her.

"I'm trying to set a good example for my baby," Jo replied. She raised the sword up over her head and brought it down in a sharp chopping motion designed to sever the demon's head from its shoulders.

And it would have, if there had been a demon there when her blow landed. But Shel sprang to his feet in a lightning-fast kip-up, going from flat on his back to standing before the pair in a blink, and he laid Jo out with an uppercut right on the point of her jaw. She fell back like a redwood toppling in a forest, and the sword went flying all the way across the ring. Jo lay on the mat, her head ringing and her vision blurry, as Shel stalked Mitch.

"Now it's just you and me, angel. Just like in the bad old days, when you killed thirty of my brothers in the Battle for the Gates," Shel said, his voice a sibilant rasp.

"I don't remember any of that, but if you want to join them, come get some." Mitch rolled his neck and popped his knuckles, bouncing from one foot to the other as he backed away from the demon.

"You know you're going to die, right? It doesn't matter how divine you are, once I rip that meat suit into half a dozen pieces, your pure little essence will just float away, scattered to the ends of the cosmos. There won't be enough of your soul to put back together. You'll be dead, angel, and I'll be left here laughing and pissing on your corpse."

"That's nasty," Jo said, struggling to her feet. "Don't you know there's a lady present?"

"Show me a lady, bitch," Shel growled at her. He swung a looping backhanded left at her and knocked her ten feet sideways.

"She said, don't call her that," Mitch said. Shel turned and Mitch swung the borrowed hammer like he was Babe Ruth in the bottom of the ninth. The silver blessed hammer head crunched into the demon's face again, and Shel crumpled to the ground like his strings had been cut.

"Nice one," Jo gasped from the floor. "But I don't think he's done." She pointed, and Mitch turned from her to see Shel rising from the mat once more. This time the demon didn't spring up, but rolled over to one knee and stood, a little shaky on its feet.

"What's the matter, big guy?" Mitch asked. "That one hurt?"

"Foolish angel, without access to your divinity, you can't destroy me. But I can destroy you. Without you, there will be no return to the Throne. That means that we get to play on Earth as long as we like." Shel smiled and advanced on Mitch. He kept his arms low and stretched out to the sides, claws extended. Mitch watched the demon's hands but had to dive to the floor when the spiked tail lashed out at his face. Mitch swung the hammer at the demon's ankles, but Shel leapt over it easily.

Shel landed with one foot on the hammer's handle, and kicked Mitch in the face with the other. He reached down and picked Mitch up, holding him high overhead with his left hand. The hammer discarded, Mitch dangled in the demon's grasp, unarmed and defenseless.

"Look upon the face of your slayer, angel. Know that I, Shelaxis, will go down in the annals of our history as the demon that slew the great Archangel Michael." Shel drew back his right hand, claws extended to rip Mitch's heart out.

Just before he struck, a blade suddenly protruded from the demon's chest. Shel looked down, his eyes going wide as he took in the tip of Michael's sword sticking through just above his left nipple. Mitch dropped to the ground, landing on his feet, and reached out to the blade. He wrapped his hand around the blade where it sprang from the demon's chest and shut his eyes against the brilliance as the sword burst into flames. Still inside the demon, the sword burned with a holy fire that consumed Shelaxis from the inside out, and within seconds, the demon was reduced to a pile of ash in the middle of the ring.

The sword clattered to the floor, and Jo and Mitch sagged against the chain link walls of the cage. They looked at one another, exchanged weary smiles, and turned for the door. Jo held the cage door open for Mitch, who picked up the sword as he walked.

"I think this is yours," he said, passing her back the hammer.

"Yep," she said. "You keeping the sword?"

"If I can figure out how to turn these damn flames off," he replied. "Otherwise it's a little conspicuous."

Jo laughed, then looked up at the bleachers. "I'm coming, Mama. It's all over. We can go home now."

EPILOGUE

"**W**hat the fuck do you mean, he doesn't know he's an angel?" the voice on the phone growled.

"Language, Harker," Jo replied. "My little girl is in the car."

"Sorry, Jo," the voice said. "Sorry, Ginny. Don't talk like me. Nice people don't talk like me."

"Are you not a nice person, Mr. Harker?" Ginny asked from the back seat of Shel's Lexus. The keys were hanging from the ignition, and Jo knew he wouldn't need it anymore.

"No, Ginny, most of the time I'm not a very nice person. Now please cover your ears while I talk to your mommy. I will probably use some other not very nice words," Harker said over the speakerphone.

Ginny did as she was told, and Jo smiled at her. "I don't know what the deal is, Harker. I put the sword in his hand, and it burst into flames, just like we thought. He used it to kill a demon, so there's definitely some divine something going on here. But he has no idea about who he really is."

"I think you people are batshit crazy," Mitch said from the

passenger seat, then winced as Cassandra leaned forward and smacked him on the back of the head. "Ow!"

"My daughter has done told y'all about cussing in front of her little girl. I might not be able to slap Harker right now, but he knows what he's got coming to him the next time I see him," the older woman said.

"Hello, Cassie." Harker's voice was softer now, with a tinge of sadness. "It's been a while."

"Almost thirty years, Quincy. Your uncle doing okay? I heard about his latest Renfield. Please pass along my condolences."

"Thank you, Cassie. I will. Next time your daughter comes back east, why don't you come along and bring that little girl? I know Luke would love to meet her."

"Quincy, as much as I love your uncle, I am not in the habit of taking my granddaughter on cross-country plane rides to visit vampires," Cassandra said with a laugh.

Harker laughed right back. "I can understand that, but I guess you're probably not in the habit of driving around with an angel in your car, either."

"You have a point, you old rascal. Tell Luke we'll get out there sometime this year. I promise." Cassandra leaned back in her seat and put her arm around Ginny. She pulled the girl close and replaced one of the hands covering the girl's ears with her own.

"I'm going to hold you to that, old woman. If you're not here by Christmas, I'll send Adam to play Santa Claus at your house."

"Oh Lord," Cassandra laughed, a rich, deep sound that filled the car. "I know I don't want that big oaf trying to fit down my chimney! Now you finish up with my baby so we can go home."

"Will do," Harker said. When he spoke again, his tone was all business. "Okay, Jo. I don't know what the deal is with your angel, but we need him back here. Put him on a plane tomorrow. I'll get you a credit card number. He'll be able to carry the sword on the flight. I'll take care of TSA."

Jo looked over at Mitch, who nodded at her. "Fine, Harker. But what are you going to do with him when he gets there?"

"Honestly? I have no idea. I suppose I'll put him in a spare bedroom and start working on breaking whatever spell has his memory blocked. It's not going to be pretty, and it's going to take a lot of time. Mind magic is complicated as—heck. It's complicated as heck, and I'm not very good at it to start with. I'm usually more the 'burn it all down and sift through the ashes' kind of magician. But we'll figure it out."

"And you have to have him there for this?" Jo asked. Mitch shot her a grateful smile.

"Yeah, I do," Harker replied. "It's not just for my research and the spell; it's to keep you safe. You got lucky killing Shelaxis. He was a low-level Pit Lord. If the folks downstairs get wind of an amnesiac angel wandering around without anybody watching his back magically, they're going to be on you like dogs on a bone. I can't let that happen."

"He's right," Mitch said. "You almost lost your mom and daughter once because of me. I won't let that happen again. I'll be on that plane in the morning."

"Good deal. I'll email you flight details and where to pick up your new IDs," Harker said, then hung up.

"New IDs?" Mitch asked.

"Yeah, welcome to working with Quincy Harker," Jo said. "He knows a guy. Doesn't matter what the problem is, he knows a guy."

"You live a century or more, sweetheart, you'll know a few of those kind of guys, too." Cassandra said. "Now let's get this precious baby home and in her own bed."

"Good idea," Jo said. She put the car in gear and headed out of the parking lot.

"Joanna?" Cassandra said from where she sat in the back with Ginny's head in her lap.

"Yes, Mama?"

"I'm proud of you tonight. You did good. Grandaddy John would have been proud, too. You carried his hammer like a Henry," Cassandra said. "I hope you don't have to take it up in violence again, but I know if you do, it's in good hands."

"Thank you, Mama," Jo said, then turned the car toward home.

II

DEVIL INSIDE

I called up "Amazing Grace" on my phone, pushed play, and set the sleek black plastic rectangle on a nearby headstone. I stepped to the head of the slightly bulging patch of ground, the sod still trying to take root even after a couple of weeks, and I started to speak.

"Sylvester Thomas Efor, IV. That was his name. That was the name he abandoned when he joined our family. It's part ritual, part homage, and part convenience that makes the name Renfield into as much a title as a moniker. It's a throwback, to be sure. It hearkens back to a time when things were less complicated, a time when it was easier to walk the night unseen, but still a time when some things had to be done in the light of day.

"When a man takes on the mantle of Renfield, we know we will outlive him. We've certainly done it before, more times than we care to dwell on. We know that our connections with the living and with the unenhanced are, by their very nature, fleeting. That doesn't stop us from making those connections, from expanding our family, from caring.

"Ren was one of us. He was family, caregiver, guardian, partner, and brewer of lovely teas. He was brave; he was funny; he was stalwart; he was loyal. It was that loyalty that led him to save my life on more than one occasion, and it was that loyalty that cost him his life in the end.

"We have avenged Renfield, but that doesn't mitigate our loss. We have balanced the scales, but that doesn't fill the hole in our hearts. We have seen the debt paid, but we still miss our friend.

"Sylvester Thomas Efor the fourth, Renfield, we will miss you. May God bless you and keep you close to His bosom, and may you find rest and all the peace you deserve."

I took a flask from my inside jacket pocket and twisted the top off. I poured the clear liquid in a continuous path around the grave, making an unbroken line around the perimeter of Ren's resting place.

"Pater noster,
qui es in caelis,
sanctificetur nomen tuum.
Adveniat regnum tuum.
Fiat voluntas tua,
sicut in caelo et in terra.
Panem nostrum quotidianum da nobis hodie,
et dimitte nobis debita nostra sicut et nos dimittimus debitoribus nostris.
Et ne nos inducas in tentationem, sed libera nos a malo.
Amen."

With a tiny flash of brilliant white light, I poured my will into the blessing, offering protection for Ren's remains and hopefully securing his soul from being dragged out of Heaven and used against us. The grave was empty, just a coffin with a light sprinkling of his ashes within, but even those tenuous bonds can sometimes be enough to conjure a shade. The blessing would hopefully keep that from happening and ensure my friend remained in the paradise he deserved.

"Amen," Rebecca, Glory, and Adam said in unison. Luke didn't say anything, just stood off to one side watching the ceremony.

I knelt on the ground and whispered, "Goodbye, old friend. May you find peace and comfort."

I walked over to where the others stood, heads bowed and voices muffled.

"Don't forget your phone," Detective Rebecca Gayle Flynn reminded me. I nodded my thanks and retrieved it from the headstone, ending the song and slipping the cell into the pocket of my jeans. We certainly weren't the most formal grouping to ever host a funeral, but when you're burying people by moonlight, the dress code gets a little more flexible.

Adam extended his hand as I walked up again. "That was well-spoken, Quincy. If I could die, I would ask that you perform my funeral."

"Well, old buddy, if we ever find anything that can kill you, it'll probably take me out, too, so I think I'm off the hook," I replied.

A grin split his scarred visage and he said, "That's probably true, Harker. That's probably true. Now I must take my leave. There are things I need to see to before I begin my hunt, and none of them are in North Carolina. We will speak soon." The giant man nodded to the women, patted me on the shoulder, and walked over to where Luke stood alone.

"That is a very odd individual," Flynn said.

"Becks, you don't even know the half of it," I agreed.

"I'm good with that," she continued. She looked at the grave and sighed. "What's Luke going to do?"

"Hire a new Renfield, I suppose. This isn't the first time we've had one die suddenly or depart unexpectedly. Luke keeps a file of qualified replacements around, and it's usually at least marginally current."

"I hope so," Glory said. "I'm not looking forward to having to wash Dracula's socks." She grinned when she said it, but I knew that living in the mundane world without her divine powers was really worrying her.

"It's okay, G," I said, trying to be encouraging. "We'll get your wings back. I mean, come on, we just stopped a demon attack in Atlanta and kept the world from coming to an end. How hard could this shit be?"

"How hard could it be to track down the most powerful of the

Heavenly Host, awaken them from their Earth-induced slumber, and convince them to find God Himself and put Him back on The Golden Throne? Nah, we should have this taken care of by lunch, no problem. Then this afternoon, we're going to fix global warming and make David Letterman funny again."

"I don't think we need to be asking for miracles, Glory. Letterman hasn't been funny in a looooong time," I said.

"You know what I mean." She folded her arms across her chest and scowled at me.

"Yeah, I know what you mean. But come on, Glory. We do the difficult in no time flat. Impossible takes a little longer."

"Harker, you sound like a Hallmark card."

"I was going for motivational. I saw it on a poster in the CMPD the last time I was arrested."

"Leave the motivational stuff to the ministers. You're built more for the magical killing."

I couldn't argue with her. I try to make it a point not to get into debates with celestial beings, even the ones who have lost their wings. I walked over to Luke, who stood alone after his brief farewell with Adam.

"Quincy," he said without turning around. That kind of thing unnerves normal people, but I've never been accused of normalcy.

"Luke," I said, walking around in front of him and sitting on a headstone. Irreverent, I know, but I've met a lot of dead people, and none of them have ever expressed outrage at the habit. Some of them have tried to kill me, but that's always unrelated to my nonchalance toward monuments.

"What's the plan?" I asked.

"Plan? I don't have a plan, Quincy. I don't have a home, I don't have a manservant, and I most certainly do not have a plan."

"Well, it's not like there's a shortage of things to do. We have a bunch of angels to find, and we need to get you a new place to live, for starters—"

"Are you kicking me out, Quincy?"

I spluttered for a few seconds before I looked at his face, startled into silence at the wry smile there. Even after all these years, I sometimes forget that Luke has a sense of humor. A very, very dry sense of humor. He got me. Again.

"No, just saying that you snore," I said, then turned and walked off. It's really the only way to get the last word in when you're in a battle of wits with someone who's outlived you by centuries. He really has heard it all by this point.

I walked back to my car with a chuckling vampire in tow and slid into the passenger seat. "Nice of them to let you keep your motor pool privileges. I didn't think crossing guards got unmarked cars," I said to Flynn as Luke got in the back seat beside Glory, muttering something about "shotgun." I ignored him.

"They didn't actually bust me down to crossing guard," Becks said. "It turns out that a good word from the Director of the FBI's Atlanta Field Office goes a long way with the Charlotte-Mecklenburg police department. I didn't even get docked vacation days; they just chalked it up to my being on interagency assignment to Homeland Security."

"Pretty sure those days are over," I said as Flynn put the car in gear and pulled us out of the cemetery.

"Oh yeah," she agreed. "The Charlotte office of Homeland is completely shut down, and the few agents who survived the encounter with you at Luke's house and were found to be free of Smith's influence were reassigned."

"What about the ones who weren't free of Smith's, how did you say, *influence?*" Luke asked from the back seat. He had a special loathing in his heart for the deceased Agent Smith, since he was the one who killed Renfield and blew up Luke's house. I shot Smith in the face, but not before he'd done plenty of damage.

"Anyone the agency even thought had close ties to Smith was sent to a secure facility for interrogation and examination," Becks said.

"What aren't you saying?" I asked.

"What do you mean?" she asked, her innocent mien fooling no one.

"You remember that I can literally hear you thinking, right?" I asked. "You'd be better off trying to lie to your mother about what you did after your senior prom."

"And I can not only hear your heart speed up when you lie, I can smell the stink of deception on you," Luke said, slipping into full-on Dracula creepy mode.

"That's a load of crap," Flynn said. She turned to me for a second. "Not you, him. I know you can hear me thinking, but I thought we could still mask specifics?"

"Is that why all I get is Kelly Clarkson lyrics? We really need to introduce you to Motorhead. You're right, he can't *literally* smell a lie. He can just smell the tiny bit of sweat that something like ninety-five percent of people emit when they tell a lie. Which is basically the same thing."

"Exactly," Luke said, leaning back in the seat. "Speaking of smells…"

"Don't say it," Flynn said. "You are in a cop car, after all. The motor pool tries, but some things don't ever really come out of upholstery."

"Don't change the subject," I said. "Where are the corrupt Homeland agents?"

"I honestly don't know. They were sent somewhere, but I have no idea where. I just know the last thing I heard when I was leaving the building after turning in my badge was somebody talking about putting them on a plane south."

"You think they got sent to Gitmo?" I asked.

"There's also a place down in the swamps somewhere near the Gulf. I don't know if it's in Florida or Louisiana, but apparently, the government has some kind of facility down there with some pretty enhanced interrogation facilities."

"Oh, you mean Fort Pontchartrain?" Luke asked.

I spun around in my seat. "You know about this place?"

"Of course. It's where the United States houses any paranormal creatures it feels the need to contain and study. It's part laboratory, part prison, all ungodly. I quite like the ambiance, personally."

"Yeah, we know your decorating tends toward eighteenth-century European creepy," I said. "So you think that's where they would send these Homeland agents?"

"Almost certainly," Luke said. "But why do you care? I thought you had angels to find."

"He does," said Glory, turning in from the window. "He has a lot of angels to find."

"Yeah, I'd just feel more comfortable if the government had found a more…permanent solution to the corrupted agents. You never know when one will turn out to be possessed."

"Oh, they will certainly discover that at Fort Pontchartrain," Luke said. "The fort has a full complement of wizards and priests. I have used their services several times over the years. They are very competent at handling possession."

"So my vampire uncle is tight with the wizards at the government's secret supernatural prison buried deep in the swamps of Louisiana. This somehow surprises me not at all," I muttered and turned to bang my head against the passenger window. Flynn didn't comment, just drove us home with a little smile on her face.

2

The next morning saw me standing in baggage claim C at Charlotte Douglas International Airport at a ridiculous hour of the morning, holding a cardboard sign that had "Mitch" written on it in my barely legible scrawl. I watched another stream of passengers ride the escalator down from the concourse, and my eyes widened as an absolute monster of a human being walked up to me.

"I'm Mitch. You Harker?"

"Yeah, that's me. Shit, Jo didn't tell me she was shipping Andre the friggin' Giant to me. Have you had breakfast? You know, did you eat a stewardess or anything?"

The big man laughed. "You think I'm big, you should see the guy we fought a couple nights ago. Last night? Shit, I dunno. The redeye always makes me all fucked up on my days. Sorry, is my language gonna be a problem? I kinda swear a lot."

I looked up at him, not really believing that somebody just apologized to *me* for swearing, then I remembered where he'd just come from. "Nah, it's fine. Jo's the only one who objects to a little spicy language, and I think that's mostly for her kid's benefit."

"And her mom," Mitch added.

"Oh yeah, you do not want to piss off Cassandra. She will fuck your shit right up. You got any luggage?" I looked at the duffel he carried, which didn't look like it held a lot in the way of clothes.

"Nah, I've got a couple things in here, but I travel pretty light."

"Is the..." I looked around the baggage claim, but everybody looked pretty mundane. I quickly opened my Sight to the supernatural world and saw nothing other than one security guard with a minor protection spell glowing around his neck. Probably a saint's medal or something like that.

"Is the sword in the bag?" I asked.

"Yeah, that's what takes up most of the space. Doesn't exactly fit in just anything, you know? How did you get them to let me go through without security finding it?" the giant asked. It wasn't that he was all that tall. He was about my height, which put him several inches over six foot. And it wasn't just that he was big. I mean, Adam was bigger, sure, but this dude was built like a damn brick wall. His hands looked like he broke rocks with his fists, and his shoulders and arms stretched against the fabric of the black fleece jacket he wore. Blond hair and a square jaw sat on a neck like a tree trunk, and he generally looked like somebody saw the *Captain America* movie and said, "I can do that. Just a little better."

"I know a few people, and the Director of Homeland Security owes me a couple of favors." Government agencies are big on promising favors and less big on paying them back, but when an entire division of the agency turns out to be working for a demon, killing that demon gives you a lot of leverage. Getting a sword through airport security wasn't a big deal. I didn't mention that the sword was magical and the guy carrying it was an Archangel. The government has plenty of ways to gather information. They don't need me telling them every little thing.

"Well, if you don't need to piss, and you don't have any bags, let's get out of here. I'm parked illegally." I turned and walked toward the sliding doors, stepping outside into the melee of airport parking and passenger pickup just as a cop was motioning a tow truck over to my Honda.

"That's me, officer," I called out, holding up my badge wallet. Just because Flynn did the ethical thing and turned in her Homeland Security credentials didn't mean I had to. I didn't let the fact that impersonating a Homeland Security official was a federal offense bother me.

"Goddammit, Harker, get this thing out of here," the cop yelled at me. I recognized him as Smith, or Jones, or some other generic-named cop I'd seen around police headquarters once or twice.

"Will do, Bob," I said, holding up a hand to stop traffic as I opened the driver's door. A horn blared from a Mercedes SUV as a little blonde realtor or soccer mom rolled right up to me before stopping. I drew the Glock 9mm from my hip and leveled it at the woman, whose eyes went wide. Her head whipped from side to side as she looked for an escape, but there were cars stacked up behind her.

I walked around to the driver's window, gun still trained on her. I motioned for her to roll down the window, and she actually did it. I will never understand people. I leaned in the open window, pistol just kinda casually pointing in her general direction.

"That wasn't very nice," I said. "You shouldn't honk your horn at people. It's not polite. There are people who would respond very poorly to such bad manners."

She stared at me and nodded silently.

"I'm not one of those people, so I'm not going to paint the ceiling of your car with what little brains are rattling around in that fucking head of yours. Let's just consider this a friendly reminder to be considerate of others while driving. Sound good?"

She nodded again. She still hadn't said a word, which was probably good. I wouldn't have shot her. Probably. But I might have turned her into a toad.

I walked back to my car, holstered the gun, and got behind the wheel. Mitch sat in the passenger seat looking at me. "That was kinda mean, don't you think?"

"You're the angel, pal. Not me," I said as I put the car in drive and pulled out of the passenger pickup line, heading for the airport exit and downtown.

Half an hour later, I walked into my apartment with an angel in tow. Another one. There were getting to be entirely too many heavenly bodies living in my building. "You can throw your bag in a corner. You'll be crashing in one of the apartments down the hall."

"You own the floor?" Mitch asked.

"I own the building," I said, going to the fridge. "You want a beer?"

"Dude, it's seven a.m."

"Yeah, you're right." I put the beers back in the fridge and pulled out the orange juice. I poured two healthy glasses of orange juice, carried them over to the bar, and topped them off with a couple shots each of Grey Goose. A few seconds with a stir stick, and I carried the drinks to the sofas. I passed one to Mitch and sat down on the couch across from him. He laughed a little and held up his glass to me.

We sipped our orange juice for a minute, then I asked, "So, you're an Archangel, huh?"

"Apparently so."

"You don't think so?"

"Man, I don't know." He took a big drink of his screwdriver. It's one of the reasons I poured us each a stiff drink. One, because I hate getting up in the morning, and two, because I thought it might loosen our boy up a touch.

"I know that stupid sword starts flaming like a Lady Gaga backup dancer whenever I touch it. I know the demon back in Phoenix sure thought I was special. Other than that, I don't know shit. I poke and prod at my memory, but it only goes back about three years. I remember working construction for a while, fighting at night, then fighting full time, but nothing further back than that."

"Do all your memories involve Phoenix?"

"Yeah. Literally the first thing I can remember is walking out of the desert, sunburned as fuck and hungry as hell, wandering up to a dude with a taco truck, and collapsing before I could even order. I woke up with a Mexican dude splashing water on my face and a crowd looking on. Some chick bought me a burrito and a Coke, some dude gave me twenty bucks, and that's the first memory I have."

"Interesting," I said. I had no idea what it meant, but his memories coincided with the time I started working with Flynn and the former Agent John Smith. "What do you think, Becks?" I asked the woman standing in the doorway of the bedroom.

Rebecca stood there, shoes in one hand and her Sig in the other, glowering at me. "I think I want to know about it when you're bringing strange men into the apartment while I'm in the shower. What if I had walked out here naked?" She wasn't naked now, but she looked good nonetheless. A pair of gray slacks and a burgundy blouse outlined her athletic figure, and her long brown hair was down, hanging past her shoulders.

"Our mornings would have been dramatically improved," I said. She didn't smile, but I felt a pleased little glow down the mental link we shared. I got up and walked over to kiss her, but she put a hand on my chest.

"Not this morning, Harker. You smell like vodka, and I'm going back for my first day on duty after being a murder suspect. I'd rather not show up reeking of cheap booze." She walked over to the couch and held out her hand to Mitch. "Rebecca Flynn. I'm Harker's…girl-friend. I'm also a detective with the Charlotte-Mecklenburg Police Department."

"Girlfriend?" I asked. I'd offered Becks a ring a few months back. She hadn't returned it, but she hadn't put it on her hand yet, either. We loved each other, and had been pretty close to inseparable in the weeks since we got back from Atlanta, but she wasn't sure where she fit with all the other weird moving parts in my life. I wasn't pushing. The last thing I wanted to do with a brilliant, smart, independent, gorgeous woman who could literally read my mind was to push her away.

"For now." She gave me a little half-smile. "As long as you don't bring too many strangers into the apartment. Especially not strangers with arms like those." She leered at Mitch, who blushed a little. "How cute, I embarrassed him! You should introduce him to Gabby. She'd like him. For lunch."

"Gabby?" Mitch asked, kinda like she'd mentioned a new type of venomous snake. She kinda had.

"Gabby is another member of the Council. The group that Jo is a part of with us," I explained. I didn't explain that Gabby was Gabriella Van Helsing, granddaughter of the legendary vampire hunter. That always got awkward, especially once they met Luke and realized exactly who *he* was.

"I'm off," Flynn said, walking over and giving me a kiss on the cheek. "Try not to get into too much trouble." She picked up her keys from the table by the front door and her jacket from the closet and out the door she went. I watched her go with no shame. She was a good-looking woman, and like the song said, I hated to see her go, but I loved to watch her leave.

"That's your girlfriend?" Mitch asked. "I guess you've got more going on than meets the eye."

"Hey!" I exclaimed. "I'll have you know that women on five continents have assured me that I am a very good-looking man."

"There are seven continents."

"I've never tried to get laid in Antarctica, and for some reason I've had shit luck with Australian women. They're immune to my charms for some reason. Now, about that sword..."

3

Two days later, I had a sword that would burst into flames on command, a mopey vampire, an overworked cop girlfriend, and two powerless angels hanging around my place. If that sounds like fun to anybody anywhere, they're on better drugs than I am.

Glory, Mitch, and I were in my apartment, clustered around my minuscule table with a laptop and a pile of Bibles and other religious research material. Becks was at work, chasing down mundane criminals for a change, and Luke was in his apartment interviewing potential Renfields. I couldn't speak for Luke or Becks, but me and the Heavenly Bodies were finally making headway in our angel hunt.

"Okay, who do we have on the list?" I asked Glory.

"There's Michael," she said. "We found him."

"For all the good I'm doing anybody," the musclebound grump chimed in.

"Hey," I interjected. "Baby steps, pal. Baby steps. Let's make sure we can find all the Archangels, then we can worry about making sure you all know who you are. Hell, for all we know, you're the only one with amnesia. Maybe the others are just lazy or having fun playing human."

"I doubt that," Glory said. "This whole being human thing sucks. I have to sleep, I have to walk places, I have to use the bathroom! Do you have any idea how disgusting the digestive process is?"

"Yeah, G," I said. "I've been digesting for over a century. I'm pretty well acquainted with the process. Back to the matter at hand…" I waved a hand at the legal pad in front of her.

"Okay, then there's Gabriel, the keeper of the chronicles of Heaven. He's basically God's scribe," Glory said.

"Okay, the Celestial Secretarial Pool. Next," I said.

"Raphael is the healer. Metatron is the voice of God—"

"I know that dude," I said.

"You do?" Glory and Mitch said simultaneously.

"Yeah, he was on *Supernatural*. Didn't the guy who played Booger in *Revenge of the Nerds* play him?"

Glory sighed. "I don't know why I even bother sometimes."

"Me neither," I replied. "Next?"

"Uriel is God's punisher, and no *Daredevil* jokes," Glory said, pointing at me. I motioned like I was zipping my lips. "Sealtiel is the herald of the apocalypse, and Azrael is the angel of death."

"He doesn't sound like anyone I want to spend very much time with, so let's leave him for last," I said.

"Probably a good idea," Glory agreed.

"So how does this whole thing work?" I asked. "Do all of you angels know each other? Is it racist to think that? Or are there like class divisions and the Archangels don't hang out with the guardian angels, and the guardian angels don't go out drinking with the…I don't know, the rescue cats from trees angels or whatever. Is there a hierarchy in Heaven?"

"There is, and it's very rigid," Glory replied. "The Seraphim rule Heaven, and they make all the day-to-day decisions. The lower-level angels, like me, don't consort with the Seraphim unless we're called upon to do something, and we never see the Archangels. Mitch is the first of the Highest Host that I've ever encountered."

"Sorry it's not a more impressive meeting," the Highest muttered.

"Don't worry, man. I'm sure you're plenty impressive…sometimes…when you know who you are and stuff." My attempt at reassurance sounded lame even to me.

"Thanks, I guess," Mitch said, leaving no doubt as to how ineffectual my words were.

"So no, I don't know all the angels. I don't even know how many there are, honestly. It's not like there's a census," Glory said, trying to get us back on something like a track.

A thought struck me, and as usually happens, I didn't bother processing it very much before I just spewed it out. "How do angels get made, anyway?"

Glory looked at me, and I could almost see the wheels turning in her head. "I…I can't talk about that, Harker. I'm sorry, but that's one of the few hard and fast rules about what guardians can and can't do. We never discuss with mortals where angels come from."

"Just tell me one thing," I pleaded. "Does it have anything to do with bells ringing?"

She laughed, and it was good to hear that crystalline bell-tone again. There hadn't been a whole lot of laughing since she got her wings sliced off and became human. But I got her. "No, Harker. Every time a bell rings, an angel does not get their wings. All that happens when a bell rings is that a bell rings."

"Okay, I can be satisfied with that. Is that all the Archangels?" I asked.

"Well…" Glory didn't meet my eyes.

"Glory…" I used my best "dad" voice, which is harder to do when the person you're talking to is both thousands of years old and just a few weeks old at the same time.

"There's another angel that technically may still qualify, but he's a little more difficult to get in touch with, and a *lot* more self-aware than our buddy Mitch here," she said, still not looking at me.

"Come on, out with it, young lady," I said. She laughed at my ridiculous attempt at authority, but quickly sobered.

"Lucifer."

"Wait, what?" I asked. I looked to Mitch, but he just shrugged and stared back at me.

"Lucifer was one of God's favorites, and he was one of the most powerful of the Host. I have no idea what status he retains in the hierarchy, or what kind of power he now possesses. But if we're listing off the most powerful angels, he definitely qualifies."

"Fuck me sideways," I said. "So if we want to get your wings back…"

"Only God can make an angel," Glory said. "I can tell you that much."

"And if want to find God?" Mitch asked.

"The Archangels are the ones with the direct communication," Glory replied.

"But I'm an Archangel, and I don't have any idea how to, I don't know, call God or whatever," he said.

"That's why we have to find the rest of them," I said. "Because hopefully one of you will still have an idea what you are, or at least how to call Dad."

"And if they don't?" Mitch prodded.

"I don't know, man," I admitted. "Maybe it's like box tops. You collect the whole set and you get a prize. I have no fucking idea. I just know there's a bunch of rogue angels trying to take over Heaven and pretty much destroy all of humanity, and we need the Big Guy to get His ass home and take care of business. Barring that, we need all the big brothers to pick up the slack and beat some angelic ass."

"So we're hunting angels," Mitch said.

"We're hunting angels," I confirmed.

"This could get dangerous," he said.

"Danger is my middle name," I quipped.

"You have a lot of middle names, Harker," Glory said. "But none of them are Danger. Now I have to pee again. I'm telling you, this body sucks!" She got up and walked to the bathroom. Mitch and I both watched her walk across the apartment.

"I have to disagree with her," Mitch said. "I think her body's pretty awesome."

"Pig," I replied.

"Like you weren't looking, too."

"I have a girlfriend."

"You're not dead. And that is a woman who can fill out a pair of blue jeans." He wasn't wrong. On either count. I wasn't dead, and Glory was a gorgeous woman.

I still didn't really think of her as a sexual creature, since not only was I in love with Becks, in my head Glory was still an angel, a sexless being who chose a gender at random. She could have just as easily decided to appear to me as a guy. Mitch obviously didn't have those hangups since he was still checking her out.

"Where do we start hunting?" Mitch asked.

"That's where I come in," said a new voice. A unicorn head with a rainbow mane and horn appeared on the laptop screen.

"Do you know how much I hate that avatar, Dennis?" I asked my disembodied hacker friend Dennis, who also answered to Sparkles the Magical Unicorn. Especially when he wanted to annoy me.

"I do, Q. I know exactly how much you hate the charming visage of Sparkles, who wants nothing more than to bring joy to the lives of good girls and boys everywhere, coming down the chimney and turning their abandoned teeth into baskets full of toys and candy."

"That's like three different myths all mixed up into one," I said.

"But you can never say I'm not a complex guy," Sparkles replied.

"What do you have for us, horn-boy?" I asked.

"I don't have any idea about the angels, but I think I found Gabriel's book. If nothing else, the book shop can help us find old Gabe."

"Is that what you did with me, used the sword to home in on my location?" Mitch asked.

"Kinda," I said. "I worked on the assumption that there would be some kind of bond between you and the sword, so I cast a spell to follow the sword to its owner."

"You were able to track me all the way to Phoenix?" he asked.

"I was able to do way more than that. Magical items like the sword of an Archangel warp the fabric of magic around them. Once I took a good look at how the sword bends the magical energy around it, I was able to pick out its unique power signature and locate you within a couple of miles."

"So it's going to be easy to find the others?" he asked.

"Not exactly," I admitted. "The spell was harder than I expected and took a lot more out of me than I thought it would. I was a little drained when we were finished."

"A little drained?" Glory said, coming back into the room and retaking her seat at the table. "He was unconscious for two days and too weak to leave his bed for the rest of a week. Just tracking you down almost killed him, and you were the most powerful of the Host. Finding anyone else would be harder because they won't bend reality around them the way you do."

"What do you mean, bend reality?" Mitch asked.

"You're not from this plane," Glory said. "So you shouldn't be here. That means that everything around you is going to actively fight your influence or bend to your will."

"You make it sound like I'm some kind of infection."

I spoke up. "Hate to tell you, pal, but you kinda are. All that chaos is the world's way of telling you to get your gringo ass home."

"Why aren't the other angels as much of a blight on the world as I am?" The bitterness in his voice crept through the joking tone. I couldn't really blame him. I wouldn't want to be told that the universe was trying to flush me from its system, either. Although I'd certainly entertained the idea on more than one occasion.

"You're the dude," I said. "You're *the* badass boss Archangel, especially after Lucifer was cast out. It was your sword that cut the Morningstar's face, scarred his perfect beauty and showed him that he wasn't invulnerable. That one slice turned the tide of the War on Heaven."

"You know a lot about a war in the sky for a dude who claims to be human."

"I claim to be mostly human," I clarified. "And I know a lot of people. Some of them were there, and they remember you very clearly. You were *the* Archangel. That's why the others aren't as reality-warping. Because they don't have your stroke."

"Yeah, too bad I don't have any of that stroke anymore."

Glory reached across the table and put a hand on top of his. "You'll get it back. That's what we do. We help people."

And here I thought all this time that all I did was chew bubblegum and kick ass. Guess I shouldn't worry about being out of bubblegum. Nowadays I "help people."

Fuck me running, I'm surrounded by celestial hippies.

4

Luke's apartment was dark when I walked in. That wasn't a huge surprise; he kept the place pretty close to pitch black most of the time. Being Lord of the Vampires came with a few perks, one of which was cat-like night vision. I didn't inherit that quality, so I reached out to flip on the lights as I walked into the room.

"Leave it, please," came my uncle's voice from the middle of the living room. I heard the scrape of a match across a box, and a flame burst into life. Luke touched the burning tip to a red pillar candle on an end table, and a soft yellow light spread throughout the room.

I shrugged and walked over to the sitting area and took a spot on the end of the sofa nearest the candle. Luke sat in an armchair, his slick hair and perfect creases at odds with the forced casual appearance of his untucked dress shirt and open collar.

"How were the interviews?" I asked.

"Dreadful." He didn't elaborate for a long time, and I didn't push. I couldn't tell what Luke needed from me right now, if he needed to talk or just needed company, but I knew he didn't need to be left alone to his thoughts. Down that path was a gauntlet of self-doubt and recrimination about why he wasn't awake and able to save Renfield when Smith broke in. We'd all been able to shove our thoughts of

Ren's death aside when we went to Atlanta to fight Orobas and keep the world from ending, but now that we were back home, we had a lot of pieces to pick up.

"Brandy?" Luke asked, rising from his chair with the fluid grace that spawned legends of him turning to smoke and vanishing in thin air. He can do none of those things, but he can move with amazing speed and stand perfectly still in a shadow, so to the uneducated eye, he can seem to disappear at will.

"No, thank you, but I'll take a single malt if you have one."

"I do not. The Council had a fondness for scotch, Dr. Watson in particular."

"I don't know if he's really a doctor, or if he's got some kind of lawyer doctor degree. Good to know who drank all my scotch, though. Brandy will be fine, then."

Luke poured me a brandy and poured himself a glass of red wine. We both knew it wasn't exactly red wine, but as long as I never drank from his glass, I didn't need to know exactly what blend of wine, blood, and anticoagulants he kept in his wine cellar.

He handed me my glass and sat back down in his chair. We sipped our drinks in silence for several minutes. I was content to wait. Luke and I have spent a lot of time together in my century and change on this Earth, and we don't have to make small talk. It's one of the things I like about being with him—no bullshit.

"Does the angel know anything?" he asked, breaking the silence.

"Nothing useful. He can turn the sword on, but he has no idea what he is. I had hoped being around Glory would spark him somehow, some kind of jump-start to his memory or something, but nothing yet."

"Do you know anything about the next angel you need to find?"

"We've come up with a list of who they are, and Dennis is searching the web for any anomalies that might correspond to their presence. He said he wouldn't have anything until the morning, so I left him to it. Glory is talking to Mitch about Heaven, trying to jog his memory of people, angels, that he should have known. Besides being boring as balls, I kinda didn't care, so I thought I'd come check on you."

"While I appreciate your concern for my hiring process, I am perfectly fine and completely capable of doing this without any assistance."

"I know that, but it's been a while since you hired a Ren—"

"Don't call him that."

"What? You always call your manservant Renfield. It's been a thing since you met my dad."

"That is over. I am no longer hiring a manservant. I am hiring a live-in personal assistant. I will learn his name, and he will become a valued member of my staff, nothing more." Luke's jaw was tight and his voice clipped. He was working very hard to keep his emotions in check.

"Nothing?" I asked after a few seconds.

"Nothing." He didn't look at me, just stared into the dregs in his wine glass. "I can't anymore, Quincy. I simply can't. I have to remain detached from these...people. I became attached to Sylvester. He was much more than a manservant or a butler. He was..."

"A friend?" I supplied the word.

"Yes. He was a friend."

"Sylvester." I rolled the name around on my tongue. It felt odd, like I was saying something wrong. I'd honestly forgotten Ren's real name until the day before. After a while, I just ignored the fact that he had another name, another life.

"Yes, Sylvester. He had an entire life before coming to me. He had a sister whom he loved very much, and he sent most of his salary to her until her death two years ago. His parents were long deceased when he entered my service, and he never married. His sister died childless, so his generation, his entire family line, ended when he passed."

"I don't know if that's good or bad," I said, thinking about the various family lines that I had running around out there. Both of my brothers died before they had children, James because his wife couldn't conceive, and Orly because he was still mostly a child himself when the influenza took them.

There were aunts and uncles scattered across England, but none that I kept track of after I started traveling with Luke. I realized that I had no idea if I was the last Harker or not. Then I realized that I had no idea if I had any children scattered across Europe and America. The twenties had definitely roared, that was a sure enough thing.

"It certainly makes my life simpler when there is no next of kin," Luke said. "Out of eight men interviewed today, four of them were married and one other had a serious girlfriend. That makes them completely unsuitable for my service."

"Yeah, someone can't exactly keep all your secrets if there's the possibility of pillow talk," I agreed. "I guess that's another reason to keep a level of detachment from your new...assistant." An idea hit me. "Have you interviewed any women?"

"Excuse me?" Luke looked genuinely shocked at the concept.

"Luke, it's the twenty-first century, get with it. You're not hiring someone to wrestle a coffin into the back of a wagon, or drive a carriage, or defend your lair against roving villagers with pitchforks and torches."

"I never have," he replied. "I believe you have me confused with Adam. He was the one chased from his home with pitchforks and torches. Although he assures me that was purely cinematic license."

"My point is that there's nothing in the job description that requires your...assistant be male."

Luke looked at me, a thoughtful expression bouncing around his face. "Perhaps you are correct, Quincy. I shall consider female applicants during my next round of interviews. I shall contact the headhunter tomorrow with new directions."

"I wish you wouldn't call them that," I said.

"Why not? It is, I believe, the acceptable term."

"It is, but just looking around at all the people and things we deal with, it might ring a little too close to true for us." Luke actually smiled a little bit at that, the first time I'd seen that in a week or more.

"What is your plan now, Quincy? You have located an angel, but he does not understand his nature. If all the Host are in such a state, then how will you manage to coerce them into helping you restore Glory's divinity?"

"Yeah," I said, taking a long pull on my drink. "That's a really good question." The truth was, I had no idea. There's only one way angels get made, and that's by the hand of God Himself. With the Big Guy AWOL, the only way to find Him was using the Archangels. If the Archangels had no idea they were angels, then the chances of their homing beacon for the Almighty being turned on were slim to none.

I let out a sigh and leaned back in my chair. "I don't know, Luke. All I can think of right now is that we need to find them all. I guess I'm hoping that if we get them all in the same place, some kind of spontaneous anti-amnesia thing will happen, and everybody will suddenly sprout wings, pick up harps, and fly off to the Pearly Gates, leaving Glory with a nice new pair of wings."

"Somehow that seems more ludicrous than even some of your worst ideas." Luke never has been one to pull punches with me.

"Yeah, I know. But I can't think of anything else to do. I have to get her wings back. I need her, Luke. I need her at full strength, I need her fighting beside me, and I need her to not have lost everything because of me. I need..." I let the words just hang there. My chest was tight, and my breath came in short gasps.

"You need to save one of them." The words were almost a whisper, but I heard them as well as if he'd used a megaphone.

"Yeah," I choked out. "I need to not have another one die, or lose everything about themselves just for being near me. I need to save one of my people. It's all well and good to save some faceless people on a Ferris wheel, or a bunch of people at a concert, but goddammit, once in a while, I need to be able to save *my* people. The folks who put their lives on the line for strangers all the time. The people who took up weapons and stepped forward just because I asked them to, because I said it was important. I need to be able to save them, too. Just this once." Tears rolled down my cheeks as I thought about the people I couldn't save, going all the way back to my younger brothers, who both died in the flu epidemic of 1918. I couldn't do anything for them, I couldn't do anything for Anna, I couldn't do anything for Dennis or

Renfield or Rebecca's dad, but goddammit, I was *not* letting Glory lose her divinity on my account.

"Then we shall find the angels, Quincy," Luke said, standing up and taking my glass. I sat silently and watched him walk across the room and refill my drink, turn to me, then return to the bar and pour me a double.

He stood in front of me, glass full of that lovely amber liquid. "Now, have yourself a nice drink, and let's figure out where we start, shall we?"

5

I pulled into the downtown Historic District of Charleston, South Carolina, around two in the afternoon a couple days later. I had the windows down and the breeze rolling across my arm as I hung it out the window of my new car, a deep red Honda Accord. I've never been a "car guy," looking at my vehicles mostly as a mode of transportation and not some expression of my soul or my worth as a human being.

When I got back to North Carolina, I realized that the junker pickup I'd bought when I went to Ohio was still in Ohio and that my old car had been destroyed in the same explosion that blew up Luke's house. Something about a door through the grill. So I took the insurance payout and a little cash I had floating around from being over a century old, and I bought myself a nice little four-year-old car. It had plenty of room, rode the highway well, and had a jack for me to hook up my phone, which meant that I had all the internet music I ever wanted. There are some bonuses to having a friend who's made up of electrons and can travel through the web.

I turned into the small parking lot of the King Charles Hotel and got out, taking a deep breath and cracking my back. I patted myself down to make sure my pistol was secure, pulled on a long-sleeve shirt to mask the gun, and walked into the lobby.

"May I help you, sir?" a young lady behind the desk asked as a bell on the door jingled my arrival. The lobby was well-appointed in what looked like either antiques or decent replicas. Nice chairs with striped upholstery and rounded backs flanked a small table with flyers for ghost tours and upscale restaurants scattered across its surface. A huge gilt mirror dominated one wall, and I smothered a smile at my recollection of Luke's face when I told him where I was staying.

He hated that lobby, most particularly that mirror. New mirrors with their acrylic and glass construction weren't an issue, but he still didn't show up in older mirrors. Something about the way the silver they used to back the mirrors reacted to the magic that sustained him. I didn't understand it, but I knew that wasn't the only reason he didn't accompany me. He was still interviewing new Renfields and beginning the cleanup and reconstruction process on his house. While I hated the reason he had to do it, I was glad he was moving forward with the project. The sooner he wasn't living in the apartment next to me, the better.

I walked over to the front desk and leaned my arms on the dark green granite-topped counter. "Room for Harper, please. I have a reservation."

She tapped on the keyboard for a few seconds, then smiled up at me. "Mr. Harper, I have you down for a king bed corner suite for seven nights. Will you be needing a parking pass?" I nodded, and she passed me a garish yellow slip of paper for my dash, then took my credit card and fake ID. I knew the feeble attempt at masking my identity wouldn't stand up to any serious scrutiny, but I had Sparkles lurking in the internet ready to alert me if anyone queried the name of Orly Harper from Battle Creek, Michigan.

Orly was a traveling consultant working with several major hotels on energy efficiency. He was in Charleston to review the power consumption of their ballroom lighting and make recommendations on how to reduce their overhead through the use of LEDs, occupancy sensors, and daylight harvesting. If that wasn't enough to bore any

Curious George chatting me up in a bar, I could go on for hours about Orly's hobby, which made Charleston *such* a fascinating section of his sales territory. Orly loved architecture, particularly French-inspired architecture from the antebellum South.

I know slightly more about antebellum architecture than I do about nuclear submarines, but only slightly. If anybody looked like they really wanted to chat me up about that crap, I was either going to have to develop an acute case of irritable bowel syndrome or kill them.

I retrieved my credit card and Michigan driver's license, signed the slip for the room rate, and pocketed my key. I took a few minutes to take my bags to the room and unpack my crap, then I walked back out to the car and slipped my pistol under the driver's seat. It was still broad daylight, and I was in the middle of downtown. If there was an ambush of pissed-off Homeland Security demons waiting for me, they would have been in the hotel lobby. They wouldn't be walking The Battery, which was where I was eventually headed.

I walked a couple of blocks from the hotel, then took a right on East Bay and headed toward the tip of downtown. I stopped by the big fountain and walked out on the pier at Waterfront Park, sitting for a few minutes on a swing until a family with a pair of toddlers wandered up really looking like they needed a seat. I walked all the way to the end of the pier and leaned out, letting the smell of the water and the slight spray of the salt air lull me into a deep sense of calm. My heart beat in time with the *slap-slap* of the waves against the rocks, and the gulls overhead pierced the peace with an occasional screech.

"Penny for 'em," a soft voice said beside me. I opened my eyes to see a young woman leaning on the rail to my left.

"Just thinking," I said, not wanting to get involved. She was too young for me, and not my type anyway.

"I could see that, silly. What were you thinking *about?*" I looked at her a little more closely this time. Dark hair cascaded down to her bare shoulders, partially obscuring a large tattooed undersea scene that sleeved her right arm in vibrant blues and greens. She wore a tank top and threadbare khaki cargo pants with black Chuck Taylor high tops and a belt studded with pouches and pockets like a utility belt slung low across her hips. She had narrow features, almost pixie-ish, but a little too angular for that. Dark eyes looked up at me, a challenge written in huge letters across the smirk she wore. There was a lot more going on in that face than just dimples, but I wasn't at all sure why she was talking to me, out of all the people closer to her age on the pier.

"My thoughts." This time I didn't bother trying to keep the "piss off" hidden from my tone. I wasn't really thinking about anything, just taking a minute to center myself before I opened my Sight and started scouring the city for an amnesiac angel. Now, as they said on *Firefly*, this girl was starting to seriously damage my calm.

I turned to walk away, and she put a hand on my arm, stopping me. I don't mean that she put a hand on my arm, and I stopped, like most people do when they're being polite. One, I'm rarely polite, and two, that isn't what happened. She *stopped* me. I couldn't break free of her grip, and I couldn't push past her.

I looked at her hand, then back at her face. All smirk was gone now, and the face that looked up at me was cold. "I'm going to need a little more than that," she said.

Well, she was about to get it. I pulled in my will and muttered *"cumulonimbus"* under my breath. Just as I clapped one hand on the pier railing behind me, a huge wind blew up, a solid forty-mile-per-hour gust that sent tourists and one hot dog cart tumbling.

It did absolutely nothing to the pixie-ish girl holding onto my arm. She waved a hand, whispered *"disperse"* like she was blowing a kiss, and the wind died down.

"That wasn't very nice," she said, her eyes taking on a deep purple glow. My arm started to tingle through my shirt, a pins and needle sensation running down to my fingertips and back up to my shoulder.

"Let go of me before I have to show you how not nice I can get," I replied.

"I don't think that's going to happen, mister. I don't like strange wizards coming into my city without going through the proper channels. That happens, and people start to think there aren't any rules at all, or that they just don't apply to them. Can't have that, can we?" She raised a fist toward my face, wrapped in that same purple glow.

I decided enough was most certainly enough. There were probably plenty of circumstances in which dancing around the Charleston Harbor with an escapee from a *Sandman* comic would be fun, but I was attached, and I had a job to do. So instead of going into my usual witty repartee, or even growling out a few manly threats, I just picked the girl up by her belt and jumped backward.

I counted on her hanging on to my arm, and that was a good guess. The second my feet left the wood of the pier, her deathtrap on my bicep tightened to almost painful levels. We hit the water with a *splash*, and her strength instantly dropped to what I'd expect from a ninety-pound woman who tops out at maybe five feet in shoes.

We popped up to the surface instantly, and I started treading water. The tide was in, so I had to swim a few yards to stand comfortably, but I dragged my witchy attacker along with me. Her magic disrupted by the salt water, she was just a bedraggled twentysomething girl who tangled up with somebody way out of her league. I held onto her belt despite her beating on my chest and shoulder with ineffective punches.

"If you don't stop that, I'm going to knock you out," I said under my breath. "Then I'll tell everybody you're my niece, you fell over the rail being an idiot teenager, and I'll carry you back to my hotel over my shoulder. Then we'll have a very unpleasant conversation where nobody can see you, and I'll make sure nobody can hear you scream."

She stopped struggling and opened her mouth to yell, but I was anticipating that very thing. "No, Delilah!" I shouted. "Don't panic, I've got you!" I wrapped one arm around her throat, making it look like I was having trouble dragging her to the shore, and tightened my grip on her carotid arteries. A few seconds later, she was out. I released the hold and threw one of her arms over my shoulder, wrapping my arm around her waist and lifting her into a perfect *Weekend at Bernie's* drunk friend carry pose. We got a few odd looks as I hauled her back to the King Charles, wrestled her into the elevator, and then down the hall to my room.

I dropped her in the center of the king bed and walked back to the door. I traced my finger around the door frame and stepped back. A whispered *"silencio"* insured that we wouldn't be overheard, and a quick *"sonjunctare"* fused the wood of the door to the frame. Nobody was getting in or out of that room without a fire axe or a chainsaw until I wanted them to.

I grabbed a fresh set of clothes and went into the bathroom to change. The last thing I needed was some kid waking up from being choked out while I'm bare-assed naked five feet away. I walked back out rubbing my head with a towel just as she started to stir. I dug through my suitcase for a pair of sweatpants and a t-shirt and threw them on the bed next to her.

"Here's some dry clothes. You might as well go into the bathroom and dry off," I said as she looked around the room in a panic.

The girl opened her mouth to scream, then closed it with a snap. I nodded. "Yes, I warded the room against sound. So why don't you go get changed and we can sit and talk about this like civilized people?"

She gathered up the clothes and went into the bathroom. A few minutes later, she came back out, rubbing her own head with a towel. "Sorry," I said. "I don't carry any women's underwear around, and anything that would have been lying around my apartment wouldn't fit you anyway. My girlfriend is full-grown."

"Fuck you, sorcerer," she said, sharing with me the accompanying hand gesture to let me know that I was number one in her book.

"You could be a little nicer to the guy who saved your life," I said.

"You're also the only person who's threatened my life today," she shot back.

"Then obviously I'm the first person you've talked to today, given your winning fucking personality."

"I don't have to take this shit," she said. Her eyes glowed purple again, and she raised her right hand.

I stood up from my chair, crossed the ten feet between us in less than half a second, and backhanded her to the ground. Then I reached down and grabbed a handful of dark hair and yanked her back to her feet. This time I picked her up by her throat.

"Let's get this very clear, little girl. I am not a nice person. I am not the guy who takes a bunch of shit and finally gets fed up enough to lash out. I am the guy who takes zero shit, gives zero fucks, and knows every incantation needed to open up a portal to the sixth circle of Hell and throw your scrawny ass through it. So unless you really think you're in my fucking league, I'd suggest you lay off the fireworks before I lose my fucking patience."

If looks could kill, I'd have been killed, reanimated, and killed a couple more times. After about ten seconds, which must have felt like an eternity to the one hanging by her throat in my hand, she let go of the power she'd summoned, and the purple light faded. I tossed her over to the bed, and she bounced clear across it to the floor.

"Sorry," I said. "I actually didn't mean to throw you that far. You seem to have a way with me." I walked back to the one chair in the room and sat down.

The girl got to her knees on the other side of the bed, still looking daggers at me. She stood up and walked over to sit on the end of the bed in front of me, just out of arm's reach.

"Good," I said. "Now who the fuck are you?"

6

S he didn't speak for a long time, then she finally took a deep breath and said, "My name is Arianne. I...protect the city."

"Like Batman?" I asked.

"Kinda, except I only worry about mystical threats. There are plenty of ways that people are defended against mundane attacks. The kinds of threats I deal with are a little more..."

"Complicated?" I offered.

"Sure, we can use that one. I deal with complicated threats to my city."

"What made you think I was complicated?" I asked. I ran down a mental checklist in my head. I hadn't cast any spells since leaving Charlotte, hadn't opened up my Sight to the magical world, hadn't done anything out of the ordinary except...*motherfucker*.

I pulled out my phone and set it on the table. I didn't have to press any buttons, I knew the ethereal bastard was snooping. "Okay, Dennis, time to fess up," I said to the phone.

"You know you have to dial those things, right?" Arianna said from her seat on the bed.

I glared at her. "It's complicated," I said, keeping with what was apparently the word of the day.

"You also know they're not waterproof?"

"Mine is. I've learned to protect my tech." I wasn't kidding. Magic is bad enough on delicate equipment, but with the number of times I've been burned, drowned, buried, or defenestrated, I caught on to the need to spend some resources on keeping my gear alive. That way it can keep me alive.

"What spell is that?" the girl asked. For the first time, she looked like she thought I might actually be competent.

I almost hated to burst her bubble. "It's called an Otterbox," I replied, gesturing to the heavy-duty protective case around my phone. "Now quit hiding in there and answer me, Dennis."

"Oh come on, Harker, don't be a dick about this." The digitized image of Dennis "Sparkles" Bolton appeared on the screen. At least he wasn't wearing his unicorn face this time. Instead, he looked like his normal moon-faced ginger self, perennially twenty-two going on fourteen with tight curly hair and about three hairs on his chin. A spattering of freckles dotted his grinning cheeks, and he used the magic of computer imaging to make his green eyes a blazing emerald.

"Why should this be any different, Dennis? I'm a dick about everything. Now why did you sic the Junior Adventurer on me?" The girl on the bed gave me the finger, and I returned the gesture.

"Arianne's good, Harker. I thought she could be useful. Especially since you're flying solo on this one." He wasn't wrong. Luke was back home overseeing the reconstruction of his new house, a process made difficult by his need to schedule construction meetings after sunset. Flynn wasn't exactly in the doghouse with her bosses at the police department, but she was on a pretty short leash nonetheless. The other Shadow Council folks were out chasing angels of their own or trying to pick up the pieces of their mundane lives. That left me on my own.

"I'm tracking down one…person, Dennis. I think I can handle it on my own. You know I've handled cases without backup before, right?"

"Oh, I remember. I think I'm the prime example of how sideways shit can go when you don't have your usual support system behind you." That stung a little, but only because it was true. Dennis was a casualty of me chasing a demonic serial killer and not being fast enough to figure out the murderer's identity. He was sacrificed in a ritual to open a doorway to Hell, and I managed to transfer his consciousness into the internet, only partially on purpose.

"So she's supposed to be Batgirl or something?" I asked.

"That's sexist," Dennis said.

"Go fuck yourself," Arianne said at the same time.

"Is that to me or him?" I asked. "I don't care. Just shut up for a minute while the grownups talk."

"Oh, one hundred percent go fuck yourself," the girl said, standing up from the bed. I put a hand on her chest, just under her throat, and pushed her back down.

"Sit. Stay."

"One *thousand* percent go fuck yourself," she said. She sprang up with her fists clenched at her sides. She was ready to go.

I wasn't. I put my hand on the top of her head this time and pressed down. She fell back to the bed, and I pointed a finger at her. "I said *stay.*"

She looked up at me and saw something in my face that made her pause. I was getting pretty irritated, so there might have been a little bit of "I can and will turn you into a toad" written across my forehead.

"What's the plan, Dennis? Do I take her under my wing, or just use her as cannon fodder?" I asked.

"I just thought it might be helpful to have someone who knows the town's players, magically speaking. So I sent Arianne a few simply encoded texts and emails with your picture, saying that a powerful and dangerous wizard was coming to her town, and I thought she might want to know about it."

"So you tell her I'm dangerous, and you expect her to just jump right in and work with me? Yeah, that seems to make sense."

"Okay, it might not have been the best way to go about it, but the end result was good, right? I mean, you guys are together now, and you can figure out how to find Gabriel and his book and then work on getting Glory her wings back, right?"

"Wait, what?" Arianne said. "What is he talking about? Gabriel? A book? Wings? Are you messing around with angels? Because I'm not messing around with angels. Angels are *assholes*."

I thought back to Barachiel, the angel behind all the shit in Atlanta, and couldn't find it in my heart to disagree. "You're not wrong," I said. "A lot of angels are assholes. But there's one who's not, and she needs my help. The only way I can help her is to find a bunch of other angels and get them to go back to Heaven and do their jobs. From what we can figure, one of them might be here in Charleston."

"Which one?"

"Gabriel," I said.

"The Archangel Gabriel?"

"That's the one," Dennis said from the phone.

"Fuck that," the girl said. "I'm out of here, and you need to be out of here, too. You don't just need to be out of this hotel room, you need to be out of my city. I'll give you until nightfall. Then I'm coming back with a bunch of my sisters, and we're going to make sure you're gone. We don't need any trouble with angels around here." She stood up, and I blocked her path to the door.

"Get out of the way."

"Sit down."

"Get out of the way." I hoped eventually she'd realize that the glowy eyes thing wasn't impressing me, but apparently, we hadn't gotten there yet.

"Please sit down, and stop trying to look badass. You're maybe twenty years old, and I've forgotten more spells that you've cast in your whole life." My powers of persuasion being what they are, that went over like a lead balloon. She shoved her hands out at me, and a bolt of pure purple energy shot out toward my face.

I closed my eyes against the glare and tapped my belt buckle. A small *pop* sounded under the crackle and hiss of magical energy, and the purple energy dissipated around me.

"What the fuck was that?" the girl asked.

"It's a dampener," I replied. "A little piece of obsidian set into the buckle of my belt. I invoke the right spell, and the stone sends out what amounts to a magical EMP, knocking out any active spells in a quarter mile and sucking away all the magical mojo for a couple hours."

"But that kills your magic, too!" The girl obviously decided that meant I was going to be old and slow, so she tried to dart past me to the door.

I might be old, but I'm far from slow. I caught her around the waist and flung her back to the bed. "Stop that," I said.

"How did you do that? Your magic should be dead, too."

"It is. That wasn't magic. That was just me being a badass." I gave her my most annoying grin, and she just gave me the finger again. I was really getting tired of seeing this kid's middle finger. I might have to feed it to her before this whole mess was finished.

"So what now, you just gonna tie me up and keep me in your hotel room?"

"Nah, I'm not into that Fifty Shades shit. Plus, I'm seeing somebody. The way I see it, we've got two options. You can either help me, or you can leave me alone. Despite my kinda dead friend's ideas, I'm pretty sure I can find one angel and one book and get them back to Charlotte on my own. So if you want to walk out of here and leave me the hell alone, that's fine."

"Sold," she said, standing up again. I dispelled the binding holding the door closed with the wave of a hand, and she rushed toward it.

I got in her way again. "You can go. I just want to be perfectly clear about one thing: I am not here to fuck with the local witches. I do not *want* to fuck with the local witches. If given the choice, I *will not* fuck with the local witches. But if you get in my way, I will rain hellfire down upon you the likes of which you have never seen."

That got her blood up again, of course. "Who the fuck do you think you are, John Fucking Constantine?"

"Kid, I make John Constantine look like John Lennon. I'm Quincy Fucking Harker, and I've been hunting big nasties since your grandparents were babies. Now I'm only going to be here for a few days, then you can get back to dancing around naked under the full moon and explaining to the mundanes why love potions don't really work."

Her eyes got big, and she took a step back. I guess she'd heard of me. *"You're* Quincy Harker?"

"Yeah, I thought I'd be better looking, too."

She didn't say anything, just ducked her head and bolted past me out the door. I closed it behind her and threw the deadbolt, then walked over to sit at the small table where I had my phone sitting.

"So…that happened," I said.

"Yeah," Dennis' voice came from the speaker.

"Looks like I'm famous."

"Not in a good way."

"Nope, she didn't even offer to sleep with me."

"You're too old for her."

"I'm over a hundred years old, Sparkles. I'm too old for everybody."

"You're not wrong."

"Think I oughta wait around here for her to come back?"

"What makes you think she's coming back? I might not have eyes, but it sure sounded like she hauled all kinds of ass out of there."

"Oh, she did. But she'll be back."

"A lot of people would think that's a misogynist attitude, that the woman can't get along without you."

"Those people would be stupid. I don't have any attitude, just proof."

"What kind of proof?"

"She left her keys on the bed with her clothes."

7

S he didn't come back in the next hour, so I went down the street and got myself an early dinner. I just ducked into a little English-themed pub, had some fish and chips that were good enough to remind me of my childhood, and downed a couple pints of Guinness. The thick stout and the vinegar on my chips were almost enough to make it feel like home, except the place was far too clean, nowhere near smoky enough, and I couldn't smell goat or horse shit anywhere. It's easy to romanticize my upbringing if you never smelled it.

The sun was setting when I walked out of the pub, so I meandered over to King Street and decided to start my investigation on familiar ground. The sign for Trifles & Folly glowed with magic even without my Sight open, so I ducked in the shop, looking around to see who was running things these days.

"Good evening," a trim young man with crisp creases in his pants and nice cufflinks called out to me from behind the counter. "Welcome to Trifles & Folly. Is there anything we can help you find today?"

We were the only two people I could see in the shop, a well-appointed antique shop with a reputation in the occult circles as the place to go to find magical trinkets. The proprietress, Cassidy, was psychokinetic, and she worked with a group of people to take dangerous artifacts off the street and either lock them away somewhere safe or deal with any malevolence surrounding the stuff. I'd met her a few times, but we tried to stay out of each other's way.

I didn't know this guy, though, so I wasn't sure how much I could say to him. "I'm looking for a book," I said.

"Well, we don't do much with rare and antiquated books," he replied. "There are several excellent used bookstores in town, including Harbor Books over on East Bay, and Battery Tales up on St. Phillips."

"This would be a 'special' book. The kind your boss often takes a particular interest in," I said, hoping that if he didn't know the deal, that he at least had enough of a clue to know that Cassidy sometimes dealt in weird stuff and would give her a call.

A shadow crossed his handsome face, and I knew he knew what I was talking about. I also knew he didn't really want to talk about it with someone he didn't know, and that seemed smart to me. I leaned forward. "Hey, look, it's cool. Why don't I leave Cassidy a note?"

He relaxed a little when I used the name, and he slid me a pencil and piece of paper across the counter. I noticed he made it a point not to touch me, and I smiled a little. Working with someone who can pick up psychic impressions off objects would give me an increased personal bubble, too.

C— *In town for a few. Nothing you need to worry about. Council stuff. Next time I'm through, I'll give you a call and we can grab a drink. Regards to S.*

Harker

I scribbled my message on the paper, wrote my cell number under it, and passed it back to the young man. "Here you go. Thanks for the tip on the books. I'll give those places a shot."

"For special books, you probably want to start with Harbor Books. Gerry over there has been known to pick up some oddball things from time to time."

"Thanks, um…what was your name again?" I asked.

"Teague," he said. "And you are?"

"Quincy Harker," I replied. "I'm an old acquaintance of the shop and the owners."

His eyes widened just a tiny bit. "I've heard the name."

I smiled at him. "All true, pal. Every word." I turned and stepped back out onto the street.

Full night had fallen, and Charleston was a different world. The bright pastels of Rainbow Row were whitewashed in the moonlight, and the whole town felt more like Victorian London than a modern American city. Even several blocks from the water, I could smell the thick ocean musk and taste the salt hanging heavy in the air.

My boots clomped across the brick sidewalks as I dodged broken stones and ankle-snapping divots. I crossed the street and headed south, turning left onto Market toward East Bay and stopping cold as I saw a shimmering figure walking into the old City Market.

"I really don't want to get involved in this," I muttered. I said it like a mantra as I walked down the street outside the open-air craft market that stood on the site near where so many men, women, and children were sold as property. I kept pace with the ghost, having no desire to leave a wandering spirit at my back, even if it was a harmless specter.

Most of them are. Harmless, that is. It's the rare ghost that can affect the material world more than a little knocking and the occasional moaning in the night. But it's a pretty rare ghost that wanders much more than a few feet from its resting place, and this ghost was moving into its third block since I spotted it, so there was definitely something odd going on.

I opened my Sight and immediately understood what was going on. The ghost itself glowed white and yellow in my vision, a pretty common color for the non-malevolent haunting types. Around its waist was the interesting thing. A band of pulsating crimson energy encircled the ghost like a belt, or a lasso, leading off down through the market. This ghost wasn't just wandering through the streets of Charleston. That happened all the time. This ghost had been summoned and was being compelled to do someone's bidding. Compelled with blood magic and necromancy, two things that ranked only slightly below "demon summoning" on Quincy Harker's List of Things that Get Your Ass Kicked. It looked like I was going to get involved in this mess after all.

I dropped my Sight, snapping my vision back to the mundane world just as I passed the delicious smells of one of Charleston's many seafood restaurants. There was a line to get in the place, and I lost sight of the ghost for a few seconds pushing through the crowd. When I finally emerged on the other side, the glowing image was a block ahead of me, passing out of the end of the market and turning down a narrow passage between two buildings. I hurried after it, only to get to the mouth of the alley and see nothing.

"Shit," I said. I opened my Sight, and the amount of magic around me left me momentarily blind. The entire alley glowed a deep red, almost the color of blood, shot through with streaks of gray, green, and a glaring piss-yellow. There was nothing good being done here, and all that not good was being done an awful lot.

I saw just a hint of white glowing amidst the darker sheen on the bricks and strode down the alley to where the last flicker of the ghost's essence lingered. A dingy metal door with heavy hinges and a thick deadbolt stood there, just the barest hint of magical essence glowing through the crack under the door. I dropped my Sight, and the ugliness of the psychic world around me faded to the normal nasty of an urban back alley with a few random garbage bags, a hint of piss wafting into my nostrils, and the acidic reek of a puddle of vomit by the opposite wall. The gray door in front of me had no identifying marks, but the new lock and well-worn scrape marks in the dirt at my feet told the story of frequent use.

I pressed my ear to the door, but it was too thick for even my enhanced hearing to pick up anything. There was no knob, just a bent piece of metal bolted to the door, so I gripped the makeshift handle and pulled. The door was unlocked and swung open with just a whisper, more evidence that not only was this entrance used a lot, but by someone who took pains to make sure their passing was as quiet and unobserved as possible.

I slipped into the building, all my mundane senses open as wide as I could manage. I kept my Sight closed off except for brief scans because there was so much red and gray pain and death magic coating the walls and floor that I could barely stand the onslaught. I stepped into a narrow corridor running the length of the building, illuminated by one flickering fluorescent tube and glaring green LED glow of the EXIT sign over my head. My boots were nearly silent on the scuffed tile floor, but I kept to the walls and shadows as best I could regardless.

There was a hallway to my right that ran to the front of the building and what looked like a simple wooden door. To my left, the corridor went a dozen yards back into the building and turned a corner, away from the street and, presumably, any prying eyes. I went left, thinking that most things done with ghosts are probably best done as far from public view as possible.

I rounded the corner only to find the hallway ran just ten more feet into a dead end. There was an open door, and a little more light fed in from the next room or passage. I crouched down to make my shadow smaller and walked to the door. I peered through the door into a large room, some kind of warehouse or storeroom. It was a huge open space, easily sixty feet on all sides, completely empty except for the naked man standing in the center of the room in a casting circle, his hands raised to the heavens.

Great, I thought. *Nothing better than fighting a naked wizard in a strange city when you're supposed to be hunting down missing angels. I guess it could be worse. I could be wrestling a nude Sasquatch.*

I drew in some energy from my surroundings, a little unsteady from the corruption coursing through the area, and released a trickle of it into the air around my hands. A bright blue glow filled the room, and the man in the circle stopped mid-incantation to gape at me.

"Who dares interrupt the workings of the Grand Barathan?"

"Is Grand your first name, or is it more of a description? I think you're the only Barathan I've met, so I don't have much of a basis for comparison. Is that a thing now? Should I start calling myself the Grand Harker? I mean, I'm the only one left, so it's not like anyone's going to fight me for the title belt or anything."

My new buddy apparently had nothing in the way of a sense of humor because he waved his arms and a dozen spirits floated up from the floor of the warehouse and floated toward me, every one of them wailing and flailing like bad guys in a haunted house.

I'm usually not very worried about ghosts. With the exception of the random banshee, most things are pretty harmless when they're dead. The exception is malevolent poltergeists, who can sometimes throw things with a lot more aim than they should have for denizens of the ethereal plane. Then there are wraiths—angry spirits summoned by necromancers. Wraiths can't cause physical harm, but they drain your life essence with every touch, kinda like Death in the old *Gauntlet* video game. Except you can't get this essence back by eating a digital turkey leg.

I blinked my Sight in and out just to confirm my worst suspicions about the spirits currently coming for me across the floor of the abandoned warehouse. Yep, every one of them had the sickly yellow-tinted aura of a wraith. So I was all alone staring down a naked necromancer and a dozen ghosts that could suck the life right out of me.

It was looking like a bad night for our hero.

8

I let loose a bolt of energy from each hand, not even bothering to coalesce it into a spell, just pouring sheer power into the wraiths. I managed to blast four of them back to the Other-world with my first shot, but that still left eight.

I leapt for the rafters and grabbed a joist, using it to swing over to the other side of the room, buying myself a few extra seconds. Unfortunately, in escaping the ghosts, I put myself a lot closer to the evil necromancer (yes, I know it sounds redundant, but I have met more than one non-evil necromancer). He lobbed a ball of fire at me, which exploded in a textbook circular blast and singed me even with my enhanced reflexes. Obviously, somebody played a little too much D&D.

The problem with tossing around fireballs inside buildings is twofold. First, buildings burn, which is generally a bad day for everyone in them, often including the person who threw the spell in the first place. Second, fire sucks a lot of the oxygen out of a room, which is even worse for the people inside than the fire. You can run away from a fireball, but it's a lot harder to run from suffocation. The bad guy's spell not only caught the walls and ceiling insulation on fire, it also made it tough to breathe between the smoke and the lack of oxygen.

I drew my pistol and shot out a couple of the windows up near the ceiling line, letting more air into the room. On the one hand, that move kept me from dying right that second. On the other hand, it gave the fire in the insulation more fuel, and it raced across the desiccated fiberglass, spreading to every corner of the room in seconds.

I looked away from the blazing ceiling to see a pair of wraiths closing on me. I called up my personal reserves of power and shouted *"begone!"* at the top of my lungs. The wraiths vanished, but I staggered as the power flowed out of me in an instant. I ran across the room, firing a couple of rounds at the necromancer in his circle as I passed. They pinged off his magical protections, but it was worth a shot. Some folks forget to ward against physical threats when they believe their surroundings to be secure, and putting a couple of bullets into the wizard would have been an easy way to bring most of my troubles to a quick resolution.

I leapt over a wraith in my path and lowered my shoulder as I approached what looked like a standard office-issue, hollow-core wooden door. I heard a resounding *crack* as I slammed into the door, but it didn't come from the door splintering into a million pieces like I'd really, really hoped it would.

Nope, it came from my collarbone as I hit a steel-reinforced door clad in what only looked like cheap wood. The door held up to my onslaught, but the surrounding wall wasn't reinforced, so the door and jamb went down, with me on top of them. I took out a solid four to six inches of wall on all three sides of the door, and the whole mess fell flat underneath me.

"FUCK!" I shouted, scrambling to my feet and spinning around to see the four wraiths gliding toward me, an inexorable tide of suck preceded by the fire racing across the ceiling at me. The necromancer was nowhere in sight, having yanked down his circle and vanishing while I attempted my escape. I offered up a brief and petty hope that his pants had already burned.

I tried to raise my right hand and summon magic, but my shoulder screamed at me, and I dropped to one knee as the pain hit me like a bullet. From a crouch, I held up my functioning left arm and drew a hasty circle on the floor in front of me with a Sharpie I carry in my back pocket. I bit my thumb and smeared a little blood across the line, invoking the circle and buying me a few seconds. The circle would keep the wraiths out, and it would keep me from burning to death, but it wouldn't do shit to stop me from suffocating, dying of smoke inhalation, or just broiling inside my own skin.

I wracked my brain for an incantation that would banish four wraiths at once, but the pain in my shoulder made it hard to concentrate. Even if I could whip up something of sufficient power to do the job, there were no guarantees that I wouldn't fuck it up in my addled state. There are worse things than miscasting a spell and being trapped inside your own circle with it, but not many.

The four wraiths surrounded my circle, not touching the mystical barrier, just surrounding it. It was like they knew I couldn't hold it forever, and all they had to do was be patient and they'd be able to get their fill of my soul. Their faces were twisted in a rictus of pain and hunger, and they bore no resemblance to the people they'd been. These were no friendly Caspers; these were monsters eager to rip my soul to pieces and feed on the scraps.

I reached out with one hand, cautiously extending my fingertips until I just brushed the surface of the glowing sphere of force surrounding me. Magical circles are kinda like soap bubbles. They have very little surface tension, but if you do it just right, you can actually touch one without destroying it. That's what I did now, I just barely connected my fingertips with the circle's inside edge. A push too hard, and it would pop out of existence, and I'd be wraith food. Not enough contact, and my silly plan wouldn't work.

I pointed my right hand toward the floor and spun my essence out through my fingers until I found what I was looking for. I lit upon a fat conduit carrying electrical wires underneath the building and drew power from it up through the floor, through myself, and poured it into my circle.

The barrier flickered, blinked a little in spots, then strengthened, its power bolstered by the power from the building. I opened the flow of energy a little, channeling more power into the circle. Like bubblegum, the sphere of energy started to expand as more and more juice poured into it. I cranked up the juice, and the circle grew exponentially faster. The wraiths whirled around faster and faster, torn between their desire to get at me and their fear of the power expanding outward.

I kept the flow increasing at a steady pace for several seconds, then cranked the floodgates wide open, drawing as much energy through myself as I could handle, blowing the circle wide open and sending a wave of energy out from myself like a shockwave from a nuclear blast. Except this shockwave was pure magical force, and when the wave hit the wraiths, it slammed into them like a hurricane wind, tearing the spirits to shreds and scattering their essence across the Otherworld.

The wraiths gone, I ran for the front of the building, found a plate glass window, and hurled myself through it. I intentionally used my already-injured shoulder, which ended up with me screaming and rolling around on the sidewalk covered in glass and soot, smoke rising from my hair and clothes.

A pair of boots materialized in front of my eyes, and I looked up the legs attached to them to see Arianne scowling down at me. *Great, from a necromancer to a pissed-off witch. This night really sucks.*

"I knew you were trouble the first time I laid eyes on you," the witch said, waving a hand at the mess behind me as if it were evidence.

Sometimes I can't keep my mouth shut when I really should. This was not the time for old Meat Loaf quotes, but I couldn't stop myself. I smiled up at her and said, "I bet you say that to all the boys."

The last thing I saw was a combat boot coming at my forehead; then everything went black.

9

I woke up with a headache, a really sore shoulder, and the smell of smoke lingering in my nose. All in all, I've had worse. I tried to sit up, and immediately, the pain in my shoulder went through the roof, and I moved right into the "worse" category. I fell back to the bed I was on, and that sent another wave of pain rolling through me. I fought desperately to keep my lunch in place as the waves of blinding pain radiated from my shoulder to my skull and back again.

"Fuuuuuuck," I groaned.

"Oh good, you're awake. We didn't want to try healing you until we could at least let you scream a little." I didn't try to sit up this time, but I did manage to turn my head to the side and look at Arianne. She was sitting in a cheap hotel chair, and by my best guess at the chair and the table beside her, we were back at the King Charles. I assumed we were in my room, but they all pretty much look the same, and I couldn't see any of my crap lying around, so maybe not.

"Heal me?" I asked. My voice cracked, and I sounded like a man who had just walked for a week in a desert. Or spent five minutes in a burning building. They sound about the same. "Feel free to start that process any time."

"Okay, but this is going to hurt," came a new voice. I turned my head to the other side and saw a young man with blond curls and a goatee sitting on the bed next to me. He held a pair of very large scissors and wore a serious expression. I didn't like where this was going.

The stranger leaned in, scissors moving toward my throat. I sucked back the agony in my shoulder enough to roll away from him and bring my hands up as I tumbled off the bed and came up to my knees.

"Back off, pal. I don't know what you're planning with the scissors, but nothing I've got going on requires surgery."

A puzzled look flashed across his face, then he relaxed and let out a little laugh. "Don't worry," he said, exactly the kind of thing a psychopath with scissors *would* say. "I have to cut your shirt off to set your clavicle. Otherwise, when we heal it, your shoulder won't work right. I don't think you want to try to raise your arm over your head right now, do you?"

I looked down at my clothes. I had just survived a fire, so it's not like anything I was wearing was really salvageable except for my trusty Doc Martens. My jeans were pretty much okay, except for a little soot and a scuff at the knee, but my shirt and t-shirt were pretty well fucked.

"Fine," I said, standing and moving back over to the guy. "Why don't we at least introduce ourselves first. I'm Quincy Harker."

His eyes widened a little, and he shot a nervous look over at Arianne. "The Reaper?"

I nodded. "I've been called that. Among other things." I didn't bother mentioning that "asshole" was chief among the other things, but he didn't need to know that.

"I'm Marcus. I'm the healer for..." He looked to the girl in the chair.

"My group," Arianne supplied.

"It's cool, doll," I said, throwing in the "doll" just to wind her up a little. Judging by the red tips on her ears, I'd say it worked. "I understand if you don't want me to know what you call your little coven. You don't have to tell me where the Hall of Justice is either."

"Let's get you patched up so we can figure out how we can help you," Marcus said.

"Or if we're just going to throw you out of town," Arianne countered.

I didn't bother responding. There wasn't any point. I just sat down on the bed and turned a little toward Marcus. "Go for it, Doc. Perform your sartorial magic on these poor garments."

He looked a little confused.

"Cut my clothes and fix my shoulder," I translated.

He nodded and got to work. First, he helped me out of the long-sleeve button-down shirt I wore over my gray *Transformers* t-shirt. Then he cut the t-shirt up the sleeve to the neck, and down from the armpit to the bottom hem, and peeled it back.

"This is probably going to hurt," he said. "Do you need something to bite on to keep from screaming?"

"Yeah, we wouldn't want the hotel security to come running, thinking we're killing you," Arianne agreed.

I opened my Sight for a second and saw that my sound-dampening spell from earlier was still in effect. It would last for a couple of days at least. I blinked my vision back to normal and looked at my makeshift doctor. "Nah, we're good," I said. "Nobody outside this room will hear anything that happens inside it as long as my spell is still going."

"Okay," Marcus said, and put one hand on my elbow. He pulled, lifted, pushed, and tweaked my elbow and shoulder for several minutes until I felt everything click back in the right spots with a sickening pulse of sheer blinding agony. Then he put his right hand on my collarbone, holding my elbow and arm stationary with his left, and closed his eyes.

"Blessed Mother, share your light and energy with this man. Mend his hurts and cure his ills so that he may once more sally forth in battle against thine enemies. Make him whole once more, and repair the source of his pain. Bathe him in your cleansing light and make him as new again."

My shoulder screamed and throbbed when Marcus began his

invocation, but as he spoke, a deep warmth suffused my arm, radiating out from the palm of his hand, pouring heat into my fractured clavicle to engulf my entire upper body in warm, pulsating energy. I *felt* the bones knit together, and the muscles strengthen, and the ligaments reattach, and even the damage to my lungs from the fire was repaired. A couple of minutes later, and I felt good as new. Better, actually, because for the first time in years, no part of my body was in pain or even uncomfortable.

I turned to look at Marcus, and he smiled at me, then passed out on the bed.

"That happens," Arianne said from behind me. "Healing takes a lot out of the healer. It takes a lot out of the patient, too, even though it doesn't feel like it at the time. I know you feel like a million bucks right now, but don't go chasing down anyone else to scrap with tonight. You'll probably die, and then Marcus would have wasted his efforts."

I stood up and could feel how right she was. I felt fantastic, but it was a very tired fantastic. I got a clean shirt from my dresser, threw it on, and pulled out a pair of sweats. "I'm gonna go get out of these smoke-scented clothes," I said. "If you're still here when I get back, we can talk about why you knocked me out, then healed me."

I walked into the bathroom, took care of some necessary bodily functions, and washed my face, neck, and arms. Then I shucked my Docs, dropped my jeans and boxers onto the floor and contemplated a shower. I decided that I was more likely to pass out and give myself a concussion than actually get clean, so I just did a quick sink bath and slipped on the sweats.

When I stepped back into the hotel room, I was alone. The kid was good, I had to give her that. I never heard the door close, and I was listening. There was a note on the bed, with an address and a time.

Meet me tomorrow. 2 p.m. We both have some explaining to do.

I couldn't argue with that. I ordered a couple of beers from room service, turned on *Law & Order* on the room TV, and was asleep before I finished the first Heineken.

10

Of course I walked around the block three times before I entered the restaurant Arianne had directed me to. I made the first lap half an hour before our meeting to see what kind of place I was walking into, checked for back exits and adjoining buildings, then took another pass with my Sight overlaying on top of my normal vision, looking for spells or magical booby traps. It all seemed safe, so I did one more trip around the building five minutes before two in the afternoon just to make sure there were no suspicious vehicles lurking or demonic portals hanging out around the perimeter.

I stepped into The Cannonball Cafe on Meeting Street at precisely one minute after two, just in case the room was set to explode at two on the dot. I'm really not paranoid by nature, but experience has taught me several things. I hate being ambushed, I really hate being blown up, and just because you're paranoid, doesn't mean that someone isn't trying to kill you.

The restaurant was nice, a real white linen tablecloth kind of place. The maître' d looked down his nose at me, which was impressive given the six inches I had on the guy. He stood behind what would be called a hostess stand in a normal restaurant, but probably had some kind of French name in this joint, and sneered at me.

"Mr. Harker, I presume?" I've never understood how somebody manages to be haughty in a Southern accent, but some folks in Charleston seem to have mastered the art.

"How'd you guess?"

"I was instructed to expect a tall Yankee with terrible taste in clothing and a perpetual scowl. You seem to fit that description. Please follow me." He turned and walked away without looking to see if I was behind him. I was, and only partly because I wanted to strangle him. I saw nothing wrong with my choice of black pants and a maroon dress shirt for this meeting. I even put on my good belt.

I followed my snooty guide up three flights of switchback stairs to a rooftop veranda with two tables set up under a white fabric awning. A large black man stood behind a small bar with a martini shaker in his hand and a white apron around his waist. I swallowed every comment that crossed my mind about progressive cities and stereotypes as Pepe le Asshat led me across the roof to a round table set for four. Three people already sat there. Arianna, Marcus, and a white-haired woman with a kind face but steel in her blue eyes, all rose to greet me as I stopped a few feet from the table.

The exposed rooftop lunch spot was not something I considered in my reconnaissance, and I didn't like being so exposed. There were a lot of buildings taller than this one in the surrounding blocks, and a sniper could easily take me out before I could raise any type of shield. Especially with a head shot.

"Have a seat, Mr. Harker. We promise not to try to kill you before you've had dessert. You simply must try the peach cobbler. It's to die for." Arianna motioned to the fourth chair as my lunch companions took their seats.

I stood in front of my chair for a moment, then extended my hand to Marcus. "I never got the chance to thank you for your help last night. I appreciate it. I felt great this morning. I hope it didn't take too much out of you."

He half-stood and shook my hand. "I was a little more draggy than usual, but I'm okay now. That's why Ari called our meeting for so late. She knows what a healing like that takes out of me."

I turned to the other woman. "I don't believe we've had the pleasure. Quincy Harker." I held out my hand. The woman just looked at it.

"I know you, Reaper. I know your uncle, the parasite, as well."

"Never heard him referred to in quite that fashion, but I suppose it's valid enough," I said, pulling my hand back and sitting. "Sorry, I suppose I missed your name."

"I am Tara, High Priestess of the Moon. And you are an interloper in my city."

"I prefer the term tourist, but whatever." The table was set with ice water and an amber beverage I assumed was sweet iced tea. A pretty safe assumption in South Carolina, where the default seemed to be tea so sweet a spoon could stand up in the glass. I sipped on my water.

"When do you plan to leave and take your necromancy with you? We find that type of magic an abomination, and its practitioners are not welcome here," Tara continued.

"I'll leave when I'm done with my business," I replied. "Are we going to order lunch, or was this all just a charade to get me here with the promise of a free meal?"

Arianne ducked her head, a tiny smile making her look even younger. There was some slight resemblance between the razor-cheeked Tara and the goth cherub Arianne, but it was pretty minor. I couldn't tell if they were distant cousins or just spent so much time together they started to look alike.

"I will not break bread with one who sucks the souls of the dead into lifeless husks for his own nefarious purposes." Tara's voice boomed across the rooftop.

"Well, I guess this is why you went for the private dining room, huh?" I asked. I stood up, and Marcus followed suit, his hand drifting around behind his back. "Calm down, Junior. There's nothing you're pulling out from behind your back that I'm afraid of, so don't even try."

His hand slipped back to his side, and he looked a little abashed. I turned my attention back to Tara. "Okay, lady, here's the deal. I'm here on a job, and I'm going to do that job with or without you. I don't know fuck-all about your necromancer problem, just that he tried to fricassee me last night, and that means he's number nine on my shit list with a bullet. So if you didn't call me here to help me hunt him down, then at least do me the professional courtesy of staying the fuck out of my way."

I turned to go and made it halfway across the roof before Tara spoke. "Wait," she said, and her tone was that of a woman who was on the edge of losing the last tiny grasp on her shit.

I stopped, but didn't turn around. "We gonna talk like civilized people over a burger with enough bacon to give bystanders cholesterol problems, or am I going to keep walking?"

"Please, come sit down, Mr. Harker," Arianne said. "I'm sure this is all just a misunderstanding."

I turned around and walked back to the table, but I didn't sit. "There's nothing to misunderstand," I said. "You fuckers have been popping up in my shit since the minute I got here. I was just minding my own business down on the pier when you decided to come down and piss on the ground to mark your territory. I appreciate the save last night, that was really helpful, but this bullshit today? Fuck you. Fuck you, and the broomstick you rode in on. You say you know me? You say you know my uncle? Then you know what we do for people who need it, and you know what we do *to* people who threaten us. So if you want to dance, let's dance. But if you're not going to help me or fight me, then leave me the fuck alone."

I stood there, the pissed-off rolling outward from me in waves, and me not giving a single fuck. I stood there watching Arianne, Marcus, and their snooty friend exchange meaningful glances for a solid couple of minutes before finally Tara looked up at me and nodded.

"Please sit, Mr. Harker. I apologize for my earlier rudeness. It was uncalled for."

"Apology accepted," I said, pulling my chair out and sitting back down. I was really glad she hadn't called my bluff. I was pretty good physically after last night's singeing, but there was no way I had enough mojo to duel three witches at once, and that's not even taking the waiters into account.

"Now," I said, taking a sip of tea and managing not to wince at the sweetness. "I met a necromancer last night who's doing some nasty shit to ghosts in your famously haunted city. What's up with that?"

Tara looked at Arianne, who made a "go ahead" gesture. "His real name is Lawrence Barathan, he now calls himself The Grand Barathan, as you heard. He is one of our former members who had designs on a greater amount of power and influence in the mundane world than we are comfortable pursuing. We cast him out, but he has continued in his efforts to influence events and gain personal wealth and authority. He seems to be using the spirits of the departed to identify objects of power, and then he works to acquire them, by any means necessary."

I could feel my brow wrinkle. "Isn't this exactly the kind of thing Sorin and his people are here to prevent? Why haven't they stepped in?"

"Cassidy and her group have been occupied with some other, more lethal, events of late. It seems that Lawrence's actions have flown beneath their radar as of yet. He has been very cautious in what type of artifact he pursues, trying to remain beneath Sorin's notice."

"Seems like a good idea. I've dealt with Sorin once or twice. Guy's a legitimate badass. So what is your pal Barry's endgame? What's he trying to do?" I asked.

Arianna leaned forward. "We think he's going to try to destroy the Coven of the Moon."

"I assume that's you guys?" They nodded. "What makes you think he wants to kill you?"

"He told us so," Marcus replied. "When we threw him out of the coven, he threatened to kill the three of us and everyone he saw wearing the symbol of the Moon." He pulled a pendant out from under his shirt, a full moon on a silver chain.

"That seems pretty clear," I said. "So why is he still walking around?"

From the looks on their faces, you'd have thought I suggested reenacting Sherman's march instead of eliminating an obvious threat to their lives.

"What are you talking about, exactly?" Arianna asked.

"Killing the bad witch before he kills all of you was the first thing that came to mind," I said.

"We are not murderers, Mr. Harker," Tara said with a haughty sniff.

"Neither am I," I replied. "But I'm also not going to just sit around and wait for some assclown with a ghost fetish to kill me in my bed. This guy has got some serious chops; I felt them last night. He almost took me out. He might have, if not for Marky Marcus and Arianne showing up when they did. So it's not murder. It's self-defense, just the magical version."

"We do not kill," Marcus said.

"Speak for your—oh, I get it now," I said as realization dawned. I stood up and once again walked toward the rooftop door. This time it wasn't a negotiating tactic; this time I was legitimately done with these fuckers.

"Wait, please!" Arianna called after me.

"Go fuck yourself," I said. "I might be a killer, but I'm not an assassin. You want this jackass dead, you're going to have to do your own dirty work."

"They can't," said the bartender, who was between me and the door for some reason. "It's not in their nature."

"Too bad," I replied. "Now step aside, dickhead."

"I don't think so, Mr. Harker."

"Oh for fuck's sake," I muttered, calling up a tiny bit of power, just enough to shove the man to the side. I gestured at him, releasing the power with a low *"sidestep."*

Nothing happened. The power struck him in the shoulder and just flowed around him.

"That's not how that's supposed to work," I said.

"Sorry about that," the bartender said, as he reached up to pull his face off, revealing the wizard who scorched me half to death last night standing in front of me. "I'm glad to hear you won't be hunting me down to kill me. Unfortunately, I've already hunted you down, so now I suppose I'll just kill you instead."

Goddammit.

11

H e looked different with clothes on, and in the daylight, and not surrounded by soul-sucking ghosts, but I was pretty sure this was the same guy who threw a fireball at me last night. Now he was three feet in front of me, dressed like a waiter, his dark skin a sharp contrast to the white tuxedo shirt he wore. A thick, ropey scar ran diagonally the entire length of his face, from his fore-head across his nose and mouth, all the way down his cheek. The way it lifted one lip in a perpetual sneer made him look a little menacing, and little like a low-rent Billy Idol impersonator.

"Lemme see if I remember this right, you're the Great Baratheon? Or is that the guy from *Game of Thrones*? I can never keep track of everybody on that show. And to be honest, I just watch it for the boobs."

He snarled and raised a glowing hand. I made a mental note to never make my hands glow again. Ever since *Doctor Strange* hit DVD, every asshole in the world with an ounce of magical ability makes their hands glow for everything. I took the hint and stepped forward, punching him hard in the nose.

"Ow!" he shouted, stepping back. The punch had the desired effect, though, scattering his attention and breaking his spell. Marcus looked like he was still pretty tired, so I didn't want him to have to heal me again. And with my magic still pretty low, punching the snot out of this asshole seemed like my best plan to resolve things quickly, and without bloodshed on my part.

"*Stoneskin!*" he shouted, and his skin turned gargoyle-gray. I checked myself before I punched him again, not wanting to break my fist.

"Really?" I asked. "The best you can come up with is a third-level *D&D* spell? You're a disgrace to magicians everywhere, and quite possibly infringing on copyright just by saying that shit."

Instead of punching him, I put one hand on his throat and one on his upper thigh and heaved him up into the air. Like so many things in a fight, this was way more difficult against a guy now made of granite. He was heavy as fuck, but I managed to wrestle him up and over my head.

The wizard thrashed around, but I got him to the edge of the roof before losing my grip. I tossed him over and turned back to the witches, who were no damn help whatsoever. At least Arianne had the courtesy to stand up and look like she thought about helping.

"Thanks for nothing, assholes," I said, clapping my hands together and walking over to the table. I sucked back the last of my sweet tea and glared at Tara.

"Now I definitely don't want to work with y'all. You didn't even..." My words trailed off as I noticed how wide her eyes were. "He's back, huh?"

This time all three of them sprang into action. Arianna moved over in front of Marcus and conjured a pair of short swords from pure energy that sprang from her clenched fists. Tara strode across the rooftop to stand toe to toe with Barathan, who was back on the roof and appeared to no longer be made of stone. She threw punches like a Jackie Chan movie, and Barathan dodged like he was the only one who knew how to control The Matrix.

It was fun to watch, but it really made me wish for my pistol. Of course, it was locked in the glove compartment of my car because that's where it was going to do me the absolute least amount of good.

I watched them try to fight for a few seconds, then pointed two fingers at Barathan and shouted "*torporus!*"

A green ball of energy flew from my fingertips and struck him right in the chest. He never stopped dodging, but his movements slowed, then slowed some more. Tara landed one punch, then another, then a knee strike, then another punch. She took a sidestep to create some separation, then drew back one leg for what looked like a devastating roundhouse kick.

A kick that sliced through empty air as the necromancer back-flipped out of range. He was slower, but still quick for a normal human. I threw a few blasts of energy at him, just to keep him off-balance, but never came close to hitting him. My slow-down spell wore off after just a few seconds, and he smiled as he drew a pair of curved knives from his belt.

"I will enjoy slicing your souls from your bodies and adding you to my reserves of power. You will help me draw nearer to my ultimate goal," he said.

"Which is?" I asked. I pulled my own pocketknife and clicked it open. It wasn't nearly as impressive as a twelve-inch curved dagger, but it's what I had. I settled into a fighting stance and stalked forward, moving left while Tara came at him from the right.

"I'll pass on the soliloquy, thanks." He clapped both hands together and set off a blinding light and a minor thunderclap on the roof, the mystical equivalent of a flash-bang. I closed my eyes and clapped my hands over my ears, but the sensory overload to my half-vampire senses still drove me to my knees.

When I could blink my eyes clear of tears, Barathan was gone, and so was Tara. I looked around the roof, and she was nowhere to be found. Arianna was still by the table, shielding Marcus with her body from any threats, but no necromancer and no high priestess.

"Well, fuck," I said. "I guess now we've got a rescue mission on our hands."

"Well, now what?" I asked Arianne.

"What do you mean, now what? Now we go get her back!" Marcus almost shouted.

"Sounds great," I said. "Where are they?"

He at least had the good sense to look chagrined. I turned my gaze to Arianne. "Any ideas, sunshine?"

"Not right offhand, no."

"Well, let's see what we can See." I walked over to a clear spot of roof and sat down cross-legged, my boots under my knees. I closed my eyes and opened my Sight, scanning the surrounding area for any magical hot spots. Trifles & Folly glowed like a fireworks display in the supernatural spectrum, all the artifacts lying around that place making it a beacon in the Otherworld. Farther away, I could see Cassidy's house, the residual magic that suffuses a place when a major Talent lives there making it glow like a gentle nightlight. There were several other shops that had a strong aura of magic around them and a few bright dots moving around downtown as several practitioners walked the streets. Nothing had the reddish-green tint of the necromancer though. I tried looking for Tara's aura, which I assumed would be a lot like Arianne's, only stronger. Nothing. No matter how far I ranged out of downtown, I could find no hint of her.

"Nothing," I reported. "Wherever he took her, he's got her hidden."

"We have to find her!" Marcus looked on the verge of tears.

"Suck it up, buttercup," I growled at him. "I'm dancing as fast as I can here." I pulled out my phone and tapped the home button. "Dennis, you there?"

"I'm everywhere, my cracker," Dennis said over the speaker.

"Dennis," I said, pitching my voice low, "you're as white as I am."

"I'm dead, man. I have transcended race. What do you need?"

"I need you to find someone for me. He goes by the name of Barathan."

"I'm pretty sure Robert was murdered, and that tall blond chick killed Tanis in the woods in season five."

"Everybody's gonna make the same *Game of Thrones* jokes, aren't they? Barathan, not Baratheon."

"Tomato, to-mah-toe. What else can you tell me about this Barathan?"

"He's a black necromancer, and he's kidnapped a witch named Tara."

"Is Willow pissed?"

"Are you just going to make TV references, or are you going to help me find this guy?"

"Pretty sure I can do both. By the way, I think necromancy counts as black magic from the jump, so your description was a little repetitive."

I looked at the phone, more puzzled than usual by Dennis' weird leap of logic, then it hit me. "No, dipshit, he's an African-American necromancer. I thought *that* might narrow the field a little."

"Oh! Why didn't you say that in the first place? Yeah, that might help, especially in South Carolina. I'll poke around and get back to you."

"Fine." I put the phone in my pocket. One bonus about having a friend who's basically a mystical pile of electrons, getting in touch with him doesn't use up my minutes. I turned to the two witches who just stood there staring at me.

"Don't you two have something to cast or something?"

"I'm a healer, man. That's pretty much the only magic I have," Marcus said.

"I've got a couple of ideas, but first I want to see how many of the coven I can pull together in case we need to throw down with this asshole," Arianne said.

"That makes sense," I replied. "I'm going to poke around a couple of the hot spots I saw in my Sight, but I've got a feeling we're going to end up back at the Market late tonight."

"What makes you say that?" Arianne asked.

"It's the first place I saw any activity from this dick," I said. "Plus, there's a lot of magic running around that place, thanks to years and years of people traipsing through there. It's past noon now, so midnight is the next strong time for magic, and the Market should be deserted then. Makes it prime time for nasty magic."

I handed Arianne a card with my cell phone number on it. "Take this and call me if you find anything. Otherwise, let's plan to meet up at my hotel at eleven. That should give us plenty of time to gear up and stop whatever this asshole has planned for your boss-lady," I said. It would also give me a little time to look around the city for Gabriel, my real reason for coming to Charleston in the first place.

The witches both nodded and headed off to do whatever it is witches do in the daytime, while I gave the city another quick scan with my Sight. The guy at Trifles & Folly, Teague, had mentioned a bookstore down on East Bay that might have something useful, so I peered over in that direction. I spotted a small place giving off a faint blue glow a half dozen blocks or so away, so I headed inside and took the stairs down to the street.

Twenty minutes of leisurely walking later, I stood in front of one of the very few businesses in the exclusive section of Charleston known as South of Broad. This part of East Bay was home to the famous Rainbow Row, the pastel houses that faced the waterfront, all with the long porches running perpendicular to the street to catch as much of the ocean breeze as possible when the ridiculous summer heat blanketed the city like a hot, damp towel.

Harbor Books was a converted house, probably worth north of a million bucks on the real estate market, but it certainly didn't seem to do very brisk business. In the ten minutes I watched the entrance, not a soul went in or out, and I only saw one old coot puttering around inside. I walked up the creaky wooden steps and looked at the sign on the door. "Open, mostly" it read, listing hours from noon until seven p.m. on weekdays and Saturdays. "CLOSED SUNDAYS" was written in large letters along the bottom of the page.

It being Tuesday, I turned the knob and stepped inside. I was instantly assailed by the papery dry smell of old books and almost knocked down by the magic in the place. The last time I was anywhere near this many magical tomes, there was a guy summoning demons for kicks who threw me out a window later that night. I hoped history didn't repeat itself. Although in downtown Charleston, there weren't any buildings nearly as tall as the one I went out of in Charlotte, so that was fortunate.

The inside of the shop was a mecca for readers and a nightmare for a fire marshal. I couldn't tell if I was in a bookstore or a documentary on book hoarding. Floor-to-ceiling bookshelves lined every wall, many of them double-stacked with tattered paperbacks from Ludlum, Clancy, Robb, King, Sanderson, Patterson, and the like. One entire shelf was dedicated to used copies of *Twilight*.

Every shelf was full almost to bursting, and hardbacks, encyclopedias, and coffee table books were stacked two and three feet high as endcaps on every aisle. The books were like multicolored literary kudzu, overtaking every inch of available floor space.

Floor lamps and tall windows provided the illumination, so there were some spectacularly shadowed corners, and as I meandered through the stacks, wandering semi-aimlessly and counting on my intuition to lead me to the most interesting texts, I uncovered various pieces of furniture scattered throughout the rooms. I felt like an urban archaeologist, unearthing settees and armchairs unseen for generations, tucked into corners with lamps behind them to provide little reading nooks all around the shop.

I saw fiction, nonfiction, memoir, biography, self-help, romance, thriller, fantasy, science fiction, science science, textbooks, comic books, manga, graphic novels, children's books, Bibles, Torah, Qur'an, and *The Book of Mormon*, both the religious text and the Broadway libretto. What I didn't see was a proprietor, unless you count the overweight and fluffy black and white cat who lounged on a chest-height stack of *Fifty Shades of Grey* paperbacks.

I reached out and scratched the cat behind its ears, and it looked up at me with a sleepy "Mrrrr?" before putting its head back down and starting to purr.

"How dost thou, sweet lord?" asked a voice from behind me.

I turned, my hand drifting to the small of my back where my pistol should have been, but wasn't, cursing myself for leaving it at the hotel. I relaxed when I saw the kind-faced old man who I'd watched through the windows standing there. He smiled at me, a little vacantly but pleasant enough, his head bobbing like a dashboard doll. He was a slight man, stooped with age and wearing a truly bizarre getup. His shoes were mismatched, one brown loafer and one white sneaker. He wore jeans, but they looked like they were patched by a psychotic clown with big fabric swatches of red and yellow sewn over the blue. An untucked dress shirt hung out lower than the pin-striped jacket he wore, and a brown tweed English driving cap sat on his head. His round face was smiling, and his deep-set eyes were rimmed with crows' feet, but his full beard was dark, and the stringy hair that I could see was brown, not gray.

"Hello," I said. "Are you the proprietor?"

He smiled at me and bobbed his head. "I like this place and willingly could waste my time in it."

Okay, not exactly what I was asking, but I guess it's close enough. "Can you help me find something?"

"Wise men never sit and wail their loss," he said, then turned and toddled off back into the stacks.

"Hey, wait," I said to his retreating back.

"Parting is such sweet sorrow!" he called back over his shoulder.

Is he answering me completely in Shakespeare quotes? Even for my life, that's pretty odd. I followed the old man through the winding stacks, past the armchairs, past piles of paperbacks that threatened to topple onto the floor at any moment, past the cat, who raised its head and meowed at me for once again disturbing its rest.

"Nice kitty," I said.

"A harmless necessary cat," the man replied. *Okay, maybe we're getting somewhere. That actually seemed to connect to what I said.*

I decided to push my luck. "Do you have any books of magic?" I asked.

"'Tis true; there's magic in the web of it," he said.

I shook my head. Nope, back to nonsense. I just kept my mouth shut and followed the old man until he stopped at the end of a long row of bookcases. I would almost swear that we had walked farther than was possible in the medium-sized house, but since we wove in and out of rooms, hallways, and stairwells, I wasn't sure.

The strange little man stood, looking up at a bookcase filled with leather-bound volumes. Some of these books looked old, and some looked downright ancient. I opened my Sight, and the entire wall glowed with a rainbow of colors. Red, blue, green, yellow, and white attacked my senses, and I staggered a little.

The little man heard the floor creak under me and turned to me, holding out a hand to catch my arm. When I caught a glimpse of him in my Sight, I saw through his mortal masquerade. Overlaid on top of the five-and-half-foot-tall human with as much curly brown hair coming out of his ears as was on his head was an ethereal image of a being wrapped in light with golden wings on his back. This batshit crazy little old man was exactly who I was looking for. This was the Archangel Gabriel, scribe of God Himself.

When I switched my vision back to the mundane world and took a good look in his eyes, I realized something else about my newfound divine entity. He was one hundred percent. USDA Grade A batshit crazy.

Now I've got a kidnapped witch and an angel with Alzheimer's. Some days I really hate my life.

I looked from the shelf, to the disguised angel, and back again. "You've got to be shitting me," I said.

"There are stranger things in heaven and earth, than are dreamt of in your philosophy," he replied, waving an arm at the books.

I let out a sigh. I couldn't read the titles with my Sight active, and I couldn't tell which ones were divine in nature with my normal vision. So I opened my third eye and pulled down all the books that glowed white, golden yellow, or pale blue. Those were usually the aura colors of positive or protective magic, the kind typically associated with the divine. I handed about ten volumes to Gabriel, who bobbled off to the front of the store in his odd little short-legged rocking gait. I took another ten and carried them myself, noting their weight.

"If anybody ever realized how strong the little bastard is, there certainly would have been some questions," I muttered as I followed him. He stopped at a large table and with one sweep of his arm knocked dozens of paperbacks to the floor. I dodged a couple, let a couple more bounce off my shins, and set my load of books down on the table by his.

"Is the information I need in here?" I asked, hoping against hope that I might get a reasonable answer.

"Ignorance is the curse of God; knowledge is the wing wherewith we fly to heaven."

"Of course it is," I said. I looked over the spines of the books and was able to immediately discard four of the two dozen as books I recognized. I set aside eight others that had titles on the spine and pulled up a chair to examine the last half more closely.

The first one was a French summoning text from the seventeenth century. Valuable, certainly, but far from the Word of God. Next was a three-volume set of spell books from the library of someone who called himself Alric the Grand. Judging by his spells, grand was not a word often used to describe him. He had spells for the shrinking of warts, spells for the reduction of passing odorous gas, spells to make himself seem more attractive, and a spell to summon a wood nymph to do his bidding.

Knowing what I do about the sexual proclivities of wood nymphs, I shuddered a little to think about him summoning one for a rent-a-date. There was no way a hornball wizard calling up a mischievous and powerful forest elemental was going to end well for the wizard. No wonder that was the last entry in his spell books.

When I whittled the pile down to three books, I turned to Gabriel. One of the books was from his stack, so I thought it was unlikely that it was his book. If our time with Michael was any indicator, as soon as he touched the book, it would manifest some outward sign, and so would Gabe. At least, I hoped Gabe would be coherent enough to do something.

That left me two books, both looking very old, and both radiating power like a mystical Chernobyl. I pulled the first one to me, and Gabe frowned, shaking his head. "Not to be," he mumbled. "Not to be, not to be, not to be."

I pushed the book away, and he relaxed. I stood and picked up the second book. He didn't look pleased, but he didn't look like I was about to shoot his puppy, either. I turned the book over in my hands, honestly a little nervous about opening the thing. If it worked like the sword, I could read it like a Stephen King novel and it wouldn't do anything in my hands. Of course, there was also the chance that it was the handwritten Word of God and would burn out my brain like an overused lightbulb if I opened it.

The book was big, encyclopedia-sized, and thick. It certainly looked old enough to have been around for hundreds of years, but it looked and felt professionally bound, so I couldn't tell if it was the original book or if it was a replica, or a manifestation, or what. There were some markings on the spine, but they looked like no language I'd ever seen before, and I can, at least, struggle through in most of them.

I opened the book, squinting my eyes to narrow slits in case I got another case of the magical dazzles, but nothing happened. Not, it didn't hurt me, but *nothing*. I just opened the book. It didn't blast me, didn't turn me into a pillar of salt, didn't call down a heavenly choir, just fell open to a spot in the middle. I looked at the pages, then back at my incomprehensible friend.

"Is this it?" I asked.

"But soft, what light through yonder window breaks?" He answered my question not just with a question, but with a completely stupid one to boot. I sighed. "This gig was supposed to be easy, you know. A simple FedEx quest, like the first few things in *A Bard's Tale*. I get a book, find an angel, put the two of you together, and *viola*, instant awesome. Instead I have Captain Incomprehensible and some old book of Enochian rituals..." I trailed off as I heard the word coming out of my own mouth.

Enochian? The language of the angels? I looked down at the book again, and sure enough, it was written in the looping characters of holy magic. "This is your book," I said, looking at Gabe.

He didn't reply, just looked at me. He kinda looked scared, to be honest.

"You have to take it," I told him. I pushed the book toward him. He sank back in his chair.

"A woman's life is in danger," I said. He shook his head and seemed to shrink in on himself.

"Fuck," I said. "I'm sorry." I closed the book, then shoved it into his chest. He put his hands up as the tome touched him, and the second he came into contact with the book, a brilliant yellow-white light shone forth from it like a miniature sun. I jerked back, letting go of the book, and covered my eyes.

Between my fingers and my eyelids, I saw the glow fade. I cracked my eyes open, then opened them wider, and my jaw dropped at the picture in front of me. The little balding crazy man was gone, replaced by a tall, muscular angel with blond curls and seven-foot wings.

"Gabriel?" I asked.

"You were expecting maybe George fucking Burns?" the angel replied, his lip curling up in a sneer as he looked down on me.

"Angels can say fuck?" Yeah, that was the part that surprised me. I mean, Glory swears, but I just assumed it was prolonged exposure to me that did it. Kinda like when you binge-watch *Deadwood* and every third word you say is "cocksucker" for the next week.

"I can say any goddamn thing I want, I'm an *Archangel*, you mewling worm." Gabriel stretched his wings and let out a huge sigh. "Ahhh, that feels good. Do you have any idea how cramped those things get while I'm wrapped in that silly form? Of course you don't. You don't know anything. You're human, why would you?"

I blinked a couple of times to rinse the condescension from my eyes, and said, "I need your help. A woman's life is in danger. Immediate danger. We've gotta go." I reached out to grab his arm, and he jerked back like I had the plague.

"Don't touch me, mortal! What makes you think you can lay hands on one of the Host, you repulsive slug."

"Wow, the Archangel's kind of a dick. Didn't see that one coming," I muttered. I looked up at Gabriel. "Look. I get that you're a little disoriented from being trapped in a crazy dude for a while, but there's a badass necromancer sucking the magic out of ghosts somewhere in the city, and he's got the High Priestess of...oh fuck it, will you just come with me? I need a little divine intervention."

"No."

No explanation, no apologetic refusal, just a flat, disinterested "no."

"No?" I repeated.

"Do I stutter? Of course not. I'm perfect. I'm an angel. Listen closely. No," Gabriel said.

"You're perfect?" This guy was starting to piss me off.

"Perfect."

"Flawless in every way?"

"Completely."

"No way to improve upon your form at all?" Oh yeah, this guy was a total douche.

"None whatsoever."

"Where's your dick?" I gave him a nasty grin as he spluttered something about choosing a form and gender being irrelevant and all the things I knew he'd say. All I cared about was that in his bluster he loosened his grip on the book for a second, allowing me to snatch it out of his hands.

The general light in the room dimmed like someone had flipped off a light switch, and Gabriel turned back into a doddering old man, looking from side to side in befuddlement.

I held the book out in front of him. "I need to borrow this for a little while."

"Neither a borrower nor a lender be," he replied, shaking his head. No borrowing was apparently a store policy.

"Then you come with me while I steal it." I grabbed his arm, tucked the book under my arm, the one not near to the masquerading angel, and turned for the door.

He struggled, flailing at me with his arms, raining useless punches onto my arm and shoulders. I held on and kept walking, practically dragging him out of the store. He calmed down when we got out onto the sidewalk, turning this way and that and staring up at the sky with wide eyes.

"How long has it been since you left the shop?" I asked. I knew angels didn't need to eat or sleep, so if Gabriel was running the interior components, so to speak, he might have been in that shop for years.

He just looked at me, confusion written all over his face. "Tomorrow, and tomorrow, and tomorrow, creeps in its petty pace from day to day."

I took his arm and walked with him, heading back to my hotel and our eventual rendezvous with the witches and hopefully not futile rescue attempt. I had no idea what this Barathan was planning, but it's been my experience that whenever somebody wants to harvest the power of a bunch of dead souls, it's never good. Like that time a crazy angel wanted to blow up most of Atlanta to tear open the barriers between Heaven and Hell. Yeah, good times.

14

I got Gabe back to my hotel without much incident, just a slight panic attack on his part when he had to cross the street. I couldn't tell if it came from being trapped as a human for too long or being stuck in a bookstore with no human contact, but it certainly seemed like my amnesiac angel wasn't just prone to speaking in iambic pentameter, but was also a little agoraphobic.

I closed the door to my hotel room and threw the deadbolt, then sealed it with a binding spell again. I was pretty sure it couldn't stop Gabriel in all his Archangelic glory, but I was willing to bet it would give Crazy Gabe a few seconds' pause at least.

"Have a seat, Gabe," I said as I walked toward the small bathroom. "I gotta visit the euphemism real quick." I tossed the book on the bed and turned the corner. I had just enough time to get unzipped when I realized exactly what I'd done. I put everything away and spun around, returning to the bedroom just in time to see Gabriel standing there holding the book. And looking *pissed*.

"I bet you're wondering what you're doing here," I said with a sheepish grin. I didn't really know exactly where on the power scale Archangels landed, but I was willing to bet two things. One, I was about to find out. Two, that it was pretty high.

"I know why I'm here, mortal," Gabriel replied. "You have some stupid quest that you cannot fulfill yourself, and you are here to beseech me for my aid."

Not technically wrong, I thought. Still no need to be a dick about it. "That's partly right. Well, I guess it's completely right, I just have more than one thing I, we, the world, needs your help with."

"No."

"No, what?" I asked.

"No, I will not assist you in whatever idiotic endeavor you think is so important. I assure you, it is not. The world will still be here long after you have shuffled off your minuscule and ineffectual mortal coil, the cities will still thrive, civilizations will still be born and die, and the Father will still sit on the High Throne of Heaven."

"Yeah, that's exactly the problem," I said, folding my arms over my chest. This guy was an asshole, but I needed him to be *our* asshole, at least until we found God and put Him back on that throne.

"What is the problem?"

"God. He's AWOL."

"What? I do not understand your stupid human words."

"Do you understand 'dick'?" I asked, grabbing mine through my jeans. "Because you're being a dick. God is on vacation, missing in action, quit, evacuated the premises. He's not sitting on the High Throne of Goddamn Anywhere, and that's why I'm in this fucking hotel talking to a fucking prick of an angel!"

"The Father is…missing?" he asked, and a lot of the asshole seemed to run out of him with that realization. The golden light that had rolled off him in waves vanished, he seemed to shrink a little within himself until he was barely taller than me, and his wings folded back into his shoulders.

"I don't know if He's missing, or if He's just on vacation," I said. "But according to very good sources, He's not in Heaven and hasn't been for a very long time."

"Balls," he said, then sat down on the bed. "He meant it?" I don't think he was talking to me but decided it might be important anyway.

"What do you mean, He meant it?" I pulled a chair out from under the table and sat with my back pressed against the door. I usually won't do that, but everybody who wanted to kill me in Charleston was going to use magic, not bullets, so I didn't have to worry about anybody going all Wild Bill Hickok on me. I was a little concerned about Gabriel trying to bolt, so I thought by putting myself in front of the door, I'd at least slow him down a little if he decided to leave.

Gabriel opened his book and flipped through pages, running his finger down the page like he was looking for the right passage. He must have found it because his finger stopped moving and he looked up at me. "He told us if we didn't take care of the humans that He'd leave it all in our hands and we could see how we really enjoyed being in charge. I think He was pissed off at Azrael for something again."

I was having a little trouble wrapping my head around the concept of God Almighty getting pissed off at one of his angels, and I'm sure it showed on my face because Gabriel laughed.

"You humans," he said, slapping his knee. Yeah, really. He slapped his knee. I suppose it's worth mentioning that he was dressed this time. In basically normal clothes, if size extra-extra-tall. He wore black slacks, a white button-down shirt, and loafers. Basic banker wear, only without the tie. "You mortals are always so baffled whenever you find one of us behaving in what you consider to be 'human' ways. Haven't you ever considered that perhaps you are behaving like angels?"

I thought about it for a second, then shook my head. "Nope, never considered it. Of course, for the first *century* I was on this planet, I'd never encountered an angel!"

"That you know of," he corrected. I got the sinking feeling that correcting was something this well-read douche of an angel did a lot.

"I'll grant you that," I said. There were plenty of times that I'd encountered a supernatural or divine creature that masked its identity from me. Most notably one asshole demonspawn that hid himself under my nose and murdered a couple of people I cared about.

"Well, we have all the same failings that you have, except for the physical ones, of course. But we are subject to sloth, anger, petty jealousy—all the emotions you feel, we felt them first."

"Especially that jealousy part," I said with a wry look.

"Yes, Lucifer and his followers were jealous of the attention Father lavished upon you mortals. As were we all, if we're to be honest with ourselves. That didn't stop just because we pitched a few rabble-rousers into The Pits. Father never liked that and told us if we didn't start acting like the older brothers He wanted us to be, that He'd give up the throne and leave us to deal with your messes all on our own."

"So you're telling me that the past few thousand years of human history have all sucked because you pissed off Dad and He pulled the metaphysical car over?" Suddenly every bit of bitching I'd ever done about the universe feeling like a ship without anyone at the wheel seemed more real than ever. Definitely one of those days that I hate being right.

"I suppose that's right. I wasn't in Heaven when He left, obviously. But if He's gone, and He's been gone for a long time, then that's the only logical answer."

"Where were you? Why weren't you in Heaven? Isn't that kinda your job, to write down all the shit that happens?" My research had referred to Gabriel as the Herald of Heaven, the Word of God, so I assumed he was kinda like a scribe.

"Not exactly," he said. He gestured to the book. "This is the repository of all the knowledge in the world, yes. I am the Keeper of the Word, yes. But I don't write the book. The book writes the book."

"That sounds very Zen."

"I think it's more Tao than Zen, but it's an easy mistake to make." Now that he was in teacher mode and not intimidating angel mode, he was a lot less of a prick. I was starting to have hope that he'd help us save the priestess and kick the shit out of a necromancer.

Gabriel went on. "Everything that happens in God's Kingdom is recorded in the book. Like I said, I don't write it. I can, however, access all of it."

"*All* of it?" I asked.

"All of it," he confirmed. "All I have to do is think about an event, open the book, and every piece of information ever gathered on Earth, in Heaven, or even in Hell, will be right there at my fingertips."

"Seems like a good book."

"It is one of the most powerful magical items ever created, as are all the Implements. Simply being near the book has completely worn through the mind of the poor human body I created to mask myself. Now he remembers nothing, save Shakespeare. He keeps that to read to me at night."

"I don't understand how he reads to you. He is you."

"It's complicated," the angel said. "Our host forms exist both with and apart from our divine selves at the same time."

"Yep, sounds complicated," I agreed. "So now what? You're an angel again, at least as long as you hang onto that book, and you know we need to get all your brother angels back together and doing your angelic duty so we can find God, literally, and get Him back to work."

"Why?" he asked.

"What do you mean, why?"

"You don't strike me as the altruistic type. So why do you want us to do all this?"

He had me there. I thought the world was running along pretty well without very much divine intervention. But it wasn't about me. "I have a friend…"

"Surprising in and of itself," Gabriel interjected.

"Go fuck yourself. Oh wait, you can't. No dick. Never mind," I shot back. "As I was saying, I have a friend. Her name is Glory. She's more like my guardian angel than just a friend. She lost her wings helping me, and apparently only God can restore her wings."

"That is true; only Father can restore lost divinity. Wait, did you say Glory?"

"Yeah, apparently my guardian angel is a *Buffy* fan."

"*You're* the Reaper?" He looked like he was trying very hard not to laugh. I was getting really tired of that nickname.

"I swear, I didn't come up with it," I said. "What the fuck are you laughing at?"

"Nothing, I'm sorry, it's just…well, I thought you'd be bigger."

"Oh, come the fuck on!" I said. "We're gonna start quoting *Road-house* now? I'm fucking six-three!"

"Well, yes, but you're terribly thin. Not very intimidating at all, to be frank. Given your reputation, I honestly expected someone...well, a little more frightening."

"I don't have to be scary," I said. "I just have to get shit done."

"Well, I will grant you that was fairly intimidating. That line, that was quite good. Still...I guess I just expected the Reaper to be...more, somehow."

"I thought you'd been trapped in the body of a nutbar bookseller for eons. How have you even heard of me?"

"Humans," he sniffed. "Still thinking of time as a straight line. Even if it were, it doesn't matter. I have the book. I read it. Don't let this go to your head, but you were foretold. You have important work to do, Mr. Harker."

"More important than restoring God to the Throne of Heaven? Because that's the current project, and it's pretty important to me."

"Fair point," he conceded. "You do realize that it will take all of us to find Father, right?"

"Yeah, all seven Archangels combining their power to locate God. I guess it's like some kind of mystical GPS, or cell phone signal, or something."

"Well, that's essentially true. Except there aren't seven Archangels."

"Sure there are. I got all their names written down somewhere. Even did the research and found out that the one with the Transformer name is really Raguel, not Metatron."

"There are eight."

I pulled out my phone and called up my notes. "Michael, Gabriel, Raguel, Raphael, Uriel, Azrael, Sealtiel. Seven."

"There are eight."

"I just named all seven."

"There *were* eight."

"Angels don't die. Well, okay, they can, but it takes Michael's sword or something...you've gotta be fucking kidding me."

"Nope. He's number eight."

"He totally doesn't count."

"I don't think you get to make that call, Reaper."

"Don't call me that. How the fuck does he still count? Wasn't he fired?"

"Still counts."

"God*dammit*!"

"In a lot of places, that would be considered blasphemy. I'm not the judging type, so I'll let it slide."

"Fucking hell."

"Exactly."

"Lucifer is the eighth Archangel?"

"Well…at one time he was the first."

"If we're getting Glory's wings back, we have to make a deal with the devil?"

"Literally."

"Fuck me."

Then my phone rang, and my day went from shitty to *spectacularly* shitty.

15

"What?" I said into the phone.

"We need you, Harker." The voice on the other end of the phone was almost panicked, but it was still mostly recognizable as Arianne.

"What's going on? It's still full daylight. There's no way anything's going down this early—"

"You ever been wrong before?" The girl cut me off.

"Yeah, once or twice." It's the kind of thing that's bound to happen in a century of wandering the planet. I even made a few fashion misplays in the sixties, but everybody was on so many drugs nobody noticed.

"Well, add this one to the list because Barathan has Tara on the steps of the old Slave Market and is ranting about burying the whole city under the waves to wash away the blood of his ancestors. Now please get your ass down here with whatever magical grenades or rocket launchers or whatever else you've managed to dig up." She hung up before I could respond, and I was left staring at a dead phone.

I turned to Gabriel. "How do you feel about mass murder?" I asked.

"Typically not a fan although I was willing to make an exception for Gomorrah, and for the assholes who destroyed the Library at Alexandria."

"Just Gomorrah?"

"I never cared that much about Sodom. They were all cool, actually. The Gomorrans were rude, so I helped wipe them out. And don't get me started on my Library. I'm still upset about that."

I just shook my head. Sometimes my life is weird even to me, and I'm the one stuck in it. "We need to go stop a psycho witch from sinking Charleston into the sea, apparently. Come on."

"No can do," the angel replied, not moving. Not even making the beginning of an attempt at moving.

"What the fuck, dude?" I asked, already at the door with my Glock in my waistband. "Are you coming or not?"

"Not."

"Is there any reason for this, or do you just feel like being a dick?"

"I can't go out there in my true form. It would cause too much of a stir. People would see me and think that Revelation has begun. It's not time for that yet, so it would not be advisable for me to leave in my current, glorious state."

"So change back into less-awesome Gabe and come on. This asshole will kill this woman, and probably a lot of other people, if we don't stop him."

"I refuse to return to that addlepated form. I have spent many years quoting that Elizabethan hack *ad nauseum*, and I will not do it any longer."

"So you're not going to de-angel?"

"I will remain in my true form, that is correct."

"And you won't go out in public like that?"

"Also correct."

"How do you plan to go to Charlotte with me?"

"I plan to travel mystically. I will meet you there."

I forgot about that whole popping from place to place thing. I always thought Glory went to Heaven, flew over to the right spot on Earth, and came back, but teleportation (or mystical travel) made more sense. "So you're not going to help me?"

"Unless you can move the confrontation to later in the evening, or this room—no."

I was pretty sure I couldn't just raincheck the guy trying to shove the entire city off into the ocean, so I just walked to the door. "Just for the record," I said, stepping out into the hall, "you're a dick." Slamming the door behind me didn't really get me anywhere in the argument, but it sure made me feel better.

I didn't bother with the car. I just sprinted down the street to the Old Slave Market. Sure enough, there was a skinny black dude holding balls of crimson energy standing in front of the building, under the big arch proclaiming it the "Old Slave Mart Museum." He'd invoked a circle in the flashiest way possible—by surrounding himself with a four-foot-high ring of fire. It had the combined effect of keeping people back and, honestly, making him look totally badass. I had to give the guy credit, he knew how to stage a photo op.

Behind him, hanging from the arch with magical bonds, was Tara, Arianne's priestess. She looked mostly unharmed, but royally pissed. I couldn't blame her, honestly. She was hanging by her wrists from magic chains in front of the whole city, looking helpless in the worst place of all—public.

Arianna stood across the cobbled street surrounded by other witches, an island of stillness against the raging tide of humanity flooding up Chalmers Street toward Church Street, trying to put the flaming nutjob behind them as quickly as possible. I skipped the normal pleasantries, just walked right up to the edge of Barathan's flaming circle.

"I think the Iron Throne is missing one asshole. They'd like you to come home as soon as possible," I said.

"I will sink this entire city beneath the waves for the crimes it has committed against my people!" the crazy wizard yelled.

It was a little hard to hear him over the crackling flames in front of me, so I waved a hand and shouted "*QUELL!*" I made a bet that his fire was really just an outer ring of flash, instead of being part of his actual circle, and it paid off as a couple hundred gallons of water condensed out of the air around us and doused the flames.

I stood in the giant cloud of steam with my arms crossed. When I could see Barathan again, I gave him a little smile. "That's better. Now, what were you saying?"

His eyes bugged out, and his face contorted into a grimace as he tried to raise his fire again and ran into my own magic stopping him. "This place is just a monument to hate and racism. This whole city was built on the backs of my people. Now their descendants will pay for what they did!" Spit flew from his mouth as he shouted.

"You do know that none of these people enslaved you, right? Oh, and by the way, you were never a slave. You're a fucking hipster millennial just looking to make a name for yourself. Get a job, fuckwit."

He turned the peculiar shade of purple I've usually associated with eggplants and one particular breed of lycanthropic Fae that I met in Lichtenstein. I've never seen it in a human before.

"Just because I wasn't a slave doesn't mean I don't know what it feels like to be hated. They killed my brother, you bastard!"

Shit. He wasn't just a run-of-the-mill magical asshole looking to get famous. He was a crusading magical asshole with what he thought was a good reason to sink Charleston under the Atlantic. If he killed Tara inside his circle, he might have enough power to do it.

Letting out a primal yell, he dropped his shield just long enough to throw a fireball at my head. He was really good at that throwing fire trick. Good thing I was prepared for him this time.

I murmured *"suffocate"* under my breath and held up my hands, palms out, at the onrushing ball of fiery doom. My magic flew right at the streaking missile and hit it square. All the air vanished from around the sphere, and the flame winked out, just like snuffing a candle. I felt a warm tingle as the magic passed through me, but there was no fire left, not even smoke.

"Nice try, asshole," I said, my mind racing. *Brother? Who killed his brother?* I looked around to Arianne for a little assist, but she and her coven had turned their attention to the fleeing crowd, trying to keep people from trampling each other and healing the folks who fell or twisted ankles.

"I'm sure your brother would have been proud of you, murdering all these people and destroying the city in his honor. That's really the kind of thing that makes somebody feel the loving memory, you know."

"Fuck you!" he shouted back. Obviously, my witty repartee was going to be lost on this one. "You don't know shit about Derek. He wasn't doing nothing, and they shot him down like a dog in the street!"

Something in the back of my head started to tickle, like I'd heard this story before. There was a kid, something about a traffic stop, and the cop thought he had a gun, and it turned out to be a wallet. The cop wasn't prosecuted, and there were a lot of people pissed off about it. Including one brother with a fair chunk of magical talent.

"You're Derek's brother?" Arianne's voice came from my left elbow.

"You probably shouldn't be here right now," I said.

"Don't act like you knew Derek, bitch!" Barathan screamed. "I will burn you to ash right where you stand!"

"I did know Derek. We had Spanish together a couple years in school. He went to West Ashley, right? Graduated three years ago? He wrote in my yearbook."

"Yeah, we both went there. I graduate next year."

Next year? This fucking kid's sixteen? Oh sweet bleeding Jesus. If he has power like this at sixteen, by the time he hits twenty, he really will be able to sink a city. This kid couldn't go to jail; no jail would be able to hold him. I had to think fast, but first I had to make sure he didn't cut Tara's throat and make Chucktown go the way of Atlantis.

"If you ever want to hold a diploma, you need to cut this shit out, Junior," I said. Maybe appealing to his sense of the future would get me somewhere.

"Fuck you, asshole!"

So much for appealing to his future self. "So what's the play, kid? You gonna cut her throat and harness her energy to open the fault line under Charleston Harbor? Crack that bad boy wide open and flatten South Carolina all the way up to Charlotte? Maybe you'd rather summon up a tsunami and just wipe out the whole coastline? That oughta run out of steam somewhere around Wilmington if you're lucky. Shouldn't kill more than a couple million people. That sounds fair, right?"

He started to look a little unsure, so I pressed my advantage. "Oh, you thought you could just, what? Dig a moat around Charleston and push this place into the ocean? You thought that wouldn't wreck anything else? Maybe you shouldn't bother trying to get a diploma. You're obviously too stupid to get out of high school. I'm surprised you've made it this long remembering to look both ways before you cross the street. I guess your big brother really did get a raw deal. It's bad enough he got killed by a cop, but he had to take care of your dumb ass his whole life, too? That really sucks."

The teenaged mage did exactly what teenagers do when you poke them enough—he lost his shit. In this case "his shit" didn't just consist of his temper or his control on his profanity, which if we're being fair, he never really had under wraps in the first place. He also lost his sense of his surroundings, so when he took his first step forward to deliver the ass-kicking I certainly deserved, and just as certainly was *not* going to receive, he broke the plane of his circle, and all his wards dropped with a *POP*.

Normally when I bait someone into dropping their shields, I step forward and knock them out. Sometimes I shoot them in the face. Sometimes I trap them in a circle of my own or send them back to Hell. I didn't do any of that to Barathan. As a matter of fact, I didn't do anything. I didn't have to.

The second his circle fell, all the other bindings and protections he'd woven into it disappeared as well. That left him standing three feet in front of a very pissed-off High Priestess, who dropped to her feet and stepped forward, conjuring a huge green glowing war hammer as she did. She laid that hammer upside Barathan's head, and he dropped to the ground like a marionette with its string cut.

I looked over at Arianne who gave me a thumbs-up. "Great work, Harker!"

"Yeah, great. Except this guy mopped the floor with us just a couple hours ago. Do you ever get the feeling that something was just a little too easy?"

I've really got to learn to keep my mouth shut.

1 ⁶

B arathan was out, but he had one last trick up his sleeve. Just like terrorists rig up secondary charges to go after the first responders to a bomb attack, he had a bomb of his own lurking in the shadows. Well, not really the shadows so much as the slave market. When his circle fell, a second wall of magical fire that had been obscured by his flaming barrier also fell. This magical barricade wasn't holding us out; it was filling the gate to the old slaver's auction house holding something *in*.

Stepping out of the darkened market into the sunlight was one of the biggest damn demons I'd ever seen. It was huge and walked on four legs, then stood up in the middle with two arms and even more badness. It looked like a cross between a lobster, one of H.R. Geiger's Aliens, and a yellow jacket. Pincers the length of my legs protruded from its midsection, and a triple row of teeth populated its mouth. It had a forked tongue and two tails, one with a club-like growth at the end, and the other one ending in a nasty-looking spike dripping green ichor to sizzle on the brick pavers.

"That's not good," I said with my typical talent for understatement.

"Nope," Arianne agreed, walking backward to get away from the thing and keep an eye on it at the same time.

"Oh yeah, that's real bad," Tara said from her spot directly in front of the monster. It swept its left pincer at her, and she managed to duck, but it right arm came across and punched her in the face, splitting her nose and laying her out across the sidewalk.

"Shit," I said, drawing my Glock. I fired eight shots in about six seconds, most of them finding a home in the demon's torso and face, but to no effect. The beastie looked over at me, smiled down from its ten-foot height, and flicked out its forked tongue to lick its lips.

"I picked a bad day to leave my guardian angel at home," I said, dropping to one knee and invoking a quick circle. The magic sprang into existence just fast enough to deflect the two pincers that were coming for me. They dug into the concrete on either side of me, making divots three inches deep and eight inches long in the sidewalk. I was protected, until my magic couldn't hold any more, but I was now stuck, unable to move, unable to cast offensive spells, unable to do anything to stop the giant lobster demon from picking Tara up in one huge claw and lifting her over its head.

The demon threw its head back and unhinged its jaw like a snake. It dangled Tara high in the air by one foot and made to swallow her whole. I dropped my circle and poured every bit of energy I could draw upon into a stream of brilliant blue energy aimed right at the demon's throat. It staggered and dropped the unconscious priestess. She hit the ground with a sickening *crack*, and I wondered briefly if I had done any saving at all, or if I'd just found my Gwen Stacy moment.

I poured power into the demon for a solid minute, drawing more energy from the city around me and adding it to the blast. It wavered, wobbled, and smoked a little, but it never fell. My power slowed from a torrent to a trickle, then all my juice flickered out, and I dropped to my knees in the street.

"Now you die, human," the demon bellowed, rising up on its back two legs to strike a killing blow.

"Not today, motherfucker," I said under my breath, and leapt up like an expanding spring. I pulled my Kershaw knife from my pocket as I vaulted the creature's head and flicked the razor-sharp blade open one-handed. I hooked my left hand in the demon's nostril and pulled myself down to drape over its head. I jabbed my pocketknife into its three-inch eyeball and grinned as it screamed in rage and pain.

It started to writhe, probably trying to throw me off at the same time, but I wrapped my legs around its thick serpentine neck and held on like a champion bull rider. It thrashed and convulsed, but I held on tight and kept jamming that little pocketknife farther and farther into its eyeball. I dug in until I felt resistance, then gave a mighty shove. I felt something crunch beneath the tip of the blade, and my hand sunk in its eyeball up to the elbow.

The demon made one last giant spasm, then went still, topping over like someone had just pulled the plug on it. Which, in a way, I guess I had. I twisted my hand around inside the demon's cranial cavity a couple times for good measure, then pulled my arm out. My fist was covered in greenish-yellow ichor and black demon blood with a sliver of brain stuck between my fingers.

Arianna walked up beside me and looked at my arm. "That might be the most disgusting thing I've ever seen."

"I wish I could say the same," I replied.

"Does it at least make the Top Three?"

"Top Ten for sure. Maybe Top Five if that smell gets any worse... yep, definitely Top Five." The demon's body was rapidly turning to a putrid yellow ooze as its soul returned to Hell and its corporeal form lost consistency. My knife wasn't any kind of blessed object, and I certainly am nowhere near holy enough to destroy a demon without one, so it wasn't dead, just banished.

"Is Tara okay?" I asked. I almost didn't want to know the answer, because I was afraid I knew already.

Arianne surprised me, not for the first time. "She will be. Marcus got to her pretty fast. Is that thing..."

"Gone," I said. "As long as nobody calls it back, it won't bother Charleston again."

"Speaking of people calling up demons..." She jerked her head over to where Barathan lay unconscious and bound across the street.

"I could shoot him," I said. She looked horrified, so I quickly went on. "I'm kidding. I swear. I know a guy. Well, it's actually his girlfriend who will be useful here. She works for a government agency that doesn't exist, if you get what I mean."

"I get it."

"Well, they have facilities where they can handle people like Barathan without them posing any more danger to society."

"Seems kinda shitty, doesn't it? I mean, all he wanted was justice for his brother."

"Don't confuse justice with revenge, Ari," I said. "I should know." Images flashed through my memory, over two hundred faces of men I slaughtered across Europe after the Nazis killed my Anna. They were bad people, they deserved punishment, but not all of them deserved to die, and no one deserved to die the way I killed the men. Except demons. Fuck demons. Kill them however you want.

I looked around at the dissolving demon, the police cars surrounding the block, the unconscious necromancer, and my slime-coated right arm, and sighed. "I think this was my last clean shirt."

"Don't you have an angel to find or something?" Arianne asked.

Oh shit, Gabriel! I turned and started sprinting up the street, hoping to get back to the hotel before he decided to smite someone. Or worse, before he put the book down and Gabe came back out to play.

EPILOGUE

Gabriel was sitting on the bed when I got back to the hotel. The book of Gabe, as I was calling it in my head, leaned against his side, but he was completely absorbed with his task. For my part, I was completely baffled by the scene in front of me. Instead of meditating, or doing kata, or basically doing anything I would expect from a divine being, he had my iPad in his hands and was tapping on the screen at lightning speed.

"You know how to use an iPad?" I asked.

"I do now. Your friend Dennis was very helpful. This internet you mortals have created, it is...quite remarkable. There are things on there that I never even dreamed possible. And the games! Astounding! This one, with the zombies eating the plants...the lawnmowers...the little catapult zombies! I love this game!" He grinned at me like an idiotic eight-year-old proud of finally learning to tie his own shoes.

"As your buddy Gabe would say, there are stranger things on heaven and earth. You ready to go?"

"Go where?"

"Charlotte. I need to introduce you to Michael, again, and maybe you can help him find himself, so to speak."

"No." His attention was fixed firmly on the screen, and he tapped furiously. If Dennis wasn't already dead, I'd kill him for teaching this angelic savant how to play *Plants vs. Zombies*.

"What do you mean, no?"

"I mean I'm not going. I don't wish to accompany you, I do not wish to participate in your quest for Father, and I certainly don't wish to see Michael again, amnesia or no. My brother is, as you mortals put it, a dick."

"I don't doubt it," I said. "But that doesn't matter. I need you to go to North Carolina with me, get Michael back in his right mind, and then help restore Glory's wings."

"No. Now be silent, human. I am trying to beat this final level, and I am down to only two lawnmowers." I assumed that was bad. I never got into video games, except for *Neverwinter Nights*. Most of the fighting games feel too much like your average Tuesday for me, and first-person shooters are way too close to home. Gabriel bent over, pouring all his attention onto the screen, and tapping with lightning speed. I hoped briefly that he wouldn't break the screen, then he sat upright and pumped his fists.

"Yes! Got you, zom-boss! Is this where we high-five?" He turned to me, one hand held up. I slapped palms with him, then leaned in for a bro-hug. But instead of pounding his back as prescribed in the Official Manual of Bro-Hugs, I reached down and picked up the tome leaning against his hip.

As soon as the book broke contact with Gabriel, there was a huge flash of light and a small *pop*. I almost fell over as the big-ass buff angel turned into the skinny little bookseller with tufts of brown hair sticking out from under a porkpie hat and a Mr. Magoo look on his face. The robe he had worn as Gabriel transformed this time into an ill-fitting brown suit with a white dress shirt, round glasses, and a brown vest with a pocket watch chain stretched across his little pot belly. He looked like a cross between the dotty uncle in a British period flick and an absent-minded college literature professor.

"Who goes there?" he asked, looking around with obviously no clue where in the world he was.

"Hi, Gabe," I said. "It's almost time to go on our trip. Are you ready to go see your old friend Michael?"

His face lit up in a huge oblivious grin, and he raised his right hand, finger to the sky. "Lay on, Macduff! And damned be he that first cries 'Hold, enough!'"

III

ANGEL DANCE

1

The last time I walked these streets, the water reached up my chest, black fingers of cold digging into my bones, threatening to drag me down into the depths of despair and death. But Lady Death has long refused to take me in her arms, and those September days and nights were different. While so many fell beneath the roiling waters of the Gulf when the levees failed, I remained, like New Orleans herself, waterlogged and battered, but still whole at the core of me.

I waded through years of pain and memories in those days just after Katrina battered the Crescent City. I was able to save some, to aid some, and to lay some to rest when they were thought lost. It was ugly work, but I am particularly well suited for such as that, being a hideous specimen myself. I slogged through the despair of a city, her waters pooling in my boots as I strode through neighborhood and business district searching for survivors.

Even in those darkest hours, I felt the life of the city thrumming under my feet, the lifeblood of New Orleans pulsing in the slow, torpid *thump-thump* of the nearly drowned. No matter how much water God poured down her throat in the torturous hours of the hurricane's onslaught, nothing could choke the spirit of the Louisiana gem.

Now I was back in New Orleans, more than a decade later, not searching for signs of life, but a needle in a haystack. I was looking for a horn in the brassy city of jazz, one instrument in a mecca for musicians, and the tune I needed it to play was more important than any heard since man first set foot outside the Garden of Eden.

There was no water filling the streets of the French Quarter this night, only jazz and the raucous sounds of tourists shouting up to or down from the balconies lining Bourbon Street. My search would begin in earnest with the dawn, but tonight I was at leisure, such as it was for me. Tonight, I walked the shadows, not a hunter, but merely an observer. I have done that often through my decades on this Earth, simply lurking in alleys and hidden corners of the cities, watching humanity rush from start to finish before me.

I am separate from the madding crowd. I do not share their everyday concerns of living and dying. I am not completely certain you can call what I do the first, and despite many attempts, I seem to be incapable of the second. I can, however, watch. So tonight, from a table in the corner of a patio in a less-traveled part of the Quarter, I settled in to watch.

I watched a quintet of bachelorettes weave along a sidewalk, bumping into an emaciated teen who leaned, smoking, against a lamppost. I watched the gangly boy slide the drunkest girl's wallet from her purse and into the pocket of his unseasonable hoodie, then spin around the light pole and stride off down a side street. I watched him slide the cash into his pocket and toss the wallet into a nearby garbage can.

I briefly considered retrieving the wallet and returning it to the woman. It would have been the chivalrous thing to do. Then I looked down at the line of stitches along my right wrist, the jagged suture line where my "father" attached the hand of a pickpocket to the arm of an axe murderer so many years ago, and I remembered how poorly it has gone for me when I have tried to interact with mundane women in the past.

I felt no need to battle through an army of pitchfork- and torch-wielding peasants to finish my task in New Orleans, so I left the wallet where it lay. Perhaps the young woman would consider the inconvenience a life lesson and pay more attention to her surroundings. Perhaps not. Either way, the hooded Artful Dodger was out of my view, and the parade of drunken mortals careening from Hurricanes to Hand Grenades to other frozen concoctions with festively destructive names continued on in its garish parade of beads, breasts, and brightly colored masks.

I motioned a waiter to my table to refresh my pitcher of water, passing him another folded twenty-dollar bill. I ordered no food and only water to drink, but as long as I paid a reasonable rent on the table, I sat as long as I liked. In exchange for being very little trouble and a very consistent tipper, the waiter kept the tables near me free of children or loud parties and left me largely to my own devices.

I watched the sea of human randomness ebb and flow until nearly midnight, then stood. I nodded to the waiter and stepped over the low wrought-iron fence surrounding the patio. My size is often an annoyance, but I will admit that there is a certain directness in being able to just walk over three-foot barriers.

I walked the Quarter, keeping to the side streets and alleys, feeling the pulse of humanity without ever truly immersing myself in it. The heat and the crowd contributed to a miasma about the area, a foggy stink of beer, sweat, and lust that permeated every corner. I stepped in front of another teen before he could slip his hand in a businessman's pocket. I tapped a thug on the shoulder and asked him for directions just as he reached for a knife to cut a purse strap. I stepped into the mouth of an alley at the right moment to startle a would-be mugger. These petty crimes I could deter, and did, through my very size and presence.

It was not enough. It was not fulfilling. I needed more. The crush of so many people, so many desires, so much sound was an unbearable pressure upon me. Perhaps leaving the patio was a mistake. This close to so much that is so overwhelmingly alive, I desperately needed to feel a part of that in myself. I needed release. Violent release.

I found it. I found it in the form of two men too greedy or confident or stupid to evaluate their situation effectively. I found it in a woman too brave or too rushed to stick to the brightly lit streets when walking back to her car, parked just one block too far from the safe spaces of the Crescent City. I found it in her muffled scream as the men converged on her just as she reached her car and thought she was safe.

I stepped into the pool of orange light cast by the streetlamp above my head. The smaller man had a curved knife in his hand, his index finger threaded through a hole in the hilt. A karambit, it was called. He held it correctly, the blade protruding from the bottom of his clenched fist, pressed up against the woman's throat. She was tall, taller than her attacker, with a lovely head of curly brown hair. He was a thickly built man, bald, with tattoos crawling up his neck from the edge of his leather jacket.

His companion hung back, watching the show and laughing. He was big, almost my height, and fat. I expected him to be slow and probably heavily armed. The big ones aren't always stupid, and when they aren't, they can be dangerous. But he was probably stupid. Most of the petty criminals are.

"You should let her go," I said from my place in the light. I wore a hoodie myself because my appearance draws unwanted attention in brightly lit places, but I took the hood down now. I wanted the attention my scarred face would bring, and the type of attention it brings was exactly the type I wanted.

"You should go fuck yourself," the big man said, turning toward me and putting a hand under his jacket. Armed. As I suspected. That added a new dimension to the encounter, but it didn't present as much of a complication for me as it would for many people.

"Not only is that not possible, it is also not polite to suggest," I replied. "You should still let her go."

"Tony, take care of this sumbitch," the small one said. "He's making my pecker wilt with his ugly-ass face." He reached up at the woman to paw her breasts, and she slapped him. He laughed and pressed the knife closer to her neck. "That's a bad idea, honey. You be nice and maybe I won't let Tony have a turn when I'm done."

"Tony most certainly will not be having a turn," I said. "And you are already done." I charged Tony, closing the distance between us in a few long strides. He got his pistol out but did not have time to fire before I bull-rushed him to the ground. I didn't slow, just planted a shoulder in his sternum and lifted my body on impact. He flew back several feet and sprawled flat on his back, where I stepped on him en route to his partner.

The smaller man half turned to me but kept the knife pressed to the girl's throat. "Take another step and I'll cut her throat," he said with a sneer. "You think you're so tough? Let's see what you do against me."

He spun in a tight circle, his foot flashing up to catch me on the side of the jaw. I let the kick turn me around, dropping to one knee as I did. I came around, and up, with my right hand extended. I picked the bald man up by the throat and slammed him down on the hood of a nearby parked car. A car alarm blared into the night, and lights flashed on the BMW. I had apparently picked a good car to abuse.

My adversary stabbed me in the shoulder with his karambit, and I let go of his throat. Tony was recovered enough to come at me then, and I felt a hammer blow to my right kidney. I lashed out with an elbow strike that pulped his nose, then reached over my right shoulder and flipped Tony onto his partner, setting off a fresh cacophony of noise as the impact shattered the windshield of the car and set off the airbag. The air filled with the stench of airbag chemicals and the groaning of two battered thugs.

I looked at the men, neither of whom looked in any hurry to re-enter the fray, then I looked at my left shoulder, a small curved knife protruding from it. I pulled it free with a hiss of pain and stabbed it into the small man's upper thigh.

"You lost this. I wanted to return it," I said, twisting the knife in his leg. He howled in pain, and Tony tried to roll off him. I let the big man drop to the sidewalk, then hit him in the side of the head with a sharp knee strike.

His head bounced into the fender of the car, and he collapsed to the ground. The little man was moaning and rolling around the hood of the car clutching his leg. I picked him up by his belt and bounced him on the hood a few times until he passed out. The car alarm gave one last plaintive squawk as I battered it into submission with the body of the mugger, and blissful quiet once again settled over the street, only broken by the woman's sobbing and the distant sounds of Bourbon Street revelry.

"Are you hurt?" I asked the woman.

"N-no," she said.

"Is that your car?" I pointed to one just past the now-defunct BMW that I had defiled with the bodies of Tony and his little friend.

"Y-yeah."

"Do you have someone at home to help take care of you? You shouldn't be alone tonight."

"My sister is there." Good. She was coherent, mostly, and seemed capable enough to drive home.

"Do you want to call the police? These men tried to rape, and possibly kill, you."

"N-no. I just want to go home."

"Then you should do that. Can you get there safely by yourself?" She looked up at me, and the fear in her eyes told me that even if the answer wasn't a resounding "yes," that I would not be the person she asked to escort her to safety.

I didn't mind. She wasn't chasing me from the village with torches and pitchforks, so that was at least a minor improvement. She got in her car and drove off. I leaned down to Tony's friend, nominally the brains of the operation, such as they were, and said to him, "I think you should consider another line of work. This one seems too dangerous for you."

Then I pulled up my hoodie and walked off into the night, the beast within satiated once again. For now.

2

M orning in the Quarter is a strange time, stranger even than the late nights. I walked the damp sidewalks, bright sun hammering my eyes through the dark glasses I wore, dodging the shopkeepers with their brilliant green garden hoses, water snakes cascading cleanliness across the face of the city, sending the sad remnants of last night's revelry pouring down the storm drains in a river of spilled beer, puke, and broken strands of beads cast aside like virtue after last call. My tattered work boots left giant wet footprints on the brick steps in front of the Sisters of the Sword Convent, an innocuous unmarked building wedged back in an alley behind a strip club and a high-end steakhouse, the dichotomy of a white linen restaurant sharing airspace with a club where the women wore less than a napkin not lost on me.

I knocked on the thick oaken door, the surface worn smooth with the touch of centuries' worth of supplicants. I waited, then checked my watch for the time. It was early enough for the sisters to still be at lauds, so I waited. Thirty minutes later, I knocked again, and moments later, a novice in jeans and a gray wimple answered the door.

"May I…help you?" She paused as she looked up, then up again, to see my face was normal. She was a slight woman, short in stature by normal standards, and I must have seemed a true giant in her eyes.

I spoke softly, as not to terrify the poor girl. My voice is a low growl at best, a grating roar at its worst, and I had no desire to be responsible for the scarring of one of the novitiate. "I am looking for Sister Evangeline. She is an old friend."

A shadow passed across the child's face, as though she were unsure how to proceed. "Um...Sister Evangeline isn't...here right now. She's..."

"She is hunting?" I asked. Sister Evangeline was a Templar, a historical militant arm of the Church. Modern-day Templars are tasked with defending a specific part of the world from supernatural threats. They are often referred to as Monster Hunters. Evangeline was the Hunter for the Gulf Coast, including New Orleans.

The novice relaxed considerably when she understood that I already knew what Evangeline was and that she would not betray her confidence by speaking freely with me. "Yes, sir. She is hunting. There is a...creature of some sort in the swamps up by Lake Maurepas. She been gone a couple days, oughta be back before long. It never takes Sister Evangeline very long to bag her...um, critter." The young nun blushed a little as she realized she may have said more than was entirely proper to a stranger. I smiled as gently as my mangled features allowed in an attempt to put her somewhat at ease.

"Thank you. I will return in a few days' time. If she returns before I come back, please ask her to call Adam." I handed her a card with my name on it, Adam Franks, and a number.

"I will, Mr. Franks. Have a nice day," she said, stepping back into the convent and closing the door.

I turned from the door and mused for a moment on the subject of names. Adam Franks is not my name, no more than Lucas Card is Vlad's, although it is what we are known by in these times. I have been called many things in my time walking this Earth, but I have had few names. Adam is what my father called me, but that was just another example of his overweening hubris. He did not think himself God, but he certainly aspired to godhood. That is what drove him to create life from a pile of lifeless parts, or to reinstall life into formerly lively parts, to be more precise.

When I was awakened, for I was never born in any true sense of the word, my father's first words were not, as popular culture has decreed, "It's alive!" No, the first utterance to pass from his lips to my ears was "I've done it." I was alive, or aware, for two days before he ever addressed me as "Adam." I have worn many names through the intervening decades, but only two words have ever truly felt like they were my name: "Adam" and "monster."

I stepped back out of the alley into the sun and put up the hood of my sweatshirt. More tourists filled the sidewalks now, and I chose to avoid the stares of the adults and the innocently horrible pointing and screeching of the children.

Without Evangeline and her knowledge of the city's seedy under-belly, I had to take a moment to reconsider my plan of investigation. Somewhere in New Orleans was a horn, a needle in the gilded jazz-infused haystack. This horn was not simply a musical instrument; it was an Implement of the Archangel Sealtiel, the herald of the End Times. I needed to find this horn, and without any magical ability of my own, I needed a guide.

I pulled out my phone and summoned an Uber. A round freckled face appeared on the screen. "You know I can do that for you, and rig it so you don't have to pay, right?"

"I know that, Dennis, but I would prefer to save your interventions for when I actually need them. I am perfectly capable of paying for a taxi service."

"Sure, whatever, bro. Just saying, if you need anything done on the internet, I'm your guy. It's not like those fingers of yours are the nimblest things in the world. Your ride's almost here. Later." Dennis' face vanished into the maze of electrons connecting almost every digital device in the world. When his body was murdered close to a decade ago, Dennis' soul had been cast into a cell phone. The phone had an internet connection, and in a real-life version of *Tron*, Dennis became truly a ghost in the machine, and an invaluable, if tempera-mental, asset to me and the other members of the Shadow Council.

A black SUV pulled up to the corner, the familiar black and white sticker on the windshield marking it as a car for hire. I opened the door and leaned in. "Are you Matt?"

The man behind the wheel looked me up and down and said, "I am. Are you Adam?"

I slid into the front seat, pushing it as far back as possible. My knees still pressed up against the dash, a situation I was well-acquainted with. "I am Adam. Do you know the address?"

"Not really, but the GPS will get us there," the man said. "It looks like it ain't the best neighborhood. You sure that's where you want to go?"

"An old friend lives there. It was a very different place when he first moved in." I didn't mention that my friend first moved to the neighborhood in question over fifty years ago or that he cared little about the condition of the sidewalk or the dilapidated state of his eaves and shutters. My friend was a blind sorcerer and saw the world only through his Second Sight. He was also one of the most dangerous practitioners of battle magic I had ever known, so I was not at all concerned about a few drug dealers and gangbangers on his block.

The driver was correct, though. The neighborhood had declined precipitously since my last visit. There were several cars on blocks stationed along the street, and a collection of young men sat on the stoop and porch of the house across the street from Oliver's home. They watched my approach with undisguised mistrust, and I saw one step inside the house and return with a sawed-off shotgun as we pulled up to the curb.

"Look, man, no offense, but I don't think I'm gonna wait around for you. If you wanna bail and have your friend meet you someplace else, we can cruise outta here right now, but if you need a pickup out of here later, I ain't taking the fare," the driver said, his head on a swivel as he tried to talk to me and watch the men on the porch at the same time.

I opened the door and got out. "That is fine," I said. "I will make other arrangements for a ride. Thank you." I closed the door and pulled out my phone.

"Dennis?" I spoke into the phone.

"Yeah, Adam?" Dennis appeared again on the screen, this time represented by his favorite avatar, a unicorn with a rainbow mane and blue eyes. I did not pretend to understand this appearance, but he held that it annoyed our friend Quincy Harker, and that was enough for him.

"Please see to it that the driver has a generous tip added to his fare."

"Will do. I've also rerouted three NOPD patrol cars to be within two blocks of the address you're in front of. The guys across the street? They're Gulf Coast Bloods, an offshoot of the LA street gang. They run the coke and weed trade for five of six blocks around you."

"I need neither cocaine nor marijuana, nor do I care about the dealing thereof, so I have no reason to interact with those young men," I replied. I turned and walked up the steps to Oliver's door.

I knocked, and after a few moments, I heard the click of several locks on the other side of the door. A young woman's head appeared in the crack between the door and the jamb, looking up at me. Everyone looks up at me. Sometimes I am gripped by an almost irresistible urge to get down on my knees before I knock on a door, just to see someone look down at my eyes for once. I never have. Perhaps someday, when I am feeling particularly frolicsome.

"Can I help you?" the woman asked.

"Hello," I said. "May I speak with Oliver?"

Her guarded expression shifted in an instant to defensive, with a hint of anger. "No, you may not. But you know that, don't you?"

I was taken aback, literally, as I took an involuntary step back. "I'm sorry, miss. I don't know what you mean? Is Oliver not home? Does he no longer live here? It has been some time since we last spoke, but I heard nothing of him moving." I kept my voice soft, both to keep our words guarded and to not sound monstrous.

She cocked her head to the side and gave me an appraising look. I took the moment to examine her as well. She was young, in her twenties, but with the eyes and set of her jaw that said she had seen many things in her years. She was a solidly built woman, with broad shoulders and thick wrists. She looked like someone who knew what work looked like and was unafraid of it.

"I'm sorry," she said after she looked me up and down again. "My grandfather passed away two weeks ago. If you hadn't talked to him in a while, I guess you might not have known. I'm Eliza, his granddaughter. Is there something I can do for you?"

I sighed and stepped back from the door. "No. Thank you for the kind offer. I am very sorry for your loss. Your grandfather was fine man, a man of strong principles and fierce love for his family."

"Yes, he was," she agreed. "How did you know him? He didn't have many...friends outside the neighborhood."

I smiled at her very polite way of saying that Oliver didn't have many white friends. "That's true, I suppose. When you grow up in the time he did, you are unlikely to be very trusting of...people outside your neighborhood." I took down my hoodie, showing her the full landscape of my scarred face. "We both had some experience with people judging us on the basis of our appearance. That made for a common bond that grew into a strong...mutual respect, if not friendship."

"Are you...Adam?" the young woman asked, her eyes wide.

"I am."

"You should come in. Papa O told me about you. He left something for you if you ever came back again." She pushed the screen door open and stepped back to let me into the house. I went inside, curious to see what Oliver thought was worth my having after his passing.

I followed the young woman into the house through a maze of boxes labeled "Goodwill" and "Keepsakes" and "Terry." Black plastic garbage bags sat piled in the corners of the living room, and I moved a cardboard box full of books onto the floor and sat in the chair she indicated.

"I'm sorry for the mess. You knew Pop, he was a bit of a hoarder," she said, sitting on a couch opposite me. There was just enough room on the couch for her wide frame between a pile of papers and another in a seemingly endless cavalcade of brown boxes.

"He was that," I said with a smile. I didn't know that. I didn't know much about Oliver, really. I have made very few attachments as I have meandered through my long life, avoiding too many connections with people destined to die long before me. I had never been inside Oliver's home before today, always meeting with him either on his porch, where he loved to sit, or at the library to research some threat or another.

"He didn't speak of you often, but he seemed to like you. He said you were a good man, and that was high praise from Pop."

"Thank you," I said. "I had a great deal of respect for him as well. He was a stalwart companion and possessed a very sharp mind."

"I guess you want to see what he left for you," Eliza said, standing. She walked to the mantle and took down a wooden box. She handed it to me, and I turned it over in my hands. I had not seen the box before, nor its contents. I opened it to reveal a silver cross on a long chain, with an unmistakable purple heart-shaped medal affixed to it.

"This is his Purple Heart," I said, giving the girl a questioning look. "He once told me he was wounded in Korea, and that injury probably saved his life."

"That's what he told us, too. He got shot in the leg, ruined his knee, and came home after just a month over there. He never walked right again, but three weeks after he got home, most of his unit was wiped out by mortar fire. He said that's when he learned to never assume anything is all bad or all good, that you have to—"

"Look below the surface of a thing," I finished with her. We shared a smile, and I remembered sitting in rocking chairs on that porch watching the sun set and drinking cheap domestic beer after a bad fight with a nest of vampires, and Oliver telling me that very thing, only about myself.

I stared down at the medal, wondering how often Oliver thought of our adventures together. Eliza cleared her throat, and I lifted my head. She had an expectant look on her face, and I stood. "I will have to be going. I am very sorry for your loss. Thank you for keeping this for me. I appreciate it very much." I turned, then paused. "How did Oliver die? Did he have a heart issue that no one knew about, or some health condition?"

A shadow fell on the young woman's face, quickly wiped away by a flash of anger. "He was killed," she said. "Some of those bastards from across the street, probably."

I made the conscious effort not to clench my fists. I didn't want to damage the medal. "What happened?" I didn't bother with the platitude of whether or not she minded my asking. I didn't care. If those thugs harmed my...friend, there would be hell to pay.

"I don't know, honestly. I came over to visit him a week ago Sunday, like always. I've been bringing him Sunday dinner every week for a while now, since I moved back to New Orleans. I got here with supper, and he was on the floor, dead."

"Shot? Stabbed? Beaten? What made you feel that the men across the street were responsible?" It sometimes surprised me how quickly the old instincts Vlad and Abraham instilled in me came back to the fore when I needed to investigate something.

"No, there wasn't a mark on him. The coroner didn't find anything, ether. Said it just looked like he decided it was time to go, and he died. I thought that was really strange. But I know those thugs had something to do with it. Look at them, just sitting around on the porch drinking beer and smoking weed all day. You know they sell drugs. And Pop had a couple run-ins with them the past few months, too."

That death didn't sound like gang violence to me, but there was no point in trying to convince Eliza of that. Her mind was made up, and I saw some of Oliver's stubbornness peeking through under her curls. It was prettier on her, but her resolve was no less steely for being sheathed in an attractive wrapping.

"That sounds very odd. I had not seen Oliver in some time, but the man I knew was not the kind to lay down and die. He was the kind to battle the Reaper with every fiber of his being."

"I know, right?" she agreed. At least, I thought it was agreement. I sometimes have difficulty parsing the grammar of young people. "That's how I know it was those Blood bastards. They won't tell me nothing, and I can't get the police to even question them, on account of there not being any evidence of foul play. Hell, the fact that my pop is dead seems pretty damn foul to me."

"I agree that something seems amiss about his death. I shall go speak to the young men across the street. Perhaps they will be more forthcoming with me."

"What makes you think they gonna tell a giant white boy anything? I mean, no offense, but you ain't exactly who they're used to having a conversation with."

I gave her a small nod and my most vicious smile. "I can be very persuasive."

3

There were five young men sitting on the porch across from Oliver's house when I stepped out his front door. One of them watched me, his baleful guise tracking my every movement as I walked down the steps and across the street. His hand drifted to the waistband of his pants as he shushed his friends and nodded in my direction.

"Hey, shut that shit off, we got us some company," he said. Another man, late teens or early twenties, reached over and turned off a speaker that was connected to someone's phone playing music.

"I need to speak to you gentlemen for a moment," I said. I stopped at the foot of the steps, still several feet away from the nearest man, but close enough that my presence could not be mistaken for innocuous. They were sitting on steps, which made them taller than me, but only just. I could still easily look them in the eye, except for the man I deemed to be their leader, the one who kept his eye on me my entire trek across the street.

"What you wanna say?" he said, standing up. I took a step back to be able to look at him more comfortably, and he took two steps forward, coming down the steps to my eye level and staring at me, asserting his dominance. Or attempting to do so, at any rate.

"I have some questions about Oliver's death. His granddaughter seems to think you or your men may have contributed in some way to his demise." I kept my tone mild, as mild as possible when your voice sounds like a bass hum through gravel.

"What you trying to say, man? You think we offed the old man?" He pushed forward at me, bumping chests in a display of aggression and dominance.

It often amuses me how humans revert to their gorilla ancestry when threatened or threatening. The bared teeth, the metaphorical chest-thumping, the thrusting themselves against their opponent: it's all very primal. And all completely ineffectual against someone who has no primal instincts, no participation in the collective unconscious.

"I do not," I replied. "But Eliza does. I would like to know which of us is correct. Would you be willing to answer some questions for me?" I have often found that exceeding politeness in a fraught situation can defuse an adversary's anger. That was not the case here.

"I ain't answering shit, man. Now you better fuck off back to whatever white boy tower you climbed down and don't ever let me see you on my street again!" He pulled up the front of his New Orleans Saints t-shirt to show me the pistol wedged into the waistband of his pants.

Growing tired of this charade, I reached down and grabbed the butt of the pistol. "I've always wondered exactly why so many people seem to want to carry a gun there," I said. "It seems very dangerous." I angled the gun to the right, then to the left. "It seems like it would be very simple for someone to make a mistake and shoot themselves in the leg, perhaps severing the femoral artery. If that happens, you'll bleed to death before an ambulance ever arrives. Even if you don't hit an artery, shooting yourself in the leg promises to be both embarrassing and painful, and that's if you manage not to destroy your knee in the process."

I turned the gun slightly to angle the barrel straight down. "And that's without even mentioning perhaps the most nerve-wracking of all possible occurrences when carrying a gun in the front of your pants, the direct downward misfire. I would certainly be concerned for my own genitals if I had a loaded handgun just inches above my private parts."

I pulled the gun from his waistband, and he let out a sigh of relief. I ejected the magazine and tossed it back over my head. I ran the slide to clear the chamber and tossed the gun aside to lie in the grass. Then I reached forward and grabbed the man directly in front of me by his testicles. "I can only surmise by the bulging eyes and the fish-mouthed gasping that you are in significant pain right now. Good. That was my intent. But just imagine how much more it would hurt if I came back here and shot your dick off." I generally dislike resorting to colloquialisms, but it seemed appropriate for the situation.

"Now, let's answer my questions, shall we?" The young man's eyes got huge and he nodded.

"What about your friends?" I asked. "Would you like them to cooperate as well?" He nodded again, then croaked out instructions for everyone there to answer my questions, no bullshitting around allowed.

"Did you or any of your people hurt Oliver?"

"Nah, man, we liked the old dude. He was kind of a dick, but he was a funny dick. We had a deal. We'd sling weed and pussy and make sure nobody fucked with the kids in the 'hood. We didn't bring nothing harder than weed onto the block, and he didn't call the cops on us. He was a cool old dude. I was sorry to see him go."

That was what I had expected. Oliver was no prude, but he did not tolerate fools lightly. He would have brokered a peace with the local thugs, and he would have kept his part of the bargain as long as they did. That meant he either died of natural causes, or someone else killed him. "Did you see anyone go into his house in the days before he died?"

"What I look like, the fucking neighborhood watch?" he asked, and I squeezed his crotch. His legs sagged, putting even more pressure on his testicles. He struggled to get his feet under him and shook his head. "I don't know, man. I don't even know when the old dude died."

"It was Wednesday a couple weeks ago, homes," one of his companions said. Every head turned to him. He was the youngest-looking of the Bloods, only the tiniest hint of a mustache shadowing his upper lip. He wore a red track suit and an Adidas t-shirt, looking like he stepped off a vintage Run-DMC album cover from before he was born.

He looked nervous at the attention, but continued. "I saw this other dude go in there Tuesday night. He was like some middle-aged white dude, maybe forty. Drove a sweet ride, a Maserati, man. He went inside, and I heard some yelling, then some shit lit up in the window like fireworks and shit, and the white dude came out. I didn't see Pops after that."

I tilted my head to one side and looked at the boy. "You called him Pops?"

"We all did. All us that grew up here, anyway. He was Pops. He took care of you, but don't let him catch you fucking around, he'd whoop your ass, then call your mama and *she'd* whoop your ass." The kid sitting next to him on the porch nodded, and they bumped fists.

The man I was holding scowled at the younger boy. "Why you ain't tell nobody that shit, Junior? You know we take care of our own. Pops was our people, man. You can't be letting some cracker mother-fucker come up in here messing with our people." I let go of his crotch, and he took a step back to sit on the steps, rubbing his sore groin.

Junior looked at his shoes, not meeting his friend's gaze. "I don't know. I thought if y'all heard me talking about magic fireworks and shit, y'all wouldn't believe me."

"Fool, this New Orleans," another one of the boys on the porch said, laughing. "Everybody know magic real, fool. We all got a granny or aunt doing the root. You don't believe in magic, you ain't been in Nola long."

A general murmur of agreement went through the young men, and I nodded. I certainly was more well-acquainted with magic than even these young men would readily believe. I looked at the young man. "Do you remember anything else about the man you saw? Any details that might help me find him?"

"Nah, man, I was pretty high. I don't remember shit." He bumped fists with one of the other boys, but the one I had released reached up and slapped him.

"I told you about getting high. You don't do that shit. You gone go to college, get the fuck out this 'hood. Tell him, big man." He turned to me.

"He is correct. You should go to college. Your friends here will very likely end up imprisoned or dead before they are thirty years old. If you leave this environment as soon as possible, you are more likely to survive and have children of your own someday." The boys on the porch glared at me, but no one spoke up to contradict me.

"What if I don't wanna go nowhere?" the youth said with a sneer.

"Going to college will still allow you to earn more money with less risk of jail than any career you can find without a degree. I see nothing wrong with recreational marijuana use, but the price typically does not agree with me." I didn't bother to mention that a side effect of my unusual physiology is a complete lack of capacity to become intoxicated. Since I am animated by magical means, my body is merely a vessel for my soul. There is no real connection between me and my body, so mind-altering substances have little to no effect on me. That is the theory Vlad, Abraham, and I crafted, at any rate.

"Whatever, man." He waved me off with the dismissive air of the internally wise teenager.

I shrugged and held out my hand to his friend. "Thank you for your help. I do not think I did any permanent damage to your firearm. I hope I did not do any permanent damage to your person."

He shook my hand. "Yeah, big man, I think both my pistols gonna be okay." He grinned at me and said, "You need a ride back into town? Frodo'll drop you." He jerked a thumb at one of the men on the porch behind him. "Frodo" waved.

"That would be nice," I said. "My Uber driver did not feel safe in this neighborhood."

"Yeah, lot of people think that," the young man said. "I think we got us a public image problem." The crowd on the porch laughed, and Frodo stood up. He walked to a black Escalade parked on the street and got behind the wheel. I walked over and got in on the passenger's side, then gave him the address of my hotel.

"Fancy," he remarked.

"Why do they call you Frodo?" I asked. "You are not particularly short." He wasn't. He wasn't tall, either, at somewhere slightly below six feet tall, but he was not a short man by any rate.

Frodo held up his right hand, and I saw that he was missing his ring finger. "Got it shot off. So now they call me Frodo."

"What did they call you before Frodo?"

"My moms named me Gerald, but that didn't sound real tough. So my street name was Skullfucker, on account of—"

I raised a hand to stop him. "Please, don't share the origin of 'Skullfucker.' I think Frodo is a much better choice."

We rode in silence back to my hotel, but could only get within three blocks. The streets were blocked by emergency vehicles and police cramming the streets of the French Quarter. Frodo pulled over, and I got out of the SUV, looking up into the sky ahead of us.

Whoever killed Oliver apparently heard that I was in town and wasn't thrilled at the news. My hotel was surrounded by firetrucks attempting to save the adjacent buildings as a pillar of black smoke rose to the sky. Onlookers crammed the sidewalks and nearby streets, all necks craning to see the inferno that was my lodging. My hotel was on fire, and I had no doubt that I was the intended target.

4

I ducked into a restaurant with a sandwich board out front announcing "Live Music Every Day!" and requested a table for one. Then I wove through the tables to the bathroom and locked the door.

I took out my phone. "Dennis, are you there?"

His unicorn face popped onto my screen and he said, "I'm everywhere, baby. Except in your hotel room, which is a good thing. Before you ask, no I can't get into the hotel security system, because the hard drives burned up and they didn't back that shit up to the cloud. And yes, all your shit is now toast, so you're going to need to find a Big & Tall Men's store to buy some new underwear."

"And perhaps a t-shirt," I agreed.

"Nah, there's plenty of 'I Support Single Moms' shirts available on Bourbon." His image on the screen changed to a stocky young man with a head full of tight red curls wearing a t-shirt with an image of a woman swinging on a pole. The connection took a moment, but when I made it, I laughed.

"I think my life can be considered more or less complete without ever owning a shirt that promotes that level of misogyny," I said.

"Okay, fine, whatever," Dennis replied, changing his avatar into a giant frowny face. "I've called you an Uber to take you to the nearest tailor that does big and tall work. They have a delivery service, too, so once you get measured and pick out some stuff, they can deliver it to your new hotel. I've already got you a reservation at Harrah's casino, with a new laptop and tablet en route to you."

"Thank you, Dennis. I will pass on the trip to the tailor for now, however. I wish to speak to these firefighters and police officers." I pressed the button on the screen to disconnect the call, but Dennis' face remained.

"Dude. You don't really think you can actually hang up on me, do you? Not gonna happen. Anyway, nobody is going to talk to you until they're sure the whole Quarter isn't going up in flames. Go get some new threads ordered and come back in a couple of hours."

As much as I longed to push my way through the throngs of people and demand answers from those in charge, I recognized the wisdom in his words. Hopefully my sartorial side trip would allow enough time for the onlookers to disperse and give me an opportunity to speak with the arson inspector. A slight delay would also remove much of the cover for the firebug if he was still in the area.

T wo hours later, I returned with a hefty receipt for a very large selection of clothing that all promised to make me look far more presentable than my normal black pants, boots, and thin sweat-shirts. I tend to wear durable clothing in solid dark colors. It hides blood better. It usually is not my blood that stains my clothes. I did choose to wear the new hat I purchased, a jaunty fedora in a dark gray check with a small feather in the hatband. I decided that it made me look somewhat less threatening than my normal appearance.

I approached a man standing near a firetruck in a heavy turnout coat, rubber boots, but without the facemask and fireproof pants of an active firefighter. "Are you the investigator?" I asked.

"Naw," he drawled. "I'm the assistant. The investigator's in there, poking around where she ain't got no business being 'til things cool down a bit. But she's always been hard-headed." The slight smile on his face and the pride in his voice told me that he considered "hard-headed" a compliment.

"Do you have any idea what caused the fire?" I asked.

He turned to me and started a little when his eyes were even with the middle of my chest. He looked up at my face, then took a step back to make conversation easier. I gave him my most reassuring smile, but that never seems to reassure anyone. He took another step back. "I'm sorry, mister...?"

"Franks," I said, reaching into my back pocket for the badge holder there. I flipped open my credentials and passed them to him. "Department of Homeland Security. I'm not official, just curious. My room was in that hotel, and I want to know if the office is going to give me too much crap about getting my laptop replaced." I tried to affect a more casual tone, to use more slang in my speech that he would perceive me as a fellow law enforcement officer.

The badge went much further toward that end than anything, I believe. It was an excellent forgery, one Dennis had created for me by a contact he knew in North Carolina.

The firefighter, or assistant inspector, nodded at the badge and handed it back to me. "You ain't working?"

"No sir, just down here to see the sights," I said. "Might be now, if anything about this looks suspicious."

"Jerry, get over here!" a voice called from inside the wreckage of the building. The assistant turned and moved at a fast walk to the sound. I looked around, then set my hat on the back of a nearby firetruck, picked up a helmet that lay nearby, clapped it on my head, and followed Jerry into the skeletal frame of my burned-out hotel.

A red-haired woman with a spray of freckles that stood out on her pale skin was bent over, cursing at a large chunk of wood. "I can't move this son of a bitch. Can you give me a hand? I need to look at the burn pattern on the bottom side of this beam."

She looked up and scowled at me. "Who the hell is this, Jerry? You know better than to—"

Jerry's head whipped around to me, and he fixed me with an icy glare. "This is Agent Franks. He's a DHS agent on vacation. He was staying here."

"Well, Agent, you gonna stand there like a lump or you gonna help us move this beam?" the woman asked.

I looked at the beam, estimating its weight. I stepped to the broken end and bent my legs. I reached down with both hands and stood, bringing the end of the beam up with me. "Where do you want it?" I asked.

The woman just pointed, her mouth hanging wide open as I hoisted several hundred pounds of charred wood and moved it sideways just far enough for her to get an unimpeded view of the floor. I rolled the beam slightly when I set it down, so she could photograph the side of the beam that was on the bottom.

"There we go," she said, pointing to a silvery residue on the alligator-like burned area of the beam. "That's phosphorous residue. It burns super-hot."

"And water only makes it burn more," I continued.

"That's right," she said. "Very good."

"So this fire was definitely set and was designed to get worse once firefighters arrived," I said.

"Or when the sprinklers kicked on, which happened several minutes before the first trucks got here," Jerry said.

"Why?" I asked.

"This wasn't just arson," the redhead replied. "This fire was set to kill someone."

I was pretty sure I knew who was supposed to end up dead. Now I just needed to find out why.

"I'm Anna Hernandez," the redhead said, holding out her hand. "Chief Arson Inspector for the City of New Orleans."

"Pleased to meet you, Inspector…Hernandez," I replied, looking at her pale skin and red hair.

She laughed. "Married name, Agent. My wife is from Chile. Now, what brings you to my fire scene?"

"I just popped by to pick up my luggage, but it seems to have been incinerated," I said.

"You were staying in this hotel?" she asked, pulling out a little notebook.

"Yes, I was."

"How many people were aware of that fact?"

"I suspect the entire hotel staff knew about it, but unless I have been followed, no one else would have been aware of that. I am not here working. I am on vacation." The lie came easily to me. I do not have the many physical tells that humans have when they are lying. My pupils do not dilate; my heart rate does not increase. Lying comes as naturally to me as breathing. This has proven very useful in my work with Quincy Harker, but sometimes provides a moral conundrum when trying to live a better life than I have in the past.

"Do you have any active cases that may cause someone to seek retribution?" Inspector Hernandez asked.

"I sincerely doubt it," I said. "I am not a field agent. I am a backline support evidence technician. I make sure that the chain of custody is followed precisely to aid in achieving a conviction. My work is essential, but not glamorous." Quincy came up with that cover story for me several years ago. His thought was that if he made me utterly boring, no one would want to delve deeper into my fabricated employment. So far, life had proven him quite correct.

Inspector Hernandez's eyes glazed over long before I finished the summary of my mythical job duties. "Yeah, doesn't sound like you were the target. But I doubt that anything in your room would be salvageable. What floor were you on?"

"The sixth. Where did the fire originate?"

"It's hard to tell with the amount of interior damage. There was so much accelerant used that it burned out a big chunk of the center of the building. So we can't tell yet what floor it started on. All we're sure of is that it was above the third, given the amount of damage on the lowest floors."

"Well, if I can be of any assistance, please let me know." I produced a business card and passed it over. It had an authentic Homeland Security logo and a fabricated office number that Dennis monitored. The cell number did correspond to the phone in my pocket, though.

I turned and walked away to retrieve my hatg and return the helmet, pulling out the cell phone and tapping at the screen. Dennis' face appeared, and I pressed the phone to my ear, since my earbuds were now melted slag in what used to be my duffel bag. "What did you find out?" I asked.

"A whole lot of nothing. Like we already knew, the hotel's security footage is literal toast, and the ATM camera across the street mysteriously went on the fritz about two minutes before the first 911 call came in."

"Mysteriously."

"Yeah, like a mysterious hand went in front of the lens, a mysterious spark came out of the hand, and the camera mysteriously didn't work anymore," Dennis said.

"Magic," I said, nodding.

"Yup."

"That sounds reminiscent of what the young boy said he saw at Oliver's the night he died. Bright flashes of light. Perhaps you could—"

"Check traffic cams in the area to see if I can find a black Maserati anywhere near the hotel before the fire? Yeah, that's a good idea. I'll hit you back. The address of your new hotel is in your phone. Your clothes are being delivered in two hours."

"I have another old acquaintance to visit. I will go chat with her, then go to my hotel to see my new threads, as you kids say."

"Okay, one—I'm not a kid. I'm a sentient bundle of super-genius electrons. And two—pretty sure nobody says 'threads' anymore. Not since 1940, anyway."

"What's seven decades between friends?" I asked. I took the phone down from my ear and tapped a query into the device's map function. It popped up the name of my next destination—Marie Laveau's House of Voodoo. It was time to visit my old friend the voodoo priestess.

5

The walls of Marie Laveau's House of Voodoo pressed in on my massive shoulders. Tourist-trap tchotchkes and bundles of decorative beads and herbs hung from spikes on the slatted display wall, and bookshelves dominated one entire side of the store. I ducked to avoid a grinning sugar skull hanging from the ceiling and addressed the young man behind the counter. He was a thin black man with an afro broader than his shoulders, bobbing his head to the reggae music that rumbled through the shop, providing a deep undercurrent to both conversation and commerce. He was reading a tattered *Shadowman* graphic novel, oblivious even to my decidedly stealth-less approach.

"I am here to see Madison," I said, trying to smile to soothe the young man as he jumped at my words. My smile was about as soothing as it normally is, and he slipped off the backless stool he was sitting on to stagger back. He knocked into a display of incense, then whirled around to catch the spinning rack before it spilled all its contents on the ground.

"I'm sorry, who are you?" he asked.

"I am an old friend of Madison's. Please tell her I am here." I handed him one of my cards. Not the one with Homeland Security on it. The one that is just my name, Adam Franks, and my cell number.

"I'm sorry, sir," he started. "We don't have anyone—"

I leaned forward, snarling at the young man. His dark skin turned ashen, and I said, "Do not play with me, child. I am here to see Madison, and you can tell her I am here, or I can injure you and find her myself. I would prefer not to do that, but you have a decision to make."

He backed up against a wall of herbs, incense, dried chicken feet, and other conjuring supplies and spun around to make sure nothing fell to the floor. Since I knew Madison kept the real supplies behind the counter, I didn't blame him for being nervous. I stood, waiting like a silent sentinel, until he turned back to face me.

"Well?" I packed as much threat into one syllable as I knew how, and that is not an inconsiderable amount. The young man gulped and pointed toward the back of the store. I followed his finger with my gaze, and my eyes lit on a narrow passage covered with multi-hued silks, a festoon of colored fabric forming a camouflaged door into Madison's work and stockroom.

"Thank you," I said, nodding at the boy. "You can call her and tell her Adam is coming back. Or I can surprise her, but we both know that is not the best option."

He gave a nod in return and picked up the telephone, pressing an intercom button and saying, "There's a giant on his way back to see you. He says his name is Adam. I'm sorry, I couldn't...okay."

He hung up the phone and almost certainly turned to me, but I was already wending my way through the labyrinthine shop to the faux door made of fabric. I heard his footsteps as he walked to the door and clicked the deadbolt in place, then I heard the slight whisper of cardboard as he flipped the OPEN sign to CLOSED. Good. Madison remembered me, and remembered that trouble often accompanied me. That trouble is frequently named John Abraham Quincy Holmwood Harker, but not this time.

This time my trouble didn't have a name as yet but seemed to have a taste for expensive foreign cars. I've noticed in my time that evil is often concerned with the trappings of wealth, while good often cloaks itself in poverty. I wonder if that is something that started with Jesus of Nazareth, or if it is a trait he adopted as well... I made a mental note to discuss that with Vlad the next time we were together, and perhaps to bring it up with Sister Evangeline as well, but then I shoved that thought to the back of my mind and stepped through the curtain of dazzling peacock silks.

Lady Madison, any surname she once possessed long lost, now merely a secret between herself and various government agencies that cared about such things, sat behind a small round table with a crystal ball nestled in a depression in the center of the table. She was a lovely older black woman, somewhere between seventy and one hundred years old, her wizened face a road map of laughter and tragedy, of love and life and loss and all the moments in between. Brilliant blue eyes shone from the crinkles of her caramel face, a parting gift from some Frenchman generations back.

She once told me that in her family blue eyes meant the child would be a powerful witch or sorcerer and asked me what the color of my eyes meant. I told her it meant that the freshest corpse in the graveyard had hazel eyes.

I looked at the small metal folding chair and smiled. "I think I'll try something different," I said. I folded the chair and leaned it against the wall, then stepped through the open doorway into the shop's tiny storeroom. I picked up four cinderblocks and brought them out in front of Madison. I arranged them into a sturdy, if somewhat firm, seat and settled my massive frame onto them.

"How are you, Adam?" Madison asked. Her voice was like warm honey, smooth and slow, seeming to flow around the room twice before it got to my ears. I had heard that voice boom and crack like a thunderstorm on the ocean, though. I knew full well the power this old woman wielded, and I was not fooled for an instant by her honey-chile sweetness and her disarming old-lady grin. This was one of the most powerful witches in the world, and she did not suffer fools lightly. I tried never to be the fool with her.

"I survive, Madison," I replied. "Despite the best efforts of friend and foe, it seems, I survive."

"You still running with that Harker fool?" she asked, and her brow knit with frustration. "I told you that white boy gonna get you killed one of these days. It don't matter how big or strong you are, if it lives, it can die. And you most definitely alive, boy."

I chuckled at that. Madison knew full well what those words meant to me, and her using them was no coincidence. "I am still working with Quincy on occasion, yes."

"You part of that mess in Atlanta?"

"I was."

"You here in New Orleans on account of some bullshit errand he got you running?"

I had to pause for a moment to consider my answer. I was, in fact, working with Harker to recover the Implements in order to restore the Archangels to Heaven and God to His throne, but I didn't look upon this quest as an "errand." It was best to be clear with Madison, however.

"I am here on his behalf, yes."

"Shit, Adam." She dragged out the curse into multiple syllables, making it sound like *sheeeee-it*. "You know that dumbass cracker magician is fucking around with things he don't understand again, right?"

"This time I fear that we are dealing with forces that none of us understand," I said. "This job involves Archangels."

"Oh, shit, son. You messing with stuff way above your pay grade now. Yours and Harker's and his damn bloodsucking uncle's, too. You Shadow Council jackasses always got to be messing with stuff. Always got to be trying to fix shit that don't need to be fixed. What you trying to do now? Bring back God?" She glared at me across the table, almost daring me to tell her that's exactly what we were doing.

And, of course, that's exactly what we were doing. "Yes," I said. There's no point trying to lie to Madison—she can sense it, even in me.

She leaned back in her chair and folded her arms over her abundant chest. "You are a damn fool, Adam. You might be the most foolish damn fool that has ever lived."

"I'm not going to argue that point, Madison," I said. "I fear at this point in my long life there is too much evidence to support your opinion. My foolishness aside, will you do a scrying for me?"

"I suppose," she said with a sigh. "I might not be done fussing with you yet, though. But you ain't here just for a scrying. I can see something is heavy on your heart today, old friend. What is it?"

Madison has always had a gift for seeing, and not just what is foretold in the cards or what appears in the crystal globe she has resting over the fiber-optic projector set into her table. She can read the body language of any mark at any card table, which led to her being banned from hundreds of casinos across the country. She can read auras from people and objects, and she can read the emotions of even a manufactured man such as myself. I asked her once how she accomplishes such a thing, and she simply replied with, "It's magic, you great big idiot."

"Oliver is dead," I said. There was no need to elaborate. She knew Oliver, in the way that all talented practitioners of magic in an area come across each other at some point in their lives. They were not friends, but I knew of no animosity between them.

"I heard about 'dat. It's a shame, it is. He was a good man and a strong wizard. He did a lot of good in that part of the city. Loved that granddaughter of his, too. You meet her? She's a fine-looking woman."

"I did meet her, and yes, she is a lovely woman," I replied. I have learned long ago that Madison has a hint of the matchmaker about her, and it is better to just let her go on about her hints and innuendos and pretend to miss the clues than it is to make any objections to her interfering in my nonexistent love life.

"But why does that have you worried, *cher*? Oliver had a heart attack, from what I hear. He was an old man, and that happens to old men. He didn't have nothing on you, of course, but you a special case." That was certainly one way of putting it. Madison and I had never gone in-depth as to my origins, but she was not an unintelligent woman, and the scars I bear in particular places make it fairly clear that I am not what anyone would consider "normal."

"He did not have a heart attack," I said. "One of the local youth saw a man in an expensive car go into Oliver's house. There were flashes of light in the windows, in many colors, then the next day Oliver was found dead."

Madison looked troubled, and I knew this was the first she was hearing about this man. "What kind of car? What did the man look like?"

"The boy said it was an expensive sports car, and all he knew about the man was that he was a white man."

"That drew some eyes in that 'hood," Madison said.

"Especially from the gang members who live across the street," I agreed.

"Too many shady white men in the Quarter to pick one out of the crowd, and ain't no parking down here, so I don't know if I'd know him if he walked in the front door."

"Well, if your security camera suddenly stop working, I would take that as cause for alarm," I said. "I believe this man was responsible for the fire at my hotel earlier today, and the security footage was destroyed."

"That makes sense, though, if it was in a fire," Madison said.

"True enough," I agreed. "But the camera on the ATM across the street also failed within a few minutes of the fire."

Madison nodded, her close-cropped white hair framing her skull as she did. "Yeah, that's more than a little bit strange, my friend. I'll keep a look out, and I'll make sure Alexander does the same."

"Please apologize to Alexander for my poor manners earlier. I was perhaps a bit intense when I spoke with him."

"Oh, it's fine. Boy needs to toughen up anyway. He's too much of a delicate damn flower. Now, you done warned me about the bad mojo man. What you want me to see for you?"

"I'm looking for a horn," I said.

"Boy, you in New Orleans," she said with a cackle. "If we didn't invent jazz down here, we damn sure perfected it. You gone need to be a touch more specific with what you asking for."

I leaned forward and lowered my voice. No matter how much Madison trusted her employee, I didn't know the boy and didn't need him knowing my business. "I am looking for the Horn of the Herald. I have to find the Horn of Archangel Sealtiel, so I can call him back to service and return him to Heaven."

Madison looked at me for a long moment, then nodded. "Well, I suppose that's a relief. I was worried it was going to be something difficult, like making the Earth rotate backward. No, all you need to do is find the Implement of one of the most powerful beings in the whole world and coerce an Archangel to return to Heaven after millennia on Earth. What do you plan to do after lunch, go to Disneyland?"

"So you can't do it?" I asked.

"Oh no, son, you not getting out this that easy," she said. "Remember, boy. The difficult we can do immediately; the impossible takes just a little more time. This is going to take a little time, but we'll find your horn. Now put your hands on the crystal. I'm going need a little blood for this."

6

Madison knew better than to try and use my blood for her invocation. Not only is it a thick, viscous substance more akin to crude oil than the sanguine stuff of human life, no one is exactly sure what it is made up of. Since my father's death, which was regrettably not at my hand, there has been no one living who knew exactly how he transformed me from my dead component parts to the walking, talking, thinking, and somewhat living creature that I am. His notes were lost in the fire that destroyed his laboratory, and I was somewhat too preoccupied with my pending incineration to rescue them.

No, she drew a small *athame* from beneath the table and pricked her thumb, bringing a small drop of bright crimson to the surface. She smeared the blood onto the crystal and pressed her palms to the stone. The cool orb immediately grew warm and began to glow with a soft amber light as her essence fused with the magic of the stone.

I have spent many years around practitioners of magic, both dark and light, and had many conversations with them about the origin of their ability to manipulate the natural forces of the world and bend the world to their whim. I have received as many answers as I have had questions as to the source of their power, and Madison was no different. She believed firmly that the spirits of her ancestors lent her their power to manipulate the world around her, and that she was merely a vessel for power and information from the spirit realm. It made as much sense as any other explanation I had received, so I merely sat mute with my hands on the still-warming crystal sphere.

"Grandmother Maybelle, hear my plea," Madison said, her voice light and child-like as she called upon one of her favorite ancestors. She once explained to me that her Mamaw Maybelle had been her favorite elderly relative when she was a little girl, that Maybelle always had a mint or a Werther's candy tucked away in an apron pocket and that little Madison would sit on her lap and dig through the old woman's pockets for the sweet, giggling along as her grandmother pretended to be ticklish at the child's quest. She called upon Grandmother Maybelle most often when I asked her for help, but I had also seen her call on the spirits of other relatives, including once her father, a big, bellicose man who she only went to in times of great need and in search of strength and power.

The stone pulsed in a deep, slow rhythm, almost like a heartbeat, and Madison's head lolled forward. Seconds later, her head snapped up, and she fixed me with a sharp gaze. "What you want now, man of dead men?" Her voice was waspish, her words more pointed, and her eyes narrowed as she spoke. "Why you back here looking to drag my grandbaby into your mess with that Harker boy?"

I started at Grandmother Maybelle's tone. She had never spoken to me directly before, choosing to communicate with Madison and let her relay her words to me. Apparently, my work with Quincy Harker and the Shadow Council had attracted attention past the mortal plane.

"Don't look at me like something done bit you on your big dead behind, golem," she ordered. "I done asked you a question, and I expect you to answer it before I start worrying myself with any of yours."

"I am here because Madison has helped me in the past, and I need her assistance once more. I seek—"

"I know what you looking for, boy, and it better to not speak of it while you talking straight to the other side. We got eavesdroppers on both sides of this rock, and I don't want to hear about you bringing any pain down on Maddie's head."

"Nor do I, but I believe that pain may be here regardless," I said. "There have been attacks against practitioners of the arts in New Orleans. That is the other reason I am here—to warn Madison." I paused, then went on. "She is a friend, and I have precious few of those. I would not see her harmed if I can prevent it."

Madison/Maybelle's expression softened, and she nodded at me. "That's good, boy. She my last grandbaby, and as much as I want to see her again, I'm in no hurry for her to cross that river, if you know what I mean."

"Only in theory," I said with a rueful smile.

The laugh that ripped from Madison's mouth was pure and loud, almost startling in its intensity. "You a funny one, golem. Maybe one day you find where that nasty man that made you tucked your soul away and you can be a real boy, just like the puppet in that cartoon."

"What do you mean?" I asked, my mind whirling at the suggestion.

"Oh child," the woman laughed again, throwing her head back. "You done spent all these years trying to find out what you are, but you got no idea what you could be. You need to take a look past the mirror someday. But for now, you can find what you seek just behind the door." Her head sagged forward, and Madison let out a long sigh. She jerked once, then sat up straight, looking around at the room.

"Did she give you anything useful?" she asked, taking her hands off the stone. Grandmother Maybelle was obviously gone, and now it was back to me and Madison in the storeroom of her voodoo shop.

"She certainly gave me things to consider," I said. "I don't know how useful the information will be, but there was a lot to think about in her words."

Madison peered at me, as always seeing more behind my words than I tried to show. "I don't think you're just talking about finding a fancy trumpet in the Quarter, are you?"

"No, I'm not. There are things your grandmother mentioned that have caused me to rethink many of the preconceived notions that I have long held about myself. I shall have to spend some significant time exploring these ideas. After we have you somewhere safe and I have located my absentee angel and his Horn."

"What do you mean, have me somewhere safe? I'm not going anywhere." She said it very matter-of-factly, like I was insane for even considering the idea.

"Madison, there is someone killing magic users in New Orleans. They have already murdered Oliver, and they tried to kill me today. This is not someone without resources or power. I would not wish to see you hurt."

"Neither would I, Adam, love. But I am not leaving this shop. Marie Laveau's is a New Orleans institution and the only place in town some folks can find the things they need to practice their rituals. We can't just shut down."

"I'm not asking you to shut down, just to take a few days off. Leave Alexander here to manage the shop while you get somewhere safe until things calm down."

"You mean until you kill this man hunting down magicians," she corrected. Her disapproval was clear on her face.

"Oliver was a friend," I said. "I don't have many of those. It makes me very protective of the ones I do have."

She stared at me for a moment, then sighed. "It don't matter. I can't leave. Xander can't run the store by himself. I got to look out for him. He's my dead sister's boy, and he's blood, but he don't have the touch. There's nothing to protect him from some of the things I keep in the back room here. He can't sell that stuff—only somebody with power can touch it without getting hurt. I leave him alone here for more time than it takes to go get lunch, and it's liable to mean his life."

I looked at my friend, and there was nothing about her that said I would be able to persuade her to leave this place. "There is nothing I can say to dissuade you from this path, is there?"

"I could ask you the same question, couldn't I, old friend?" She gave me a slight smile, and I nodded.

"That is fair," I said. That settled to no one's satisfaction, I changed the subject. "Your grandmother said something about looking for what I seek behind the door. Does that mean anything to you?"

Madison thought for a moment, then shook her head. "Not a damn thing, Adam. I'm sorry, but you know how ghosts are. Sometimes I swear they like to be obtuse just for the pure hell of it."

I smiled and stood up. "I do, yes. Thank you, Madison. Please try to stay safe in the coming days. This man, or whatever he is, burned down an entire hotel in an attempt to do me harm. I have no doubt that he will be at least as serious in his attempts to eliminate you if he deems you a threat."

She chuckled. "If he don't think I'm a threat, then he's a bigger damn fool than you are," she said. "Oliver was my friend, too. More than that, back in the day." A wistful smile crossed her lips. "I will miss that grouchy old bastard. If that son of a bitch comes for me, he'd better come heavy because I'll set the ghost of Queen Marie her damn self on his sorry ass." She gave a real laugh then. "We'll see how the son of a bitch likes that."

"Take care, Madison. Do not underestimate this man. He is dangerous."

"So am I, Adam son of no man, so am I."

I looked in her eyes, and there was no fear there, just the steely resolve of a woman who has spent a lifetime dealing with powerful forces and still stood to tell the tale. I gave her a nod and left the back room, pushing through the rainbow silks into the main part of the shop.

"She's going to need some water, and you'll need to make sure that shotgun stays loaded," I said to Alexander as I stretched my back, stiff from sitting on the cinderblocks for so long.

"It's always loaded," he said, reaching beneath the counter. His hand came up with a bottle of Aristocrat vodka. "And she don't never drink water. You can let yourself out." He walked past me into the back room, and I wove between the counter and the display to the front door. I flipped the sign back to OPEN and stepped out onto the sidewalk.

Somewhere in New Orleans was a missing angel, a magical trumpet, and a man who wanted to kill me. I needed to find them all, and I had no idea where to look. I turned left out of the shop and headed toward Jackson Square, unsure if I was trying to clear my head or just make myself a more visible target.

7

The square surrounding the park was crowded in the mid-afternoon sun. Tourists milled about, stopping here and there to listen to buskers or to admire the art hung on the wrought iron fences by the street vendors. One enterprising band of youths combined a pair of young men beating on buckets with drumsticks with a group of four teens dancing and leaping in choreographed chaos, blending capoeira combat dance with breakdancing and hip hop dance moves. I stopped to watch them for a few minutes and dropped a five-dollar bill in a hat before I moved on.

Near the southwest corner of the park, I came upon a young man playing jazz, the sun glinting off the chrome of his trumpet's bell and flickering into my eyes to draw my attention. He played energetic covers of rock songs with a jazz flavor, and behind him, a homeless man shuffled a little flat-footed dance in time to the music. On the ground before him sat an upside-down fedora in front of a chalkboard sign. The sign read, in big pink chalk letters, "TONIGHT - One Night Only - The Alley Club - behind The Famous Door - Thunder Travis Blows Blues – 9 PM"

I stopped cold as my brain processed the words on the sign. Behind The Famous Door. The trumpet gleaming in the sun. It all clicked together in my head in an instant. This was the man I sought. Or at least the instrument I sought. Now I just had to convince him to either accept his true form as an Archangel, or give me the trumpet so I could find Sealtiel with it.

Thunder Travis, as the sign named him, was a large young man, a Clarence Clemons-sized musician, only with a trumpet instead of a saxophone. His dark skin glistened in the sun, and tattoos ran the length of his bulging arms, sweat obscuring the details and dampening the front of his white tank top. His short dreadlocks stuck out from his head at all angles, and a long silver chain with an ankh on it hung from his neck. He wore cargo shorts and sneakers, and generally looked like a college kid out for a good time, only he was here working to make ends meet blowing jazz for tips in the middle of the afternoon.

I pulled out my phone and aimed it at the man playing the trumpet. "Dennis, are you there?"

"I'm always here, big buddy. What can I do ya for?" the unicorn head on my screen asked.

"I need you to access my phone's camera and get me any information you can gather on the man playing the trumpet," I said.

"You get that's not really how facial recognition stuff works, right? I don't just beep a few times like R2-D2 and then spit out this dude's home phone number and address."

"You always tell me how amazing you are, Dennis. I am merely providing you with an opportunity to prove yourself correct."

"Sometimes I think you gave Harker asshole lessons when he was a kid," my electronic unicorn companion muttered.

"Any of his formative years are purely the fault of Abraham and Vlad. I was merely a witness to their corruption of the young Harker. What do you know about this musician?"

"Jesus, dude, gimme at least a minute, will you? Okay, he doesn't come up in a scan of military records from the last ten years, same for any wanted posters, ditto any TV star websites or major search engines. It looks like your dude is just a dude, playing jazz in the park trying to make a living. Sorry."

"Is there anything else you can do to try and find out more about him?" I asked. "Driver's license records, anything like that."

"I'm scanning the Louisiana and Mississippi DMV records now, but there's nothing. Sorry, Adam. I've got nothing. I'll start a deep scan, see what I can see on Facebook and other social media stuff. I mean, it's not like the guy is trying to stay out of sight, maybe he just doesn't drive. I don't know. I'll let you know what I find."

"Thank you," I said, then slipped the phone into my pocket. I sat on a nearby bench and watched the crowd pass by. People of all shapes and sizes walked along the sidewalk in front of me, never looking twice at the huge man in the hooded sweatshirt sitting there watching the world. Men, women, children, all absorbed into their own little worlds, their attention often dominated by the tiny screens they held in their hands.

A man stepped up to the musician, bent down, and dropped a bill in the hat. He sat on another bench for a time watching the musician and his dancing homeless man, a dirty shuffle-stepper scuffing his worn shoes in some semblance of time to the music. The spectator sat in the shade, only his wingtip shoes catching the bright sunlight, the patent leather shining to an almost blinding gloss. He wore an expensive suit, with an Italian tie and a matching pocket square. His watch cost more than everything I wore combined, and likely didn't smell of burning hotel. His hair was immaculate and his face shaved so smooth I wondered if one could use his cheekbones as their own razor.

He was a fiendishly handsome man, and his attention was not locked on the musician, as mine so often was, but skipped across the crowd, the musician, the sidewalk artist making a three-dimensional image on the ground in nothing but chalk, an impermanent masterpiece to be washed away with the next rain. The man's gaze even fell on me once or twice, and he gave me a friendly nod as we locked eyes. I nodded back, acknowledging him, and returned to watching the trumpeter and his dancing hobo.

After thirty minutes or so, the man set his trumpet down on a small folding stand and took a long drink of water from a plastic bottle at his feet. Then he opened the case next to his water bottle, lay the trumpet inside, and slid the case and stand into a small backpack. He transferred the money from his hat to his pocket, then put the hat on his head. He stood, slipped his arms through the loops on the backpack, and picked up his sign. He turned to the man in the suit, gave him a slight bow, then did the same to me.

"Like the sign says, I'll be at The Alley Club tonight at nine. Hope y'all can come join us. Bring a friend. Don't bring too many friends, though. The place isn't that big." He laughed, downed the last of his water, and tossed the bottle into a nearby wastebasket. I watched the young man walk off up the sidewalk, whistling a tune as he went. His dancing homeless man stood around for a moment watching him go, then wandered off back the way I came, toward the restaurants and bars of the Quarter.

I waited until he had almost vanished from view, then stood. I noticed the well-dressed man walking ahead of me, his languid gait belied by the way his head never wavered from his target. He was following the young musician, pursuing the same quarry. I pulled my phone from my pocket and held it to my ear.

"Dennis?"

"Yeah, big guy?"

"Have you found anything on our young Mister Travis?" I asked.

"Who's Mr. Travis?"

"The trumpet player," I replied. "His name is Thunder Travis."

"Do you think you could have told me that any later?" Dennis' voice rose in my ear.

"I'm sorry," I said. "I thought you were amazing."

"I am *amazing*," he retorted. "I'm also incorporeal and trapped in the internet. It's not like I can just hop out of here on a lightning bolt and take a look around."

"But wouldn't that be interesting?"

"Yeah, that would be great," replied my disgruntled disembodied friend.

There are very few times in life that I enjoy tormenting people, but for one reason or another, they always seem to center on either Dennis or Quincy Harker. Perhaps it is the fact that they are so high-strung. It is just a simple matter to wind them up a little more and watch them go around in circles.

"Okay, here we go," Dennis said. "Jermaine 'Thunder' Travis was a standout running back in high school, second-string at LSU, good enough to get a scholarship for all four years, but nowhere near good enough to play in the pros. He graduated LSU six years ago with a degree in music education, worked for three years at a high school in Baton Rouge, then moved back to New Orleans…looks like he came back to take care of a grandfather who was sick. Grandpa was the original Thunder Travis, a popular sideman in New Orleans in the fifties and sixties. He was in the house band at The Famous Door for a little while, played in the Preservation Hall band for a couple of years, then quit playing as he got older. He died about a year ago. Jermaine was his only living heir."

"What happened to Jermaine's parents?"

"Looks like not much record of his dad being involved. He's listed on the birth certificate, but he's lived in Montana since 1999. Dad is remarried, has a couple of newer model kids, looks like he sent a check every month until Jermaine turned eighteen, but no real contact. Mom…whoof, that's a bitch. Mom died six months before Grandpa. Grandma died before Jermaine was born. No other relatives that I can find, no wife, no serious girlfriend according to social media. Looks like he's pretty much a loner."

"Send me the address of his grandfather's house," I said. If he was headed home to sleep before his gig that night, I could take an Uber and beat him there. I didn't know why the man in the expensive suit was following him, but anyone paying that much attention to the bearer of the Horn of the Herald was probably someone I didn't want getting to Jermaine before I did.

"Uber's around the corner," Dennis replied. "And it's paid for. Don't worry, I didn't hack anything. Except Harker's debit card, that is."

"Well, if it's Quincy's money, it's all the better. I believe he still owes me money from an old poker game."

"The one where Hickok got shot?" Dennis asked.

"I'm not that old," I replied, hanging up the phone.

"You know you can't hang up on me!" I heard from my pocket as Dennis worked valiantly to get the last word in.

I got in the Uber, glad once again that Dennis knew to specify an SUV to accommodate my seven-foot height. The driver didn't try to make small talk as he drove, letting me lean my head back and relax after a morning spent surrounded by people. I let the soft faux leather of the seat envelope me as I closed my eyes. I didn't sleep, not even a doze, but I did manage a small moment of meditation, working to center myself after being battered by crowds almost since rising.

The Suburban pulled up to the curb two blocks from Jermaine's house, as instructed, and I got out. I walked down the sidewalk toward the address Dennis listed and stepped into the shadows between two houses across the street. It was a typical city neighborhood with houses crammed as close together as any sense of privacy would allow. Jermaine rode up on a dark red bicycle about ten minutes after I began my surveillance, chaining the bike to the pipe-built railing of his front steps and walking up to enter his house. Jermaine opened the door, and a flash of light exploded from within, hurling him back through the air to slam into a panel van sitting at the curb.

The wooden door was obliterated, nothing more than a smoking hole in the front of the house, and stepping through it was a demon. Not just a little, run-of-the-mill Reaver or even a bigger, badder Torment Demon. No, this was a nine-foot-tall Demon Warrior, a soldier of Hell's armies, complete with a flaming sword and armor so black it seemed to absorb all the light around it, making the entire world feel darker, more gray.

I sighed and stepped forward, looking around for a weapon. The last time I'd gone toe-to-toe with a demon unaided, it hadn't ended well, but it was worse for the demon. Ripping something's head off with your bare hands tends to ruin its day. I just hoped this demon wasn't about to ruin mine.

8

I ran to Jermaine's side and knelt beside his unconscious form. He lay sprawled on the grass beside the dented van with blood oozing from a small cut on the back of his head. The demon stood at the top of the steps, looking around for its prey, then its glowing red eyes locked on me. The thing was nearly two feet taller than me and broad in the shoulders. It was fully encased in what looked like obsidian plate armor with a flaming black sword in one hand. A horned helmet covered its entire face save a slit for its crimson eyes to glare through, and smoke hissed from a grate where its mouth should be, spewing sulfurous stench across the yard.

"Remove thyself from my field of battle, mortal, and I shall spare thy life."

I stood and faced the demon. "I can't do that, demon. This man is not yours, nor shall he be as long as I live."

The monster laughed, a chilling, hollow sound coming through the armor from the bowels of Hell. "Then he will be mine in mere seconds, human. For that is all the longer you shall live!"

He leapt off the steps and charged me with his sword. I turned, ripped the passenger door off the panel van, and brought my makeshift shield around to intercept the charging demon. We slammed together with a mighty crash, and I managed to shove him back. My reprieve lasted less than a breath as he slashed at me with that terrifying blade. I got the door up into its path, but his fiery sword sliced through the metal like it was butter. I gaped at the two hunks of van clenched in my fists, and for the first time in many decades, thought I might actually die.

I threw the chunk of door in my left hand at the demon's head, and he swatted it away with his sword. That exposed his left side, and I slammed into his knee with the other chunk of door, feeling a grim smile stretch across my face at the satisfying *crunch* that came from the joint. The impact bent his greave on that leg as well, and he was unable to straighten his leg. He spun around, dancing on one foot and the toes of his left leg, and swirled his sword in a deadly arc before him.

"It seems I underestimated you, human," he said, his voice sounding like an earthquake mating with a forest fire, all pain and disaster and wreckage, crackling through his throat.

"I won't give you a second chance to make that mistake, demon," I said, lowering my shoulder and slamming into him with the remnants of my door-shield. The glass shattered all over the back of my head, and the heat from his sword caught my hoodie ablaze, but I had him at a bad angle to strike, and he could do nothing but tumble backward onto the concrete steps of what remained of Jermaine's house.

I fell atop the demon and grabbed his right wrist with mine. Agony shot through my palm as the spikes on his gauntlet pierced all the way through the back of my hand, but I knew to let go was to most likely die. It had been many years since I had battled alone against a foe that could possibly take my life, and I didn't intend to go easily, if at all.

The demon growled in my face, and its rotten-egg breath wrapped around my face in a foul miasma. It thrashed, and kicked, and howled, and still I sat astride it, pressing down with the van door into its chest, trying to punch it somewhere that would do more damage to the monster than to my fist, but its armor thwarted me at every turn. It bucked in one giant convulsion, and I flew off to the side, only connected now by my grip on its wrist and the spikes through my hand. The pain was immense, tearing at my palm and grinding the bones on the metal studs that protruded through the back of my hand. I rolled onto my side and gripped that right arm with my other hand, grabbing above the wrist this time so as not to destroy my other hand.

I wrapped both hands around the creature's forearm, planted both feet in its ribcage, and pulled with all my considerable might. The demon let out an anguished scream and thrashed about on the grass, starting small fires and scarring the sidewalk with its intense heat. I felt its other fist slam into my shin once, twice, again and again, the spikes on that gauntlet ripping deep furrows in my calf and lower leg. I bent forward, relaxing the tension for an instant, then snapped back, giving one huge yank, and with a shriek of pain and rage, and a squeal of rending plate mail, I pulled the demon's arm off at the shoulder.

Black blood spurted from the wound, and every blade of grass that blood touched smoked and died away down to the dirt in an instant. The gouts of demon blood sizzled on the sidewalk and melted part of one of my shoes, burning my toes and sending yet more pain through my battered body. I got to my knees, turned the demon's hand around in my bloodied grip, and plunged the obsidian blade into its wielder's chest. The blade pierced the breastplate with a *crunk*, and the demon let out a howl of rage and pain that shattered every car and house window on the block.

The demon stared up at me, its red eyes growing dim, and as the light winked out, I heard it hiss, "I will remember you." Then its eyes went black, and the demon's body turned to nothing more than black soot and ash. I knelt on the grass, somehow still holding the gleaming black demon sword, and looked over at Jermaine. He was unconscious, probably concussed, and would need medical attention quickly. And that's without even beginning to address the damage I had endured. I fumbled in my pocket and pulled out my phone. The screen was shattered, but as I pressed a button on the side, it lit up in a few places.

"Dennis?" I croaked.

"Holy shit, Adam!" The face on the screen was his human face, and concern was written in every line. "How the hell are you still alive? That was—"

"I know," I managed to gasp out. "We need..." I couldn't speak any more. The pain was too great.

"Hang on buddy, I got people coming to get you. Just hang on, big guy, they'll be there..." Anything else he said was lost as I toppled sideways to the ground and blackness filled my vision.

I woke on a hard surface in a bare room. It was as much a cell as a room, except there were no bars on the door. There was no door at all, just an arched entry into the tiny room, so I did not consider myself a prisoner in any way. It is usually better for the structural integrity of the building if my egress is not impeded. The floor was bare concrete, with a drain set in the center. I lay on a metal "bed" for lack of a better word, with a pillow of sorts under my neck. I looked up at the bright white fluorescent light, then at the stark walls, and let out a dry chuckle. I was in one of the cryptid autopsy rooms at Sisters of the Sword.

The Sisters were not just a militant arm of the Church and the home of the Hunter for the Gulf region. If that were not enough for one small collection of nuns, they also were, to a woman, research scientists dedicated to the study and understanding of cryptids, supernatural or paranormal or simply odd beings that defied conventional understanding of science in some way.

I had stood on the other side of one of these stone walls, watching via video feed, as a Sister had autopsied, or attempted to autopsy, a rogue vampire. It did not end well. The problem most humans have with studying the body of a deceased vampire is that such a thing does not exist. Vampires are already dead by definition, so when the magic that animates them is removed, they either crumble to dust, or if they are more recently turned, they explode in a shower of blood and gore.

You can't really autopsy a vampire because it's still alive after death. But you can, with the proper precautions, take tissue samples from an animate vampire to study. Most creatures take exception to being participants in vivisection, however, and vampires are very strong. In the case I witnessed, a pain-mad vampire who already had exhibited no compunction against taking human life, ripped his arms off to get free of his bonds, then chewed through the throat of the Sister attempting to perform the autopsy. It took four of us to put the vampire down, even with no arms. It only took two to dispatch the Sister once she turned. She was much fresher than the original vampire.

Now I found myself in a similar room, the major exception being the lack of door. I sat up and waved to the small video camera mounted in a corner. "Hello. Thank you for tending my wounds. I would like to speak to Sister Evangeline now."

A tall nun in full wimple came into the doorway a few moments later. She was a severe-looking woman, the reputation of nuns as disciplinarians notwithstanding. She did not speak, simply gestured toward the open door.

As I stood, the sheet covering my lower body slipped to the floor, and I realized for the first time that I was nude. "Pardon me," I said, retrieving the drape and fastening it around my waist. "I seem to have lost my clothes. The nun showed neither surprise nor disgust at the patchwork landscape of scars, stitches, and seams that made up my skin, so I merely hiked the sheet up to free my feet and passed through the doorway into the hall.

This passage felt somehow as if it were underground. The muffled sounds of our feet on the stone floor, the slightly musty smell that pervaded the entire area, and the light chill in the air all contributed to a sense of a tunnel or catacomb. It was well-lit with electric light, so there was no gloomy flicker of torchlight or choking smoke to sting my eyes. My feet slapped along the cool slate paving stones until I came to a door ahead of me.

I turned to my escort, who stopped several feet behind me. "I am to enter?"

She nodded.

I raised my hand and knocked. A cheery "Come in!" rang out from the other side of the door, and I lifted the handle and pushed on the thick iron-bound wooden door. The hinges swung noiselessly, and the thick oaken door glided open to reveal a library with a vaulted ceiling and a roaring fire in a fireplace.

Two armchairs sat on a round area rug before the fireplace, and a plump smiling nun occupied one of them. "Come in, come in, love. And close the door behind you. We don't want to let Agatha's chill follow you in!" The woman's voice was bright and crisp, like sunlight dancing on water, and I felt something for her that I almost never felt when dealing with mortals, particularly those associated with religion. I trusted her and felt safe in her presence. Something resonated within me, making me feel as if no harm would come to me as long as I was with her. I felt an unfamiliar warmth on the flesh of my chest, and I looked down to see the medal Oliver's granddaughter gave me lying on my bare skin.

The Purple Heart was glowing with a faint white light, just enough for me to see it. I touched the medal, and it was warm. Not the warm of being in contact with living flesh, as I give off very little heat, but a gentle radiance that came from the amulet itself.

"You are Oliver's friend. Adam, I believe he said your name was." I tore my eyes from the necklace and stared at the woman. She stood before her chair, her eyes fixed on mine.

"My name is Mother Eunice. I'm glad to see the child gave you that necklace. I think you're going to need it. Please, sit down. We have quite a lot to talk about."

9

"**I** am happy to join you, but before I do, may I have my pants?" I asked.

Eunice's laughter was a thing to behold. It swelled from within her copious bosom like a geyser, rippling out from her in waves and infusing the entire room with joy. I smiled as she laughed, but I remained standing. I did, after all, want my pants.

"I am sorry, my son," she said after a moment of mirth. "Your clothes were either burned horribly or torn to shreds in your fight with the demon. Then there's the matter of the demon blood eating through much of the fabric, and your own blood soaking the remainder. There really was very little worth saving. We have nothing here to fit a man, much less a man of your size. Your friend Dennis is having some clothes delivered from your hotel. Once those arrive, they will be brought to you."

"You have spoken with Dennis?" I asked.

"Oh yes, my son," she said. She reached over to a table between the two chairs and held up my abused cell phone. "I would hand this to you, but I am aware of the lack of pockets in your current wardrobe." She put the phone back on the table and motioned to the other chair.

"Won't you sit by the fire? I find these tunnels to be a little chilly, and it helps my arthritis to stay warm."

I moved to the chair and sat, then asked, "If it is uncomfortable for you down here, why not simply work aboveground?"

She waved an arm around us at the bookshelves. "The books, love. I can't take the books upstairs into the humidity. The Louisiana atmosphere would destroy this old paper in a heartbeat. We are digitizing everything as fast as we can, but it's not a quick job. So as long as the collected knowledge of the Sisters resides here, I stay underground, and every once in a while, I stoke the fires with another copy of this drivel." She gestured to a kindling box near the fireplace, where a stack of popular, and well-worn, romance novels stood. "I do, of course, have to read them all multiple times, just to make sure they're drivel. Wouldn't want to torch a literary masterpiece by mistake."

"Perish the thought," I said, feeling an unaccustomed smile stretch my features. Something about this funny little woman put me very much at ease. I found myself enjoying her company, with her romance novel habit and her arthritis. She was obviously hard at work down here, protecting the accumulated knowledge of her order, but she just as obviously loved her work.

I cleared my throat and drove on toward my initial purpose in New Orleans. "I had hoped to speak with Sister Evangeline," I said. "Her assistance would be welcome in my current endeavor."

"Finding the Horn of the Herald?" Mother Eunice asked. My face must have registered my surprise because she laughed again. "When I spoke with your digital friend," she nodded to my phone, "he told me who you are and what you are doing here. We typically stay far from Council business, but this seems important. Evangeline isn't here, however. She is hunting in the swamps. We have had several bodies appear in recent weeks, and the most recent was a teenage boy who went out frog gigging last weekend. His body was found Wednesday. His legs were not."

"I am sorry to hear that," I said. "Do you think you could help me?"

"Our archives and my knowledge are at your disposal, but Evangeline is the Arm of the Order. She is the only Sister who bears weapons. The rest are all pure researchers."

This took me aback, and I let that show. "I was led to believe that the Sisters of the Sword were a military order."

"We are," Eunice replied. "But we are much more the weapon development side of the military. All our Sisters are trained in the arts of war, and all *can* bear arms if the situation warrants it, but unless the end times are truly upon us, Sister Evangeline is the only armed one among us."

"So, I can use your library, but you won't stand with me against whoever is calling demons in New Orleans," I said.

"Unless His Holiness in Rome orders us to do so, which I doubt even your friend Luke could persuade Him to do."

So she knew about Luke. That almost certainly meant they knew exactly who and what I was and had plans to deal with me if I became unruly. That put a damper on any arguments I had planned, so I switched tactics. "You knew Oliver?" I asked, pointing to the necklace I wore.

A sad smile crossed her face. "I did. We know most of the major practitioners in the city and have traded knowledge with them over the years. Oliver was a good man, and he cared deeply for his friends. He spoke often of you, wishing that you would visit more frequently."

"I wish it, too, now." I found the words to be true. No matter how diligently I worked to avoid human connections, the stolen heart in my chest kept drawing me back to the short-lived candles. It was just like a fire, warm and comforting right up to the second it burns. That is exactly how humans are to me. They are sources of such inspiration and joy, and the source of almost all my pain as well.

"I think whoever called the demon today is the same person that murdered Oliver," I said. I hoped that this information would persuade Eunice to join my hunt for his killer.

"I believe you are almost certainly correct," she said.

"And still you will not aid me?"

"I will lend you every bit of aid that we can. We have healed your wounds, added a number of impressive stitches to the patchwork quilt of your flesh, and I am here to walk you through our library in search of any information you need. But we will not become involved in your quest, either the one for vengeance or for the Horn."

"Not vengeance," I said. "Justice."

"Be careful that you can tell the difference between the two," she replied. "Many men cannot."

"I have known both in my time," I said, remembering the feeling of a delicate throat beneath my fingers. Murdering Victor's bride had been vengeance. There had been no justice in taking her life. She never harmed me, and killing her did not balance accounts between my "father" and me.

"Do you know who this man is that is killing magic users in New Orleans?"

"I do not," she replied.

"Do you know if he is the one who summoned the demon to attack Jermaine?"

"I do not," she repeated. "But it seems likely."

"Where is Jermaine?" I asked.

"He is here. We can keep him here, or you can take him to Evangeline. If this man is as dangerous as we believe, then it may be best if he is not within the city."

"Where is Evangeline?"

"She's up by Baton Rouge in the Atchafalaya Wildlife Refuge. There have been reports of a black gator up there that's gone man-eater. She went up three days ago. We confirmed this morning that she is staying at a cabin in the swamp, hunting the creature."

"I've never heard of a black gator," I admitted.

"I would be surprised if you had. It is not a natural gator," she said. "It's a zombie gator. Some of the priestesses out in the swamp raise them up for security. They're big, strong, and terrifying, but they tend to be very docile as long as their creator maintains tight control over them. That has not happened in this case, and several people were killed by the creature. Evangeline is also looking for the person who raised the alligator. She has expressed a desire to have a conversation with them."

I was not surprised by this. I would be surprised, however, if the voodoo practitioner left the "conversation" unscathed. I had seen the results of Evangeline's conversations before. They often featured brass knuckles, and once or twice, a shotgun.

"I will take Jermaine to stay with Evangeline in the morning," I said.

"Why do you wish to wait? If you leave as soon as your clothes arrive, you could go and get to Evangeline before full dark."

"Jermaine has a show tonight," I said. "I would hate to deprive him of that income, particularly since part of his home was destroyed today."

She smiled at me, a tight, mirthless grin. "And you think that the man you seek may come to this show, giving you an opportunity to kill him."

"Killing a man in a crowded nightclub, even if the man murdered one of my few friends, is not something that I would consider a wise choice." I paused and touched the medal hanging on a chain around my neck. "But I would not speak ill of fate should it place me in an alley with the man who attacked Oliver." I offered up a mirthless smile of my own.

"Well, far be it from us to keep you from your chosen path of destruction, Adam." She stood, and I got the distinct impression that I had disappointed her somehow. I felt a brief pang for that, but it subsided quickly. I have spent over a century disappointing people; it has become almost second nature to me.

"I will go to the club, watch Jermaine's set, and make sure that he is not attacked and that the Horn remains safe. Tomorrow morning, we will set off to find Evangeline, and hopefully she will be able to keep him safe until the threat has been resolved."

"You will not offend me if you use the word killed, Adam," she said with a smile.

"I doubt you have such delicate sensibilities," I said. "But some things are better left unsaid."

Eunice stood and motioned for me to follow her. "Let me escort you to a room where you can change. I believe the delivery man should be here with your clothes by now."

We stepped into the hall and walked down a different corridor than the one I had taken to her library. "Is there anything you can tell me about this medal?" I asked, fingering the heart with the cross affixed to it.

"I don't know very much about it," Eunice admitted. "I blessed the crucifix in the waters of our sanctuary, and I believe Oliver mentioned fashioning some protective spells into the medal, but if it possesses any mystical properties, I am unaware of them. Why? Does it bother you?"

"It doesn't bother me, but when we first met, it glowed and grew warm to the touch, as if letting me know that you meant me no harm."

I saw her nod, but could not see her face, walking behind her in the narrow hallway. "That seems like the type of protection Oliver would have imbued the medallion with. He was very concerned with some of your associations. He felt that many people would attempt to manipulate you, and that you may not always be sophisticated enough to see it, given the isolation you typically prefer."

I closed my eyes against a rising tide of annoyance. Oliver spent decades working to convince me that Vlad was the monster the books made him out to be, and nothing I ever told him would change his mind. I had no doubt that he, or Harker, was the manipulator that Oliver intended to protect me against.

"Well, I don't need a personal good intentions meter, but if it contains any additional protective capabilities, I would be a fool to discard it," I said.

"It may well be the thing that kept you alive this afternoon by dissipating the demon warrior's fire just enough for you to slay it."

"I wouldn't mind if it had dissipated a little of the piercing agony I had in my hands, but I suppose that is too much to ask," I said.

"It is a very small necklace, Adam. It can only do so much." She stopped before an unmarked door and opened it. A room very similar to the autopsy room I awakened in lay before us, but this one had a pair of shopping bags on the bed. I ducked through the doorway and turned back to Eunice.

"Thank you," I said. "I appreciate your help. Were it not for your healing magics, I would undoubtedly be incapacitated, and that could prove ruinous to our quest. I do not wish to seem ungrateful, for I certainly am thankful for your aid."

She smiled, a warm thing that spread across her face like dawn. "Of course, Adam. Some of us are required to walk a darker path while some of us are fortunate enough to stride through the light. Your path is a shadowed one, but you may take some of our light with you on your journey." She reached out and placed a hand on my chest, covering the amulet Oliver left me. I felt the medal grow warm and saw a golden light bleed out through Eunice's fingers.

"Go with God, Adam. May He watch over you always." She turned and walked back down the hall as I stepped inside the room to dress.

"Thank you, Eunice," I whispered as I closed the door. "But He might not want to see all the things I have to do in His name."

I stepped out into the evening air, the muggy Louisiana heat fading with the moonrise, and pulled the new phone from my pocket. I pressed a button on the side, and Dennis' unicorn face appeared.

"How's it hanging, big guy? Don't answer that. You can get kinda literal at times, and there are some things I really don't want to know."

"I'm fine, Dennis. I don't know what the Sisters did to me in there, but my wounds are mostly healed."

"From what I understand, they prayed a lot, gave you like eight units of blood, and then shocked your heart back to pumping with some ridiculous amount of electricity. I think I'm going to need to make a donation to the convent just to help them pay their power bill next month."

"That is quite a lot of blood," I said.

"Yeah, most people have like twelve units in them, at most. You're bigger than most people, but you were running on empty by the time they got you here. And there was a lot of blunt force trauma going on, and a bunch of shredded tendons. Whatever prayers they sent up, they must have been answered. I didn't think you were going to be moving for days, and I figured it would be at least a week before you could use your hands again," Dennis' face morphed into his human guise, and the concern was evident on his digitized mien.

I looked at my right hand where I had gripped the demon's armor and driven spikes clear through the back of my palm. There were fresh white scars all over it, crisscrossing my skin with more reminders of the punishment I have inflicted upon myself over the years, but I felt no pain. The fingers flexed, the wrist bent, everything worked perfectly. "I suspect there may have been more than simple prayers at work in that convent, Dennis."

"Well, you know the Templars, Adam. They've got all their ancient rituals and spells and shit. At least some of them do. That big goofball in Georgia seems to get by on dumb luck and large-caliber bullets."

"There are worse ways to go through life," I replied. "How far am I from the club where Jermaine is playing tonight?" I wanted to move the subject from my miraculous recovery before we got too far down the rabbit hole of contemplating my existence. That road never takes me anywhere good.

"About six blocks," Dennis replied. "He's already there, holed up in a back room. The ER docs said he didn't have a concussion, so they cleared him to play. I made sure the bills were covered. You know jazz musicians aren't exactly rolling in money."

"I do not approve of theft, Dennis."

"I do not care, Adam. Besides, I stole it from David Duke's offshore bank account. If you can't steal from a former Klansman to pay for a black horn player's hospital visit, who can you steal from?"

I had to admit, the concept did have a certain ironic appeal to it. "I suppose I can let that go this time," I said, calling up a map on my phone and walking toward the blinking lights of the nightclub. "Dennis, I have to ask. What in the world made you decide upon these clothes?" I was dressed in the ensemble provided by the Sisters, which they assured me was sent over by "my associate." I wore a New Orleans Saints black hoodie with "Who Dat?" on the chest in huge letters, a pair of neon green and purple high-top basketball shoes, and a pair of blue jeans with patches of various colors on them. Under my zip-up hoodie was a black t-shirt with a silhouette of a woman swinging on a pole and a caption that read, "I support single moms." The entire chaotic mess was topped with my fedora. The overall effect was, in short, awful.

"Do you like 'em?" Dennis asked. "I just thought about something I'd like to wear after almost dying at the hands of a demonic warlord and super-sized it. I thought the feather in the hat really topped off the outfit nicely. Gives you kind of a rakish vibe, you know?"

His face looked so enthusiastic, so genuinely happy at the spectacularly awful things I wore, that I couldn't bring myself to tell him what I really thought. "They're lovely, Dennis. I couldn't have picked out a better outfit myself."

He looked at me for a brief moment, then doubled over with laughter. "Dude," he exclaimed. "That was great! You looked like somebody had switched your sugar with salt and you just put three spoonfuls in your coffee. Yeah, I know it's all awful. Except the t-shirt. I thought that was hilarious. It was the first shop I could find with enough crap in your size to get you out of the convent not wrapped in a sheet. You've got plenty of time to get to your hotel and change before you go make sure nobody murders Jermaine. There should be a room key in the pocket of those pants. Here, I'll reroute your map."

I looked at the screen, and a detour appeared, showing my hotel. "Thank goodness," I said. "I was afraid I was going to have to wear these horrible shoes all night."

"Hey, cut me a little slack. Size nineteen shoes aren't easy to come by on short notice, so try not to wreck everything in your room this time. I'm gonna have to raid the Saints' equipment room if you need more clothes. I think New Orleans is now officially out of size 4XL, Tall."

I walked to my hotel and changed, then headed to the club. I was now dressed in a much more subdued pair of black cargo pants, black t-shirt, and black combat boots. I kept the Saints hoodie to make me look more like a tourist than a Delta Force operative and had a pair of oversized brass knuckles in each pocket. I also had Oliver's medal around my neck under my shirt and a long silver dagger in a sheath hidden in the small of my back.

I stepped into the alley beside The Famous Door and pulled a five-dollar bill from my pocket. I handed it to the doorman at the aptly named Alley Club, and he looked up at me.

"Please don't start anything," he said. "I don't want to find out which one of us is the baddest man in the room."

"I have no intention of starting anything," I replied. "I just want to hear Thunder Travis play."

"That's good, man. Thunder's good, dawg. He can blow that horn, man. Here's a ticket for a free drink. On me." He passed me a small orange carnival ticket with the smile of man who has been in many bar fights in his time and has no desire to be in any more. I took the ticket with a nod and ducked into the club.

It was a small room, maybe thirty feet by twenty, with a long bar down one wall and windows lining the opposite. A low stage, perhaps twelve inches high, took up most of one end of the room, with a narrow hallway leading back to what I assumed was a dressing room or green room area. A dozen or so round tables were scattered around the room, and I took a seat at one that allowed me to put my back to the far wall and maintain a clear line of sight to the rest of the room. Once the room grew crowded, it would be more difficult, but as long as the crowd was small, or seated, I could see the stage and the entrance perfectly.

I ordered a whiskey and water from the young waitress and passed her the ticket and two singles when she brought it. She smiled and tucked the cash into her front pocket, then dropped the ticket onto her tray and hurried off to deliver more drinks.

The room began to fill up as nine o'clock drew near, and shortly after the hour, Jermaine stepped on stage. He wore a dark suit, with gleaming white shoes and dark sunglasses, a far cry from the itinerant street musician I'd watched play in the park earlier that day, and a different person altogether from the terrified young man I'd seen after the demon attack. This was a cool cat, a calm, collected musician about to ply his trade in front of room full of adoring fans. Admittedly, the room was only about half full, and the fans were more intoxicated than adoring, but he was still very much a man in control of his destiny. At least as long as I could keep him alive.

"Good evening," he said into the microphone. "My name is Jermaine Travis, but my coaches used to call me Thunder."

Polite applause rippled across the gathered listeners, and I watched one overweight man wearing several dozen strands of colorful Mardi Gras beads lean over to the emaciated woman next to him and whisper something in her ear. I could almost make out "LSU" from his words and assumed he was a football fan.

Jermaine put the trumpet to his lips and started to play. He was, as I saw that afternoon in the park, a good musician, but there was nothing extraordinary about his playing. I detected no magic coming from him other than the magic that all talented musicians bring to their performances. His band was tight, full of obvious professionals, but it was just as obvious that playing gigs in bars was likely the pinnacle of their careers.

The spark that transforms a pleasant night listening to music with good whiskey into a memory, the tiny flame that fans into a life-changing talent, that was nowhere present in these men. They were good, perfectly enjoyable, but there was no hint of the divine in them. This was not my missing Archangel. But judging by the heat growing in the amulet pressed to my chest, *something* supernatural was nearby.

I looked around, shifting my focus from the band on stage to the room around me, and noticed two things. First, the bouncer had left his post at the door to roust a homeless man from hanging around outside the bar's alley window, and second, that the well-dressed man from this afternoon was now sitting right next to me.

I turned to him, looking up and down at the interloper at my table, and he smiled at me. The song ended, and he extended a hand. "Pardon the intrusion, friend, but I saw your table was empty and thought you could maybe spare the seat."

He made no threatening moves, and I had no desire to cause a scene in the crowded bar, so I just nodded at him. I took his hand and said, "You're welcome to join me. I'm Adam."

"Thank you. My name is Martin." He drew his hand back, and I noticed a spot of brown on the French cuff of his shirt, just by the diamond-studded cufflink.

He saw my gaze and pulled his jacket down to cover the spot. "Sorry," he said with a rueful smile. "I had a po' boy for dinner and got a touch of sauce on my sleeve."

I could read the lie, but not the reason, so I let it stand. I cared not a bit about the man's dinner, just his plans for Jermaine. Everything about him made my senses scream, but this was not the time or place. I turned back to the stage as Thunder and his Lightning Bolts began a new tune, but my pocket began to vibrate. I stood, pulling out my phone, and wove through the tables and out the front door.

I tapped the screen and held the phone to my ear. "Hello?"

"Adam?" The voice on the other end was female, and frantic. "Adam, it's Madison. Come quick. Something killed Xander. Right here in my shop, Adam. Something got in here through all my wards and murdered my nephew."

11

I got to the back entrance on Marie Laveau's less than five minutes after Madison's call, and there was already a crowd gathering in the tiny courtyard behind the narrow building. A large black man with a shaved head and a pistol on his hip stepped into my path, putting one hand on my chest and the other on the butt of his gun. He was dressed in black tactical pants, black boots, and a black t-shirt. Everything about him screamed former military, particularly the flat glare he gave me as he looked up into my eyes.

"The store is closed, sir. There's been an emergency. You'll have to come back later." He pushed against my chest, but I just kept moving forward.

"Where is Madison? Is she hurt?"

"Sir, I'm going to need—" I swatted him aside, knocking him into another guard and taking them both down. He did everything right, working to control my movements, shift my momentum, all the things he should have done to stop me without causing harm. He just didn't take into account exactly what he was dealing with.

"Adam?" I heard Madison's voice and turned to see her sitting at a round wrought-iron table. A white man in a suit knelt beside her, and he was taking a blood pressure cuff off her arm as I went to her.

"What's wrong, Maddie? Are you okay? Did it hurt you?" I heard the questions tumble over my lips faster than anyone could hope to answer, but I couldn't stop myself. The torrent of words poured forth, and I recognized a rarely-felt emotion in myself: fear. I was afraid for her. Afraid to lost another one of my very few friends to violence. A violence that I may very well have brought into her life.

I knelt beside her and took her hand. It felt even smaller than usual, and I could feel the butterfly wingbeats of her pulse in her wrist. Her heart raced as she looked up into my eyes, too tall to look directly at even on one knee.

"I'm not injured, if that's what you mean. Frederick just wanted to make sure I wasn't having a heart attack." She patted the leg of the man, who now stood slightly behind her. Madison turned back to me. "Whatever got in there, Adam, it tore Xander to pieces. It was...horrible. I've never seen so much blood."

Coming from Madison, and knowing the sanguine nature of some rituals she had performed, that was saying something. "Can I go in?" I asked. "Are the police coming?"

"No." The voice came from behind me, and I turned to see the big security guard standing there. He looked angry, and his gun was in his hand now. It was pointed down at the ground, but it was definitely positioned to raise and fire faster.

"No, I can't go in? Or no, the police aren't coming?" I asked, rising. I probably could have avoided the macho posturing, but I was upset, and feeling guilty, and it brought out my inner masculine idiot.

He stared up at me for long enough to count to twenty, and it felt like none of the other people in the small courtyard breathed. There was a sense of anticipation in the air, like a fuse had been lit and an explosion of violence was imminent. Finally, just before I thought I was going to have to smear this man across the walls like spackle, he let out a deep breath and holstered his pistol.

"No, the police aren't coming. I would prefer if you didn't go in there, but I won't try to stop you."

"Thank you," I said, and I could see the surprise in his eyes. "I think this part of New Orleans has seen enough violence for one night."

"I think there's still a little violence to be meted out, myself," he replied with a tight smile, and I knew he didn't mean to me.

I nodded, and we silently acknowledged each other in that way that men who shed the blood of others regularly have. I turned back to Madison and knelt beside her.

"Was he alone, Maddie? Or were you here?" I asked, keeping my voice soft. The rest of the alley didn't need to know these things.

"He was alone, Adam. I left him here cataloging some herbs and some new books that we got in. Harmless things, not anything with true power of their own. I never let him mess with the real magic. He didn't have no power to protect himself with, so I couldn't let him mess around with anything that might be carrying a curse."

"Do you have security cameras? Do they show anything?" I asked.

Maddie looked up at the big man, who dropped to a knee beside me. "There are cameras. We haven't reviewed the footage yet. It's one of the first things we'll do after we..." He looked at Madison. "Um..."

"He trying to say they got to get Xander's body out the way first," she said. I noticed her accent was heavier than normal, the stress of the night making her slip back into some of the patois she was raised around.

"I have people coming," the security man said.

"I would like to see the scene without any disturbances," I said. "I won't move anything, and I certainly won't touch anything," I said. This last was to Madison. I knew there were very potent magical items around the store, and some of those things could be triggered by contact with human blood, or by being in the presence of death. Her entire store would be on a hair trigger, only needing one misstep to bring about a magical devastation the likes of which had been unseen in the United States since the Great Chicago Fire.

"You can go in," Madison said. "Be real careful by the door, though. There's a big puddle of blood there. I wouldn't want you tracking that all over my store." She tried to smile, but it broke down into a sob. I stood, patted her on the shoulder in a gesture I hoped appeared more supportive and less awkward than it felt, and walked across the courtyard to the back door of the shop.

I motioned the security guard over. "Keep an eye on her. If anything comes at her, do not hesitate, just shoot it. Shoot it and keep shooting it until you are out of bullets. Then run like hell. I will try to be back out here as fast as I can. Do not try to fight this thing, just put as much lead into it as you can and don't let it get to Maddie."

He nodded, and I turned and walked to the back door. Another guard stood there blocking my path, but he stepped aside after a second of alpha male posturing. I let him posture. I had nothing to prove to the assembled crowd, and he and I both knew how much I cared about whether or not he looked tough.

I pushed the red-painted wooden door open with an elbow and stepped inside. The coppery scent of blood twined with the visceral stench of death to curl around my throat and draw my gorge forth. I took a moment just inside the door to adjust to the dim light and the foul miasma of odors coming from the shop, then stepped into the tiny storeroom. I flipped on a light switch beside the door, and blazing cool fluorescent light illuminated the shelves and the bare wooden floor. The storeroom was clean and seemed undisturbed. Either Alexander was the attacker's target, or it had found its quarry elsewhere in the store.

The passage to the back of the store stood before me, a cascade of discarded Mardi Gras beads fashioned into a curtain over the years by Madison and her predecessors. I pushed my way through the clicking barrier into the small room where Maddie did her readings and scanned the area for anything out of place.

The room was in slight disarray, but far from ransacked. The crystal orb in the center of the table had a huge crack running through the center of it, but it remained intact, except for the new flaw. The box of prognostication implements Madison kept beside the table was overturned, her Tarot cards scattered on the floor, and herbs and runestones tossed across the tabletop. The shelves of books were untouched, and the furniture stood upright. Again, the signs of a casual search.

The front of the store was a different matter, I could see that from the doorway. The curtain door of silks was matted with blood and gore, and as I passed through it, I saw the true savagery that had been unleashed. Alexander was not simply killed, he was *destroyed*. His limbs were torn from his body and cast into the corners of the room, painting the walls and shelves with arterial blood.

His chest and abdomen were ripped open, not by a knife or anything that would leave a clean slice, but by something jagged, something tearing. The front section of his ribcage was ripped from his body and flung at the front door so hard it shattered into pieces no larger than a finger bone. His heart and entrails were removed from his body and placed on the altar to Marie Laveau, his heart's blood smeared over the painting of the Voodoo Queen that sat in an alcove in the store. Alexander's intestines were piled on the altar in a slimy heap, a bastardized offering to the Queen, defiling both her store and her altar.

Worst of all was his head. Whatever had killed Alexander had ripped his head from his body, taking part of the spine and esophagus with it. This gruesome trophy, with eyes wide and mouth fixed in a permanent scream of agony, was given a place of pride atop the cash register, jammed down over the plastic and metal construct hard enough to be immobilized on the makeshift stand.

I reached out and closed his eyes, my one concession to human sentiment. Otherwise, the horrible scene affected me not at all. It was far from the first time I had seen dismembered bodies, some of them at my own hand. This was not my work, though. This was not the work of any human, either. The sheer strength required to pull some-one's head from his shoulders is immense, only possible for someone with strength born of the deaths of many men, or the souls of thousands.

I took a deep breath, letting all the scents of the bookstore-turned-abattoir fill my nose. There it was, underneath the blood and the shit and the guts—sulfur. The stench of the Pits confirmed my suspicions. This was the work of a demon. I wondered briefly if this was connected to the attack on me that afternoon, then pushed all thoughts of investigation aside.

More pressing business demanded my attention—Madison's

safety. I twisted and turned my way through the narrow shop and emerged into the small cobblestone courtyard.

I walked over to where Madison sat with three security guards around her. The one who traveled with me held and stroked her hand while two others stood over her shoulders, their heads on a swivel.

"Madison, we have to leave," I said, standing over her.

She looked up at me, her eyes red-rimmed. "Where can we go, Adam? I won't be safe anywhere. Whatever hurt Xander got through all my wards, got past my threshold, everything."

That was impressive. Threshold magic is old magic, powerful, and not many magicians today can create it, especially in a public place like a store. But Madison was not like many magicians, and that may be the only thing that would keep her alive.

"You have to leave, and you have to leave now, Maddie. That thing was not after Alexander; it was after you. We should not mince words, so I will not call it a thing. We should just call it for what it is. It is a demon, Maddie. I fought a Knight of Hell this afternoon, and barely survived, and now there is another demon in New Orleans, and it means to kill you. So come with me if you want to live."

12

It was either my persuasive argument or my uncharacteristic popular culture reference, but Madison agreed to leave the city with me. Her security team, who she referred to as members of her congregation, provided us with a battered passenger van and a pair of armed escorts. We rolled north out of the city in a twenty-five-year-old Ford van with "2nd Antioch Missionary Baptist Church, Metairie, LA" emblazoned on the side in faded white script letters. I drove, Madison rode in the front bench seat behind me, and one of her "congregation members" rode shotgun. Literally, as he carried a pump-action shotgun and a scowl. The other congregant sat on the rear seat facing out the big back window with an AK-47 on the seat beside him and enough ammunition to invade Lichtenstein.

I have been to Lichtenstein many times. It is a lovely country but offers very little in the way of military might. It is quite possible that I could invade the country with an old van and two armed men by my side. Having a witch along with us would just be overkill.

We rode north for several hours, until my passengers were all fast asleep. I remained perfectly alert, as I require very little sleep. I was unable to contact Evangeline or any of her people, but Dennis assured me that he had a lock on her position, and as long as we made it to her camp before sunrise, she would still be there. While speaking with him, I asked that he maintain surveillance on Jermaine while I was gone, just in case our predator went after him in my absence. I had no reason to believe the musician was in danger, but in light of recent events, I felt justified in being overly cautious.

So it was that I pulled an antique church van up in front of what appeared to be an old bootlegger's or smuggler's cabin deep in the swamps of Louisiana in the predawn glow. I stopped the van, and my cargo came awake with a groan. I rolled down my window, and the thick scent of swamp moss and over-still water rankled my nose. The early morning sounds of bullfrogs and owls echoed through the clearing, and I heard a small splash as something dropped into the water nearby.

"Oh sweet Jesus on the cross, Adam, why did you let me fall asleep?" Madison groaned from behind me. She grinned at me and stretched, the bones along her spine crackling with stiffness and age.

"I was not in a position to stop you, Madison," I replied. "Besides, you needed your rest. You had quite the shock last night."

"You can say that again," she replied, her smile vanishing. The two gunmen got out of the van and fanned out in opposite directions, guns held low and heads sweeping from side to side. I thought about calling out to them, but decided to let them test their training and ability against that of a sleeping nun. I have often been accused of having no sense of humor, but I found the concept of Sister Evangeline disarming two militaristic members of a voodoo cult hilarious.

Perhaps I simply have a more well-developed sense of humor than most people.

A series of thuds and a small *crack* came from one side of the shack, and I opened my door and slid out to the ground. "Don't kill them, Evangeline," I called out. "It's Adam. They're with me."

"Shit, *cher*," a rich voice said from behind the shack. "I been out here nine days and ain't been able to kill anything. I was hoping a little voodoo thug blood be what I needed for gatorbait."

A minute later a striking woman came around the corner with one of Madison's security draped across her shoulders. Sister Evangeline dumped the unconscious man on his back in the front yard of the cabin and shot me a grin. I smiled back, unable to help myself. Evangeline was a lovely woman, with skin the color of coffee with two creams, long black curly hair, and almond-shaped violet eyes that told the story of her mixed African, French, Asian, and something indeterminate heritage like a roadmap of the world.

She was a tall woman with broad shoulders. Strongly built, she had little trouble carrying the unconscious man and her ever-present twelve gauge at the same time. She was dressed for the swamp in high mud boots and a tattered t-shirt, her hair pulled back in a long ponytail. She walked over to me and wrapped her arms around my waist, squeezing tightly.

"It's good to see you again, you big idiot," she said into my chest.

I felt a warmth suffuse me at her words, and I returned her hug, albeit much more lightly. I am not known for my approachability, and I am far from what one would consider a "hugger," but Evangeline cared nothing for that, or for anyone's personal space. If she wanted to hug you, you were getting hugged. And at that moment, I was very definitely getting hugged.

After a brief moment, she stepped back and extended her hand to Madison. "Ms. Laveau, I'm Sister Evangeline. I'm the Hunter for this region."

Madison cocked her head to the side and looked Evangeline up and down. "How you know my last name, girl?"

"Like I said, I'm the Hunter for dese parts, ma'am. I make it my business to know everybody in my city." The two women looked at each other for a long time, and I got the distinct feeling that something was passing unsaid between them, but I neither knew nor cared.

"Evie," I said, and Evangeline's head snapped around at my uncharacteristic use of her nickname. "We need your help. There is a demon in New Orleans, and it's after Madison."

"Could you be a tad more specific, *cher*? Is this a new demon, or is this one of the regulars?" Evangeline asked.

I will admit, I was taken aback by the question and had to blink a few times to collect myself. "I'm sorry," I said. "You have regular demons?"

"Well, not in the sense that they customers or something, like I run a bar, but there's some demons that live in the city, yeah. One runs a tattoo parlor out by the airport, but he ain't nowhere near strong enough to make you run out of town, even if he decided to stop tattooing and start harvesting the old-fashioned way. Then there's a couple in the Quarter, but they mostly just pouring beers or playing jazz. One's a hooker at the casino, but she's just a run-of-the-mill succubus. I reckon couldn't none of the local demons make you nervous, much less leave town. I reckon that makes this a new one."

I looked at Evangeline, not quite understanding how to proceed. A Hunter, a Knight Templar, with demons living in her city, and she allows them to remain? She saw the confusion writ large upon my face and laughed.

"Oh good Lord himself, Adam, cut a girl some slack. These demons just want out of Hell. They ain't causing no trouble. Not like whatever got you so riled up. So tell me, what brings the son of Frankenstein and the granddaughter of Marie Laveau out to the swamp to chase down one stupid ol' nun?"

I explained the situation, how I believed a sorcerer or demon murdered Oliver, the attack on me at Jermaine's house, Alexander's dismemberment, and how I brought Madison to her for protection. When I was finished, Evangeline looked up at me, shaking her head.

"Man, Adam, that Quincy Harker, he get you into some of the stupidest things. You must really feel like you owe him something."

I nodded, then said, "It is much more to do with what I owe his uncle, but yes, I do owe Harker and the Shadow Council a debt."

"And I owe one to you, so I reckon this is where you call dat in," she said with a rueful smile.

"I was of the hope that you would help me because it was the right thing to do, not to balance any ledgers between us," I replied.

"Whatever helps you sleep at night, you big ox." But she smiled when she said it, a genuine smile this time, full of the warmth I had come to expect from the salty monster-hunting nun. "I'll keep an eye on the voodoo princess, but you got to help me finish something first. I can't dedicate no time to looking out for her while I still got a man-eating gator in these swamps."

"You want me to hunt an alligator with you?" I asked. I will admit to feeling a slight thrill at the idea. I had never battled an alligator but had always had immense respect for the creatures. Nearly unchanged for eons, the alligator has always been a fascinating creature to me. Their muscled bodies, their armored skin, it all combined to form a brilliant hunting machine. I found myself looking forward to engaging one of these legendary beasts.

"Yeah, and to be honest, I might need you with me," the nun replied. "I found the wreck of an airboat this beastie got hold of yesterday, and it was pretty wrecked. Last I heard, there were three old swamp rats going out lookin' for this bad boy the day before I got here, and by the looks of this boat, they found him. Or he found them, rather. There weren't enough left of any of them boys to Carbon-14 date, and unless you can match dental records to three teeth, we ain't ever gonna be sure if it's them, but I found an airboat tore into half a dozen pieces and painted with blood, and one old Caterpillar boot with a foot and ankle still in it. That's all that was left of them boys. Made me think this critter might be more than I can handle on my own."

That was a sobering thought. Evangeline had been the Hunter for the Gulf Coast region for more than a decade, and I had known her to battle vampires, lycanthropes of all variety, shades, ghouls, more zombies than a season of *The Walking Dead* extras, and at least one banshee. All without batting an eye. If this alligator was giving her pause, it would certainly be a challenge.

"I will be more than happy to assist you, but we need to make sure that Madison will be safe here without our protection," I said.

"She oughta be fine," Evangeline said. "I don't know how you found me, much less how anyone else would get to this place."

"I have some…unusual resources," I replied. She gave me a questioning look, but I did not elaborate. Dennis was a very useful associate, but I felt that his peculiar existence may be objectionable to the Church, and Evangeline was, after all, a nun.

"Well, your resources must be pretty damn unusual indeed," she agreed. "'Cause this place ain't on no maps, or no property records, and my cell phone oughta be untraceable. Evidently not, though."

I did not reply. I merely turned to Madison. "What do you think? Can this shack be defended with only two men?"

Evangeline held up a hand. "Hold up a second before you answer that." She turned to go into the small building and waved for us to follow her.

We did, and once we were inside the shack, many of my doubts about the security of the small patch of swampland faded away. What appeared from the outside to be a one-room shack was, in fact, the top floor of a multi-level reinforced concrete bunker, complete with metal blast shutters to close over the windows, sealable airlock hatches separating the floors, and a front door worthy of a bank vault. On the lowest level was a command center with multiple displays showing views of the entire perimeter from hidden security cameras; an armory with a full complement of guns, blades, and one rocket launcher; and shelves with enough food to last for at least a month.

Madison looked up at me and said, "Somehow I think we'll be just fine."

I turned to Evangeline. "Then we can go hunt your killer alligator, then I can return to New Orleans and hunt a killer demon."

She laughed and said, "Adam, I don't know if you really are immortal, but I swear you keep running with that Harker boy and you damn sure gonna find out. Let's go get us a gator."

13

The brownish green water rippled out from the sides of the airboat as Evangeline steered us into the narrow channel. I glanced behind us to see the reeds already popped back into place and the wake dying to leave no hint of our passing except the silence of the birds and the frogs behind us. Spanish moss hung down from huge live oak trees, masking the snakes that undoubtedly nestled above us, just waiting to drop from the branches onto our unsuspecting heads and necks. Every ripple in the water was a moccasin, every splash another alligator. The mosquitos were the size of small birds, and not for the first time I was very happy that my blood did not flow normally.

We delved into the heart of the swamp for nearly an hour before Evangeline cut the engine and allowed us to drift. "This is where the monster was last seen," she said, standing up from her pilot's seat and hefting her shotgun. "I don't see no sign of it, but I reckon if it heard our boat, it'll take it a minute or two to come looking after us."

I scanned the water for ripples, knowing nothing better to do. I have never been an aquatic creature. My mass makes it difficult for me to float, and I do not disrobe in public for fear of frightening crowds, so trips to the beach have never been my chosen vacation. I can swim if need be, but as I do not require breath for anything other than speech, if I must traverse a body of water, oftentimes I simply walk across the bottom.

A splash from behind and to my left caused me to spin around, bringing my own shotgun to bear on the sound. Evangeline laughed, a deep, throaty sound full of mirth, but no malice.

"It's alright, *cher*," she said, her voice cutting through the muggy air like a knife. "Just chumming the waters, as they say."

I looked at her and saw her with one hand deep in a white five-gallon bucket at her feet. She pulled her hand out, and I saw it held a fistful of entrails. I gave her a questioning look.

"Pig guts, *cher*. How we gonna catch a predator if we ain't got no bait? Unless you want to jump in the water and splash around a little bit?" She grinned and lobbed the mass of innards into the water on the other side of the boat.

"Have you any concern with attracting other predators too numerous to handle?" I asked.

"Nah, baby," she said, an easy smile playing across her lips. "Anything stupid enough to share the water with a black gator gonna get eat up real fast, so we either gonna get some little nasties, which I figure we can handle easy enough, or we gonna get one great big nasty, and that might take more work." She flicked on the flashlight slung under the barrel of her Mossberg and pointed the gun back at the water. The flashlight's beam only penetrated a few inches into the swamp water, the brown and greens of muck and algae too much for the sharp, blue-white light.

We drifted, listening for any sign of the man-eater, following the gentle currents of the swamp for nearly an hour before Evangeline waved a hand at me. I looked where she was pointing and saw nothing but an enormous rock protruding from the surface of the brackish water. I peered around the boulder for any sign of the gator, then started when the boulder itself opened one eye and cast a baleful gaze at us. The head, easily six feet long, rotated around, and the massive creature heaved itself to its feet. At least twelve feet of alligator loomed above the surface of the water, with none of the tail visible.

"Mary, Mother of God," I heard Evangeline whisper behind me.

I turned to her and said, in all sincerity, "I think we're going to need a bigger boat."

"And bigger guns," she replied with a nod.

"And perhaps a tank," I agreed.

The gator slid into the water, moving with surprising speed and silence for such a massive creature. Its tail coursed through the water, and I could see that it was at least as long as the rest of the alligator. We had somewhere in the neighborhood of twenty-five feet of massive, toothy lizard swimming toward us, and two shotguns with which to handle it. I felt uneasy about our chances, and by the look on her face, so did Evangeline.

"Did you know it was this big?" I asked.

"The guide who took me to the wrecked airboat told me it musta been at least twenty feet long based on the bite marks in the hull. I thought he was exaggerating. Ain't never been no gator more than twenty feet long, according to the official records."

"I suppose this little fellow is making unofficial records, then," I said. I thumbed on the flashlight on my own shotgun and aimed the beam at the water. The gator's tail disappeared as it approached, and Evangeline jumped down from the pilot's chair.

"Be careful, he might have dove down to—" Her words were cut off as a huge *THUMP* came from beneath the boat, and the shallow craft rocked hard to one side. The airboat flipped, and Evangeline and I flew out in opposite directions. I held onto my gun but saw hers spin through the air, leaving her defenseless.

I hit the water on my back and sank like a stone. I managed to right myself in the few seconds I had before making contact with the bottom and opened my eyes to find the alligator. The murky water made it very difficult to see anything, but the thrashing mass about eight feet in front of me looked like the most likely spot for my quarry.

I took two steps toward the thrashing gator and raised my shotgun. The chamber was loaded, with five more slugs behind, so I stood on the bottom of the swamp and pressed the gun into my shoulder. I squeezed the trigger, and a cloud of bubbles issued from the barrel of the shotgun as it exploded in my hands. Pieces of the shattered barrel whizzed by my face, and a few fragments of shrapnelized Mossberg lodged in my chest, arms, and legs.

I stared at the ruined weapon as the gator emerged from the cloud of silt and air bubbles that had hidden it from view. I dove to my right as the creature bit down on empty space that I had occupied seconds before, then skidded backward, falling to my rear and then throwing myself flat on my back as the gator spun around unbelievably fast and snapped hundreds of razor-sharp teeth shut right above me.

The monster whirled around again as I scrambled to my feet, this time heading straight for me with its mouth open wide enough to fit half of my torso inside with one gulp. I jammed the gun between those massive teeth as its jaws slammed together, wedging the beast's mouth open. The jagged edges of the destroyed barrel pierced the gator's soft upper palate and its tongue, and the shredded metal stuck fast. The monster jerked its head back, bringing me with it, as I had not let go of the gun. It swam backward, dragging me along and thrashing all the way. Then it spun around, and I was forced to let go of the gun with one hand and reposition myself astride the beast's head.

The alligator swam through the swamp, thrashing and rolling and contorting and twisting to free itself from the thing biting its mouth and the nuisance on its back, but neither I nor my gun would be dislodged.

The monster thrashed, but I held on. It rolled, throwing huge clouds of sand and muck into the water, but I held on. It worried me like a rag doll hanging from a St. Bernard's mouth, but I held on. After almost a full minute of wrestling with this enormous predator, my strength began to flag. My arms felt leaden, my back and legs were battered and ready to give, and my lungs filled with mucky water and algae stirred up from the bottom of the river.

The gator swam forward, shoving me back. I slid along the bottom of the swamp bed, leaving great parallel furrows in the brown water. I clung to the shotgun as though my life depended on it. It likely did depend on it, given the size of the alligator. For the first time in many years, I actually thought I might not survive a fight. Even battling demons with Harker, I always thought that I would eventually prevail. I was much less certain about the outcome of this battle.

I felt the uncertainty morph within me into something different, something I had not felt in decades. I felt a prickle of fear, and a rush of excitement coursed through me. My lips pulled back in a fierce grin, and the muscles in my arms and shoulders grew taut with fresh, exhilarated blood. I shifted my weight and planted my feet, halting the creature's forward progress. It thrashed from side to side, but the shattered barrel was jutting through the alligator's snout at one end, and wedged tight between two teeth at the stock. The creature could neither open nor close its mouth, just flail wildly trying to free itself from the thing that pained it.

I let go of the gun, releasing the huge reptile. It spun around in a flash, and I lunged for its back before it escaped. My fingers gripped the scaly spines at its front shoulders, and I was hauled off my feet as the alligator swam toward the far shore, dragging me with it. I pulled myself up along the creature's back, slowly climbing closer and closer to my goal, fighting the rush of the water as the gator swam at enormous speed. It slammed into the riverbank with its snout, trying to dislodge the gun from between its jaws. When that didn't work, it lurched up out of the water and rolled on the bank, its tremendous weight crushing me into the earth as it lay on its back and writhed from side to side. I held on, though I both felt and heard ribs cracking under the beast's onslaught.

The alligator righted itself, and I pulled myself farther forward, until I finally sat astride the thing's shoulders, with its head and snout in front of me. I punched downward with one fist, caving in its right eye with a single blow. I slammed my left fist into the other eye, blinding the creature and sending it into another paroxysm of pained thrashing. I leaned forward, pulled my right fist back, and pounded its head and orbital socket again and again until finally I felt the bone crunch beneath my blows.

I unclenched my bloodied and battered fist, made a tight spike from my fingers, and jammed my hand into the alligator's eye socket. My hand met resistance inside the orbital socket, but I leaned forward, wrapping my left arm around the alligator's snout and pressing forward with my entire body weight. I shoved my hand in and in, harder and harder, until finally, with a resounding *crunch*, I shoved my hand through the monster's eye socket into its brain. The beast gave one last mighty shiver, then collapsed, its brain mangled by my fist, dead.

The alligator slumped to the ground, and I rolled off to the side, slamming into the mud and the reeds with a splash. I lay there, staring up at the green canopy, listening as the sounds of life came back to the swamp as our mighty battle, so enormous to me and the gator, was forgotten by the other creatures almost immediately. A smile crept across my face as I lay there cataloging my injuries. I counted three broken fingers; one dislocated pinky; innumerable scratches, scrapes, and cuts; four broken ribs; and what felt like three loose teeth. And one shotgun, dead on the scene.

"Adam!" I heard Evangeline's voice calling for me from somewhere nearby.

I groaned, then when making that much noise proved to not be harmful, I called out, "Here!"

"Where are you?"

"Can you see the gator?"

"Yeah, I see him. He looks dead."

"That's because he's dead," I replied. "I'm lying next to him."

"You two need some alone time?" the nun asked. I frowned for a moment, then understood her question and laughed.

"Ouch. Don't make me laugh," I said.

"It only hurts when you laugh?" Evangeline asked, now standing over me. She was soaked to the skin, but looked otherwise unhurt.

"No, it hurts no matter what I do, but it hurts in extra places when I laugh," I said.

She walked around the gator, inspecting the monster's corpse. "Adam, what in the holy hell happened to your shotgun?"

"I tried to shoot the alligator with it."

"While you was underwater?"

"Yes. It seems that was a poor choice."

"You, my friend, are a master of understatement. But, and I will admit that I'm almost afraid to ask, but I'm going to anyway…how exactly did you kill that gator? It looks like you reached in its eye socket and yanked its brains out."

I lay there for a moment trying to come up with a less barbaric way to phrase it. It didn't exist. "I reached in its eye socket and yanked its brains out."

Evangeline looked down at me for a long few seconds, then said, "I'm gonna go get the boat. You lay there until you feel like you can stand up, then you go wash that arm off. You are not dripping gator brains all over the bottom of my boat."

That sounded like an absolutely fantastic idea.

14

Several hours later, I was in Madison's battered church bus headed back to New Orleans with the sun setting over the swampland all around me. I had spent an entire day with Evangeline, hunting a giant alligator, killing said alligator, and then cleaning alligator brains from under my fingernails. When I left, Madison and her two-man security detail were gearing up for a marathon bridge session with Evangeline, a bottle of whiskey sitting in the center of the table with the cap tossed somewhere into the far corners of the shack. I felt the irony of leaving my friend the voodoo priestess in the care of my friend the nun, but they seemed to be fast friends.

I set my phone on the center console of the van and pressed a button. "Dennis, can you hear me?"

"Yeah, I can hear you, but you're a little muffled. What did you do to your phone this time?"

"I wrestled an alligator. The phone was in my pocket. I am surprised it still works."

"It better work," he said. "That case cost me a hundred bucks."

"You steal all your money from Harker, or corporations you don't like," I pointed out.

"Doesn't mean I want to overpay for stuff," he replied. "What do you need?"

"Do you still have surveillance on Jermaine?"

"Thunderlips?" he asked. "Yeah, I've got him."

"I think he only calls himself 'Thunder,'" I corrected.

"I know, I was...never mind," Dennis sighed. I smiled into the windshield. Frustrating my electronic friend was fast becoming an enjoyable pastime, almost on par with making Quincy wonder if I understood his feeble attempts at humor. Most of the time I did, I just didn't think he was funny. That made it better.

"Okay, I've got eyes on your guy," Dennis said. "He's at the club, cleaning up. He's booked to play starting at ten tonight."

"Is there anyone else there? And have you seen them before?"

"There's a couple of touristy looking guys in khaki cargo pants, looking like soccer dads. There's a young couple making out between bites of crème brûlée, a homeless dude sitting at the end of the bar with his head down, and one guy in an expensive suit sitting alone with his back to a wall. He's not there for the food or the hurricanes, I can tell you that much."

"Why is that?"

"He's got an untouched po' boy in front of him, a glass of water he hasn't touched, and his head is on a swivel. He's trying real hard not to look like he's watching Jermaine, but he picked a table with an unobstructed view of the entire joint."

"Does he look familiar?"

"Yeah, it's the same dude that sat next to you the other night."

"Martin," I said, remembering the man, his graceful movements, and the spot of dark red, almost brown on the cuff of his shirt. "I do not trust that man."

"Me neither, but I don't trust anybody. Call it a side effect of getting murdered by a homicide detective, but my trust level is shot to shit."

"Understandable. My own caution is an outgrowth of being chased from my home by a rampaging horde of villagers with pitchforks and torches," I replied, remembering the smell of smoke pouring into my home, driving me farther up the narrow, winding staircase until I reached the roof of my father's manor house. I could hear the chants of the mob below me, the crackle of the flames and the shattering of windows from the heat as the only home I had known was consumed in the fire that threatened to devour me. I felt the rush of water envelope me as I dove from the roof into the rushing river far below, then the crushing impact as I crashed and bounced into the rocks as the current swept me away.

"Hey, Adam!" Dennis' voice yanked me from my reverie, and I focused once more on the present, and the immediate future.

"Yes, Dennis?"

"You with me, buddy?" There was honest concern in his voice, the usual snark gone.

"Yes, I apologize. I was lost in memory for a moment. Is there anything else happening?"

"Nah, just Thunder straightening up, waiting on the bar customers, and every once in a while going over to the stage to polish his horn. And, man, am I glad that is not a euphemism for something else. Is Madison all squared away? Evangeline has her place so damn locked down I can't even get a satellite image of the place."

"Yes, Madison is safe. But if the camp is blacked out, how did you find it in the first place?"

"I looked for the black hole in my net. There's a blackout zone a half-mile in diameter that I figured was centered on Evangeline's camp, so I pointed you to the middle of it."

I thought for a moment. "What if it had been something else? Something unfriendly?"

"Well…that would have been bad," Dennis admitted. "But it wasn't, so we're good, right? Good deal. Talk to you later, pal!" He disconnected the call before I could point out the errors in his logic. And he was right, it had all worked out, so there was no point in harassing him about it now.

I left Madison's church van in the public parking lot that her people designated, then proceeded on foot to the French Quarter. The club was busier by far than Dennis had described, but I still found an empty table with little trouble. I placed my back to a wall, making sure I had clear sightlines to both the stage and the man who introduced himself as "Martin."

He still sat at a table alone, an untouched sandwich and drink before him. I observed a waitress walk over to him, reach for his glass to clear it, and him wave a hand to stop her. A folded bill and she nodded and walked off, shaking her head at his behavior but obviously content to ignore him as long as he continued tipping.

I sat, ordered a drink, and kept watch on the room. Jermaine ducked out from behind the bar as his replacement showed up, then a few minutes later, he stepped onto the small stage, drawing a smattering of applause from the crowd.

"Hey, y'all," he said, leaning down into a microphone before him. "I'd like to thank y'all for coming out tonight. We gonna play some old stuff, some new stuff, and a few originals. I hope you all have a good time. So now, without any further ado, I'm Thunder Travis, and these are my Lightning Bolts!" He pressed the trumpet to his lips and blew out the first few notes of an upbeat jazz number. The band picked up the rhythm, and they were off to the races.

Thunder and the Bolts played the crowd as much as they played their instruments, dropping into slower, cooler jazz when the crowd was thin, pumping things up when the crowd was hopping, and generally keeping everyone in the room dancing, drinking, or at least tapping toes for the next two hours. Everyone but me, that is. Everyone but me and the businessman in the corner, who kept his head on a swivel as if he were waiting for someone in particular to show up.

After a long set, Jermaine leaned into the mic and said, "Thank y'all! We're gonna take a short break, but we'll be back in twenty minutes or so. If we don't give Ellis a break every couple hours, he sobers up, and the last thing you want in a jazz band is a sober drummer!" The crowd laughed along with the drummer, a stout bald white man in his fifties, who waved at the crowd with a big grin on his face.

The band stepped off the low stage and wove through the crowd toward the bar and the restrooms, accepting congratulatory backslaps and handshakes as they passed happy drunken revelers. Jermaine paused at the end of the bar to exchange an elaborate handshake and hug with the homeless man I had seen in the park the day before. He'd been sitting on the same stool sipping water through the entire set, eyes closed and swaying in time to the music.

I turned my head to resume surveillance on "Martin," only to find his chair empty and his table cleared. I scanned the room but could not see him through the throng of people. I stood, and my height made it a simple thing to spot the man in the expensive suit near the stage. I saw "Martin" pick up Jermaine's trumpet from the stand on the stage, tuck it under his coat in a horrible attempt to mask the thing, and start for the door.

I moved to intercept and cut off his route in the middle of the crowd. "I don't think that belongs to you," I said, nodding at the oddly misshapen lump beneath his suit coat.

"This is none of your business, freak. Get out of my way before you get hurt." His voice was low and gravelly, with an inhuman growl behind it.

"I've been hurt before," I said. "It all heals. And that doesn't belong to you."

"You are meddling in things beyond your ken, mortal," he hissed, and now it sounded as though his tongue was forked, the sibilance taking over his diction.

"There is at least one misconception in that sentence," I replied, then punched him in the face. He staggered back and crashed into the clumped humanity behind him.

"That's for running out on my sister, you dick!" I bellowed, advancing on the well-dressed man as he struggled to get back to his feet and hold on to the trumpet at the same time. I threw an uppercut that lifted him off his feet and flung him back through another clump of people. I stepped into the punch, swinging from my heels and putting nearly my full strength into the blow. If he were human and merely a trumpet thief, that punch would have decapitated him.

It didn't. He flew back, his arms flying out from his body as he lost consciousness for an instant. The trumpet flew from his hands and landed in the arms of a woman in the crowd, who turned and set it on the bar. The man struggled to his feet, shoving away the hands of people trying to help. His eyes glowed red for a brief second, then he rocked his head from side to side and gave me a nasty grin.

"Martin" glowed with a red and purple aura for a brief moment, then red light blazed from his form. When the dazzle cleared, the well-dressed businessman was gone. Standing in his place was a humanoid form, only larger, nearing my own seven-foot height. His skin was the darkest ebony, with short horns extending from his forehead. His mouth stretched preternaturally wide, almost from ear-to-ear, with fangs extending down past his lower lip. He wore chain mail and carried a curved sword in one hand. A long narrow tail hung down nearly to the floor, until he twitched it up over one shoulder to point the needle-sharp spike on the end of it straight at me.

"That was a mistake, mortal," he said, and his forked tongue flicked out across his fangs.

"Again, you have some misconceptions about me, demon," I replied.

"What would those be?"

"You assume that I didn't mean to expose you for what you truly are. Then you assume that I am mortal." I waded forward against the crush of humanity rushing for the exits and got almost within grappling distance of the demon before throwing my first punch.

He ducked, far too fast for my impeded punch to score a hit, and slashed across my forearm with his tail. The sea of onrushing humanity split apart around us, and I found myself with a clear space to fight. The demon grinned at me and ran his tail spike in front of his face. We locked eyes as the creature licked my blood from its tail and grinned at me.

"Are you ready to die, human? Will you die screaming like the little bitch you are, or can you hold on to some shred of dignity like the old man?" the demon asked. There was no question in my mind that he meant Oliver, and the grin that stretched across its disgusting face said that he expected me to die horribly.

For the second time in as many nights, I found myself fighting a stronger opponent in unfamiliar territory with insufficient weapons. Perhaps Evangeline was right. It seemed I needed to re-evaluate my life choices.

Then the demon charged, and the time for thinking was past.

15

How does one battle a demon in a crowded bar? There are no rulebooks on this type of combat, and no amount of travel to ancient masters of meditation can prepare one for having a mammoth demon warrior attack with flailing sword and razor-sharp tail. Sparring with the world's oldest and most decorated vampire, who also happens to possess centuries of battlefield experience does prove useful, however.

The demon charged straight in, the bullrush of a monster accustomed to being the strongest and most fearsome creature in every battle. In that sense, the terrifying unstoppable force met the horrific immovable object because all I did was plant my feet and throw an elbow at the beast's onrushing forehead.

The point of my elbow crashed into "Martin's" head with a sickening *crunch*, and I spun on my heel at the impact. "Martin" dropped like a stone, falling flat on his face to the hardwood floor. I shook my numb right arm, then pounced on my momentarily downed foe. I drove a knee into his spine, hearing another set of grotesque crunches as I broke at least four ribs. I wrapped my left arm around the demon's throat and pulled upward, bending his body almost to ninety degrees. I drew back my right fist for what I hoped would be a killing blow, then bellowed as hot agony shredded my wrist and hand.

I looked up to see the monster's tail spike protruding through my wrist, my thick blood coursing down my forearm. It withdrew the spike, causing fresh fire to run through me, then it jabbed the spike at my face, forcing me to launch myself sideways off the demon's back. I skittered back on my rear, narrowly avoiding losing an eye to the tail's jabs, and pulled a table in front of one fierce thrust. The tail slammed into the dark wood surface of the table and stuck, allowing me a moment's grace to scramble to my feet.

"Martin" had regained his footing as well, looking considerably the worse for wear. Mere seconds into our battle, and he was clutching his ribs, had blood streaming down his face where my elbow split his forehead to the bone, and had a round table stuck on the end of his tail, effectively negating that weapon.

I was in better shape, but still far from whole. My elbow throbbed from the impact with the demon's skull, and my right hand was essentially useless and was dripping blood all over the floor, making my footing treacherous. Nevertheless, I persisted. I stomped toward the demon, picking up a splintered chair leg as I went. Armed with my makeshift club, I squared off against the monster.

"I will accept your surrender at any point," I growled to the demon. Quincy tells me often that I need to improve my mid-fight banter, but I often find myself clinging to my shreds of humanity by the most tenuous of threads, making conversation difficult.

"I will eat your heart with pralines, monster," the demon hissed back. It dragged the table around in front of itself, planted a foot on the edge, and yanked its tail free. Thus unencumbered, it charged me again, vaulting over the table and covering the twenty feet between us in two leaping strides.

I stepped to the right and swung the chair leg at its knees with my left hand. I heard a resounding *crack*, like small-arms fire, as I connected, and "Martin" went sailing into the far wall. A pulling sensation along my face followed by a line of fire drawn along my cheek told me the tail had scored another hit even before I reached up and drew my fingers away red.

The demon fetched up against the wall in a heap, but righted itself instantly. I looked down at the shattered club in my fist and dropped it. My right arm was almost usable again, my healing sped along by whatever strange magics kept me alive and ambulatory long after my component parts should have decayed.

I felt the pain subside, replaced by a familiar fury. This monster didn't belong here. This monster was too small and puny to challenge me. This *monster* must die! A red haze suffused my vision, and I attacked, lowering my shoulder and charging the demon. I slammed into the monster, pancaking him into the plaster wall, then fire erupted in my neck and abdomen, and I staggered back.

I looked down, and saw the demon's ebon blade protruding from my stomach. I had impaled myself in my fury, not the first time rage and pain had obscured the dangers of my actions. I felt another ripping in my flesh, this time in the junction of my neck and shoulder, and turned my head right to see the tail spike pulling out of my mangled flesh.

The demon stepped forward, driving the sword through the meat of my left shoulder. The tail flashed forward, jabbing through my neck sideways, the point coming out in a pointed parody of the neck bolts Boris Karloff wore in the film depiction of me. My grinning opponent yanked both the sword and spike free at the same moment, and I fell. I collapsed backward, my knees bending in a painful outward splay, and my head impacting the floor with a hollow *thunk* that was certainly a commentary on my empty-headed frontal assault on a demon.

I knew better. I wasn't the wild-eyed monster I once was. I knew how to attack a superior enemy, how to distract the demon, how to feint, how to draw it into fighting me on my terms. But in the moment, when I saw an opportunity to destroy Oliver's killer, I lost my way.

The demon stood over me, a wicked grin splitting its midnight-black countenance. Its eyes flickered red with the fires of the Pits shining from within the monster's darkened, condemned soul, and its smile was the stuff of toothy nightmares.

"Time to die, creature," the demon said with a low chuckle. "I'll eat your spleen, then I'll hunt down that magical bitch you've got tucked away in the swamp somewhere. When I'm finished with her, I'll have all the time in the world to hunt down the Horn of the Herald without interference."

It raised the black sword high overhead, my blood running down to spill off the cross guard, and as the blade started to fall, I whispered one thing.

"I'm sorry, Oliver. I failed you, my friend."

Then the sword flashed down, and as the tip cut though my shirt and touched the medal lying on my chest, a white light shone forth with the force of a supernova, and I was suddenly wrapped in a gold-and-purple cocoon of light and power. The demonic blade shattered against my shield, and I felt the healing light course through me. My wounds were flashed closed, and I felt the power trapped in the amulet knit my shattered bones and stitch torn tendons back together.

New strength flowed through me, and I felt power the likes of which I hadn't known since that storm-filled night of my birth so many years ago. I sat bolt upright, hearing two voices mingled in my ears. One, my father's demented, prideful screeching, "I've done it!" The other, a softer, subtler voice with the slightest lisp and the scent of the Gulf in every word saying, "Live, my friend. Live!"

Victor Frankenstein animated me in a thunderstorm many decades ago, and for that, I will never forgive him. My friend Oliver Rambeoux resurrected me in the middle of a battle on an autumn night in New Orleans, and for that, I will always be grateful. I stood, glaring down at the demon lying sprawled on the floor of the small jazz club, and in his eyes, I saw a most familiar and welcome sight. I saw the thing that had filled most every eye to land upon me for more than a century. I saw it, and for the first time, I welcomed it.

In the demon's eyes, looking up at me as he held the hilt of his broken obsidian blade, I saw fear.

I picked the monster up by his throat and hefted him up over my head. I slammed him into a nearby table, turning it to splinters. I hauled the demon to his feet, then spun him around and slammed him face-first into a wall. I drove his horned head into the surface of the bar, then pounded his ribs with knee strikes until his ribs were ground glass. I shattered the monster's spine with a brutal double-fisted hammer strike that drove him to the ground and left a horn snapped off in the front of the bar.

I rolled his limp form over with an ungentle nudge of my boot, then I hauled the demon up to look me in the eye. Its head lolled on a shattered neck, and it was barely able to speak through its shattered jaw, but I didn't care. I wanted this thing to look me in the eye as I dispatched it.

"Are you ready to return to Hell, demon?" I growled.

"Yes, send me home, fool," it said with a grin. "You can't kill me, so just send me back to the fires where I shall be re-forged into a stronger weapon for my Lord to use against you foolish mortals! Nothing you can do will ever truly hurt me!"

"What about me?" a soft voice said from my left. I looked, and standing in front of the stage was the homeless man from the end of the bar. He held Jermaine's trumpet in his hands, and there was a pale white light surrounding him.

"Can I hurt you, Ezariem, Lieutenant of the Seventh Army, Baronet of the Pits? Can I hurt you, my poor, beaten, broken cousin?" The man's voice was soothing, like the mist after a summer thunderstorm, and the expression on his face was beatific. Tears streamed down his cheeks as he raised the trumpet to his lips, and he began to play.

The melody was soft and low, almost inaudible. I *saw* the magic as it flowed from the Horn, wrapping around the demon in my grasp and gently prying loose my fingers. Blue, white, and golden light surrounded the demon, Ezariem, and he floated in midair, rotating slowly like a glowing top. He spun faster, picking up speed and glowing brighter with every revolution. He spun faster, and as he spun, he began to scream. He screamed in terror, then in agony, then in the silent shrieking of someone undergoing so much torment that their voice is simply shattered. He spun, and screamed, and glowed, and flared brighter, and shrieked higher, and spun faster until, with a silent explosion of multi-hued dust, he vanished.

I turned to the homeless trumpeter, who now stood before me a six-foot-tall woman in white robes with huge golden wings sprouting from her shoulders, and was amazed to find tears still pouring down her face.

"Why are you crying?" I asked, wanting very much to reach out to her, but also terrified of defiling this glorious creature with my touch.

"He was my kin," she said, and the sound of her voice at the same time filled me with peace as I had never felt, and the horrible anguish of loss that I had never escaped.

"I am sorry you had to hurt him," I said. "But I am grateful for the assistance. Sealtiel, I presume?"

"I am Sealtiel," she confirmed. "I am the Herald, and if I am needed, then these must indeed be dark times."

"You are needed. You are *all* needed," I said.

"Then I will come." She turned and walked over to the bar, where Jermaine cowered. "You may come out now, Jermaine. You are safe."

The big man's head poked up from under the bar. He looked around and shook his head at the destruction, then took another look at Sealtiel. "Steve? Is that you?"

"Yes," the angel replied. "You knew me as Homeless Steve, or Stevie Shoes, and you were always kind to me. That is appreciated, Jermaine. I must go, and I must take the Horn of the Herald with me." She motioned to the trumpet she carried, and Jermaine nodded.

"I always thought there was something special about that horn, man. I mean, ma'am. I mean, Your Angelness. What am I supposed to call you?"

"You may call me Steve, if that is easier."

"Thanks. Yeah, Steve, I always knew I wasn't as good on any other horn. There was just something about that one, ya know?"

Sealtiel looked at the trumpet in her hands and smiled. "I do know. But I would not leave you without an instrument." She gestured to the stage, where a new trumpet sat on Jermaine's stand, gleaming in the spotlight from one of the few unsheltered bulbs in the building. "I think you will find it satisfactory."

"Wow, um, thanks!" Jermaine said. He vaulted the bar and almost slipped in a puddle of demon goo.

"That will not do," Sealtiel said. "The people here were kind, unlike many I have encountered." She waved a hand, and the bar was restored to its former state, with no sign of the devastation the demon and I had wreaked upon it. I was beginning to understand why Quincy often traveled with a guardian angel. If nothing else, they were good for cleanup.

The angel stepped over to me, her eyes fixed on the medal around my neck. "Curious," she said, reaching out to touch the Purple Heart. "Do you know what this is?"

"I thought it was just a memento from a friend. I now believe it to be much more."

"Yes, much more indeed." She looked up into my eyes. "Shall we go? I believe my brothers are in need of me." Then she turned and walked out of the bar, her wings fading with each step until she took the form of an ordinary, if very pretty, human woman.

I turned to Jermaine. "Now that the demon is gone, you should be safe. If you need me, just dial 'Adam' in your phone."

He looked confused. "How did you get in my contacts list?"

"I have a friend," I said, and walked out into the street after my angel to meet the sunrise over the Crescent City.

IV

RUNNING WITH THE DEVIL

1

"This is so not my scene," I said, sipping a Stella Artois and looking around, feeling spectacularly out of place. I've been all over the world and seen all manner of wonders and horrors. I can converse in several languages and have dealt with heads of state, heads of corporations, and heads of dark covens. I've been arrested, celebrated, intoxicated on six continents, and gotten laid on five (never did the deed in Asia, oddly enough). But Purgatory was very much not my scene.

Not the metaphysical dimension between Heaven and Hell, though that may very well be an apt description of my life. No, this Purgatory was Purgatory 124, the Carolinas' longest-running fetish party, held in a converted warehouse set off the beaten path in an industrial park in Charlotte. Part rave, part S&M club, part geek convention dealer room, and part mosh pit, Purgatory was the kind of place where the freak flags flew loud and proud. There were more nipple rings on display than earrings, and the last time I was around that much leather, it was still part of a cow. I stood at the bar, my Doc Martens, long black coat, black dress shirt, and black jeans letting me blend in just a little, but I was pretty sure I stuck out like a sore thumb.

Maybe if you didn't stare so much, you'd fit in more, Detective Rebecca Gail Flynn said through our mental link.

Maybe if you weren't walking around in leather pants and boots straight out of a teenage boy's spank bank, I wouldn't stare. And that's not even mentioning that bustier. Where'd you get that thing, anyway? And why haven't I seen it before?

Don't be crude, Harker. We're on the clock. Flynn danced out of my line of sight, much to my chagrin. She was a good-looking woman in sweats and a burlap sack, but tonight she looked like sex on two legs. I really wanted to get this gig over with, find the missing Archangel Uriel, and get Becks home so I could show my appreciation for her help. And her wardrobe.

"You need another drink, honey?" a short woman with pale skin and brown-and-green hair asked from my elbow. I looked down at her and got a view straight down her open blouse to the leather bra she wore. When I tried to look somewhere a little more modest, I realized that her blouse was see-through and that she was wearing nothing more than the blouse, bra, matching black leather panties, a garter belt, and fishnets. I didn't look at her feet. Frankly, I didn't give a shit what kind of shoes she was wearing, if she wore shoes at all.

"Nah, I'm good," I said, trying very hard to look at her eyes.

"Then how about a spanking? I'm Mistress Amy, and I have a few minutes before my next appointment." She gestured over to a wooden apparatus that looked like a waist-high bench with four leather cuffs. It took me a minute to figure out how everything was supposed to line up, but I eventually realized that she was inviting me to lean over it so she could paddle me.

"You know, another beer sounds great, now that I think about it," I said, draining mine in a long gulp.

Mistress Amy laughed, a gentle, high-pitched giggle that was infectious. I found myself smiling as the bartender put another Stella in my hand. "What are you having, hon?" I asked her.

"Oh, I never drink when I play. I don't want to dull the sensations," she said with a smile. I found myself smiling back. This was not what I expected from a fetish party. "Is this your first time here?"

"Does it show?" I replied with a smile of my own.

"Oh yeah, sweetie. It definitely shows. Plus, the newbies always hang onto the bar like it's a life raft. It's kinda cute."

"Yeah, this is a new one for me. I…a friend invited me, and now I can't find him in the crowd."

"If you think this is crowded, just wait until things really get going. DJ Spider is up next, and she always brings the fun." She pointed to the stage, where a gorgeous woman stood behind a pair of turntables. She was dressed as the superhero Dazzler and must have been over six feet tall in her sparkly platform shoes. She touched a few buttons on the DJ rig, and Rob Zombie's "More Human than Human" blared from the speakers. I bobbed my head to the music and drank my beer, scanning the crowd for anyone who looked like they might be an archangel in disguise. There weren't many candidates in this crowd.

I opened up my Sight, peering at the throng of dancing humanity in the supernatural spectrum. I saw a dozen or so minor charms, probably designed to enhance attractiveness or lower inhibitions. There were several moderately powerful witches peppered through the crowd, and one minor demon who looked around in panic as soon as he felt my Sight on him. He bolted through a side exit and was gone seconds later. I spotted a couple of vampires and what might have been one succubus, but nothing divine.

Well, until Rebecca sidled up next to me, reached out with her slender hand, and wrapped her caramel-colored fingers around the neck of my bottle. I released my grip as she pulled my beer to her lips and turned to her, admiring her graceful neck as she swallowed. She was out of my league on my best day, and we both knew it. I was a moderately good-looking guy of somewhere north of a century old, and she was a beautiful young woman with her whole life ahead of her. I decided not to dwell on that too long and stared at her boobs instead. Much happier topic.

Of course, it being a crowded bar, I wasn't the only one looking. "Can I buy you a drink?" the meathead next to her asked.

"I've got a drink," she said, holding up my beer and waggling it in front of the guy's face. "And a date. But have a good time." She turned her back on the guy and handed me back my beer. I looked at the meathead, and if there was anybody who looked more out of place than me, it was him. He wore a bright red New England Patriots t-shirt, and a Boston Red Sox baseball cap on backwards. He was rocking khaki cargo shorts and flip-flops, the official uniform of the American fraternity douchebro, and I wondered for a second if he just happened to stagger into the wrong bar.

Then he put his hand on Becks' shoulder, and I knew I was going to have to break somebody tonight.

"Hey," he growled. "I was talking to you."

Before I could step around her to deal with the idiot, Becks whirled on him, jabbing three fingers into his throat and one knee into his groin in one smooth motion. As he collapsed, she leaned forward and caught him. "If you ever lay a hand on a woman without her permission again, I'll find out. Then I'll hunt you down and wear those tiny little balls I just crushed for earrings. Do you understand me, asshole?"

Meathead nodded, and Rebecca let go of his shoulder. He dropped almost to his knees but caught himself on a bar stool before he went all the way down. After a few seconds of gasping and wheezing, he straightened up and wove his way through the crowd for the door. I motioned for the bartender to bring us another pair of Stellas and gestured to the stool. Becks shook her head, so I sat. "Nice shot," I said.

"You're a bad influence on me. A couple years ago, I would have just slapped his face. Now I had to restrain myself from putting that idiot in the hospital."

"Then I'd say I'm a good influence. He deserved a lot more than you gave him. Besides, fuck that guy, we've got important angel hunting to do. And you've got more dancing to do."

"You just like looking at my boobs in this top." She was smiling when she said it, so I figured whatever moment of introspection she was in was over.

"Nah," I replied. "I like looking at your boobs no matter what top you're wearing, or even if you're not wearing one. I'm an equal-opportunity ogler."

Becks shook her head and sipped her beer, giving me a smile as she did. "Yeah? Well, what kind of opportunity was Miss Lingerie giving you when I was dancing?" She nodded over to where Mistress Amy was paddling a chubby guy who was strapped into her apparatus. The solid *thwacks* coming from that direction told me she was swinging for the fences, but if the grin on the guy's face was any indication, he was into it.

"She had a cancellation and wanted to know if she could work me in for a spanking. I told her I appreciated the offer, but I passed."

"Good idea. Nobody kicks your ass but me, Harker."

"Oh, if only that were true," I said with a smile.

"Any luck finding our angel?"

"Nothing," I said. "There's some magic running around, but nothing divine. No big surprise there."

We stood at the bar people-watching and drinking for a while, then wandered upstairs where there were a few vendor tables set up. I skipped over the displays of paddles and nipple clamps to check out the jewelry stand manned by a smiling African-American man with long dreads. I picked up a silver ankh on a long black leather thong. "How much?"

"Twenty-five," he said. "I made it myself." I paid the man and slipped the necklace on over my head. I'm not much of a jewelry guy, but having a little bit of bling helped me fit in. Besides, he was nice.

"Your first Purgatory?" he asked.

"Am I wearing a sign?"

"No, but there aren't many men here wearing jeans," he said.

"My ass-less chaps are at the cleaners," I said, tipping my beer to him. We both laughed, and I sidled up behind Becks, who was browsing a display of corsets.

"What do you think of this one?" She held up a garment for my perusal, and I raised an eyebrow.

"I think you'd look great in it," I said, giving her and the corset appraising glances. "But I'm not sure where you'd hide your gun."

"I think if I wear this, I'd just knock people dead with my boobs," she replied with a smile.

"But what a way to go." I grinned back at her. We wandered off from the vendors and leaned over the rail, looking down into the crowd. "Maybe this is a bust. The seeing I cast really made it look like it would be here tonight, though. You ready to bail?"

"I'm good to hang out for a while," Becks said. "This is kinda fun. Like a walk on the wild side, but safe, you know?"

"Okay, then lemme grab us another couple beers." I walked over to the upstairs bar and ordered two Stellas, returning to the rail just as a dark-haired man with a goatee stepped up to the microphone.

"Ladies, gentlemen, and perverts of all persuasions, please welcome to the stage, for a demonstration of whip play, the amazing, the inimitable, the one and only...TORCH!"

Applause erupted as a man of about forty stepped out onto the stage, wearing leather pants, a black leather vest, and a top hat. In his hand, he held a bullwhip, which he spun around his head and cracked to even more thunderous applause. The second the whip cracked, I felt a tingle along all my magical senses that had nothing to do with the beautiful scantily-clad woman on my arm.

I opened up my Sight and looked to the stage, dropping back to the normal spectrum immediately to keep from being blinded. The glow from the stage was bright as the sun. I leaned over to Flynn. "The guy with the whip? That's our angel."

"Ummm, are you sure, Harker? I went to the Purgatory website. That's the guy that runs this show."

"Well, then the founder of Charlotte's largest fetish party is also the Archangel Uriel. That's awkward."

Then the doors burst open, a dozen religious zealots charged in, and things got really awkward.

2

They came in dressed all in white, but without the hoods I've come to expect from people wearing white after Labor Day. Close though, since they did wear bandannas covering the lower half of their faces, Western bank robber-style. Where do you even buy a dozen white bandannas? I guess if they're all white, they're hankies. So these religious zealots burst into the room wearing hankies on their faces, and the party went to shit in a hurry.

One of the assclowns reached over to the wall by the door and slapped the light switches, bathing the room in a bright white fluorescent glare that isn't conducive to any kind of sex, kinky or otherwise. If you ever want to throw cold water on a party that involves a lot of black leather and handcuffs, fluorescents and Jesus are a great combo for that, believe me.

Four of the jerks ran straight for the stairs and to the balcony, then began showering the people below with what looked like religious tracts. One fat guy in a white t-shirt with his belly hanging out (it's okay, his belly was almost as white as his shirt, so he was still all the right color), white jeans, white shoes (after Labor Day, no less), and a hankie around his face shoved a tract in my hands. He yelled

"Repent!" in my face, getting so close that I could smell the broccoli on his breath.

I did what I usually do when assholes get in my face. Okay, maybe not exactly what I usually do, since I didn't shoot him. But I did punch him right in the nose, screwing up his monochromatic life by putting a splash of red all over his hankie. He dropped to the floor, and I turned around, looking for the angel.

"Son of a *bitch*!" I growled. "Becks, I gotta get down there," I said as I watched my quarry stage dive all two hundred fifty pounds of himself right onto a pair of the invaders. He took them out, but more swarmed him, screaming about patron saints of sin and dragging him toward the front door.

"Easier said than done, Harker," Flynn said from beside me.

I turned and sighed as I saw the entire place erupting in chaos. The dozen dickweasels who came through the front door had been joined by another twenty or so streaming in from the back, and the whole place, balcony included, was turning into a vicious mosh pit. Only with mosh pits, most people don't really want to beat the shit out of everybody else. Not so much the case with these guys. The backdoor assholes swung bats and two-by-fours while the partygoers armed themselves with paddles and whips from the vendor tables. Some of them just wisely hid behind the bars or under the tables, but a solid two or three dozen gleefully joined the fray.

"Back off, fuckwit," I heard Rebecca say, and I turned back to her. A white-clad douchebag held a slab of lumber over his head, looking like he wanted nothing more than to crack her skull.

I stepped forward, snatched the board from his grip, and back-handed him across the face. He spun around and dropped to one knee, but came back up and stepped up to me again, doing that stupid thing where guys bump their chest into you. That's never a good idea against someone who actually wants to fight you, and I really wanted to hit somebody right then. So I gave him a headbutt to the face, hearing a satisfying *crunch* as his nose pulped under the impact of my forehead. Our assailant staggered back, hands pressed to his face, and I kicked him in the jewels. He dropped to his knees, and I slammed my fist into the hinge of his jaw, probably dislocating it, and definitely rendering him unconscious. He slumped to the floor, and I turned back to the balcony rail.

"I gotta go," I said to Becks. "Try not to shoot anybody." Then I vaulted the rail and dropped into the fight on the ground floor.

The last thing I heard before I went over was her saying, "Where the hell do you think I could hide my gun?"

I landed on the back of two scrapping partygoers, driving them to the floor. "Sorry," I said, getting to my feet.

One of them, a big guy with a shaved head and a goatee that reached halfway to his bellybutton, got up and glared at me. I looked up at him, giving him my best "that's a bad idea" glare, and he got the hint. Something cracked across my shoulders, and I went down in an explosion of pain. I rolled over, both to see who I had to kill and to try and avoid getting my head bashed in, and saw an albino asswipe with a baseball bat standing over me grinning. His white clothing hid everything but his blue eyes, and they crinkled at the corners as he smiled down at me.

"I will drive the sin from your soul with pain and justice!" he yelled, raising the bat.

I called up a red-tinged ball of energy and flung it at his chest, slamming him into the air and setting his shirt on fire. I got to my feet, calling up enough power to make myself glow with a crimson aura. I stalked over to the bat-wielding dickhead, enhancing my voice so my words were easily heard even over the Skinny Puppy blaring from the speakers. "I will send you to Hell for all eternity, you cowardly ratfuck bastard. I will shove that bat so far up your ass you get splinters in your retinas. I will use your ears for handgrips while I skullfuck your eye sockets, you miserable bag of excrement. You have three seconds to get the fuck out of this time zone or I will mutilate you so bad even dental records won't help identify your body."

Then I started throwing magic at him. I flung bolt after bolt of bright colorful energy at the jerk as he skittered along his ass trying to get away from me. I tossed yellow, red, blue, green, purple, white, pink —every color I could imagine. The bolts didn't do anything more than singe his ass and cripple his pride, they were more for show than anything else, but my little display had the desired effect. Every motherfucker in the room stopped fighting and focused their undivided attention on me. I hit the Babe Ruth wannabe with one last rainbow-hued energy bolt, which was really just a sleep spell with fireworks wrapped around it, then turned to examine the room and the shocked combatants standing frozen while they gazed at me in shock and awe.

I threw a blast of power at the sound board, and with an explosion of sparks, the music stopped. "Who is responsible for this bullshit?" I bellowed.

Nobody moved. I saw some of the white guys carefully not looking at one guy on the stage, so I knew it was him. "WHO?" I shouted, punctuating my question with a blast of power flung at the stacks of speakers on the sides of the stage. They were harmless sparkler-spells, but nobody needed to know that I was just playing the modern-day equivalent of Gandalf at Bilbo's birthday party. The last thing I needed was some fool of a Took getting in my way.

The guy nobody seemed willing to look at stepped to the center of the stage. "I called this rally. We are here to bring an end to this den of filth in our community. We shall have no truck with the devil, and we wish to see this type of perversion brought to a close immediately." I was fifty feet away from him, and I could see even at that distance that I had the worst kind of opponent on my hands—a true believer.

"Do you have a problem with fun? Or just public fun?" I asked, walking forward both to get closer to the stage and to get a better line of sight on where the guy I'd pegged as the Archangel ended up. I couldn't see him, but that didn't really mean anything. There were a lot of guys with goatees in black leather around.

"I have no problem with fun. I have a problem with perversion!" the man thundered. He had a big voice for a skinny dude, and I hoped he didn't have too much of a bad habit of his mouth writing checks his ass couldn't cash. If he'd gotten away with this kind of shit too often, it was unlikely I was going to be able to talk him into leaving quietly and letting these folks get back to running angle grinders over metal brassieres and using people as swingsets.

"If you have a problem with kink, then don't get kinky. But don't go telling these folks how to live. That's not cool, man." I tried to keep my voice level, but the more I scanned the crowd, the more I didn't see the guy they called Torch anywhere. If this doucherocket got my Archangel disappeared, I was really going to beat his ass.

"I don't care about cool—" he started, but I interrupted.

"I can tell. I mean, your wardrobe alone gives that one away."

His face turned red, bringing a little color to his ensemble at least. He yanked his hankie down and scowled at me. "I will not be mocked. You are just another sinner, and you will be brought to the way of the Lord. By force, if necessary! Lightbringers, show this fool his sin!"

Half a dozen of his white-clad thugs rushed me, and I figured the time for talking was over. This was a lot tougher than most of my fights because I couldn't just kill these idiots. I couldn't shoot them because my gun was sitting useless locked in the glove box of my car, and I couldn't just rip their spines out because they were human. I never thought I'd say it, but sometimes it's just easier fighting demons.

I threw out a quick side kick and caught one guy in the gut. He went down, and I ducked a big looping roundhouse from a giant in white. Where the hell did they find an Andre the Giant lookalike willing to wear all white and beat up freaks on a perfectly good Saturday night? I kicked Andre in the knee, and he did what all giants do when they can't stand up—he fell down.

Two of them grabbed my arms, but they expected a normal human level of resistance. I'm far from normal, and not completely human, so I pulled my arms around in front of myself and slammed the goons together. Then I punched them both in the face, and they collapsed in a heap of bloody noses. Pro tip—don't wear all white to a fistfight. Red shirt and brown pants are recommended. The stains don't show as bad.

That left two assholes in white standing in front of me. I rushed one of them and bowled him over. Unfortunately, he dragged me down with him, and we hit the floor in a heap. I said a silent thanks to Uncle Luke and his psycho wives for my enhanced immune system because a bar floor on a Saturday night is no safe place for man nor beast. I bounced my opponent's head off the floor a couple times, then turned around, looking for the last asshole.

He was already down, his baseball bat laying on the floor beside him, and my girlfriend, the always-awesome Rebecca Gail Flynn, standing over him in leather pants and a spiked corset. He was unconscious, so he couldn't even enjoy the view, which, trust me, was stunning. "Nice work," I said, getting to my feet.

"Thanks. Looks like your little debate partner flew the coop."

"Not surprising." I looked around. Most of the white-garbed dickheads were gone, and a fair number of the partygoers were streaming out the back door as the first members of the Charlotte-Mecklenburg Police Department came through the front. They had their tasers out, and Flynn made her badge appear from somewhere beneath her corset.

"You seen the angel?" she asked.

"Not since the fight broke out and he decided to stage dive into the fray," I said. I opened up my Sight and scanned the room. "Fuck,"

"What is it? You see him?"

"No, he's gone. But there's demon sludge in the air." I could see the taint a demonic entity left behind, like an oil slick across our plane. Not only was the angel gone, but it looked like a demon took him. Now I had to not only find the Archangel Uriel, I had to rescue him from demons.

3

An hour later, I sat on the couch in Luke's apartment with a bag of frozen peas on my Saran-wrapped to my right fist and a tumbler of Maker's Mark in my left hand. Becks sat across from me on the other couch in a pair of my old sweatpants and a ratty old *Hellblazer* t-shirt. Luke puttered around the living room, straightening cushions and generally looking grumpy. The sun would be up in a couple hours, so he was nesting. This was a new thing for my uncle, better known as Count Vlad Dracula, the most famous vampire in history. But ever since the last Renfield died and we saved the world from getting turned into a conduit between Hell and Heaven, Luke had been downright domestic. It was a little creepy.

"Why do you even have frozen peas? You don't eat," I asked, more to get him to sit down than anything else.

It worked. He stepped around the overstuffed armchair and sat next to Rebecca. "I have you in my life, Quincy. That has led to innumerable adventures, no small amount of joy, and an appreciation for first aid that would otherwise be unknown to me. I have a bag of frozen peas in my home for precisely the application you are using them now, to reduce swelling and conform to difficult to bandage body parts. You are prone to injure yourself in new and interesting ways, and I cannot always spare the blood to heal you immediately."

"Not to mention you like to watch me suffer," I grumbled, taking a long sip of my whiskey.

"There is also that," Luke agreed. "Now, tell me again what happened at the club."

He wasn't being a dick, making me repeat shit over and over just out of spite, or trying to catch me embellishing my fighting prowess or anything stupid like that. This had been a part of our post-combat ritual for decades. Luke makes me repeat a story at least three times, and he listens for the new bits each time, the pieces that don't pop out in the first telling. Sometimes pertinent details get glossed over by the front brain, but if you poke at a story long enough, the lizard brain brings them out. That's what Luke was pushing by making me tell the story over and over again—my lizard brain.

I got to the part where I started to scrap with the half-dozen assholes, and Luke stopped me. "What did he call his minions?"

"Lightbringers," I replied. "I said that."

"You said that this time. But not the first time you told the story." And just like that, we had a clue. I looked over at Rebecca.

"On it," she said, grabbing the TV remote. She pointed the remote at the wall-mounted fifty-five-inch LCD "smart TV" and fired up the internet-connected device. "Dennis, you there?"

A giant unicorn head with a rainbow mane popped onto the screen. "Technically, yes and no. I'm always here because there isn't really a 'here' here, if that makes any sense." Dennis Bolton, often called "Sparkles" because of his tendency toward stupid internet avatars, was the disembodied soul of an old friend who was murdered during one of my first fights with the demon Orobas and his minions. I transferred his soul into my cell phone in an attempt to save it, and he hopped out of my phone and into the internet. It was kinda like *Tron* with less glowing Frisbees and more demons.

"Not in any relevant universe," Flynn said. "What do you know about a group of religious zealots called Lightbringers?"

"One second," he said, then the unicorn head spun around, emitting a shower of rainbow-colored sparkles and cartoon stars. "You like my new effect? I've decided to do that anytime I come up with the answer to a question. Do you love it?" Sometimes I think my disembodied thirty-year-old friend is actually the soul of a k-pop fashionista and not an American tech wizard who happened to get murdered by a demonspawn and sent into the Matrix.

"I love it," I said, my voice James Bond martini-dry.

"Perfect!" Sparkles said. "If it annoys Harker, then I love it." These are my friends. My enemies are nicer; they just want to kill me.

Sparkles started talking, and I leaned forward. "Okay, *Lightbringer* is a series of fantasy novels by a guy names Brent Weeks..."

"Nope," I said.

"It's also the name of a sword on George R.R. Martin's *A Song of Ice and Fire...*"

"Is that like *Game of Thrones?*" I asked.

"You have read a book once in your life, right, Harker?" Flynn asked.

"If it's worth a shit, they'll make a TV show," I said. "Regardless, that's not it."

"Okay, this one should be a little closer to home," Sparkles said. "Lightbringers are the militant arm of an ultra-conservative Evangelical Christian Church based in Fort Mill, South Carolina, called the League of Light."

"That's gotta be them," I said. "This douche sounded like a bad street preacher."

"That's pretty much what he is. Their leader is Pastor Rob, who started off as a twenty-something crusader against immoral behavior and condoms in schools. His views are somewhere to the far right of Rush Limbaugh, but he couches his words in so much hip language and flashy lights that his followers have no real idea what they're cheering for. He's made Jesus cool for thousands of people around the country, thanks to his YouTube channel and streaming video of his sermons."

"And now he's crashing BDSM parties?" I asked.

"That's not a new thing," Dennis said. "The scale is bigger than most, but he's led marches outside sex shops and adult video stores, protested movies that he deemed inappropriate for the community, and picketed burlesque shows at comic cons."

"Wow," Flynn said. "This guy needs a hobby."

"Or a girlfriend," I said. "Oh wait, he's a religious leader. He probably has more sex than anyone in this room."

"Given the fact that one of us is undead and another is a disembodied soul, that's not hard to accomplish," Luke chimed in. "Has this League of Light become violent before tonight?"

"There are no records of it," Dennis said. "But there are a lot of emails flying back and forth between members advocating for beating up pornographers and perverts in the lead-up to the 'Raid of Shame,' which is what they're calling their attack on Purgatory."

"Yeah, it's a shame they showed up and all the hot girls in leather pants left," I remarked. "What do we know about this Pastor Rob dude?"

"Just a second, you're getting a visitor. I'll be back." Dennis vanished from the screen in a shower of digital glitter and rainbows just as the buzzer from the condo building's parking garage sounded. I bought the building a while back, and when Luke's house was destroyed a few months ago, I vacated the top floor of the place and moved him into one of the apartments up here. The secure elevator led from the parking garage directly to this floor with no exposure to sunlight, so he could use it even in daytime. I don't know what he would want to do in the parking garage in the daytime, maybe change a tire, but I made it happen.

I looked over to Luke. "You gonna see who it is?"

"Go ahead," he said. "It's for you, anyway."

"How do you figure?"

"There are only a few people who know about the elevator, which is hidden in a room clearly marked 'Authorized Personnel Only.' Out of those people, three of them are in this room, one is a disembodied digital spirit, and the rest are the Shadow Council, all of whom have access codes to use the elevator. Therefore, anyone who knows about the elevator, and the hidden door that disguises it from anyone randomly curious enough to snoop in the mechanical room of an apartment building, but does not have an access code to get up to this floor, must have been told about it by one of those people. Dennis obviously didn't do it since he vanished immediately upon seeing this person. Rebecca has shown no indication that she knows what is happening, no one on the Council would ever give out information about my living quarters without my knowledge, and I didn't tell anyone. That leaves you."

"I hate it when you get all Sherlock on me," I said.

"Well, I did know the man and was not only impressed by the deductive leaps he was able to undertake but was also a student of his methods." Luke leaned back on the sofa and crossed his arms, a slight smile on his lips. He loved being the smartest one in the room, and when you've got as many centuries under your cape as he does, it's a pretty common occurrence. But this time, I had a surprise for him.

Looking back from the video display was a trim African-American woman in her late sixties or early seventies. I certainly wasn't going to ask her exactly how old she was. She had white hair pulled back in a bun and a no-BS look on her face. I pressed the button beside the screen and said, "Glad you could make it. I'll buzz you up. When you come up the elevator, come to Number Four."

"I can do that," Cassandra Harrison replied with a smile. "I'll see you in a few minutes, Quincy."

"Who did you just invite into my home? At less than an hour before sunrise? You know I like my rest, Quincy. This is most unusual." Luke stood beside me at the screen, but the display was blank, Cassandra having already stepped into the elevator downstairs.

"Your new Renfield is here, Uncle. She'll be up in a couple of minutes." I walked to the fridge and dropped another ice cube in my glass, then took a tumbler out of the cabinet and poured an ice water for Cassandra.

Luke stood by the door, staring at me. In over a hundred years of living, I'd almost never seen my "uncle" speechless. But there he was, mouth hanging open like a twelve-year-old who just discovered internet porn. "My new...what?"

"Your new Renfield," I said, setting the ice water on the kitchen counter and walking over to my uncle. I took him by the elbow and walked him over to the armchair. He sat, looking up at me like I'd grown another head.

"Quincy," he said after his words returned. "As I am sure you understand, the search for a new manservant is one that I have undertaken with great diligence, interviewing countless individuals for the post. As of yet, there has not been a suitable applicant, but I have the utmost faith that the right person shall reveal themselves in due time."

"Yeah, whatever. The right person is about to walk through that door in about minute and a half. I've already hired her, so you might as well get used to it." I made sure I was out of arm's reach before I dropped that last bombshell on him.

Good thing, too, since he shot up out of his chair like his ass was spring-loaded. "You cannot hire someone to be my manservant! The position of Renfield is a time-honored one, immortalized in literature for decades. The role requires the utmost discretion, plus a certain level of intellect and physical ability that not everyone possesses. This is not a role you can advertise on your Craigslist, or wherever it is that you found this woman. And a woman? Be serious, Quincy." He looked at Becks, who just stared at him. I didn't envy my uncle in that moment. Flynn's glares can intimidate even the Lord of the Undead.

"No offense, Rebecca, but a manservant is, by definition, a *man*. There are things that I require that a woman simply cannot do."

"Name one," I challenged.

Luke looked at me, opened his mouth, closed it, opened it again, closed it again, then sighed. "I cannot think of them right at the moment, but I am certain that this will not work. Send this woman on her way." With that, he folded his arms across his chest and turned away from me, doing everything but stomping his feet in his little vampire temper tantrum.

A knock came at the door, and I walked across the room. I opened the door, and there stood Cassandra Harrison, granddaughter to John Henry, the legendary steel-driving man and demon hunter, mother to Jo Harrison, member of the Shadow Council, and the newest Renfield.

"Hello, Quincy. A pleasure to see you again. Hello, Lucas." Her voice was warm, but there was iron in it. I got the feeling, just like I did every time I was in Cassie's presence, that no matter what, this woman had her shit under control.

I saw Luke's back stiffen, and he turned. His eyes were wider than I'd ever seen them, and he looked across the room at his new Renfield. "Cassandra? You?"

"Me, Lucas." Her soft tones melted my uncle's resolve, and he blurred across the room.

"Gods above, woman, why didn't you tell me you were coming! It is so good to see you again. How is your granddaughter? What is her name again?"

"Ginny. She's good, she's good. Her mama is bringing her out next week."

Luke looked to Cassie, then to me. "What is going on here? Is Joanna moving here?"

"We all are, Luke," Cassie said. "After what happened out west, Jo wanted me to be somewhere nearer to powerful people so that Ginny and I would have somewhere to go if she ran into more trouble in her work for the Council. So, when Quincy told me about his friend's death, I came here. I'm your new Renfield. Am I good enough, or do you still want a man?" The corner of her mouth turned up, and I could tell she enjoyed making Luke squirm as much as I do.

Luke straightened himself and took a step back. "Well, I suppose you will suffice. After all, you already know all my secrets, so the learning curve will certainly be simpler."

"Suffice?" Cassie raised an eyebrow. "Vampire, you need to get your behind to bed and let me get some work done in this pigsty. Then I'll show you 'suffice.'"

Luke and Cassie both laughed, then Luke did something completely out of character. He hugged the slim woman. "I am glad you're here, Cassandra. Thank you." Then he blurred his way off into his bedroom to sleep through the day, but before he went, I was pretty sure I saw a glint of a red tear in the corner of one eye.

4

S everal hours later, I stepped up to the nondescript door on the side of Mort's Tavern. The parking lot looked a lot worse than the last time I was here, with weeds peeking up through cracks in the concrete. I pegged that as a solid metaphor for life in Charlotte these days, and maybe the whole planet, and knocked on the door. The panel in the door slid open, and Doug the Door Demon's eyes came into view.

"Goddammit, it's too early for this shit," he muttered, his raspy voice cutting through the morning air like a buzz saw. The panel slid shut with a metallic clang, and I heard deadbolts unlock from the other side. "It's open!" Doug yelled, his voice muffled.

I pushed the door open and stepped through. "What's wrong, Doug? You don't love me anymore?"

"I hate your fucking guts, Harker, and you know it. You've broken my nose more times than Tiger Woods broke his marriage vows."

"Yeah, and you're uglier than my backswing," I said, walking to the inner door. "Is he in?"

"He hasn't been anywhere else in months. Whatever you fuckers did in Atlanta, the boss didn't like it. The vibe's real different now, Harker. Watch your ass."

I stopped cold. Doug wasn't lying. He really did hate me. "Why are you giving me the heads up? If there's something in there likely to kill me, wouldn't that make you happy?"

"I don't want to see you dead, Harker. I want to see you live an even longer life than you have. Preferably blind from syphilis and with your dick swollen to three times its normal size thanks to the clap, with a couple of bleeding anal warts thrown in for good measure. If you're dead, I don't get a chance to torture you. And that sucks. But as long as you're alive, my dream of ripping off your jawbone and taking a shit straight down your throat lives on."

"You're a fucking prince, Doug." I opened the door, but not before I sent a small bolt of magical energy into Doug's desk chair. Every bolt in the thing fell to the floor, leaving it primed to dump the fat fuck right on his slimy ass the second he sat down. Petty, I know, but that's just the kind of prick I am.

I could see the truth in Doug's words the second I stepped into Mort's. What used to be a paragon of mediocre decorating was now just a shithole. Tables with broken legs stacked up against the far wall, piled with the remains of chairs shattered in brawls that never would have happened with Christy behind the bar. But Christy was dead, another victim of the asshole demonspawn "John Smith," who served the demon Orobas. He murdered Christy, Mort's bartender and, much to my dismay, daughter, in an attempt to destroy the world. She'd been the enforcer of Mort's Sanctuary status and made one hell of a Bloody Mary. I missed her every time I smelled tomato juice.

There were other signs of Mort's decline in the place. The floors were dirty, spots of last night's blood and puke lingering in the corners. The lights were dim, about half the bulbs burned out, and the smell of old grease and half-rotten food permeated the air. Then there was the new bartender. I could tell from the second I walked in that he was going to be a pain in my ass.

"We're closed," said the musclebound half-dragon without turning around.

"I'm not here to drink," I replied.

That got his attention. He turned around, and his hands dropped below the surface of the bar. I called up a little rivulet of power and sent a tiny bolt of electricity out to zap him on the nose. "Don't do that," I said.

"Do what?"

"Touch the shotgun under the bar. I know it's there, I know it's loaded with silver flechette rounds, and I know that I can cook the scales off your ass before you can squeeze off a shot. So let's pretend we've gone through all the bullshit and you just let me back to see Mort."

"Mort's not here."

"Go back and tell him Quincy Harker is out here." I hoped dropping my name would get a reaction, and I wasn't disappointed. Of course, like so many reactions, it didn't exactly go as I'd planned. The half-dragon spread his wings and came at me over the bar, claw and fangs bared. I drew my Glock and fired off four quick shots, but the bullets didn't even nick his hide. He was on me before I could holster the weapon, and my pistol went clattering across the floor as I went down under four hundred pounds of muscled-up, pissed-off dragon-man.

I didn't have any idea what this guy had against me. I'd never seen him before, and I hadn't fought any dragons since Europe, and those were Scandinavian Ice Dragons. This guy looked like a South American Red, maybe even a Mayan Feathered Dragon, but nothing I'd ever scrapped with. "What's your fucking problem?" I croaked out as I tried to keep his clawed hands off my throat.

"You motherfucker, I'll rip your lungs out," he growled, smoke billowing from his mouth with every syllable.

I turned my head to the side to get a breath of non-scorched air, then headbutted the draco right in the nose. Bad idea. Dracos, or half-dragons, have thick ridges of bone running up their faces right above their noses. This reinforces their skulls against things they might run into while flying and also makes their noses really strong. Instead of breaking his nose, I made myself see stars, and my arms went slack for a second.

That's all the time he needed to wrap his huge hands around my throat and start to dig in with his claws. I kicked and flailed, but even my enhanced strength was useless against a draco's power. I started to see spots around the edges of my vision, and just as the pain started to overwhelm my anger, I pressed my index fingers into his armpits and channeled lightning again. This time a lot more, and a lot closer.

My finger-tasers sent thousands of volts of electricity coursing through the half-dragon, and he jerked and danced like an epileptic at a rave, but didn't let go of my throat. His grip slacked enough for me to suck in one deep breath, then he was back on me, rage filling his eyes and smoke pouring from his mouth. He drew in one deep breath, and I knew what was coming—a face full of dragonflame, hotter than lava and able to burn my skull to a cinder.

As his mouth opened wide, I gasped out one word, hoping it wasn't going to be my last. *"Conglacio!"* It came out more a croak than a command, but it had the force of my entire will behind it, and as the power surged through me, a blast of crippling cold rolled from my mouth, right into the draco's throat. He froze, literally, from the inside out. The magical blast of ice froze the fire in his esophagus and everything around it. His throat, mouth, tongue, lungs, and heart turned to solid ice instantly. His eyes went wide in a second of what must have been incredibly agony, then they went blank as the life fled from them. He dropped onto me, knocking even more wind out of me, dead as a stone. I struggled out from under the corpse of the dragonsicle and struggled to one knee. I knelt on the disgusting floor, gasping for air, just waiting for the next attack, but nothing came at me. Maybe killing a half-dragon before noon gave me a little bit of badass street cred. Then I looked around the room and realized that the dragon and I were the only ones there. So much for street cred.

"Goddammit, Harker, why'd you have to kill him? Do you have any idea how hard it is to find someone who can mix a decent drink who's willing to tend bar for a bunch of demons?" Mort's voice came from the doorway into his back room.

"Do you have any idea how very few fucks I give? Your little shithead of a barkeep tried to burn my face off!"

"Well, Stewart was a little impetuous."

"And lazy. This place looks like shit. Next time, maybe hire somebody who knows which end of a broom should touch the floor."

"Maybe next time don't get my fucking daughter killed." I looked up at Mort, and the pain on his borrowed face was heartbreaking. Sure, he was a demon, and a hitchhiker at that, jumping from body to body on a whim, but he wasn't what I ever really thought of as a "bad" demon. If he was, I wouldn't be talking to him. Not outside a protective circle, anyway.

"I'm sorry about Christy. I liked her, Mort. She was good people." Well, only half-people, since she was Mort's daughter and, therefore, half-demon, but that didn't seem important at the moment. I stood up, giving Mort a good once-over. He looked like refried shit. The body he inhabited wasn't up to his usual standard, to start with. It wasn't famous, or good-looking, or even funny, like the time he was a cat for a year. He looked like some middle manager, or maybe an accountant. He had brown hair, a scruffy beard that looked like he was dirty instead of looking hip or cool, and he had a little paunch. I mean, whatever, you be you and all that, but the last time I saw Mort, he was riding in the body of an NFL quarterback. Now he looked like a featured extra on *The Office*. I guess losing Christy hit him harder than I thought.

"What do you want, Harker? I'm assuming you didn't come here just to kill my bartender and make my life difficult."

"I need information, Mort. This used to be the kind of place where people heard things. Of course, it also used to be a Sanctuary, but I guess the fact that your bartender tried to fucking kill me puts the lie to that idea, huh?"

"Oh, it's still a Sanctuary, just not for you. My baby girl is dead because of you, Harker, so you don't get any protection. Ever."

"Fucking Hell, Mort, I thought we were good!" I protested. "We fought Orobas together. We beat the fucker and shit all over his plans. Together. Remember Atlanta? Bad traffic, raining corpses from the Ferris Wheel, explosives in the Georgia Dome? Any of that shit ring a bell?"

"Oh, I remember it all. I remember cutting a deal with a Lord of

Chaos to serve him once I killed Orobas. So, I never killed him. But it turns out keeping one of your fellow demons prisoner and torturing him on the material plane is kinda a no-no to the legions of Hell. And it turns out the forces of Chaos don't like people who poke loopholes in their contracts. So, I've got a couple million demons back home pissed off at me for torturing Oro, and I've got all the Chaos Lords pissed off at me for not just killing the bastard." The smell of pine trees almost knocked me down when he spoke, and I understood more of what was going on. It takes a *lot* of fucking booze to keep a demon drunk. Their metabolisms burn it off even faster than mine. Even faster than Luke's. But Mort was shitfaced, and obviously had been for a while. That kind of shit plays hell on the mind, even a mystical one.

"And this is my fault…how, exactly?"

"Because you got Christy killed!" Mort blurred out of sight, then reappeared right in front of me, his eyes blazing red. Shit, he was *fast*.

"I had not a goddamn thing to do with that, and you'd know it if you'd crawl out of the fucking gin bottle long enough to think shit through, you lush."

I hated to do it, but there was only one thing to do if I was going to get the information I needed without fighting Mort. I kinda liked the silly hitchhiker demon, I didn't want to chop him into hell-kibble if I could help it, so I drew in my will and placed a hand on each side of Mort's head. I poured magic straight into his skull and whispered, "*Sobrietas.*" Cleansing magic poured out of my hands, and Mort's red eyes cleared in an instant. He spun around, puked violently on the nasty tile, then whirled back around to glare at me.

"You miserable fuck. What did you do that for?" Then he dropped to his knees, wracked by sobs. I sighed, more in sympathy than frustration, and knelt down beside the grief-stricken demon. I wrapped my arms around his shoulders as he poured out his grief in the middle of the bar.

5

H alf an hour later, I was seated at a table in Mort's back room with the door locked and warded for silence. More to keep the sounds of Doug the Door Demon eating the dead half-dragon out than to keep anything Mort and I said in. Doug was a messy eater. "You feeling better?" I asked.

"Not really." Mort finally looked at me, the first time since he broke down in the bar that he'd managed that. "She was my baby girl, Harker. You don't know what that's like."

"No, I don't." I kept my answers simple and didn't want to argue with him. Besides, he was right. I've never lost a child, since I've never had any children. In all my conversations with Luke, we don't know if I even *can* have children, or how they would turn out. The magic that Luke's "wives" had with my dear old dad, not to mention Luke's own interactions with my mother, made some fundamental changes in my DNA that gave me long life, magical power, incredible strength, heightened senses, and a resistance to many forms of physical damage. The charm is all mine. But we don't know if I can procreate, and frankly, I've never wanted to.

"It's the worst thing I ever imagined. And I've been to Hell. Like, literal Hell. Lakes of fire and all that shit? Been there, done that, bought the pitchfork. Losing Christy was worse. She was with me for centuries, Harker. I know you're old for a human, but she and I watched the *pyramids* going up. Did I ever tell you those were supposed to just be big squares? I fucked with the engineers. My best gag until I came up with disco."

I let him ramble, figuring he'd either get to the point and give me information about these Lightbringer assholes, or he'd let something slip that I could use. After he waxed poetic about his daughter, who I always thought was only part demon, but the way he was talking today made me think otherwise. Demons. Lying sacks of shit, every one of them.

Finally, he blew his nose one more time and looked over at me. His eyes were red-rimmed, but clear. "Okay, Harker. You've listened to me bitch and moan about my dead daughter for half an hour, and I think you even believed some of what I was saying. So what do you want?" The tone of his voice made it clear that the whole conversation had shifted. We weren't drinking buddies commiserating about a lost buddy; we were now in the business portion of our relationship, and doing business with demons is a place to tread lightly.

"I'm looking for information."

"On who?"

"A bunch of religious kooks called The Lightbringers. They're led by some douchebro who calls himself—"

"Pastor Rob," Mort cut me off, with a look on his face like he'd just bitten into something rotten. "Yeah, I know him. And his band of assholes. What do you want with those twats, Harker? I promise, if you're going to kill them, I'll give you a discount on any information I give you."

"What's your beef with them?" I asked. "Aside from the obvious Christianity thing, of course."

More looked genuinely offended. "What makes you think I have anything against Christianity? I love the Christians! Shit, Harker, belief is currency to my kind, and nobody believes more in demons and Hell than dickhead Sunday morning Christians who fuck their secretaries every Friday before they go out to the strip clubs and pay for hand jobs in the VIP rooms while their wives stay home raising their kids. Those dickheads keep my people in business!"

"Makes sense," I said with a shrug. "So why do you hate Pastor Rob?"

"I just hate hipsters," Mort said. "I like my bad guys to wear fedoras and trench coats, smoke cigarettes, and carry a gat. This kid uses more hair product than I do deodorant and wears skinny jeans. I hate skinny jeans."

I leaned back from the table and folded my arms across my chest. "What aren't you telling me?"

"Do I need a reason to hate somebody? I'm a demon, remember?"

"Yeah, I remember. I remember that you're a hitchhiker demon, and you buy and sell rides within the meat suit of the week. I also remember that I just watched you cry your eyes out over the death of a half-human demonspawn and that I fought side-by-side with you to keep other demons from turning our dimension into a freeway. So you aren't exactly what I would call a 'normal' demon." Sometimes I take a minute to realize that my life includes me using the phrase "normal demon" in a completely sincere fashion, and I regret all of my decisions.

Mort looked around the room as if he were about to say something he didn't want overheard. "Alright, so…yeah, there's something fucked up about that guy. You remember when I was a cat?"

"How could I ever forget? How does that work, anyway? I thought you had to inhabit a willing vessel, or one without a soul. Do cats not have souls?"

"Nah, they've got souls. They just don't give a fuck. Cats will let you come in and hitchhike for a while as long as they have a pretty good idea that you're going to do something fucked up, or at least interesting. They're assholes by nature, so as long as there's potential for chaos, cats are always willing vessels."

Like I said, my life is weird. "So, what does you being a cat have to do with Pastor Rob?"

"There were a bunch of guys coming and going through here last year, all of them bitching about how tough it was to score new souls.

They were all blaming this Pastor Rob dude. Word on the street was that he was giving people hope, and lots of it. That kind of thing really fucks with the normal ebb and flow of a city, at least in our line of work. We need a certain baseline level of despair to get enough souls sold to us. It's why we don't do much in Canada. Those fuckers are all too polite and happy. Can't make deals with people like that."

"Except Quebec," I grumbled.

"Yeah, they're great!" Mort agreed. "Fucking miserable people, always happy to sell their souls to shit on their neighbor. Totally my favorite province. But anyway, my customers were having a tough time collecting souls, and that's not good for me. No souls, the guys downstairs get pissy and yank the boys back home to tend the Pits. No demons, no customers in the demon bar. No customers, no new PS5 for Morty."

"You're all heart, Mort," I said. "So what did you do? Go have a come to Satan meeting with Pastor Rob?"

"Nah, that wouldn't do fuck-all. I was a cat, remember? Nah, I decided to do what cats do. I stuck my nose where it didn't belong."

So Mort had been inside the Lightbringers' main facility? This oughta be *good*. "What happened?" I asked.

"I snuck in there one Thursday night. The Bible-thumpers are crawling all over that joint on Wednesdays, between evening service and choir practice and circle jerk practice and whatever else bullshit they practice. But Thursdays are pretty quiet. So, I waited by the door until the cleaning crew showed up around ten—I'd gotten their schedule from an imp who was fucking the sister of one of the cleaning crew guys. When the janitors went back out to their van to bring in the vacuum cleaner, I slipped inside through the front door. Let me tell you, Harker, this lobby was nicer than a few mansions I've been in. I mean, we're talking marble floors, half a dozen flat screen TVs on the walls, coffee bar by a giant reception desk—the whole place looked more like a plastic surgeon's reception area than a church."

I wondered how many plastic surgeons' offices Mort had been in, then thought about how many men and women would sell their souls for a little extra here, or a little less there, and figured probably a lot.

The demon went on. "I crept around behind the reception desk when the guys emptied the trash cans, and that's when I got my first surprise. Harker, this joint has better security than Fort Knox. There were a dozen monitors set into the front of the desk, and they cycled through what must have been a hundred or more cameras scattered all over the building, including in all the offices and bathrooms. That was my first clue something was off with that place. My second was the guns hidden under the desk."

"Guns?" I asked. "Plural?" It's North Carolina, so one firearm randomly scattered around in a public building was no surprise, but two hidden at the reception desk of a church? That was weird, even for the South.

"Yeah, *guns*." Mort drew out the "s" sound for emphasis. "There was a pistol mounted in a quick-release holster under the desk's surface and a sawed-off shotgun hanging under the desk on clips right behind the pistol. I never met the receptionist, but she was ready for shit to go down."

So maybe kidnapping archangels masquerading as S&M moguls wasn't that far out of character for these guys. I motioned for Mort to continue.

"I poked around the lobby for a while until the guys opened a door to the sanctuary. I gotta tell you, being a cat is cool for having claws and basically being expected to shit in the shoes of people who annoy you, but not being able to reach a doorknob was a pain in the ass. The sanctuary was pretty basic, for your modern-day rock and roll church with a ton of lights and enough sound equipment to run Woodstock without a strain. There were padded movie theatre-style seats, video projectors all over the place, and a clear Lucite podium with Pastor Rob's face emblazoned on it. I swear, Nero didn't have nearly as high an opinion of himself as this little peckerhead does.

"Anyway," Mort continued. "I poked around in the giant monument to ego that was the sanctuary for a while, then wandered backstage. There was a door standing open, and the lights were on, not that I needed much in the way of light, being a cat and all. I slipped through the door and found myself in Pastor Rob's office. And there, sitting behind his desk in all his skinny jeans-wearing glory, was the man himself. Contrary to what I'd been led to believe, he didn't have a halo, and there weren't dozens of virginal Christian girls throwing themselves at his feet. Or virginal Christian boys, for that matter. Nah, he was just a good-looking dude in his early thirties, sitting at a huge computer watching YouTube videos and making notes.

"Of course, the videos were all of violent rioting in the streets from all over the world and all throughout history, and he was making notes with one hand and holding a big goddamn pistol in the other. I sat on the floor looking up at him as he watched police beat the shit out of protestors in Egypt, soldiers shoot a crowd of civilians in Iraq, a kid in China stand in front of a tank, and a bunch of cops drive tanks through the streets of Missouri. The worse the videos got, the bigger Pastor Rob's grin got. I swear, Harker, I thought at any minute he was going to start jerking himself off, the way he was fondling that .45 pistol. He must have watched that shit for fifteen minutes with me watching him, but when he finally noticed me, he swung that big pistol around and aimed it right between my pointy little ears.

"'I know you're not a cat. So whatever you are, you have about fifteen seconds to get the fuck out of here before I spray kitty brains all over the carpet. And I like this carpet.' He didn't raise his voice, didn't even make any real threatening moves, unless you count pointing a Colt 1911 at my fuzzy little face, he just told me exactly what he was going to do unless I made myself disappear. So I did. I arched my back and hissed at him, just like a normal cat would, but I hauled ass out of there. I'm telling you, Harker. That dude was bad mojo. He pegged me for supernatural the second he laid eyes on me, and I have no doubt he would have splattered me all over the walls of his office if I hadn't run like hell."

I looked at Mort and raised an eyebrow. "I've known you a long time, Mort. What aren't you telling me?"

"What do you mean?"

"You're a pain in the ass, arrogant, braggadocios hitchhiker, and I've never known you to play down your involvement in anything. But you're really just giving me the highlights of this dude. So spill it. What's the rest? Did he do something? Kick you and break your kitty ribs? Have you spayed?"

Mort sighed and didn't meet my eyes for a long time. Finally, he looked up at me and said, "I clawed him."

"What?"

"As I was leaving, I jumped up on his desk and took a swipe at him. I tagged him right on the side of the face with my claws—ripped him a good one. Then I ran like hell before he shot me."

"Okay, so he's got another reason to want to kill you, since you fucked up his pretty face," I said.

"That's just it, Harker. I didn't. I laid into him good. It should have scarred up that face enough to make your pal Adam look gorgeous. But he didn't even bleed. I sat on his desk, paw hanging in midair, and watched the skin knit right back together like I'd never touched it. That's what made me run like hell, not some stupid pistol. I don't know who this Pastor Rob is, Harker, but he ain't human, and he's powerful as fuck."

"And now he has his own personal archangel, unless I can get Uriel back." Now I not only needed to know where Pastor Rob was holding Uriel, I needed to know what he was planning, or shit could get real bad, real fast.

6

So after a demon warns me to stay away from the charismatic pastor and his oddball church, what's the first thing I do? Break into their main sanctuary, of course. I suppose "break in" is a pretty strong term for what I did, since it was the middle of the day, but I'm sure nobody would have signed me up for the All-Access Pass I granted myself.

I walked in the front door, just like any random schmuck off the street. A perky blonde sat at the desk, a cute twenty-something with her hair pulled back in a sensible ponytail. I couldn't help thinking about the armaments Mort said were tucked under that desk. The image of a grim-looking shotgun didn't mesh well with the girl I saw. She looked way more like she should be rushing a sorority than anyone who should be slinging lead at bad guys. Or good guys, depending on what side of the lead you're on. But that's when bad guys are effective—when they don't look like bad guys. Somebody walks in wearing a black trench coat in July with dark sunglasses, combat boots, and a flak jacket, and people are going to have their guard up. But when Bible-Thumping Barbie whips out an Uzi in the middle of her prayer meeting, nobody expects that crap.

Except me. I don't trust prayer circles.

I walked up to the desk and leaned on the polished marble surface with my elbows. The receptionist looked up from her command center and chirped, "Hi! Welcome to Lightbringers Ministries! How can I help you?" The level of cheerful she exuded from every pore was somewhere above "high school pep squad" and slightly below "eight-year-old girl watching a sea otter video."

I tried to push my face into something more like a smile than something small children ran away from and asked, "Hi there! How are you? I'm looking to speak with Pastor Rob, is he in?"

The plastic smile dropped from her face like a curtain on a bad opera, and she gave me a wary look. "I'm sorry, sir," she said, in a voice indicating she was anything but sorry. "Pastor Rob isn't at this location today. I believe he is visiting some of our church members in the hospital, or he may be doing some volunteer work somewhere in town. He's hard to keep track of." She gave me one of those "I'm just a long-suffering secretary" smiles that let me know she was completely aware of Pastor Rob's whereabouts at all times, had no intention of giving me any information, and would tolerate little to absolutely none of my bullshit. I liked her. Not enough to feel bad for what I was about to do to her, but a little bit.

I summoned up my will, waved my hand in front of her face, and said, "*Dormio.*" My magic pulsed from my palm in a gentle blue orb, floating toward her face like a big glowing dandelion puff, until the necklace around her throat flared with a reddish light, and my spell was sucked into it like it never existed. *Well, that wasn't supposed to happen*, I thought.

"What the hell are you doing?" Barbie asked, leaning forward and reaching under the desk. Thanks to Mort's little story, I knew she was either pressing an emergency call button, reaching for a pistol, or both. None of those courses of action were good for me.

"Well, shit," I sighed. "Sorry about this." I leaned over the desk, reached out with my right hand, and cupped the back of her skull. I slammed her forehead down onto the desk's wood surface with a serious *crack*. Barbie slumped to the floor, out like a light and hopefully with no serious brain trauma. Keeping an eye peeled for security or anyone else who may have noticed our little scuffle, I hurried around the desk and shoved Barbie deep under the desktop where a casual observer wouldn't see her. I did a quick check to make sure she was still breathing, then I grabbed the medallion hanging around her neck, intending to yank it off and study it in depth at home later.

"*Fuck!*" I hissed, snatching my throbbing hand back. I looked at my palm, and the outline of the pendant was seared into the flesh of my hand. "Fuck me," I muttered. "I gotta stop getting burned. That shit hurts." Looking closer at the necklace, I couldn't pick up anything out of the ordinary about it. For all I could see, it was a simple silver cross with a red jewel in the center. Behind the cross was a sun design that matched the Lightbringers logo emblazoned somewhere every twelve inches along the walls of the lobby. I took a picture of the cross with my phone, hoping that Dennis would snoop as much as he usually did and have some info on it when I was done snooping.

Looking up under the desk, I saw that Mort hadn't exaggerated the arsenal under there. I pulled the pistol from its holster and unloaded it, slipping the magazine into my back jeans pocket. The shotgun was a little tougher, but with a serious grunt, I managed to bend the barrel enough to be way more hazardous to anyone trying to shoot it than to any potential targets. Since I thought there was a good chance I'd be the next target, that was good enough for me.

Barbie's computer was password-protected, so I got nothing from there, but the security videos showed the sanctuary as completely empty. I figured if they had Uriel stashed on site, it would be in one of the rooms Mort told me about backstage, so I headed into the main worship center to poke around.

It was everything Mort described, and then some. I paused just inside the entrance and took a good look around, soaking in the smell of millions of dollars as a shrine to God and ego, in distinctly unequal portions. The room was shallow, but wide. At the back of the church, I was still probably less than a hundred feet from the stage. And this was no pulpit, this was a *stage*. Easily fifty feet wide, with a Lady Gaga-level lighting rig hanging over it, the stage was littered with microphones, music stands, instrument stands, and various chairs. A drum kit that would make Keith Moon drool sat on a riser upstage center, with a huge percussion kit off to one side. There was a multi-keyboard rig, a baby grand piano, three Marshall guitar amps, a Fender bass head, and a small set of chairs arranged like a jazz ensemble. Two dozen chairs in rows on one side of the stage made for a choir area, and the whole thing focused on a clear podium made of plastic and gleaming metal, with that same cross etched in the front of its Plexiglas surface, a red gem gleaming in the center like a dormant Eye of Sauron.

"One church to rule them all," I muttered, walking toward the stage. I put one foot on the four steps leading up to the platform, then all hell broke loose.

"Hey!" came the shouted voice from behind me. I turned, and there was Barbie, five feet of fury with a lump on her forehead and a Sig Sauer in her hand. Of course, I didn't search the desk for extra magazines. Who in their right mind would keep extra ammo for the pistol strapped to the underside of their desk? This ignores the fact that most people with guns strapped under their desks aren't in their right mind.

Seconds after Action Figure Barbie burst in with her ponytail and Pepto-pink sweater, the other rear door to the sanctuary flew open and a pair of armed security guards came through, drawing their guns and aiming them in my direction. *Great, now not only do I have a pissed off receptionist with a concussion and a gun, I have two bargain-basement Barney Fifes with poor trigger discipline.*

I drew in my will and flung orbs of pure energy at Barbie and the Renta-Cops, but red light blazed from necklaces around each of their throats, and my magic dissipated like my hope for getting out of there undiscovered.

"Surrender now, and we won't have to use deadly force," Renta-Cop Number One said, but the way his finger twitched around the trigger said all he really wanted to do was to pour hot lead into my ass. Fortunately for me, most people shoot for crap under stress, and I felt pretty good about my ability to avoid getting killed by this guy. I felt less good about none of the three of them catching me with a stray bullet, so I put my hands up.

"Okay, I surrender. I'm really sorry about the whole desk thing. I just really, *really* want to meet Pastor Rob, so I can tell him what a ginormous positive impact his teachings have had on my life. I think I'm almost ready to move up in levels, and I just need to know what it costs to progress." They kept moving forward in a steady, crouched heel-to-toe walk that made me think they'd all received at least some training in tactics. Maybe this wasn't going to be as easy as I thought. Like taking down three armed attackers was ever easy, especially when they had amulets that made my magical attacks useless.

Useless on them, maybe, but not on the things around them. While Barbie and the security dweebs kept their eyes and their guns trained on me, I kept my hands pointing to the heavens. Maybe not straight up, but definitely toward the ceiling. And toward the hundred-foot lighting truss that they walked directly under as they approached the stage.

About two steps before they passed directly under the truss, I let fly with a burst of my will and a shouted *"Abrumpo!"* The chains holding the lighting rig in the air snapped with a loud *TWANG*, and several tons of metal and electronics came crashing to the ground. The guards and receptionist dove for cover, and the metal monstrosity missed them entirely as it sent plastic light parts and aluminum shards whirring through the air to lodge in the backs of seats and the front of the stage. I threw up a quick shielding spell to keep from getting brained by my own brilliant idea and sprinted to the backstage office area.

The darkened hallway seemed deserted, a fact I confirmed by whispering *"lumos"* and summoning an orb of light to float along beside me. From the sanctuary, I heard the sound of guards calling for backup and Barbie using some very un-churchy language as they tried to get over or around my roadblock. I peeked in a few doors, but they were your basic offices. Just a few desks, chairs, family pictures, that sort of thing. One held a circle of chairs, a coffeemaker, and a table with an empty Krispy Kreme box, the universal signs of an AA meeting.

I came to the end of the hall and opened a door marked "Pastor Rob." No last name, no title, just "Pastor Rob." I thought about it for a moment, then realized that I'd never heard of Pastor Rob *having* a last name. It was weird, but everything about this whole deal was weird. The door was locked, but a little extra *oomph* and the knob twisted off in my hand. I pushed the door open, not really caring about any alarms I might trip. At least, not any mundane alarms. I did give a quick sweep of the area with my Sight, but nothing showed up. Just your average demon-tainted room in the back of a rock and roll church.

Yeah, more demon taint. This room practically reeked with it, making me think that there was a lot more our buddy Pastor Rob than just thumping the Bible and passing the collection plate. What was conspicuously absent, however, was any hint that Uriel, or anything divine in nature, had been in that office ever, much less in the last twenty-four hours. I scanned the bookcases, flipped through an blank day planner, and generally came up completely empty as far as clues to the location of my missing Archangel or to the long-term plans of a demon building a megachurch in my hometown.

I turned to go and found myself in a position I'd occupied many times before—staring down the barrel of a Sig Sauer .40 pistol held by a uniformed member of the Charlotte-Mecklenburg Police Department. Between dating Detective Rebecca Gail Flynn and working for an official, albeit heinously corrupt, branch of Homeland Security for over a year, I'd forgotten exactly how much I disliked cops pointing guns at me. I mean, let's be honest, I hate anybody pointing a gun at my face, but something about one of the good guys drawing down on me particularly annoys me. I guess it's because we're supposed to be on the same team or something.

"Let me guess," I said. "This isn't about that parking ticket Detective Flynn said she was going to take care of for me."

"Get on the ground!" the cop shouted. When he raised his voice to talk to me, barely ten feet away, I got a good look at just how young he was. *Fuck.* He was barely out of the Academy. He'd probably never even fired that gun off the range. I sighed and got down on my belly, fingers laced behind my head. The last thing I needed was to get shot in the face by an overzealous rookie. I didn't know if it would kill me, but I wasn't in a mood to find out.

"Quincy Harker, you are under arrest for trespassing, breaking and entering, assault with a deadly weapon, and anything else we can think of to throw at you." The voice was familiar, but the last time I'd heard it, it hadn't come from a uniformed officer. I looked up, and my heart sank. Standing in the doorway behind the rookie was Darrell Grizzle, a former detective who I thought got fired after the whole Agent Smith debacle, since he worked closely with the man who turned out to be a half-demon murderer. But there he stood, smirking up at me and holding his sidearm trained on my face.

"You're the reason I got busted back down to patrol, asshole. I know your bitch girlfriend will have you out sooner than I want, but let's see how some of my buddies in the holding cells treat you tonight." I think I would have had better luck if I'd just burst into the office and found a demon. So off to jail, and a pretty guaranteed beating, I went.

7

I n all my dealings with Detective, now Officer, Grizzle, I never
thought he was evil. Lazy, yes. Stupid, maybe. Vindictive, absolutely. So, when he tried the old trick of slamming my head into
the roof of the car while trying to "gently" push me into the back seat,
I knew how to go completely limp at just the right moment so he
didn't "accidentally" crack my skull. He cursed and tried to maneuver
my dead weight and keep me from falling to the ground while I
pressed down on the arch of his left foot with my left heel, grinding
the bones in the top of his foot together.

"So sorry about that, Officer. I lost my balance," I said from the
back seat of the squad car as he and the rookie took their spots in the
front seat. Squad car back seats smell pretty universally bad, and the
advent of methamphetamine just added a stink of rancid cat piss to
the miasma of flop sweat, vomit, blood, and shit that roils around in
every cop cruiser I've ever been in. And there have been a lot. I'd say
I've probably been riding around in police cars in America since
within a couple of decades of the invention of the police car.

"Go fuck yourself, Harker," Grizzle growled from the front seat.
"We'll get your ass taken care of at the jail."

I leaned back into the stinky seat and tried to recap what I'd learned. It didn't take long since there was practically nothing learned. Pastor Rob was either a demon or possessed by a demon. That wasn't exactly news since Uriel's abduction site fairly dripped with demon taint all over the building, but knowing that the source was Pastor Rob complicated life just a little. He was a public figure with a *lot* of people looking at him all the time. Any demon driving him or just masquerading as him had to be powerful to hold that illusion in place consistently. Perhaps more disturbing was the lack of demonic magic I sensed anywhere else in the church. That meant the trigger-happy security guards and the Rambo Receptionist were completely human, unpossessed, and just batshit crazy. Not to mention highly armed. I had to wonder how many other of Pastor Rob's pals would be packing, and probably heavier artillery than just pistols.

We pulled into the underground parking deck at CMPD Headquarters, and the rookie got out of the passenger seat and hurried to the back door to let me out. I guess he decided that police brutality was passé and he'd just follow the Geneva Convention. I slid out of the car and handed him the cuffs. The kid gaped at me as I walked toward the elevator. "Don't worry about me, kid. I know the way to the booking sergeant's desk."

"Take another step, and I'll blow your goddamn head off, Harker," Grizzle said, and I heard the hammer click back on his Sig Sauer pistol and turned around. He was in a classic Weaver stance with one hand cupped under the other on the butt of the gun. The forty-caliber pistol was center on my head, and I got pissed. I really don't like it when people threaten to kill me, especially when I know they want to.

So, I decided it was time to remind Grizzle who the Alpha dog was, no matter who was wearing the badge. I let my eyes glow red, sending tendrils of magic out to waft through the air around my face. "Go ahead, Darrell. Pull the fucking trigger. See what happens. You remember how life turned out for your pal Smith when he pissed me off, right? Well, I don't like being threatened, and you're *really* starting to piss me off."

I cut my eyes over to the rookie. "Don't touch that goddamn pistol, kid. You've acted like a decent person all night, let's not fuck it up now." I turned my attention back to Grizzle. "Now, Darrell. This can go down one of two ways. You can shoot me, which is just going to piss me off and scare this rookie. Then I'll have to get unpleasant. Or you can holster your weapon, and we can go upstairs, where you book me on charges you know will be dismissed before nightfall, and you can try to have somebody murder me in the holding cell. That's not going to get you anywhere either, but it's the option that doesn't end with your head sitting on your patrol car as a goddamn hood ornament. Now let's go upstairs and get this charade underway."

I turned to walk to the elevator, then turned back. "Unless, of course, you'd like to see if your life expectancy is any better than your buddy Agent Smith's after *he* tried to fuck with me."

I stared at Grizzle for almost a full minute, then he finally holstered his weapon and stomped past me to the elevator. The metal doors slid open, and the three of us stepped in.

We stood for a few seconds in an uncomfortable silence, then the kid drew in his breath to speak. I held up a hand and cut him off. "Don't ask, kid. If you ask, I'll tell you, and there are lot of things in this world that you're better off not knowing. Just trust me on that one."

He stood there contemplating my words long enough for the elevator to rise the two floors to the booking desk, and I stepped out and walked over to my old buddy Sean, the sergeant in charge of booking. Sean had been taking my prints and processing my arrests for well over a decade, and we were friendly, if not friends. And I didn't blame him—it was probably frowned upon to be friends with a guy he arrested all the time. Lucky for me, incarceration was never really my style. Banishment and immolation were more my bailiwick.

"What is it this time, Harker?" Sean said with a sigh. "I thought we were done going around in these circles with you once you and Flynn got cozy."

"I did, too, Sean," I replied. "But your buddy Darrell over there didn't get the memo that I'm one of the good guys now, so here we are again."

"Fair enough," Sean said. Sean Fitzpatrick had been around the block enough times to not even bother sticking his nose into political crap. He was a solid cop—did his job, didn't try to pull anything over on anybody, and was just biding his time until retirement. I remembered Sean as a young tyro twenty-five years ago, chasing the biggest collars and the most dangerous assignments. Then he caught an arrow to the knee in an armed robbery of a sporting goods store, of all ridiculous things, and that put an end to his adventuring days. Now he pushed papers instead of chasing purse-snatchers, and he'd turned into one of the most efficient desk sergeants Charlotte-Mecklenburg PD had on their roster.

Sean walked me through the process, taking my prints (again), taking my mug shots (again), then handing me over to Grizzle to take me back to holding. "Darrell, I know you've got issues with this man, but he needs to come out of that holding cell in the same shape he goes in."

"No worries on that one, Sergeant. He'll still be an asshole when he comes out." Grizzle laughed and led me down the hallway to one of the holding cells. He perp-walked me past three empty cells before stopping in front of the one farthest from the door. His rookie partner opened the door, and four giant men that looked like a cross between brown bears and Hell's Angels stood up. It was feeding time at the zoo, and I was the entree.

"Let me guess," I said. "This is the one in the security cameras' blind spot?"

"Nah, this is the one with the biggest drain in the floor. It'll be easier to wash the blood away when they're done with you." Darrel shoved me through the open cell door. He tried to trip me as I went in, but I stepped over his foot. The shove did put me most of the way into the cell, and I heard the heavy *clang* of a steel door slamming shut behind me.

"Try not to let him make too much noise," Darrell said, his leather shoes slapping across the tile floor as he walked away from the cell. "I'd hate for anybody to hear your ruckus and interrupt you." With a creak of hinges and the thud of another heavy door closing, I was alone with four men who probably weren't interested in a rousing game of gin rummy.

"Hi fellas," I said, backing up to make sure none of them could get behind me. "We don't need to make this unpleasant, do we?"

"Unpleasant is what we do," one of them said, a giant at nearly seven feet tall with a cascading black beard and arms the size of my thighs. His eyes glowed red, and I know that Grizzle's days of consorting with demons hadn't ended when I put a bullet in his boss's head.

"I guess there's no point in me asking if you want to do this the easy way, is there?" I asked. The jolly demonic giant laughed, and I threw a fireball in his face. Then the others came at me, and the shit really hit the fan.

8

"*Inifiernos!*" I shouted, leaping to my left. I flung out my right hand, and a ball of flame the size of a volleyball shot forth, catching Blackbeard right in the face. I didn't expect much reaction and didn't get much. Demons are pretty used to being on fire, after all. But it bought me the moment's distraction that I needed to get my back into a corner and limit the thugs' angle of approach even more.

The demons stopped chuckling and concentrated on their attack. Blackbeard was busy putting out the fire on his face since it turns out no matter how impervious you are to fire, your beard won't be, but that left three demons to come at me. And come at me they did. Two smaller men shed their human forms, literally ripping the fleshy disguises into piles of disgusting skin and clothes, then sprang at me with razor-sharp claws. Reaver demons. I hate Reavers, more even than a character in a Joss Whedon space western. These little buggers had claws the size of steak knives and twice as sharp. The first one went high, and I ducked his slash.

Of course, that put my face right in line from the stabbing strike of the Reaver who went low, but I knew he was coming. It wasn't my first Reaver fight, and I knew that without serious weapons, I was going to be sporting several new orifices before the end of the day. With that in mind, I grabbed the demon's right arm and used those razor-bladed nosepickers to slice off its left hand at the wrist. Blood fountained from the severed limb, but I grabbed my newly created weapon and jabbed a still-twitching demon finger into its owner's left eye. The Reaver shrieked like Lucifer himself was wielding the whip and scuttled backward, flailing around like it couldn't decide whether to hold its perforated eye, or try to stem the bleeding with its remaining hand. Life's tough for the one-handed man with two fatal injuries.

The demon pulled back, but I held onto the severed hand, the claw sliding out of its face with a wet squelching sound. The other Reaver drew back for a downward slash at the back of my neck, and I dove to my right, whipping the severed hand up and toward the remaining Reaver. I missed, and the hand flopped around on the floor of the cell, dripping blood into a pool right by the drain. Nice of Grizzle to comment on the ease of cleanup. At least I wouldn't have tormenting the janitor on my conscience.

Reaver Two came at me again, and I barely pulled in enough energy to thrust power wildly at the little shit before he impaled my spleen on his fingertips. He staggered back, knocking into the third man, who still looked mostly human, except for his obsidian skin and gleaming red horns and teeth. I didn't recognize his type of demon, but since he wasn't currently trying to remove any parts of my body, I put him firmly in the "deal with later" column. Reaver Two recovered way faster than I wanted him to and dove at my knees this time, bowling me over and opening up cuts all over my thighs and calves with his claws. I went down, driving an elbow into his back on my way down. That, at least, stunned the little bastard for a couple of seconds, giving me enough time to suck in a breath, press my hands to the sides of the demon's head, and croak out a strangled *"conglacior."*

A blast of crippling cold flowed from my hands, plunging the Reaver's temperature into the negatives in a heartbeat. Its eyes glazed over, and it let out one last mist of breath before its entire skull froze from the inside out. I pushed myself up to my knees and slammed the demon's head into the concrete floor. It shattered into a million disgusting pieces, and its entire body dissolved into steaming pools of black ichor.

I scrambled around until my back was to a wall again and looked for Blackbeard. He was nowhere to be seen, at least not in that form. Instead, what faced me was the thickly muscled form of a Greater Pit Fighter. "Fuck me," I muttered, my brain scrambling for a way out of this fine mess.

The Pits of Hell are a real thing, at least from what I can find in my research. I've never actually been to Hell, although I'm pretty sure I've been a few places that were in the same zip code. The Pits are more than just lakes of fire where sinners are punished and theoretically absolved of their transgressions. I say theoretically since I've never found record of anyone who has ever expiated their sins and moved on to Heaven.

Never.

No one. In millions of years, no one has ever made it from Hell to Heaven.

That makes it pretty obvious that the Pits are for more than rehabilitation. They're also for the enjoyment of the greater demons, the Dukes, Archdukes, and Lords. Think the Roman Colosseum, only with a lot more lions and a *lot* more bloodshed. New souls that show a predilection for murder and mayhem get tossed into the Pits, where they get matched up against increasingly stronger opponents to fight for the entertainment of the masses. Since they aren't alive, they can't die. Whatever injuries they receive heal, albeit slowly and in the most painful ways possible. Hell, remember.

Well, after a few thousand years of getting their asses kicked, most souls either give in to despair and refuse to fight anymore, at which point they get moved on to other, more horrific punishments, or they get good at kicking ass. If they choose the latter, they move up through the Pits to fight demons instead of just the souls of human assholes. If the souls excel there, they can get turned into demons themselves.

This isn't much better, from what I hear, except that you're the one doing most of the tormenting, and you have the ability to leave Hell once in a while if you get summoned or find a crack in the walls, which happens way more often than I would like. So, what stood in front of me was a damned soul, who was enough of a badass to get promoted out of the Pits after a few thousand years into becoming an actual demon, then he was either strong enough or cunning enough to find a way out of Hell.

Things were not looking good for our hero. The literal only thing I had going for me was that the fourth demon had removed himself from the field of battle, at least as much as one could in a twenty by twenty holding cell. He sat on a bench fastened to the far wall, his hooves feet folded underneath him, just watching the proceedings with what looked like only the mildest of interest. I didn't mind that much. The less interest I could draw from another creature determined to rip my spine out and beat my head in with, the better.

"You burned me, human!" Hulk Hogan Demon bellowed, and even from ten feet away, I could smell the charred death on his tongue. Seriously, what do these guys *eat*?

"Yeah, but your little friends cut me up, so you wanna just call it even and play pinochle?" I don't even know how to play pinochle, but if it would mean I didn't have to fight a demon hand to hand in an enclosed space, I was willing to learn.

Hulk didn't respond, at least not with words. He did raise his huge hands over his head and charge me, so I took that as a hard "no" on the pinochle. I crouched into a little ball and hid behind a curved shield of my magic, letting him punch himself out on my shield as I fed the magic coursing through the building into my defenses. I don't do it often because it's pretty unethical and has the unpleasant side effect of sometimes accidentally killing people, but when I'm in a pinch and really short on power, I can leech energy off whoever is around me. It's kinda like what Luke does to survive, in that I'm actually consuming the life force of the people around me. The difference is that I don't need a bib, and I only replenish my magical stores with it, not any of my physical strength. But since this was a matter of life and death, I figured the rest of the guys in the jail would cut me a little slack. Nah, I didn't even think twice about it. I just reached out and sucked power into my shield so I could survive Hulk's initial onslaught.

HIs fists slammed into shield again and again, then he lifted his arms over his head and bellowed in rage. "I will crush you to paste!"

"Not if you keep taking your eyes off your opponent, asshole," I muttered, and dropped my shield. I might be over a century old and stronger than most things on Earth, but I know my limits. I am never, *ever* going to be able to take out a Pit Fighter in a fair fight. Good thing for me, I don't fight fair.

I sheathed my fists in magical energy and shouted, "*GLADIO!*" Blue-white energy flared from my hands in a pair of two-foot magical short swords. I thrust my energy swords into the demon's legs just above the knee and twisted with all my strength. I felt the tendons sever beneath my summoned blades, and the demon bowed at the waist like a puppet with his strings cut. I let the swords dissipate back into the aether and sprang up from my crouch, laying both of my magically wrapped fists under the demon's jaw in an uppercut that would have made Rocky Balboa proud.

I didn't just swing from my heels, I *launched* myself into that punch, and it showed. The demon's forward fall arrested, he straightened up and flew backward a good three or four feet before he slammed to the concrete floor in a puddle of Reaver blood. His head hit the floor with a sickening *crack*, and his entire body shuddered, then lay still.

I've been in a lot of fights. It's a byproduct of having generally poor impulse control, associating with vampires, animated corpses, and magicians for over a century, and still having the nagging voice of Abraham Van Helsing in the back of my head like a grim Germanic Jiminy Cricket, constantly pointing out injustice and horrors in the world that needed to be corrected. Thanks to all that horrible life experience, I learned a long time ago not to believe an opponent was dead until you'd taken the second bite of his still-beating heart.

Metaphorically. Okay, mostly metaphorically, but there are few things in the world tastier than fresh werewolf heart. So, I walked over to the apparently dead demon, but I wasn't relaxed. I held a ball of glowing magical energy in my right hand and had a shield spell readied with my left. I was totally prepared to pour enough power into the monster's head to turn him into a red smear on the concrete, but I didn't have to. I was still a foot or more away when he dissolved into smoking black sludge, filling the cell with the stench of sulfur, cooked demon blood, and burned hair.

I dropped my shield and my ball of power, backed slowly across the cell, and sat down on the bench. I looked across at the last demon, who just watched me, his gaze completely ignoring the dissolving bodies of his three fellow denizens of Hell. His eyes locked onto mine, and he unfolded his legs and stood up. I didn't get up. One, I didn't want to give him the courtesy, and two, I was fucking tired. Drawing that much power through me left all my nerve endings feeling raw and abused, and casting spells with that much juice behind them gave me a headache. So, I sat there as the demon approached, stepping through the puddles of Reaver and Pit Demon like they weren't even there.

I readied another shielding spell and prepared to summon another blade of magical energy, but there's nothing in the world that could have prepared me for the next words to come out of the demon's mouth.

He stood right in front of me, his black skin glittering in the fluorescent light. He bent his head down to me, and I looked up into his black pupil-less eyes. He smiled, which was made more nerve-wracking than usual by the fact that there was no malice in it. He looked genuinely happy that it was his turn.

He's happy that I killed three demons in five minutes and now he gets his shot at me. I am so fucked, I thought, then did what any sane person would do—I smiled back.

"Hello there, human. Would you like to play a game?"

I know I should've been shit-scared, and I pretty much was, but all I kept thinking about was how this dickhead probably had no idea he'd just dropped a *War Games* reference on me. Yup, one-hundred percent fucked.

9

"Ummm…sure?" I said. "As long as the game isn't called 'Eat the Human,' I think I'm good with that."

The demon smiled, one of the most unnerving sights I've ever experienced, and said, "That depends on whether you win or lose, I suppose, doesn't it?"

I couldn't argue with his logic. But I still wanted to know a little more about what, or who, I was dealing with. "What are you called?" I asked. I've learned through painful experience not to ask a demon for its name because it will lie. Names, true names, have power, and demons hate more than anything giving up power to another creature. But the names of many demons are also well-known, which makes it worth trying to figure out who you're dealing with. And since most demons are glory-hungry little pricks, they want you to know who you're dealing with, so you'll be intimidated and fuck up into promising them something you really shouldn't give away. Like your soul.

It's convoluted, but they're basically immortal beings, and assholes at their very core, so they spent a lot of time parsing semantics and coming up with more and better ways to screw with mortals. I was interested not only to see what this particular asshole's plan was, but also who he was.

"My apologies, John Abraham Quincy Holmwood Harker, I see I have you at a disadvantage. I am known as Zepar, commander of fifty legions of Hell's armies, and the greatest lover of women, and men, your pitiful world has ever known." He made a deep, florid bow, almost sweeping the floor with his ebon knuckles.

Fuck. I knew about Zepar. In my line of work, it paid to know all the legit badasses among Hell's ranks, and Zepar certainly qualified. He was overstating his importance a little, unless he'd managed to seriously rise through the ranks recently, but he was still a serious mother. He was one of the Fallen, not a demon made from the waters of the river Styx, or forged in the fires, or a pitiful human who fought his way out of the Pits. Nope, the guy standing in front of me used to be an angel, picked the wrong side in the War on Heaven, and followed Lucifer down into the flames for it.

"Pleased to meet you, Zepar. You can call me Harker. Or Q, if we both live long enough to get friendly. But I doubt that's the plan, is it?" I stood up and held out my hand anyway. Just because two beings really want to kill each other is no reason to be rude.

The demon shook my hand, an act that took all my willpower not to run screaming from. His glassy black flesh scraped along my skin like the edge of a knife, just to the point of making me fear he was going to rip me open, but not quite. As we shook, I felt the evil coming off him in waves. It felt like a roiling mass of tar, or lava, only ice cold. The sense of *wrongness* that spread across my hand and up my arm was like dipping my whole fist in a vat of acid, the burning sensation pricked in all the way down to my bones.

I didn't scream, and I didn't pull away. I shook his hand and sat back down, resisting the temptation to wipe my hand on my pants. I kept my eyes locked on his, trying to discern something, anything, about his intentions. "So, what's the game, Zepar? If it's not going to be 'Eat the Human,' what other games do you know?"

The demon smiled at me again, and the flesh along my spine crawled like it was trying to make a break for it. "The game is simple.

We shall tell riddles. If you cannot guess one of my riddles, I get to kill you without a fight. If you somehow manage to tell a riddle that I cannot decipher, then I will leave this plane, taking all evidence of your disagreement with my compatriots with me."

Riddles. Well, that was different. I'd fought demons, bargained with demons, wrestled one or two, shot a *lot* of them, and done my level best to outwit a few of them. But I'd never had one want to play at riddles before. I took a moment to think about my options, maybe a moment longer than Zepar thought was appropriate, because after less than a minute, he cleared his throat.

"If you would rather duel in some other fashion, I suppose we could move straight into single combat. But I was one of the Host before my Fall, and I have battled alongside Michael himself. Trust me, Quincy Harker, you at least have a chance at besting me in riddles."

He had a point. There was no chance I was going to beat this guy in a fistfight, and my magic would likely slide right off of him like a watergun shooting an elephant. "Okay. What are the rules?" There are a lot of races that you can enter an agreement with before you know every detail of the rules. Demons are not on that list. Neither are female police detectives, but that didn't stop me.

"I will begin. I will tell you a riddle. If you can figure out the answer, you get to tell me a riddle. We alternate until someone can't answer the riddle, or can't come up with a riddle of their own and surrenders. All riddles must have a legitimate answer, no Mad Hatter's riddles are allowed. You may make one incorrect guess per riddle, but if you guess wrong twice, you lose. If the loser does not agree that the proffered answer is valid, then a new riddle may be provided. This may only be done once. I would suggest that you take care."

I mulled it over as I looked at Zepar's ebon grin. He had something in mind, but I couldn't for the life of me figure out what it was. Oh well, if I didn't like the way it was going, I could always just fight him. At least that way I'd die quickly. "Okay," I said. "I'm in. Hit me with your first riddle."

"What is so delicate that even speaking its name will break it?" Zepar asked, and I knew he was going easy on me to kick things off.

"Silence," I said with a smile. "That's an old one."

"Well done, Harker. Now it is your turn." He walked a few feet away from me and sat cross-legged on the floor, facing me where I still sat on the metal bench. I had no illusions about getting away, even if I could get out of the cell. One of the Fallen was going to be way faster than even my vampire-enhanced speed.

I thought for a moment, then decided to see how far I could bend the rules. "Okay, here's an oldie but a goodie," I said. "What's in my pocket?"

Zepar actually chuckled. "Tricksy hobbit, that's not a riddle. I couldn't possible know, or guess, but I know it isn't The One Ring. Try again. I'll give you a free pass because it was moderately clever, but Tolkien you are not."

"Fair enough. What walks on four legs in the morning, two legs in the afternoon, and three legs in the evening?" Another old standby, but at least this really was a riddle.

Zepar gave me a steady look, as though slightly insulted. "A man. He crawls in childhood, walks on two feet as an adult, and walks with a cane in his old age. Do try to be more original. I taught that riddle to the Greeks."

"Okay, fair enough. I'm not going to trip you up with anything too old or easy. Your turn." I folded my arms across my chest and waited, my mind tumbling over trying to think of another riddle.

"I travel the world 'round, yet I never leave my corner. What am I?"

I had to spend a little time on that one. *What travels, but doesn't move? What corner? A bus? No...a bus driver? No, that's too easy, too. Besides, he gets off the bus. Okay, think less literal. What kinds of things travel? Information travels—* "A stamp!" I exclaim without a second's hesitation.

Not bad, Harker. For the first time all day, I felt Becks in my head. Sharing my blood made a mental connection between us, one that had only grown stronger as our relationship blossomed, but she'd been strangely absent all day.

Where have you been? I asked in my head.

There's something blocking me. I don't feel cut off, but it's hard to communicate. I'm in the building now, so it's easier. I'm trying to get down to spring you, but Grizzle is cock-blocking me at every turn. He's really got a mad-on for you.

He's still working for demons. Don't come down here. This guy will tear you apart.

"Tell Detective Flynn I wish her the best. And tell her goodbye," Zepar said, and I felt a wall slam into place between Becks' consciousness and mine.

"I guess now I know what was keeping her from contacting me," I grumbled.

"Oh, you most certainly do. I can't have you getting an unfair advantage over little old me, can I? I mean, it's bad enough that you get to spend your life above ground, with all the myriad experiences humanity has to offer. Why should you be allowed to cheat in our little contest, as well?"

"I'm not the demon in the room," I replied. "I think I should be the one worried about getting cheated."

"Well, worry later, after I've eaten your kidneys with rice. For now, get on with the game. Unless you choose to forfeit?" His glittering smile was colder than a Frost Giant's breast milk, and I racked my brain trying to come up with a riddle.

I thought and tumbled old jokes and riddles around in my brain, trying to come up with something useful. Finally, a hint of something came to me. "Many have heard my voice, but none have ever seen me. I only speak when spoken to. What am I?"

Zepar actually looked like he was thinking for a few moments before he turned that chilly grin on me and said, "An echo. And that's what you'll be soon, Harker. Just an echo of yourself, floating around in people's memories."

"Nice," I said, smiling at the demon. "You trying to psych me out, since you know you can't beat me?"

Zepar's grin faded as he said, "I suppose it's time to end this, and it seems only fitting that the riddle that brings about your end starts with the one that brought about your beginning—your pitiful God."

"Wow, bringing the big guy into our little conversation? I must really have you rattled."

He didn't reply, just launched right into the riddle. "What is greater than God, and more evil than Satan? The poor have plenty of it, the rich need it not at all, and if you eat it, you will certainly die?"

I had nothing. A complete blank. Not a single idea came to me. I sat on the metal bench for at least a minute, feeling the cold radiating from the demon seeping into the metal and chilling my skin. I got up and paced, but still no ideas came. I drew in a breath, sure that the inspiration was right on the tip of my tongue, but again…nothing.

Then it hit me, and I felt like a complete idiot, in the way that only riddles can. I turned to face the demon. "I've got nothing, buddy."

He smiled big enough to show me both rows of pointed teeth. "You surrender, Harker?"

I returned his smile with the biggest shit-eating grin I could muster. "No, of course not. I told you the answer—nothing. There's nothing greater than God, nothing more evil than Satan. The poor have all the nothing they could ever want, and the rich don't want any more nothing. If you eat nothing, you'll die, and you're going to starve today because there will be no bits of Harker on your menu." I sat back down, grinning as the demon fumed.

"Your turn," he growled, glaring at me. His eyes began to flicker red, but the cold still poured off him in waves.

"No problem," I said. "Here's another old one for you. A hunter leaves his house and walks south for one mile. He encounters a bear, which chases him east for a mile before he finally shoots and kills it. This incredibly strong hunter then drags the bear one mile back to the front door of his cabin. What color is the bear?"

"What?" Zepar looked at me like I'd just grown another head.

"What color is the bear?" I repeated the question.

"How in the world am I supposed to glean that from the information you gave me? Or am I just supposed to guess? Guessing games aren't allowed. This isn't Samson's game, Harker. There has to be a correct answer that can be discerned from the information at hand. Try again."

"No," I said. "All the information you need is in the riddle. You just have to figure out the color of the bear. Or do you surrender?" It was my turn to smile, even though antagonizing demons isn't the smartest pastime I've ever picked up.

He mused on it for a little longer, then stood up and began to pace. Zepar muttered to himself, going through all the random permutations of bear coloring before finally turning back to me and saying, "I have no idea, Harker, what color was the bear?"

"You give up? You concede that I have won the contest?"

"As long as the answer is fair, then yes, you have won. What color is the damnable bear!" I loved watching the steam almost literally come out of his ears, but decided not to torment him too long lest he decide to ignore the rules of his own contest and beat me to death with my leg.

"White," I said. "The house was located on the North Pole, so the bear was a polar bear. It was white."

"Then how do you...the North Pole," he said, and that scary grin came back. "When he ran east, he actually ran in a slight curve, so he was still a mile directly south of the cabin."

"Yep," I said, waving at the gore behind him. "Don't forget to clean up your mess on your way out."

Zepar turned to me, his frozen grin sparkling white in his inky black face. "Don't worry, Harker. I never forget. *Anything.*" With that, he waved a hand and vanished in a cloud of sulfur. I blinked my eyes against the stinking cloud, and when my vision cleared, the cell door stood open, and all evidence of four dead demons was gone.

Harker? I heard Flynn's voice in my head as clear as ever, probably because the demon wasn't around anymore to cause interference.

Here, babe. I outwitted the demon, so we're good. I'll be up in a minute.

Yeah, you will, but not why you think. Captain Herr has Interview 1 set up for you, and he's on his way down right now.

What did I do now?

I think it's about me. And you. Us, I mean.

Shit. The last thing I need while trying to track down a fetishist Archangel was relationship counseling from my girlfriend's boss. Well, the last thing I needed was to play a game of riddles with a goddamn Fallen Angel, but dealing with Captain Herr was a close second. The door at the end of the hall clanged open, and my day went from bad to worse in an instant.

Herr walked to the open door of my cell, looked around for the other men who had occupied the cell with me until mere moments ago, and shook his head. "Harker, and am I ever going to hear your name without thinking about how fucked up my life is that I have to deal with you?"

"Probably not, Bennie. How've you been?" I asked, stepping out of the cell into the hallway.

"Worse every day that you're in my life. And don't call me Bennie."

"No problem, Shirley," I replied.

"I really want to shoot you." It wasn't the first time a cop had said those words to me, and I believed pretty strongly that it wouldn't be the last. But I didn't feel like getting shot at that particular moment, so I let Herr's comment slide. He looked me up and down, noting the tattered remnants of my sleeves thanks to the Reavers' claws, but said nothing. He just let out a sigh, then turned and walked up the hall back the way he came.

I followed close behind, more curious than anything. Why did Herr come to get me himself? Did he know there was more corruption in the building than just the dead Agent Smith? Did he know I was innocent, well, kinda innocent? And what did he care about my relationship with Rebecca?

I didn't get any answers, from Herr or through my mental link with Becks, as I followed the captain up two flights of stairs to the interview room. I don't know when they stopped calling them inter-rogation rooms, but now they're "interview rooms." The furniture is still the same—one chair on the side of the table facing the big two-way mirror, one table bolted to the floor with a thick metal ring through the table's surface to affix a suspect's handcuffs to. There were not more tape recorders, but there were two cameras in the corners of the room, trained on the center of the table and focused right where the suspect's face would be were he or she sitting in the chair. There were usually two chairs on the opposite side of the table, but this time there was just one. A pair of plastic tumblers sat on the table, with a pitcher of water between them.

Herr sat in the chair across from the "perp seat," and I took the suspect's position. It wasn't an unusual one for me—I'd sat in this chair dozens of times over the years. Up until a couple years ago, it was almost always Detective Rebecca Gail Flynn sitting across the table from me, trying to make charges stick when the evidence, and victims, had a bad habit of turning to dust. I'll admit, I made life diffi-cult for Becks before we started working together. But she was pretty much a giant pain in my ass, too, which I figured it was only fair.

"Water, Harker?" Herr asked, pouring himself a cup.

"Sure," I said. I opened my Sight as he poured, but I saw nothing out of the ordinary in the glass. A murmured *"purificent"* and a slight push of my will into the water, and I was mostly certain that there were no poisons or drugs in my drink. I took a sip, letting the cool liquid soothe my parched mouth. Fighting demons always dehydrates me for some reason.

I set my cup down on the table and looked across the scuffed surface at Herr. "What's up, Captain? I know what Grizzle wanted with me, but why are you here?"

He looked around and pulled a remote out of his front pants pocket. He aimed the black rectangular hunk of plastic at the cameras in the corners and pressed a red button on the device. The red lights on the cameras winked out, and Herr put the remote back in his pocket. He turned around to the big mirror and said, "Turn on the lights so Mr. Harker sees there's no one in the room, then get out."

Lights flickered on behind the mirror, throwing the surveillance room into dim light. There was a video camera on a tripod pointed at the glass, and two people in the room. I watched as a trim woman in a police uniform spun the camera to the ceiling and walked out of the room. The balding cop sitting at the lone desk in the room took off a pair of large over-the-ear headphones and followed her into the hall, leaving the light on.

"Now," Herr turned back to me, "you see that there's no surveillance. This isn't being recorded. You're not under arrest, and you're not under investigation for anything. The Lightbringers aren't pressing charges for trespassing or assault, and there's no proof that the lighting rig falling from the ceiling is anything other than a freak accident. It apparently just happened to occur while you were in the room. Because that's what you are, Harker, just a world of coincidence."

"I can't help it, Captain. I just end up in chaotic situations a lot. It's the burden I must bear." I spread my hands to show my innocence.

Herr wasn't buying it. "Yeah, whatever. I don't give a shit about whatever kind of weirdness you had with Smith. He was dirty, and he took some of my guys down with him. Maybe even fucked up some guys that didn't start off working with him, and now I've got some cancerous fucks floating around my division that I've got to root out."

"What does that have to do with me, Captain?" This wasn't going anywhere that I expected. I had no real idea what Herr wanted out of this secret conversation, so I just sat back and waited to see where he was going.

"Let me lay all my shit on the table, Harker. Flynn has a bright future in this department. She's a hell of a detective, and she can go a long way. As long as she doesn't have any kind of stink of corruption on her. The Smith thing is bad, but he snowed a lot of people up and down the food chain from Becca, so it's not going to stick to her too much."

It sunk in then, to Becks as well as me. I heard her in my head just like she was in the room. *That motherfucker. Who does he think—*

I cut her off, which is even harder to do when somebody's in your head than it is in real life. *Hold on, Becks. Let me just hear him out.*

But he—

He hasn't anything yet, I replied. *Besides, he's just your boss. I'm the one you're stuck with in your head, no matter what the day job says.*

She didn't reply, but I felt a surge of warmth come across our mental connection. She withdrew into the background, and I turned my attention back to Captain Herr. "Let me get this straight. You're saying I shouldn't see Detective Flynn outside of a working relationship, or it could have negative ramifications on her career? Is that what you're saying, Captain?" My voice was low and steady, and I locked eyes with the captain. I was pissed, but anyone looking in from the outside wouldn't be able to guess.

Herr got the message loud and clear, though. "I'm not saying that. I'm simply saying—"

"You're saying that being around me is bad for her career. Well, Captain, let me lay this out for you. I know you might not believe in everything that I deal with. But don't kid yourself into thinking that you have any fucking idea how the world works. There is shit out there, shit that I've seen, that would make you rip your own eyeballs out if you ever had to deal with it. I take care of the nasties that you and your people aren't equipped to deal with, and Detective Flynn is more than just my girlfriend, she's part of my team. I have stood shoulder to shoulder with that woman and fought literal demons, and I know she's got the goods. So not only will I not stop dating Flynn, and I won't stop sleeping with her, I can't afford to cut her from my team. She's too damn good, and the stakes are too damn high. If that fucks her career, I hate it, but if her career is the sacrifice we offer up to save the world—again—then so be it. Now, are we done?"

Herr sighed, pushed back from the table, and stood up. "I suppose we are." He walked to the door, then stopped with his hand on the knob and turned back to me. "Can you do me one favor, though, Harker?"

I stood up and looked him over. His uniform hung loosely on his wiry frame, and there was more gray in his temples than I'd noticed just last year. "If it's something I can do, Captain, I'll give it a shot."

"Don't get her killed." With that, he opened the door and stepped out into the hall, leaving me alone in the interrogation room to wonder if I had any chance of keeping my girlfriend alive.

I t was full dark by the time I made it out of the police station. I walked down the front steps with my belt in one hand and a brown paper bag containing my personal belongings in the other. Becks and Luke stood at the bottom of the steps in front of Luke's new car, a mammoth 1973 Dodge Monaco in pristine condition. The land yacht gleamed black under the yellow streetlights, its engine rumbling like a tiger's purr.

"Tell me again why you bought the absolutely biggest, most garish vehicle possible?" I asked, opening the passenger door for Becks then sliding into the back seat.

Luke got in the driver's seat and pulled the door closed with a solid *thunk*. "Because, dear nephew, the more I am around you, the more important it seems to surround myself and my belonging with as much reinforced metal as possible."

I didn't have an answer to that. That's one of the problems with hanging out with people who are centuries older than you—they always have the last word. I swear sometimes that Luke spent the entire 1760s just thinking up snappy comebacks. I had to give him credit, though, the big car rode like a dream. I was just nodding off in the spacious back seat when Rebecca spoke.

"What did you think of what Herr had to say?"

I sat up a little straighter in the seat. The simple fact that she'd spoken aloud instead of just communicating through our mental link told me that either she didn't want me hearing her thoughts on the matter, or that she wanted Luke's opinion. I wasn't going to mention that a dude who kept three psychotic vampires tucked away in a Romanian castle as his "wives" might not be the best person to go to for relationship advice.

"I don't know," I answered honestly. She'd know if I was lying anyway, and it's usually just easier to tell the truth. Way less to keep track of that way. "I mean, there are few things that I know. I know your career has already taken a hit from your association with me. No matter how much good you do, you'll always be tarred with the Agent Smith brush, and I'm sorry for that."

"That wasn't your fault—" she started to protest, but I cut her off.

"It wasn't completely my fault, but we both know that part of the reason Smith brought you into his division was because you and I had worked together, and he wanted to use you to keep an eye on me." I took her silence as agreement and went on. "And he as much as said that if you continued to hang around me, you're never getting captain's bars on your collar. I know that's not what you got into policing for," I said, forestalling another protest. "But you and I both know that if you're going to do something, you want to be the best at it. So, knowing that your association with me will hurt your advancement in the department, that's a real drawback."

I took a deep breath and let it out slow, then said what I really wanted to get across. "But here's the deal. I love you. I love you and am a better person with you than I am without you. If I have to move Heaven and Earth for us to be together, then I will. I understand if your career is more important than some old man and his crazy band of magical misfits, but if you decide that I'm what you want, that this life is what you want, then I'm all in."

"As am I, Rebecca," Luke said, reaching across the long bench seat and patting her knee. From me, that kind of gesture would end in me slapped in the face with my own hand for being a patronizing douche. Luke pulled it off. Another bonus to living forever, I guess.

She sat silent for the rest of the drive home, not that it took more than five minutes. We pulled into the underground parking deck for my building, and Luke parked in his reserved spaces. His car took up the room of two modern cars. Becks got out of the car, then stood leaning with her elbows on the hood while Luke and I stood by her. After at least a minute of standing there in silence, she stood up and looked me in the eye. "All I've ever wanted to do was be a cop. To catch the bad guys. Especially after my dad was killed. I want to make sure that no other little girl has to hear that her daddy isn't coming home because a bad person did a bad thing, and he couldn't quite stop it."

I remembered the night her father died. I remembered the rain, the smell of his blood, the way he looked up at me and asked me to take care of his little girl, to make sure she knew he loved her. I remembered when the light fled from his eyes. That same fire that left her father's eyes that night burned in Rebecca's eyes now. "I lost my father because of a bad *thing*, not a bad person, and if it weren't for you, I never would have known those things existed. So, if Herr wants me to stop seeing you, to stop associating with the man who pulled back the curtain and showed me the real darkness, the real bad guys, the real reason I became a cop...well, if Herr wants me to turn my back on everything I've ever wanted to do, not to mention turn my back on the man I love, then he can kiss my ass."

"Does this mean you're not breaking up with me?"

"Quincy Harker, you are a certifiable asshole," she said, then threw her arms around my neck and kissed me like there was no tomorrow.

After a long kiss that answered all my questions about her sincerity, I pulled back. "If that's how I get treated for being an asshole, I'll have to do it more often," I said with a smile.

"Well, when you figure out how to cram more hours into the day, I'm sure you'll manage," Luke said from the elevator. "Now let's go upstairs. I'm feeling peckish, and I'm either going to the apartment for dinner, or I'm going around the corner to the sushi restaurant." Flynn and I hustled to the elevator. If there was one thing I knew about Uncle Luke, it's that when he mentioned going to the sushi restaurant for dinner, fish was not on his menu.

"This is a bad idea, Quincy," Cassandra said as I sat across from her in Luke's apartment.

"Why?" I asked. "He likes you, he respects you, and there are very few safer places in the world than the headquarters of a shadowy organization filled with monsters, wizards, and large-caliber weapons."

"Luke is not what concerns me. You are not what concerns me, and by now you should know me well enough to understand that I am not a woman who is easily cowed by things that go bump in the night."

"I seem to recall that from a few adventures you had with Jo's father back in the day," I grinned, remembering Cassandra in her youth. She was a fiery woman, and as lethal with a pistol as her husband had been with his hammer. Unfortunately, longevity is not something the human members of the Shadow Council are often blessed with, and I remembered the call when Alex, her husband and Jo's father, was killed by a lycanthrope in Utah. I buried the body myself, after severing his head with a silver blade to make sure there was no chance of him turning.

"That was a long time ago, Quincy. I'm an old woman now."

"Where's the nearest weapon, Cassie?" I asked, a game I played with her many years ago. She didn't answer, just smiled at me and tipped her chin down. I leaned to my left and saw the pistol pointed at me from her lap. "I thought so. What were you worried about, again?"

"Ginny," she said, and I saw true fear in her eyes. "I don't know if I can have my grandbaby growing up around all this. This insanity, it changes a person, makes them hard in ways I don't want her to be. This past year, it's been hard on Jo. A lot of things got more real for her after y'all's trip to Atlanta, you know? Before that, she would fight monsters, and she knew she was in danger, but I don't know if she understood the stakes you all play for. But Atlanta…"

"Atlanta was rough," I agreed. "It brought a lot of things home for a lot of people. But that's why I need you here, Cassie. You know what's at stake. You know how bad things can get if there's nobody to stand up against these things and the people that help them. I need you around *for* Jo. You keep her grounded. You can do the same thing for Luke. Bring Ginny around, let her get to know him. You know how he loves kids."

I could see the memories in her face. The few times Luke and I spent the holidays with Cassie and Alex when Jo was a little girl. I was pretty sure Jo didn't remember any of it, but I knew full well Cassie did. After a moment of smiling reflection, she nodded. "Alright, Quincy, you win. I'll let Ginny play with Luke from time to time, no matter how much the old bat complains. And we'll stay. For a while, at least."

She leaned forward and her eyes became chips of black flint. "But let me tell you one thing, Quincy Harker. Joanna is a grown woman, and she can make her own decisions. God knows she's told me that enough times. But if you let anything bad happen to my grandbaby… well, there ain't enough magic in the world to save you from the Hell I will unleash on your sorry ass."

I held up my hands in surrender. "Not a problem, Cassie. I promise on my life that I will protect that child as though she were my very own." With those words, I felt a tingle run through my hands, and they were surrounded by a white glow for just a second, then it was gone.

"What was that, Quincy?" Cassandra asked.

"I have no idea. I didn't cast anything, at least not intentionally."

"Well, I guess you're Ginny's godfather now, and I expect you to take that seriously. Now if you'll excuse me, I have to go down the hall and see if *Master Luke* is finished with his snack. I don't know if that old fool expects me to tuck him in and read him a bedtime story or what, but we are going to have a conversation on the duties of a personal assistant in the twenty-first century sooner rather than later." She stood up and walked to the door. She stopped, not looking back at me, and said, "Thank you, Quincy. Thank you for looking out for my family."

"Thank you for looking out for mine," I replied, and could almost hear the smile stretch across her face as she opened the door and stepped out into the hall.

F our hours later, I was nearing exhaustion and feeling further and further away from any kind of solution. I stretched out on the floor of my living room, my bare heels breaking the chalk circle I'd spent the last forty-five minutes sitting cross-legged inside. I heard the crackle of my spine stretching and settling as I lay on the hardwood floor feeling every one of my hundred-plus years. "Fuuuuuck," I said as my everything tried to realign itself.

"What's wrong, old man?" Becks asked from the counter by the kitchen, where she sat on a barstool watching me and reading a book on her Kindle.

"Aside from my ass falling asleep, my back killing me, and my left knee locking up, something's wrong with my magic."

"What do you mean?"

"Something's not working right," I explained. "I cast a spell to locate divine magic, which should have pointed me to Uriel's location, or at least narrowed down the part of town that he's being kept in."

"It didn't find him?"

"Well, it's more than that. Not only did it not find Uriel, it didn't find anything."

Flynn set her Kindle on the counter, slid off the barstool, and came over to sit on the couch by my head. "Do you mean you didn't find Uriel, you didn't find any angels, or you didn't find *anything?*"

I sat up, my butt wiping out more of the circle. Annoyed, I stood up and wiped my hands, ass, and feet off with a small towel, then dropped it on the floor by the circle. I sat on the couch facing Flynn and leaned forward, my hands on my knees. "I kinda mean all three. I sensed the angels in the other apartments here and a trace of the divine coming from Glory, but that's it. Nothing else."

"Okay, then maybe you should look somewhere else. Broaden the search. Could be the Lightbringers took Uriel farther afield than you were expecting."

"Farther afield than twenty-five miles from the center of town? I doubt it, Becks. Their center of power is here. They're pretty damned unlikely to skip town. But that's not the only problem."

"It never is," Flynn said with a shake of her head. "What else?"

"There's no divinity. Not even the baseline of minor artifacts that I can usually sense with that kind of locator spell. Even that's missing. It's not just that the Lightbringers have taken Uriel, they've somehow sucked all the divine magic from the entire city."

Flynn looked concerned, but then brightened. "Maybe there just isn't any to find? I mean, there are a lot of churches around here, but Charlotte isn't what I would call a holy city by any stretch."

I laughed. "You're right about that, but it's got a fair number of minor artifacts floating around, not to mention enough things that have proven to be articles of faith to get imbued with divinity from the belief of people nearby over the years."

Becks leaned forward her curiosity obviously piqued. "Yeah, like what? What kind of things can become holy just by people being close to them for a long time?"

"Well, anything that people talismanize, actually. Howard's Rock in Death Valley Stadium had a ton of divine energy just because of decades of football fans pouring their hearts out for their team. The Ben Long fresco in St. Peter's Church downtown was a huge source of divine energy until it got wrecked a few years ago. The JFG Coffee sign off John Belk Freeway has a little bit. It used to have more, but when they took the sign down for years, it leached away. It got put back up, but it's a different city now, so a lot of the faith and connection that people felt to the sign is gone, so it has less power."

"So anything that a lot of people connect to, feel strongly about, has this energy to it?"

"Yeah," I said. "Maybe 'divine' isn't the right word, especially if God really is MIA, but it's as close as I've got with my limited vocabulary. The only thing is, now it's all gone. There's none of this energy anywhere around Charlotte. Usually even if there aren't any major artifacts, the pulpit of every church holds a little bit of magic. But not anymore. Not here. The only source of divinity in the city is in this building."

"What does that mean?"

"I don't know, and my best resources, or at least, *sources* of information, are all kind of insane."

"Yeah, they're nuts, but they're your nuts, Harker. I'm not going anywhere near those jerks." She stood up from the couch and walked toward the bedroom. "Besides, I've got to be at work in two hours. I'm going to go take a shower. Too bad you've got to go talk to angels, you could help me wash my back." I watched her back, among other parts of her, sway with a rhythm both beautiful and dangerous as she walked away. I hated to see her go, but like the song said, I loved to watch her leave.

"I wish I could, darling. I wish I could in ways I can't even express. But I don't think I have a whole lot of choice in the matter."

That's how I came to knock on the door of an Archangel's apartment in the early morning hours, and I didn't even bring doughnuts. Sealtiel answered the door, still wearing the guise of a gorgeous human woman that she was using when Adam brought her to my building a couple weeks before. "Good morning, Quincy. How are you today?" She stepped inside and gestured for me to come inside. I did and smelled the most glorious aroma to pass my nostrils in hours.

"Is that fresh coffee?" I asked, more a grunt than a question. Between my run-in with the Lightbringers, my fight with demons in the jail cell, and my fruitless spellcasting, it had been a long time since I'd seen my bed, with or without Flynn in it. I was running on fumes, and the ones coming from the coffee maker on Sealtiel's counter were just what the doctor ordered.

"It is indeed," Sealtiel replied, reaching into the cupboard above the sink and passing me a mug.

"Hey Stevie?" a rough voice came from behind me.

I spun around to see a shirtless Mitchell Carson standing in the doorway of the apartment's one bedroom. Mitch wore a pair of black boxer briefs and a slightly embarrassed expression on his face. But that was all.

"Yes, Mitchell?" Sealtiel, apparently keeping the "Stevie" nickname for now, replied. She didn't look the least bit embarrassed, and I wasn't really sure she even understood the concept.

"Hi, Mitch," I said, giving him a wide grin as I filled my mug.

"Harker." Mitch nodded at me. "Um, Stevie, I was just going to ask if you had any more clean towels, but..."

"Oh, I'm sorry, Mitchell. I was coming out here to get some spares from the closet by the front door, but Quincy came to visit. I think we'll have to postpone our shower while I speak with him. Or, I suppose you could shower alone, but as you explained, that is horribly inefficient when the shower is certainly large enough to accommodate both of us at once."

"Yeah, Mitch, that's really inefficient. Why don't you throw on some pants, and maybe a shirt, and come out to chat? I just need a little information, then when I leave, the two of you can make sure your backs are plenty clean."

Mitch looked everywhere but at me, acting like a teenager swiping his dad's *Playboy* magazines instead of a grown man. Hell, given the fact that he was really the Archangel Michael, he was even older than Luke. But he didn't remember anything before his Mitchell Carson persona was created, so it was almost like dealing with a human. "Ummm...yeah, I'll do that." He turned around, the tips of his ears flaming red enough to act as turn signals, and ducked back into the bedroom to get dressed.

I turned to look at Sealtiel, leaning against the far counter, her arms crossed over her pink t-shirt. She was simply dressed, with her blond hair pulled back in a loose ponytail. Long tanned legs poked out of the cutoff sweatpants she wore, and a mischievous smile flittered around on her face. "You're a naughty angel, aren't you?"

"I can't help it, Harker," she protested. "You know we don't have gender when we're in our true form, and I was Stevie Shoes for so long, I just wanted to remember what human women felt like! And Michael was always such a stick in the mud as an angel, I thought it would be fun to play around with him a little while he's human. Besides, he's so *cute* when he blushes."

"You seduced the Archangel of War, Stevie. I think that's a little more than 'playing around.'" I was not exactly sure how to deal with a flirty angel wearing a human suit, especially not before eight a.m.

"Probably," she admitted. "But I was right. It's a lot of fun sometimes, wearing these human bodies."

"Don't remind me," I grumbled. "I could be upstairs right now conserving some water of my own, but I'm down here trying to find out what's fucked up in my city."

"This time," Sealtiel added.

"Huh?" I grunted. "This is coffee number one, Stevie. If you're being all snarky, I'm not smart enough for it right now."

She grinned, and the whole room lit up. If this was the woman that was supposed to herald the end of days, all she had to do was smile like that, and all of humanity would go willingly. "I just meant that there's always something wrong with your city, so you need to find out what's wrong *this time*."

"God, I wish you were wrong," I said, reaching for the coffee pot. Sealtiel put out her hand and slapped the back of my wrist.

"Mitch hasn't had any yet. Share and share alike, Quincy. I promise, when he's done, I'll make another pot. Now what do you want our help with?"

Mitch came back out of the bedroom wearing a pair of sweats and a Charlotte Hornets t-shirt. Not having to look at his abs certainly made my life a little less self-conscious. Stevie poured a cup of coffee and handed it to me, then waved me over toward the couch while she set to brewing another pot. "I can hear you from here. Go sit with Mitchell and tell us why you're here."

I did as I was told, even unaccustomed as I was to being told where to go and what to do by an Archangel in pajamas. But I went with it because my life is just weird sometimes. I took the armchair, leaving Mitch to sit on the sofa with enough space for Sealtiel to perch there when she joined us. "The divinity is gone," I said, pitching my voice loud enough to be heard in the kitchen.

"I don't know what that means," Mitch said.

I explained the whole thing about divine magic to him, finishing up just as Sealtiel came in and perched on the arm of the couch. "It means that whoever took Uriel is far, far more powerful than Quincy expected, and shit is about to get real," she said, holding out one of the two mugs in her hands. "Now I wish I'd spiked the coffee."

"Me too, sister," I agreed.

"You can't sense *any* divinity? Anywhere in the city?" Sealtiel asked.

"Outside of this building, there's just the faintest glow around some of the oldest churches. St. Peters has a touch, but that could be trace from the Ben Long fresco that hung there for so long. The theatre downtown, Spirit Square, it has a glimmer, but it went from being a church to a theatre."

"And both of those are holy places, just not always to the same people." She nodded. "But you sense nothing from any artifacts, no relics of power, nothing like that?"

"Nothing that would help me pinpoint Uriel's location," I said.

"What about that demon bartender you hang out with sometimes?" Mitch asked. I glanced at him, but there didn't seem to be any condemnation in his question, just trying to help.

"Mort's not answering his phone, and the recording at the bar says they're closed until further notice. If I didn't know better, I'd say that Pastor Rob has him scared shitless and he's laying low until one of us kills the other one. Mort's a good hand in a fight, but unless there's something in it for him, he's probably not jumping in."

"Can't say as I blame him. People that jump into fights around you people tend to find their lives turned upside down," Mitch said, a bitter twist to the corner of his mouth.

"Sorry, pal," I said in a tone that I sincerely hoped showed exactly how not sorry I was. "Once we've convinced the Almighty to get back to doing His job and gotten Glory's wings back, I'm sure you can mind-wipe yourself again and get back to breaking noses inside an overgrown dog kennel. But until then, either lend a hand or shut the fuck up."

He stiffened, and I held up both hands. "Sorry," I said, and I meant it. "That was out of line. I haven't slept in about thirty-six hours, and I don't know how the hell I'm going to find this angel before the demon masquerading as a televangelist tears my city apart."

"It's okay," Mitch said in that gruff way that guys accept the half-assed apologies we give each other. "I was being a dick, too."

"If you two are quite finished," Stevie interjected before our bromance could truly flourish in her den. "Quincy, why don't you go get some rest, then we can reconvene in a few hours and investigate the mysterious black hole of divinity."

"Yeah, that's a good idea," I said with a yawn. "This coffee hasn't even made a dent in my...wait a second, what did you say?" Something was tickling the back of my head, but I couldn't quite pin it down.

"She said go get some sleep," Mitch said.

I waved him off. "No." I turned to Sealtiel. "Repeat exactly what you just said." She did, and the pieces fell into place. "That's it! Stevie, you're a genius. You two go take your shower and meet me in my apartment in forty-five minutes. So don't fuck around with any lengthy back-washing, just do what needs to be done and get some clothes on. I gotta go." I put the mug on the coffee table, then almost knocked it off with my knee as I stood.

"What are you going to do, Harker?" Mitch asked, standing up as if to catch me.

I steadied myself and headed to the door. "I gotta go cast a spell to find what isn't there. Then we're gonna go kick some demon ass and save the world. Again."

Ninety minutes later, I stood outside the back door of a nondescript warehouse on the south side of Charlotte with a pair of angels standing behind me, ready to commit burglary for the second time in twenty-four hours. That might have been a record, even for me. I opened my Sight and looked around the building but saw nothing out of the ordinary.

"Is there an alarm?" Mitch asked.

"I have no idea," I replied. "I was looking for magical traps and things I care about. I just assume I'm getting arrested again for this shit, so I wasn't worried about that."

"You're pretty blasé about getting arrested. Were you like this before you were sleeping with a cop?" Mitch asked.

"I was this way before said cop was born," I said. "I've seen the inside of more jail cells than most people have seen states. It doesn't bother me that much anymore. Until they put demons in the holding cell with me. That was a buzzkill." I put my hand on the doorknob, and it turned easily. I pushed the door open and stepped through, motioning for the others to follow.

I took a few steps, then realized I was alone. I turned back to the doorway, where Mitch and Sealtiel stood. "You guys coming?"

"I'm sorry, Quincy, we cannot," Sealtiel, still in her Stevie guise, honey-blonde hair spilling down over her shoulders and concern in her green eyes. "The vacuum of divine magic that you sensed does indeed emanate from this building, and it begins at the threshold. We cannot enter without our divinity being severely compromised."

"That doesn't sound good," I said.

"If we lose too much of our holy magic, we will disappear entirely. I am not sure if we will become ethereal and return to the Heavenly plane, or if we will just cease to exist. Regardless, that is a chance I would rather not take. While this body is new to me, I rather enjoy it." Mitch let a little smirk flicker across his face, and I gave him a lot of credit for not mentioning how much he enjoyed Sealtiel's body.

"Shit," I muttered. "Okay, then you two stay here and make sure I'm not surprised by anything coming in behind me."

"I can still come in," Mitch said, stepping forward. Sealtiel grabbed his belt and jerked him backward before his foot touched the threshold.

"No, Mitchell, you cannot. While you have no recollection of being Michael, the fact remains that you *are* the Archangel Michael, Defender of Heaver, Dispenser of God's Justice, and the wielder of the one sword that we can least afford to be without in the upcoming conflict. So no, you may not go in."

I nodded at the stunned man. "She's right. We can't afford to lose anyone else, and who knows what will happen to that oversized toothpick on your belt if you bring it in here? I've got a pretty good idea, and it's pretty bad news. My gut tells me that we're going to need that sword, and the angel that wields it, a whole lot in the days and weeks to come, so you're benched for this one, pal." I turned to head into the warehouse, my backup just eliminated without ever throwing a punch. I love going into a fight when I don't know the combatants, the territory, or the schedule.

I closed the door on a pair of disappointed angels and ventured into the building on my own. The section I was in looked like a basic warehouse with a couple of rollup doors at the loading dock near the door I came in. There were a couple of pallets of what looked like random office equipment sitting shrink-wrapped on the concrete floor. Oddly arranged fluorescent lights flickered in the ceiling overhead, casting bright light across the huge empty space. I opened my Sight again, and aside from a few smears of demon-taint here and there across the floor, nothing struck me as odd.

Until I looked up. "Fuck," I said, my voice barely more than a whisper. Glowing in my Sight, but invisible to the naked eye, was a huge casting circle hanging over my head. I immediately understood why the lights were arranged in such a weird pattern—to keep them from breaking the boundaries of the circle, easily the largest permanent magic structure I'd ever seen. A fifty-foot diameter circle was scribed into the ceiling, double-walled with Enochian symbols between the walls of the circle. A pentacle with Norse, Enochian, Hebrew, and Aramaic runes and symbols in each corner was nestled inside the circle. This was created for a major working, more major even than the biggest summoning circles I'd ever seen.

"What the fuck?" I asked, my voice barely above a whisper.

"Impressive, isn't it?" came a familiar voice from the end of the warehouse. I dropped my Sight and looked over to where Pastor Rob stood silhouetted in a doorway on the far wall. I recognized him from his website and his YouTube videos, but he somehow looked even more smarmy in person. I couldn't tell from this distance if he was the one who led the raid on Purgatory and kidnapped Uriel, but he certainly didn't seem surprised to see me.

"I gotta give it to you, it is that," I said. "I've seen a lot of assholes gaping wide and spewing their shit across the planes, but this is the biggest, brownest shithole I've ever seen."

His face darkened for an instant, then the perma-smile was back. "I've heard about you, Quincy Harker. I've heard that you're crude. I've also heard that you're very powerful. I have to admit, I'm not impressed so far." He walked toward me, stepping into the well-lit warehouse so I could get my first good look at the man all the fuss was about.

He was good-looking dude, I'll admit. He was tall and trim and moved like his joints were well-oiled. Dark, curly hair was tousled artfully atop his high brow, and his eyebrows were so perfect I wondered if he plucked them. His jaw was chiseled and covered in the type of stubble that you know wasn't grown, it was trimmed down to be perfectly symmetrical. His full lips gave just the slightest feminine cast to his features, and his razor cheekbones made him look more male model than worship leader. He was dressed in a long-sleeved white dress shirt, open at the collar, skinny jeans just frayed enough at the knee to be cool, and dress shoes that cost more than my car. Admittedly, I have crap taste in cars, but those were handmade and Italian or my dad never banged a vampire.

He walked all the way over to me, his sly smile never wavering. He stalked as much as walked, prowling the room like a big cat, all predator eyes and slow swagger. I didn't move. I'd seen his type before, all quiet confidence and sleek smiles until it was time to throw down. Then he'd go for a one-shot kill, probably a blade to the throat or something equally flashy. If he didn't take me down in the opening attack, I had a good chance to making it through the night.

"Nope, not impressed." He paced around me, the heels of his shoes clicking across the floor. I felt his breath on my neck as he got close and breathed deep. "You smell nervous, Harker. What's wrong?" The mocking lilt of his voice was familiar, but I couldn't remember where I'd heard that tone before.

"That's my asshole repellant. I put it on every morning with my deodorant. I guess today's dose has worn off."

He was back in front of me now, out of easy reach but still close enough to close the gap in an eye blink. "You're funny, Harker. Why don't you give up all this and come work for me? We could run this town. Hell, we could probably run this whole country if you play your cards right. You can be my right-hand man, sitting next to the throne, enforcing the law, slinging spells and kicking ass, just like you do now. Only it would pay a lot better."

"I'm not short on cash," I said, keeping my voice low and slow. The longer he talked, the longer I had to figure out his end game, and the better chance I had to piss all over his cornflakes.

"But your girl, she's having some job troubles, right? I could make all that go away. Maybe induce a vacancy in the department, move a few pieces around on the board to put her in a better position...you just tell me what her favorite position is, and I'll make it happen." His smile stretched ear to ear, and I pushed down the swell of rage I felt when he mentioned Becks.

Keep calm, idiot. He's baiting you. I wasn't sure if the words were coming from my head or if Flynn was listening in, but either way, it was the truth. I let out a deep breath, resolved not to let this asshole throw me off my game. Then he pushed the wrong button, and shit went red.

"Or maybe I'll just introduce myself and find out what her favorite position is myself. Tell me, Harker, is she a screamer? She will be."

The words were barely out of his mouth before I was on him. I didn't reach for magic, didn't try to cast any kind of spell, I just shot forward, covering the ten feet between us in less than a second, clutching his throat with my left hand and pulling my right back to pummel his face to powder. I looked in his eyes, which widened with surprise, then narrowed in anger.

"Oh no, Harker," he growled. "That is *not* how this is going to go." He let me push him back into a pallet of copy paper, of all ridiculous things, then he brought his right hand up in a sweep, knocking my grip from his throat like I was a gnat. He grabbed the front of my shirt, pulled me so close that our noses almost touched, then the smug fuck *smiled* at me. "That's not how this is going to go at all." He flexed, no effort apparent in his movements at all, and I found myself airborne.

I crashed to my back on the concrete floor and slid a good six feet before I came to a slow stop. Pastor Rob, whatever he was, stepped forward away from the pallet of paper and glared at me. "We were having such a nice chat, too. Then you had to go and spoil it. Now I have to be unpleasant. I don't like to be unpleasant. I try to get my way through persuasion, through negotiation, through coercion if I must. But now I have to be unpleasant. And that's not fun for anyone. Well, maybe for the boys."

He snapped his fingers, and four hulking brutes came through the door at the back of the warehouse. "Boys," he said with a sweeping gesture to the goons, "teach Mr. Harker here the consequences of being unpleasant to me."

The thugs advanced on me, and Pastor Rob turned and walked back into the room at the back of the building where they came from. I got to my feet, drew my Glock from under my leather jacket, and got ready to get unpleasant.

Four demons, one Harker. If I kept this up, it was going to turn into its own internet meme. They looked mostly human, except for every damn one of them being over seven feet tall. All these big guys made me long for the days of scrapping in enclosed spaces with Reaver demons. Oh wait, that was yesterday.

"Hey guys, can we talk about this?" I said, walking backward, keeping the thugs in my sight the whole time.

One of the two in the middle just growled, while the far left goon took three rushing steps forward, his arms held low like he wanted to body-slam me.

"Guess not," I said. I raised my pistol and fired four quick shots to this chest. He jerked with the impact and went down to one foot, but didn't drop. No blood came from the three holes in his chest, and he ripped his black t-shirt away, giving me a great view as the flesh closed in a few seconds and pushed the spent bullets out of his chest to *plink* on the floor.

"Well, shit," I said, tossing the gun at his face. He swatted it out of the air, but it gave me the distraction I was looking for. I reached for my magic, but the second I touched it, I felt it flow out of me as though a vacuum was latched onto my soul. My eyes wide, I staggered and released my hold on the energy.

"Looks like the little wizard found the portal," the far right goon said with a chuckle. "Go ahead, wizard. Cast a spell. See who get hurt, us...or you."

I didn't need to investigate that possibility any further. I knew how that shit was going to go. Shrugging out of my leather jacket, I turned and sprinted for the back door. As expected, the demons charged after me, but I wasn't trying to escape. The last thing I wanted was these assholes running around in my city. Even if it did give me backup in the form of Sealtiel and Mitch, I wasn't sure how much help they would be, since they couldn't touch their magic. I wasn't even sure what would happen if Mitch invoked his sword. Would it work? Would it be drained, just like my magic was? Yeah, getting Archangel Michael's sword busted sounded like the very pinnacle of bad ideas.

So I ran. But before I got to the door, I jumped, channeling every episode of *American Ninja Warrior* I'd ever seen, and ran up the wall. I made it a few feet, but when I pushed off the wall into a backflip, my naturally enhanced strength and agility let me flip over the heads of the pursing demons to land in a crouch behind them. I whipped out my pair of matched fighting daggers from the back of my belt and slashed through the hamstrings of the two center demons. Their flesh and tendons parted easily under the silver-edged blades, which I said a silent prayer of thanks for. If these buggers had some kind of protection against harm by unsanctified weapons, I was screwed. Even so, with their ridiculous healing, they would only be out of the fight for a minute at the most.

Desperately needing to end this quick, I leapt on the back of the nearest standing demon and wrapped my arms around his neck. I could feel the laugh rumble through his chest, until he felt me bury the pair of daggers in the sides of his neck. I wrapped my legs around his chest, leaned back, and pulled my hands together, drawing the knives through his neck and severing his head from his shoulders. The blades scraped through his spine, showering me in the wretched stench of black-green demon blood. I jumped off his back turned to the last demon standing, gore dripping from my face and hair.

I let the grin stretch across my face and called up just enough magic to make my eyes glow red. "Okay, motherfucker, you're next."

He wasn't scared. I really wanted him to be scared. "Is that supposed to scare me, wizard? I can make my eyes glow, too." And he did. His eyes blazed orange in his otherwise human face, and when he opened his mouth, a stream of fire shot out, bathing me in red-orange flame.

I dove out of the way, but not before getting thoroughly scorched. I'm sure there are things in the world that smell worse than burnt demon blood, but I've never smelled them. I gagged and rolled on the floor, putting out my burning clothes, and scrambled to my feet, singed but not hurt too badly. I turned to face the dragon-demon, who stood grinning as his two buddies now drew themselves up to their feet, hamstrings mended and attitudes significantly worsened.

"Well, shit," I muttered, then ran straight at the nearest goon. His human mask was slipping, letting a little of his gray skin show through as he used more energy to put himself back together from his injuries. Gray skin meant he probably wasn't a big-time Pit Lord or anything I really needed to stress over, except for the part where there were two of them and I couldn't draw on my magic to bail me out. I got within about eight feet of him and sprang forward, thrusting out one leg like I expected to do some kind of awesome kick.

I didn't expect to do any kind of awesome kick. I know me. I'm a badass, but I'm no Chuck Norris. What I expected to happen was for the demon to snatch me out of midair and slam me to the hard concrete, knocking me breathless and ringing my bell pretty solidly. Since I was expecting it, it didn't knock me as senseless as it normally would, leaving me enough presence of mind to jam both knives into the demon's forearms, wedging the blades into the tight space between the arm bones. I pulled the blades apart sideways, snapping the forearm bones and leaving the monster's right hand dangling by a few strands of muscle and flesh.

The thug let his human guise drop completely as he let go of me and shrieked in pain. He clutched his ruined hand to his chest and fell to his knees, screaming and spraying blood around the warehouse like a firehose. I stood up and charged the other demon, who looked at the ruins of two of his compatriots and turned tail. He was bigger than me, stronger than me, and probably could have taken me out with a little help from his fire-breathing buddy, had he not been a chicken-shit hellspawn pansy. He was stronger, but I was faster, and I ran him down in seconds, jamming my knives into his back and opening him up like he had a zipper on either side of his spine. I opened a big enough hole in his back, then jammed my right-hand knife in his kidney, freeing up my right hand to reach into his chest and yank his beating heart out through his ribcage. He collapsed to the floor, his soul already back in the fires and his body starting to dissolve on the warehouse floor.

I turned to the firebreather, gore-splattered and panting with exertion and battle rage. "Okay, fuckwit, your turn."

He didn't speak, just opened his mouth and spat a gout of flame as big around as my leg at me. I called up a shield and sent the power straight into the floor. I marched toward him, his fire burning hotter with every step. Whatever vacuum for magic they had working in this joint was taking a serious toll, and I struggled to hold my shield against the onslaught of fire and the constant drain on my power, but I pushed on. I got to within a few feet of the demon and angled my shield to pour the fire right back in his face. I knew it wouldn't cause him any real harm, but it did burn his human suit off, leaving him standing in front of me in his considerable lack of glory. I drew back, then slammed my magical shield forward, knocking him onto his ass and cutting off the stream of fire.

The demon looking up at me from the floor was actually a lot less intimidating in his true form. As a human, he was a buff giant, carved out of muscle and attitude, with glowing red eyes. Once his concentration on that illusion was shattered, he reverted to his true form, which looked more like an evil Danny DeVito than something out of the pages of Revelation. He sat on his butt, glaring up at me, butt-naked with a huge gut spilling out over his junk. His skin was a mottled gray, with tufts of wiry black hair sprinkled over him like patchy grass or mangy fur. His lower jaw jutted out, and a pair of short fangs stuck up. His eyes were still red, but they are narrow, beady things, more pathetic than frightening. All in all, he looked like a cross between a cherub and a fat gargoyle.

"What the fuck are you?" I asked, then shook my head. "Fuck it, I don't care," I growled, then stabbed him right in both beady eyes. I twisted the blades for good measure and felt the heat in the room start to dissipate as his soul fled back to his home plane.

I turned to the crippled demon, still whimpering and trying desperately to regrow the bones in his wrist and hand. "You have two choices, pal. You can flee this plane and go dive back into the fires you crawled out of, or you can find out why they really call me the Reaper. I don't give a single fuck which one you pick, but make a decision, because as the man said in the movie, it's nut-cutting time." I can't help it, I thought *ZombieLand* was brilliant.

He looked at me, looked down at his hand, still hanging by a few threads of meat, and then looked around the room at the scattered remains of his three demon buddies. "Fuck this place, I'm going back to Hell where it's safer," he said, and his eyes went dark. A black mist rose from the demon corpse's eyes to dissipate into the aether, and the body it once occupied began to decompose into really smelly demon sludge, just like his three buddies. Within an hour, there would be nothing left of them but puddles of goop, and within four hours, even that would evaporate, absorbed back into the magical energy of the planes.

I wiped off my blades and tucked them back into the sheaths on the back of my belt, knowing that I'd be dousing them in holy water, then salt water, then holy water again before I buried them in a churchyard when this was all over. Silver is potent magically, but the last thing I needed was a pair of knives hanging around my apartment that had carved up four demons. That kind of taint lingers, no matter how much you cleanse a weapon. Come to think of it, I'd better just have these things consecrated then melted down. I let out a sigh at this realization. Good knives are hard to come by.

I looked around the warehouse with my Sight, but there were no other surprises waiting for me. Not out here, anyway. So I dropped back into normal vision, retrieved and reloaded my Glock, and walked across the deserted warehouse to kick down a door and fight to the death with a demonic evangelist wearing skinny jeans.

So I did just that. I planted a size eleven Doc Marten just to the left of the doorknob and kicked the door in. The cheap hollow-core door splintered and slammed open with a satisfying crunch, and I stepped through into a scene straight out of Hannibal Lecter's wet dreams. Uriel was pinned to the far wall, hanging from spikes driven through his wrists. He was trapped in a circle drawn on the drywall with what looked like blood, and from what I could see, he provided every drop.

The angel seemed trapped in his human form, and it looked like he'd gone ten rounds with Mike Tyson in his prime, then another ten with Ali. His face was pulped, his jaw hanging loose and spilling blood and drool down his chin and chest. His eyes would have been swollen shut from the bruising around them, except his eyelids had been sliced off and stapled to the wall on either side of his head. Judging from the bruising all over his torso, I'd guess at least most of his ribs were broken, and probably both legs. I wasn't close enough to see his fingers and toes, but given the dedication Pastor Rob had shown to his craft, I assumed the nails were gone and all the digits at least dislocated, if not broken.

"That's impressive, Pastor," I said, stepping into the room. "The last time I saw somebody fucked up that sincerely, they were under a doctor's care. Admittedly, the doctor was Josef Mengele, so you've reached a pretty high bar."

"I'm glad you like what I've done with the place, Harker." Pastor Rob turned from a long table set along one of the room's side walls. As he stepped away from it, I could see the surface littered with knives, spikes, cleavers, needles, and other implements of torture, all stained brown with years of bloody work. Pastor Psycho wore long rubber kitchen gloves now, to protect his delicate skin from blood spatter, and a white apron with a picture of Darth Vader on it that said, "Come to the Dark Side. We have cookies." There was a lot more red on the apron than there was visible white, but I did appreciate the irony.

"I didn't say I liked it, I said I was impressed. Not the same thing," I replied, moving into a clear space in the middle of the room. Part of me wanted to keep my back to a wall, but with as flimsy as the door was, I didn't trust the wall to stop anything I was afraid of.

"Oh well, you can't please all of the people all of the time, right? But forgive me, I'm being rude. Have you met my guest, Uriel? I think you know him better as Torch, legendary local pervert, deviant, malcontent, and loudmouth." Rob covered the distance between himself and the battered archangel in two long strides and grabbed a fistful of Torch's curly red hair. He jerked the man's head up, forcing him to look at me with his reddened, blood-soaked eyes. Tracks of tears and blood carved rivulets down his face, dripping through his red goatee and down the front of his scarred and naked body.

"Uriel, say hello to Quincy Harker," Rob said. "He's here to rescue you from the nasty demon that kidnapped you and stole your little toy."

Uriel hung there, silent except for the sound of his labored breathing. A wheeze came from his mouth, but his shattered jaw couldn't form words.

"What's that, Uriel? Cat got your tongue? Oh, no, not a cat, a rat! That's right, you can't say hello to Mr. Harker because I ripped your tongue out and fed it to the rats last night. Silly me, I forget."

"Hhhhuuuuuuuukkkkk ooooooooooo," the angel panted, the hatred on his face perfectly clear even without words.

"I think he doesn't like you very much, Robbie-boy. If your guest is so unhappy, why don't you just let me gather up his belongings and take him over to my place. Maybe being around some of his own people will make him a little more pleasant." I stepped toward a table against the other wall, one with a whip lying in the center of it.

"Maybe you shouldn't try to take things that aren't yours, wizard!" Rob snapped, extending a hand in my direction. Force hit me like a hurricane wind, lifting me off my feet and slamming me into the wall above the table. I crashed down, the cheap particleboard snapping under my weight like I was the star attraction at a pro wrestling show. I groaned and rolled over, picking up the whip as I struggled to my feet.

"Well, if you didn't want me to have the whip, I don't think throwing me on top of it was the best plan, pal." I shook my wrist, and the black braided leather unfurled across the floor. The whip was a dark, hungry thing that felt alive in my hand, like a sinister snake just waiting to lash out at something, and not too particular about its target. I raised my hand, snapped my arm forward, and with a flick of my wrist, the tip sliced through the air, breaking the sound barrier with a resounding *CRRRRACK*. The whip continued toward Rob's face but halted its flight in mid-air just inches from his cheek.

"That's not going to happen, Harker." He stretched out his right arm, palm up, and the whip's handle flew from my grasp to slap into his hand. He twirled his wrist, and almost before I could see him move, another *CRACK* rang through the room, and my face burst into flame as the braided leather cut a slash the entire length of my cheek.

I took a step back, blood streaming down my jawline to mix with all the other blood spilled on the room's stained floor. I saw his hand twitch this time and ducked, but that was no defense against the whip wrapping around my left ankle. I crashed to my back on the concrete, my head smacking the floor with a dizzying crunch. Pastor Rob just stood there grinning as he pulled me to him, coiling the whip as I skidded along on my ass.

I grabbed at the nearby table, but he yanked me free. I tried to reach my ankle, but he was on me before I could untangle myself. He reversed his grip on the handle and used it like a club, slamming the polished wood across my face two or three times before I collected myself enough to draw power and blast him off me. I blasted raw magic into his chest, and he flew back, slamming into the wall and collapsing into the table of torture tools. He got to his feet while I was still freeing myself from the whip, casting aside broken table chunks and various knives in all directions.

"That wasn't nice, Quincy. Can I call you Quincy?" he said, walking toward me, that predator's swagger again suffusing his every step.

"Can I call you fuckwit?" I shot back, drawing my Glock. I centered the front sight on his chest and squeezed off three quick shots. He was gone before the third pull of the trigger, moving faster than I could hope to see.

"That's not nice, Quincy," Pastor Asshole whispered in my ear before he snatched me up by the back of my collar like a naughty kitten. He held me up, my feet dangling in the air, for several seconds before hurling me to slam into the wall beside Uriel.

I slid to the ground, covered in a slick smear of commingled angel and human blood. "You wanna get your divine on and help a brother out?" I asked the ruined man. He looked down at me, bloody tears leaking from the corners of his lidless eyes. No help coming from that quarter.

I struggled to my feet and looked around for my pistol, then raised my head as Rob cleared his throat. "Looking for this?" he asked, twirling my gun around on his index finger. "Don't worry, you don't need this anymore." He put one hand on the grip, the other on the barrel, and bent the gun until it shattered and sent shards of plastic and metal all over the room.

Then he was on me again, right up in my face, slamming my back to the wall and shoving me up the vertical surface until my face was level with Uriel's. "Should I just hang you here, Quincy? Just leave you suspended by your wrists next to the angel you were trying to save?

Crucify you and let your lungs implode like that stupid carpenter you people rave about?"

"Or you could just give me the whip and the angel and crawl back to whatever rock you've been hiding under," I said, gritting my teeth to get the words out.

"Always the funny man, aren't you, Harker? You just always have to have a quip, no matter how fucking bleak the situation. Doesn't that get old after a while?"

"Not yet," I panted, reaching to my belt and drawing the knife there. "But if it does, I'll give you a call." Then I jabbed the knife into his gut. The demon dropped me and stepped back, yanking the knife free from his belly and glaring at me. He snatched the apron off and poked his finger through the hole in his shirt, glaring down at his belly as if it had offended him somehow. He pulled his finger out and held it up to his face. There wasn't a drop of blood on it. I hadn't even drawn blood, much less injured him.

"I *liked* this shirt," he spat, then charged me. He stepped slightly to one side and lifted his knee into my ribcage. I bent at the waist, and he used the same knee to shatter my nose. I stood up straight, and he grabbed me by the jaw, slamming my head against the wall once, twice, three times before I lost count. Drywall dust showered down over my face, mixing with the blood pouring from my nose to make a disgusting paste that coated my mouth and jaw.

"I" *slam* "liked" *slam* "this" *slam* "shirt!" he yelled into my face, then he jerked me free of the wall and tossed my limp body aside like yesterday's dirty underwear, tumbling bonelessly across the floor. The demon turned to me, hellfire blazing in his eyes now, and stalked me like a jungle cat, all lithe muscle and bad intentions.

"There aren't many things I really like, Harker. I like listening to the screams of innocents as they realize there is no hope for them and their pain will never really end. I like the smell of brimstone in the morning; it smells like freedom from tyranny. I like the taste of angel's blood on my face as it sprays from the soon-to-be dead flesh of my enemies. And I like a nice linen shirt, freshly pressed with a perfect crease in the sleeves. Do you understand how hard it is to get a perfect crease in linen? It doesn't want to crease, Harker, and that makes it very difficult. But if there's anything I ever learned from my no-good, shiftless, absentee judgmental cock of a father, it's that anything worth having is worth working hard to get. And now I don't have this very nice linen shirt with the perfect crease. That makes me angry, Harker. When I get angry, people get hurt." He turned his head from side to side. "Oh look, you're the only person in the room. I guess that means this is going to hurt."

He held out his hand, and the whip flew into it. He held it high for a few seconds, and it began to glow with the same crimson light that came from his eyes. "Oh yes, Quincy Harker, this is going to hurt. You know what Uriel's role was in the Host, don't you? He was God's Enforcer. He was in charge of meting out the punishment of the Almighty. And he used this whip to do it. The very same whip that I'm going to use to strip the flesh from your bones, one agonizing strip at a time. Right after I do...this."

Demon Rob spun on his heel and lashed out at Uriel with the whip. The leather lash wrapped around the imprisoned angel's neck three times, and Rob gave the handle a vicious yank. Uriel found some way to force a shriek through his shattered, tongue-less mouth as his wrists pulled from the wall, straight over the fat ends of the spikes still driven into the wall. Rob flicked his wrist, and the bound and bleeding angel skidded right to the demon's feet. Pastor Rob knelt down by Uriel's side and pressed a hand to his chest. For just a hint of a second, so brief I thought I imagined it, I saw regret flicker over the pastor's glowing red eyes, but it vanished in half a heartbeat.

"I'm sorry, brother. I'm not quite finished with you, but the sound of your bleeding and moaning is terribly distracting. And I'm sure you'll agree that Mr. Harker here deserves my undivided attention. So please, Uriel, brother dear, *SHUT UP.*" Then he slammed the angel's head into the concrete hard enough that I heard the skull crack from all the way across the room. The demon stood and turned to me. "Now that we won't be disturbed again, let's wrap up our business here so I can get on with killing everyone you've ever met."

He lashed out with the whip, and it shredded my shirt and carved a line of fire into my chest. I didn't even bother trying to be tough—I screamed. I screamed profanities that I haven't uttered in years, and when he whipped me again, I switched into languages I thought I'd forgotten. I tried to call up enough power to give myself a little bit of a shield, but he picked up the pace of his whipping and I couldn't concentrate enough to do anything but yell and curse. Again and again the whip fell, faster than any weapon like that should be capable of, but between the demon's inhuman speed and the whip's inherent magic, all the laws of physics were shattering on my back and chest today. I rolled over and over, seeking some tiny respite from the brutality he unleashed on me, but there was nothing forthcoming. Just more pain, more blood, and more screaming, until finally, when he decided that I'd been sufficiently flayed, he stopped.

I looked up at him from my position on the floor, curled up in a fetal position trying to keep as much of my flesh attached as I could manage. I watched his feet as he strutted over to me, that feline arrogance oozing from his every pore.

"I'm sorry, Quincy, I truly am. I had such high hopes for our relationship. But you see, I just can't tolerate subordinates speaking to me like you did. So, it seems we can't be friends. And that's all I have in this world—friends. My friends live long, fruitful lives full of riches and the finer things in life. Those who think to style themselves my enemies...well, they don't live long enough to style themselves as anything. Just like you won't."

Pastor Rob, the only sign that I'd even tried to fight him a tiny hole in his favorite shirt, knelt down beside me and put his left hand on my forehead. He pressed my skull against the concrete and started to push. I felt pain radiate out from the back of my head like a spiderweb, arcing out and around my head as he inexorably increased the pressure, slowly, steadily mashing my head until I was just seconds away from my head popping like a grape.

The demonic minister leaned down so that his face was just inches from my own, and said, "Goodbye, Quincy Harker. I promise that when I kill every friend you've ever had that I'll make them suffer just for knowing you." Then he smiled, and I knew in the pit of my soul that he meant every word. He drew in a deep breath, and I felt the muscles in his arm tense as he readied himself for the final thrust that would destroy me and, by extension, everyone I'd ever cared about.

Then I heard a muffled *crack*, and the pressure on my head disappeared. I saw boots with trim female legs in them stomp past my field of vision and heard a voice prettier than any chorus of angels. "Okay, you son of a gun, you have two choices...Nah, screw that, you don't get any choices. Time to die."

I rolled over enough to get a decent view of the action as a dark-skinned woman with very good timing slammed a very large hammer into Pastor Rob's chest. Another *crack* rang through the warehouse, and Rob staggered back. I managed to pull myself into a sitting position just as the glorious Rebecca Gail Flynn stepped up to Jo Henry's side, the Sword of the Archangel in her hand.

Becks, you can't bring that in here, I thought. *It'll get destroyed.*

Too late, idiot. I'm already here. And since I'm not an angel, I don't turn on its full power, so it looks like we're okay. Ignoring the other feelings coming across our mental link, mostly relief and concern, Becks turned to Rob and leveled the sword at him. "Go ahead, asshole. Give me an excuse."

"Oh, my dear detective," Demon Rob said with a grin. "You don't need an excuse. Just my being here is all the excuse you should need. But I can read a room. I know when I'm not wanted. After all, I am, as they say, a man of wealth and taste. Discernment is one of my many virtues." With that, the demonic preacher lashed out one last time with Uriel's whip, this time wrapping it around the legs of the dead angel. Then he held up his hand, drew a few symbols in the air in front of the wall, and perfectly round opening appeared in the air. He stepped through the portal between the planes, dragging Uriel's body with him. I looked through the glowing circle briefly and wished I hadn't. That portal led nowhere I'd ever been, but I've seen enough Francis Bacon paintings to recognize it. Pastor Rob had just opened a doorway to Hell and carried a dead Archangel through it.

I looked to Jo and Becks, who had managed to arrive just in time to keep my brains from becoming an omelet on the floor, and then everything that happened in the past few days, together with Rob's last words, all clicked in a horrifying conclusion. *A man of wealth and taste...fuck.* The terrifying realization was just too much, and my body, having sustained a decade's worth of abuse in the past ten minutes, decided that enough was fucking enough, and shut down.

My last thought as I slid into unconsciousness was that we were exceptionally fucked.

EPILOGUE

"Wait, *what?!?*" Becks tried to stand, but couldn't move, since I was currently lying with my head in her lap. My heavily bandaged head, which went well with my heavily bandaged everything else. I still hurt like a mother, but after I came to at the scene of my fight with Rob, I managed to summon up enough magic to heal myself a little. Sealtiel threw a little angelic mojo on me, too, once Flynn and Jo got me out of the warehouse. Then we all piled into two cars and hauled ass back to my place.

Now the whole gang, minus Luke, who was still sleeping, was gathered in the apartment we'd converted to a conference/war room. I was stretched out on one sofa with Becks; Jo and Mitch were on the other sofa with Cassie sitting beside them. Sealtiel and Gabriel sat in armchairs at the end of the sofas, and Dennis looked down at us from the LCD TV on the wall.

"So you're saying that Pastor Rob, the leader of the fastest-growing evangelical church in the Carolinas, is actually Lucifer?" the sparkling unicorn head said from the display.

"Unless you know anyone else that's likely to use *Sympathy for the Devil* as an exit line," I said.

"Nah, I got nothing. I also looked up his records, and there's nothing on Pastor Robert Stellam prior to his appearance in Charlotte twelve years ago."

"Stellam..." I mused.

"Star," Gabriel chimed in. He was in his angel mode, so it wasn't the full-on *non sequitur* of his human guise, but I still looked at him askance. "Stellam is Latin for star."

"The morning star," Jo said. "Son of a bitch." She flinched as her mother held out her hand. Jo reached in her pocket and handed Cassie a dollar for the swear jar. I just put a hundred-dollar bill in it every Monday. Saved time.

"He was flaunting it the whole time," I said, struggling to an upright position on the couch. "His name was Star, short for Morningstar. The church was called Lightbringers, another name for Lucifer."

"And he was so damn pretty, no way was he not dangerous," Flynn said.

I looked at her sideways, but Jo reached out and pounded fists with my girlfriend. If I were a lesser man, I'd have felt insecure. Although I guess since I was missing half the flesh on my torso, I probably *was* a lesser man, but I figured Luke could fix that with a few drops of vampire blood when he woke up.

"So, now what?" Jo asked. "I mean, we have three of the Archangels, but you said he killed Uriel. I mean, can that even...can y'all..." Her words trailed off as she looked at Mitch, Gabriel, and Sealtiel in turn.

"I don't know. I still only halfway believe I am what you guys say I am," Mitch said. "But Harker's paying my way, and I get to hit things, so I'm good for now."

"We cannot be truly destroyed," Gabriel said. "Our physical bodies can be destroyed, but our essence will simply return to Heaven and reconstitute."

"Just like demons," I said. The angels whipped their heads around to look at me, and I felt like I *really* needed to explain myself. "I mean, when the demons die, they just go back to Hell to rebuild. Is that what you do?"

"Exactly," Sealtiel said, putting a hand on the arm of a glowering Gabriel. I got the feeling that the arrogant angel didn't like me very much. I didn't mind. The feeling was mutual. Sealtiel went on. "We cannot be destroyed on this plane. We would simply return to Heaven and craft a new vessel for ourselves."

"But what about in Hell?" I asked. The angels looked at me, their eyes wide. "Rob, I mean Lucifer, he dragged Uriel through the portal to Hell with him."

"Was Uriel dead when he went through?" Sealtiel asked, leaning forward in her chair, her blond curls spilling across her shoulders.

"I don't know, but I don't think so," I said. "Rob said something about not being finished with him, then smashed his head into the concrete. Everything gets a little fuzzy after that because of the never-ending agony and all."

"That's a problem," Sealtiel said, leaning back in her chair.

"Indeed, sister," Gabriel agreed, folding his arms across his chest.

"Want to explain things to the humans in the room?" Jo asked.

"And the ones that don't really believe they aren't human?" Mitch added.

Sealtiel got up and started to pace. I've seen enough shit in my life that not many things worry me anymore, but when something has a no-shit Archangel freaked out enough to pace, I worry.

"Lucifer was the strongest of all of us. Even stronger than Michael, not that we mentioned that very often. Michael was a little sensitive," the beautiful angel said as she wore a path in the carpet. "When he was cast out, Father took his implement, the Star of the Morning, and destroyed it. The only way Lucifer could ever return to Heaven was if he somehow got his implement back."

"Or someone else's," I said. "Like Uriel's whip."

"Not quite, but close," Gabriel said, his tone making it clear that he was impressed that a lesser being like me even got that close to understanding something. I mentioned he was a douche, right? "Our implements are attuned to our divinity. As long as we live, no one else can effectively wield the implements to their full power."

"But if one of you dies, really dies…" Cassie said.

"Then any other divine creature can take up the implement and take the deceased angel's place in the Host," Gabriel said.

"Then we're fine," Dennis said. "Lucifer isn't divine. He's the devil. Problem solved!" The rainbow-maned unicorn did backflips on the TV.

"Not so much, Dennis," Becks said.

"What do you mean?" the unicorn looked perplexed.

"There's no real difference between the divine and the demonic," I said. "Lucifer is still an Archangel. He just fell from grace. So, he can use the whip."

"So, now he can get back to Heaven?" Dennis said.

"And without God on the throne, he might actually manage to take over this time," I said.

"Fuck," Dennis whispered, then his head snapped up. "Sorry, Cassandra. I'll put a dollar in Ginny's college fund, I swear." Cassie just nodded. None of us ever asked where Dennis got the money for the virtual swear jar. Some things, it was better not to know.

"So what do we do?" Mitch asked. "I mean, I might not know much about being an angel, but I know that Lucifer getting into Heaven doesn't sound good for anybody."

"We keep doing what we've been doing," I said. "We're going to need the entire Host behind us if we're going to face Lucifer head-on."

"Head on?" Flynn asked, looking at me.

"Yeah, Becks. Head on. We've got to find the rest of the Archangels and fast. Because we're going to have to take the fight to Lucifer, and that means going straight to Hell."

TO BE CONTINUED

IN SALVATION - QUEST FOR GLORY PART
2 - COMING IN 2018!

V

REDEMPTION SONG

BONUS QUINCY HARKER SHORT STORY

REDEMPTION SONG

A QUINCY HARKER HISTORY

Time stopped when the man first showed up in the Golden Grin Saloon. It was one of those between the raindrops moments, when everything fell silent for an instant, and everyone's attention landed on the same spot. Big Bob, the piano player who took an Ohlone arrow to the knee that ended his trapping days, finished one Stephen Foster tune and began leafing through a tattered Dan Rice songbook for another song to play. The man stood in the doorway, hat pulled down low over his eyes and a long leather duster hanging well past his knees. He looked like a man who had been rode hard and put away wet—thin almost to the point of gauntness, and so pale one could see the veins in the back of his hands if they let their eyes linger long enough, something not many were inclined to do.

He stood motionless, nothing about him even twitching except his eyes. Those chips of flint flickered back and forth across the room, taking in Leila and her dancing girls on the tiny stage in one corner near Bob, JR sitting at his faro table flipping cards and stacking chips, and Smilin' Bill behind the bar polishing a glass in his eternal battle against the grime of the street. The man held the gaze of every soul in the Grin for a long heartbeat, then he stepped forward, and with the jingle of his spur the spell was broken. Big Bob launched into an old minstrel tune that had the girls high-kicking, JR flipped over a Queen to top the bettor's nine and take his last chip, and Smilin' Bill set the glass down on the bar and poured a slug of whiskey into it.

The stranger put one foot onto the bar rail and leaned on the polished oak. Smiling' Bill gave him one of his trademarked grins, gold tooth sparkling on his lower jaw, and slid the whiskey into his hand. "First one's on the house, friend. You look thirsty," Bill said. "I'm Bill Evans, owner and proprietor of the Golden Grin Saloon, the finest drinking establishment for at least a hundred feet in any direction!" Bill laughed at his own joke, and a couple of the regulars at the bar joined him out of either manners or a hope for a free drink of their own.

"Thanks," the man said. He slammed back his whiskey and dropped a golden eagle to spin on the bar. "Another." His voice was more a rasp than speech, like the sound of two sheets of paper scraping across each other in the wind.

Bill poured another and slid two quarters across the wood. The man made a gesture to him, and Bill nodded his thanks as he slipped the four bits into his apron pocket. "Where you from, stranger?"

"East."

"Well, son, we're in San Francisco, 'bout everything's east of here!" Bill laughed, but not quite as loud as the first time. There was something a little off about this stranger. Something about the way he talked, or didn't talk, or maybe it was just those eyes, the way they never stopped moving. Either way, this fellow wasn't quite right somehow, and Bill hoped he wasn't planning on staying long.

Audrey Reese hadn't taken her eyes off the stranger since he appeared in the doorway. And that was the right word for it - *appeared.* No one heard his boot clomp up the steps. Not a hint of a spur jingling announced his coming. There was no creak of a swinging saloon door to herald his arrival. One minute the doorway was empty, the next he was standing there, alabaster skin looking like it was carved from marble, not flesh. His perfectly black pants and coat seemed to absorb all the light from around him, as if a young gunfighter like him could just step sideways into his own shadow and disappear.

Audrey shuddered on the lap of Rich Spence, her current beau and the man sitting behind the biggest pile of bills, coins and chips at the poker table in the far corner of the Double G, as the locals called it. *Goose walked over my grave,* Audrey thought as she tried to adjust her bustle so her movements wouldn't distract Rich.

"You okay, darling?" Rich asked. His voice rumbled deep in his chest, like distant thunder. She liked to lay against him when he talked, feeling that thunder peal across her face as he talked aimlessly in his deep voice. But now that voice had an edge to it, and Audrey looked down at her man. He caught her gaze and jerked his chin at the stranger by the bar. "You know him?"

"No, baby. He just . . . looked like somebody I used to know for a minute. But I don't know him at all." *Do I? He looks . . . But that can't be . . .*

"Maybe you need to go on over there and see what he looks like instead of squirming around on my lap like some little brat. I'm trying to work here." Now Rich's voice was hard, his words grating on one another like granite, and Audrey felt the fear blossom in her chest.

"No, Rich, baby. He's nobody. I'll just sit here and watch you take all these nice people's money." She flashed a smile at the two miners and one trapper that shared the table with Spence. The trapper had already lost most of his winter stake, and the miners were down to one small bag of gold dust between them. The bigger one, that Audrey had heard called Jeremiah, was fingering a stack of papers in his jacket pocket and she hoped against hope he wasn't about to wager his claim against Spence. Rich Spence was a good enough poker player to take most everything these men ever owned or ever would own without any help, but when he put Audrey to work distracting his opponents, he could cheat like an honest to God magician.

There was a flash of black in her vision, and when she looked up, the stranger was just *there.* She woulda sworn he hadn't walked across the saloon to stand in front of the table, one minute he was at the bar, leaning over a whiskey like a respectable human being, the next he was right in front of her, standing there with a handful of five-dollar gold coins.

"You got room for one more?" He asked, and that sandpaper voice crawled down Audrey's spine like a spider, sending another shiver through her.

Crack! Spence's palm slapped her on the butt, hard. "Woman, I told you to sit still or get gone. Now what's it going to be?"

Audrey shrank in on herself, becoming very small and still on Rich's lap. "I just want to sit here with you, Rich, baby. That's all. I'll be good, I promise."

Rich smiled, an oily grin that never reached his empty blue eyes. "You do that, honey, you be good and we won't have any problems. But you keep that tight little ass still or I'll have to teach you how to be still. Now you don't want any lessons tonight, do you, sweetheart?"

"No, Rich. I don't want any lessons, please. I'll sit still."

"Good." Rich turned his attention to the stranger, who stood motionless over the table, his hat obscuring his eyes and the upper part of his face form the table. "Now, stranger, you want to play some poker? I believe we might be able to accommodate you, what do you think, boys?" Rich unleashed a wide grin on the table that made him seem like the affable gambling buddy instead of the man who'd been cheating them out of their very livelihood for the past six hours.

The miners both nodded and scooted their chairs over, while the trapper stood up and said "You can have my seat, friend, but watch his hands when he deals." The trapper pushed past the stranger and headed for the door, his last few dollars clenched tight in his fist. The newcomer pulled Matthias' abandoned chair out from the table and sat, every motion smooth as glass, almost like he didn't have any bones in his body whatsoever.

"Matthias?" Spence called from his seat.

The trapper stopped. He slowly turned to face the gambler. "What, Spence?"

"Tip your hat to a lady when you leave the table, you mannerless cur." Spencer's voice was cold and low, but it cut through the bustle and music of the bar like the crack of a whip.

The man called Matthias stiffened at the insult, but he nodded to Audrey and tipped his coonskin cap. She gave him a polite nod, and Matthias turned to go.

"Matthias?" Spence called again.

Matthias turned to find Spence standing beside his chair, Audrey staggering back from being dumped off the man's lap. Spencer's coat was brushed back over his hip to show off the mother-of-pearl grips on his Peacemaker. Matthias looked down at the gun, and at Spence's hand dangling beside it.

"W-what you want now, Spence?" The trapper asked.

"It seems to me that you might have felt that I wasn't dealing fairly as we played cards. That hurts my feelings, Matthias, to think that you would accuse me of being a cheat. And to do so right here in the Grin, where I do most of my work. Why, that might be considered in some circles as downright insulting. And I don't appreciate being insulted."

"I didn't mean nothin' by it, Spence. I's just mad on account of I lost and now I got to go back up in the hills and git more pelts instead of spending some time with Miss Audrey's girls like I had planned to do this winter."

"But is that my fault, Matthias? Is it my fault you gambled with money you couldn't afford to lose? Is it my fault you aren't the poker player you thought you were? Is it my fault you are too stupid to quit while you are no flat damn broke?" The gambler had taken a step forward with every sentence until he was right on top of Matthias.

The trapper looked up at the tall man, his eyes darting about for an exit. "No, Spence, that ain't your fault!" His words tumbled out quickly, like a stream babbling over stones and skipping over syllables.

"Then why in the world would you call me a cheat?" Spence's hand rested on the butt of his forty-five.

Matthias looked around the bar as if for help, but all the other patrons were very studiously not looking at him or Spence. Just as he drew a breath and steeled himself to clear leather on the gambler, a voice came from the table.

"You gonna play cards or you gonna kill that man? Whatever it is, I wish you'd get on with it. I'm bored." The grating sound of the stranger's voice cut the silence like a bullet through flesh.

Spence cocked his head to one side and turned, very slowly, to face the stranger. His hand never left the butt of his gun. He looked at the stranger like a dog examining a bumblebee, trying to figure out where the noise was coming from. "Did you . . . say something, stranger?"

"I told you to get on with whatever you were about. I came here to play cards, not to watch a floor show. And if I'm going to watch a couple of jackasses dance around a saloon, I hope at least one of them has better tits than y'all."

Spence stared at the man, now seated at the table with a stack of gold coins in front of him. He stood there unmoving as a statue, eyes locked on the stranger's own grey orbs. Neither man blinked for a long time, then Spence threw back his head and laughed. It was a big laugh, that broke the room free of its stillness. "God-*dammit* that is the funniest thing I've heard in a coon's age! Bill, you grinnin' idiot, bring us another bottle! We got a *gambler* in the house tonight!" He stomped back over to his seat at the table, swept his coat over the back of the chair with a flourish that both drew attention to his fine clothes and let him keep his gun swinging free, and sat down.

"Matthias!" Spence called, patting his knee for Audrey to sit.

The trapper turned. He was almost at the door and hadn't looked back since the stranger spoke. "Y-yeah, Spence?"

"You watch your goddamn mouth next time. You ever call me a cheat again and I'll shoot you right here at my poker table."

The trapper nodded, turned, and half stumbled, half ran out the swinging doors. Spence turned his attention to the new arrival.

"Well, howdy, stranger." Spence stuck out a hand. The pale man just stared at it and after a long moment Spence dropped his arm. "My name's Spence. Richard Spence. You got a name?"

"Yup."

"You care to share it with the table?"

"Let's play cards."

"Well, I like that!" Spence said, slapping his leg. "Come on over here, Audrey. Don't you like a man who gets right down to business?"

"I do, Rich. I like that." Audrey sat down on his leg, but her eyes never left the newcomer. She couldn't see his eyes under the wide brim of his black hat, but she thought that she could feel his gaze on her, measuring, judging somehow and finding her wanting. She didn't enjoy that feeling, that sense of not being quite good enough for this smooth-walking stranger with the gravelly voice, but she wasn't quite sure why it bothered her so.

"Let's play cards, he says." Rich grinned as he reached for the deck. "Let's play cards indeed."

The pale man's hand flashed out, quick as a blink, and he snatched the deck out from under Rich's grasp. "She deals," he said, never looking up.

"You don't trust my dealing, stranger?" Rich glared at him.

"I don't trust anybody," the man replied. "She deals, and she sits there." He pointed to a chair exactly between himself and Spence, a chair currently occupied by the smaller of the two miners, a man called Morris who fidgeted like his chair had bugs, or he did.

"Morris is sitting there," Spence said.

"Morris has lost enough for one night," the man said. "Right, Morris?"

Morris looked from Spence to the new man and back again. Audrey could almost see the moment when he decided his money had a better use somewhere else. He gathered up his last few gold nuggets and a couple of loose coins and shuffled off over to the bar, where he ordered a whiskey in a shaky voice and very quickly commenced to forgetting all about the pale man in the back corner.

Spence turned his attention to Jeremiah, the last remaining gambler from his original game. "What about you, Jer? You decided I've taken enough of your money for one night, or you gonna throw down the deed to that claim you been fiddling with for the last half hour?"

Jeremiah opened his mouth, but a ten-dollar golden eagle flew across the table and spun down in front of him. "Jeremiah is going to join his friend at the bar and drink until he's blind while we get down to business. Isn't he, Jeremiah?"

Jeremiah glared at the stranger and opened his mouth to speak, but then he caught sight of the man's eyes. The big miner blanched pale and grabbed the coin, along with three nuggets and a depleted sack of gold dust. He stood up, shoved his gold in his pockets, and tipped his hat to Audrey. "I think it's about time for a drink. You two have fun." He turned and headed over to the bar. Smilin' Bill set a shot glass down in front of him and filled it to the rim with amber liquid. After the fourth shot Jeremiah stopped seeing the pale man's eyes.

"Now we got that all settled, we can play cards." The pale man said.

"You ran all the easy money off the table, mister. How do you plan on making a profit now?" Spence grinned around a cigarette.

"Since you done took everything they got, I figure now I'll just take everything you got." A slow smile crept across the man's face as he slid the deck across the felt to Audrey.

"Stud poker, nothing wild. How's that grab you?" Spence asked, tossing a dollar coin into the center of the table. "Ante's a dollar."

The pale man didn't speak, just nodded to Audrey and tossed a dollar to clink against Spence's. Audrey dealt a card to each man face-down. Spence peeled up the corner to see his card, the ten of clubs. He looked across the table at the stranger, but there was nothing to see. The man gave nothing away, no hint of whether he had an ace or a three. Audrey dealt the first face-up card, a Jack of spades to Spence and an eight of diamonds to the stranger.

"Jack bets," Audrey said, with the calm manner of a woman who has sat at many card tables.

Spence threw out a dollar. "Just a dollar," he said. A little feeler bet, to see if the old boy liked his cards or was going to be pushed around. The stranger barely took time to breathe before he tossed a dollar back out, calling the bet.

Audrey dealt out the next card, a nine of spades to Spence and a five of hearts to the stranger. "Jack is still high," she said, motioning for Spence to bet or check. He tapped the table, indicating he checked. The stranger checked behind, giving nothing away. Spence cheer the inside of his lip a little—this one wasn't going to make it easy on him.

The fourth card came down, a ten of spades for Spence to show a possible straight and possible flush but really giving him a pair of tens.

"Jack bets," Audrey said, motioning to Spence, who already had money in his outstretched hand.

"Five dollars," he said, dropping the coins onto the table one at a time with a *clink*.

"Call," said the other man, tossing a single coin into the pile. Spence studied his opponent but still saw nothing. He nodded to Audrey, who dealt the last card face up. Spence showed the Queen of spades, filling the flush if he had a buried spade, filling the straight if he had a King or an eight underneath, but leaving him with just a pair of tens. The stranger caught a five to pair his board, and the action went to the high hand.

"Pair of fives bets," Audrey said, motioning to the newcomer.

The pale man tossed out another five-dollar coin, and Spence looked hard at him.

Spence stared at his unmoving opponent. What was he holding? There were a lot of hands that beat him here. A five in the hole made trips, but would he have stayed on every street fishing for trips? Did he catch two pair on the river to sink him? What did he have under there, and was it worth a call to find out? Spence's head went back to something his Granddaddy told him when he was a little boy learning the game at his knee. "The worst thing you can ever do, tadpole, is call a bet. You want to play poker, you bet or you raise. But men don't ever call."

Spence grabbed up five five-dollar coins and shoved them forward. "Gone cost you more than that to bluff me, stranger," Spence said with a grin as he leaned back in his chair.

"I never bluff," the stranger said as he slid four golden coins into the center of the table. He turned over a five of spades for trips and leaned forward, looking dead at Spence.

Spence took his cards, turned them all facedown, and flung them over to Audrey. "You got it, stranger. Good hand." He tapped the table in a show of respect and anted up a dollar for a new hand. The stranger raked in the pot and slid a dollar into the middle, then flung a dollar to Audrey.

"That's for you, dealer," he said, with one corner of his mouth tweaking up just a hair. Audrey caught the dollar in midair and slid it into the purse on her hip. She smiled and nodded at the stranger, then dealt the cards. The men played poker for hours, neither gaining a significant advantage over the other. Some hands the stranger would come out ahead, some hands Spence would find himself raking in double handfuls of golden dollars. They had long since foregone using chips to keep track of their bets, preferring the jingle of real currency and the pain of real loss on their opponent's face.

The sun was peeking over the low horizon when Smilin' Bill wandered over to the table. "You boys going to finish up anytime soon? I'm thinking I might shut her down for a few hours before we have to go again tonight."

"Bill Evans if you don't get away from this table right this second I swear to God I will shoot you in the face," Spence growled. "Can't you see we got us a pot here?" There was indeed a sizable pot building, and quite the run of cards. Spence had a three, four and a five showing, with a deuce in the hole for an open-ended straight draw. The stranger had three spades up, with one of them the King for a high flush draw. The bet was on Spence, and his once-mighty stack of coins and bills had dwindled over the course of the night until he as sitting behind less than a hundred dollars in cash and the small sack of gold he took off Jeremiah so many hours before.

"I reckon I'm gonna bet it all, stranger," Spence said as he shoved the rest of his money and gold into the middle of the table.

Audrey took a minute to count it all out. "One hundred six dollars and three ounces of gold, comes to one hundred sixty-six dollars."

The stranger stacked his coins and slid them into the middle of the table. "That's one hundred fifty dollars," he said. Then he twisted the wedding band off his pale left hand and placed it atop the tallest stack of coins. "There's almost an ounce of gold in that ring, so if you'll agree, we can call that even."

Spence looked at the pile of coins and gold in the middle of the table, more money than he'd ever seen at one time, and nodded at the stranger. "That'll be good, partner. Audrey, deal the river."

Audrey flipped over the last card for each man and slid it to him. Spence's card was the Ace of spades, making his straight. The stranger's card was also a spade, this one an eight for a flush if he had a spade buried.

"Well, friend, it seems like this was not your lucky night," Spence said, flipping over his deuce to show the five-high straight.

"I reckon it wasn't at that, but it wasn't yours, either," the stranger said as he turned over his hole card. Spence's eyes went big and he flew out of his chair as he saw the card, the Ace of spades.

"What the hell is going on here, son?" Spence shouted. "How long you been cheating me?" He pointed to the table, where two Aces of spades lay next to each other.

"I ain't never cheated you, Richard Spence. Not like you've done so many men for so many years, but I ain't cheated you. I ain't the one dealin' the cards." He picked up the deck of cards and flipped them over one at a time. Ace, Ace, Ace, every card was an Ace of Spades. Every card was Death.

Spence turned to Audrey, who was on her feet and backing up. "What is this, Audrey? Is this some kinda trick? Who is this man? What are you playing at?"

"I swear I don't know, Spence! I ain't never seen him before..." Her voice trailed off as her own eyes went wide and all the blood drained from her face. She stood, staring at the stranger, who was on his feet and for the first time since he walked into the bar, not wearing his hat. His cold blue eyes were set deep in his brow, and his dark hair was cropped close to his head. But it was the scar that ran through his left eyebrow that held Audrey's eyes. The scar he got when...

"Ashley?" She whispered.

"It's me, darling," the stranger rasped.

"But they killed you," She said, her voice quavering.

"I got better," he replied. "You know me now, Richard Spence? You recognize the scar you gave me when you shot me? You recognize the man you cheated at cards, then murdered him and forced his wife to run with you and steal from these poor dumb bastards all over California?" He ran his fingers along the puckered line of flesh that crept through one eyebrow and arced back over his head to disappear into his hairline.

"What do you want?" Spence asked, his hand brushing the handle of his pistol. "I killed you once, you son of a bitch, I can do it again."

"This ain't about you, Spence. You can go to hell for all I care. I'm here for Audrey. It's time to go, darling."

"She don't go anywhere without me, and you don't go anywhere with my money, you cheating bastard!" Spence's hand dropped to his gun, but he staggered backward before it ever cleared leather. The stranger drew and fanned the hammer twice quicker than lightning, and red bloomed across Spence's vest. He collapsed into the chair behind him, and stared up at the newcomer with dying eyes.

"Ashley!" Audrey ran to the pale man, who staggered as she wrapped her arms around him. "Are you all right?"

"I'm fine, honey, but you have to go now."

"What do you mean, go?" Audrey bit her lower lip and her jaw quivered a little. "Can't I stay here with you?"

"No, darling, because I'm not staying. Spence is gone, and this place is going soon. We have to go. Do you trust me?" His voice lost some of the rasp and when Audrey looked up into his eyes he was almost the man she married again.

"I trust you," she said, her eyes brimming with tears. "I'm so sorry, Ashley. I never...he tried to make me, but I wouldn't...I only ever loved you."

"And I only loved you, darling. Now go." He closed his eyes, placed a hand on her head, raised the other to heaven and chanted "On behalf of this woman, who cannot speak, I beseech you clear her passage into heaven and allow her to ascend to sit beside her husband Ashley, who has waited patiently for many years. Glory, if you're listening, please cut the red tape for this one. She's a good lady and deserves a little help." His hand flared with white light, and when he opened his eyes again, Audrey was gone.

The pale man turned to Spence, who lay bleeding out in the chair.

Spence looked up at him and laughed. "You ain't Ashley Reese. I killed that poor bastard."

"You're right, I'm not. I'm just a man who put on his wedding ring to do a job. And now his wife's spirit is free. And you? You can go to hell." With those words, the man's right hand flared with a red glow and power streaked from him. Crimson energy flooded the room, and Spence was gone. The pale man looked around, nodded to Smilin' Bill, and walked out the swinging doors into the sunrise.

"Y ou okay, Harker?" The words jolted me the rest of the way back to my time, my reality, and my crappy little kitchen. The taste of the desert was still in my mouth, and the Charlotte humidity made it suddenly hard to breathe.

I jerked my hands off the table, and stared at the woman across from me. She was pretty, but not my type. I prefer them a little more broken, and with less baggage than me. Cassidy Kincaide missed on both fronts. Besides, she hung out with some unsavory characters. But she was cute, though...

Perv, came the accusatory thought from somewhere outside my head. I rolled my eyes and told Detective Rebecca Gail Flynn, member of Charlotte's police department and sometimes hitchhiker in my head, so screw off. I blinked a couple times to get the last of the Old West out of my eyes, or my Sight at least, and pointed toward the fridge. Cassidy, a brilliant and talented woman, or at least a woman who'd spent more than five minutes with me, understood my universal signal for "beer" and grabbed a couple of Sam Adams seasonal out of the door. She popped the top on the edge of my counter, guaranteeing me another lecture from Ren when he came over to make sure I had food and toilet paper later, then she handed one beer to me and sat down across the table.

"How did it go?" She asked.

"I managed it. It wasn't easy, but I got it done. They're clean." I waved my hand at my scarred Formica kitchen table, where an antique Colt Peacemaker and a wedding band rested on a velvet cloth. "How did you know they were haunted?"

"I don't know that they were, until recently." Cassidy replied. I cocked an eyebrow at her and she laughed and went on. "I've had that wedding band for years, and it never showed any signs of any possession or even a particularly interesting history. Until recently."

"When the gun came in," I supplied.

"Exactly. Once the two pieces came in proximity to each other, strange things started happening."

"Makes sense," I said. "The woman tied to that ring had a serious hate on for the man who carried that gun. He murdered her husband and basically made her his slave until she caught him with his guard down one night and killed him in his bed."

"That sounds pretty justified to me," Cassidy said.

"Me too, but her ghost didn't see it that way. She felt like she'd betrayed her husband somehow, and only he could forgive her."

"So how did you get her to move on?"

"I forgave her."

"But you weren't her husband. Or were you?" Cassidy asked.

"I'm not that old, Kincaide. So no, I was never her husband. But she didn't know that." I drained half my beer in one long swallow, trying to get my voice back to normal.

"So you lied to her." I didn't have to look at her face to see the disapproval I knew was there. I just stayed focused on my beer. I'm used to disapproving looks from women, regardless of species.

"I lied to her, and now she's at peace. For me, that's worth it."

"I guess so. Anyway, thanks for this, I appreciate it. " She gathered up the ring and the gun and put them into an oversize purse.

"No worries," I said, draining the last of my beer before I walked her to the door. "And Cassidy?" I asked as I opened the door.

"Yeah, Q?" She stopped at the top step and turned around.

"Tell that vampire buddy of yours he owes me one."

KEEP IN TOUCH

If you want to stay up to date with all my latest escapades and appearances, go to -

http://www.subscribepage.com/g8d0a9 and join my newsletter & get a free short story!

ACKNOWLEDGMENTS

Thanks as always to Melissa Gilbert for all her help, and for trying in vain to teach me where the commas go.

Many thanks to the amazing Natania Barron for this cover. You should go buy her books, they're badass.

The following people help me bring this work to you by their Patreon-age. You can join them at Patreon.com/johnhartness.

Sean Fitzpatrick
Noah Sturdevant
Mark Ferber
Andy Bartalone
Nick Esslinger
Sharon Moore
Sarah Ashburn
Wendy Taylor
Sheelagh Semper
Charlotte Babb
Andreas Brücher
Butch Howard
Wendy Kitchens

Andrew Bolyard
Darrell Grizzle
Larry Nash
Delia Houghland
Douglas Park, Jr.
Travis & Casey Schilling
Michelle E. Botwinick
Carol Baker
Leonard Rosenthol
Lisa Hodges
Patrick Dugan
Noella Handley
Leia Powell
Melissa Cole
Bob Dobkin
Robin Castellanos
Vickie DiSanto
Jared Pierce
Jeremy Snyder
Candice Carpenter
Theresa Glover
Salem Macknee
Trey Alexander
Brian Tate
Jim Ryan
D.R. Perry
Andrea Judy
Anthony Hudson
John A. McColley
Mark Wilson
Dennis Bolton
Shiloh Walker & J.C. Daniels
Andrew Torn
Sue Lambert
Emilia Agrafojo

Tracy Syrstad
Russell Ventimeglia
Elizabeth Donald
Samantha Dunaway Bryant
Shael Hawman
Steven R. Yanacsek
Scott Furman
Rebecca Ledford
Ray Spitz
Lars Klander

FALSTAFF BOOKS

**Want to know what's new & coming soon from
Falstaff Books?**

**Join our Newsletter List
& Get this Free Ebook Sampler
with work from:
John G. Hartness
A.G. Carpenter
Bobby Nash
Emily Lavin Leverett
Jaym Gates
Darin Kennedy
Natania Barron
Edmund R. Schubert
& More!**

http://www.subscribepage.com/q0j0p3

ABOUT THE AUTHOR

John G. Hartness is a teller of tales, a righter of wrong, defender of ladies' virtues, and some people call him Maurice, for he speaks of the pompatus of love. He is also the best-selling author of EPIC-Award-winning series *The Black Knight Chronicles* from Bell Bridge Books, a comedic urban fantasy series that answers the eternal question "Why aren't there more fat vampires?" In July of 2016. John was honored with the Manly Wade Wellman Award by the NC Speculative Fiction Foundation for Best Novel by a North Carolina writer in 2015 for the first Quincy Harker novella, *Raising Hell.*

In 2016, John teamed up with a pair of other publishing industry ne'er-do-wells and founded Falstaff Books, a publishing company dedicated to pushing the boundaries of literature and entertainment.

In his copious free time John enjoys long walks on the beach, rescuing kittens from trees and getting caught in the rain. An avid *Magic: the Gathering* player, John is strong in his nerd-fu and has sometimes been referred to as "the Kevin Smith of Charlotte, NC." And not just for his girth.

Find out more about John online
www.johnhartness.com

ALSO BY JOHN G. HARTNESS

The Black Knight Chronicles - Omnibus Edition

Paint it Black

In the Still of the Knight

Man in Black

Scattered, Smothered, & Chunked - Bubba the Monster Hunter Season One

Grits, Guns, & Glory - Bubba Season Two

Wine, Women, & Song - Bubba Season Three

Year One: A Quincy Harker, Demon Hunter Collection

The Cambion Cycle - Quincy Harker, Year Two

Fireheart

Amazing Grace: A Dead Old Ladies Detective Agency Mystery

From the Stone

The Chosen

Made in the USA
Middletown, DE
14 September 2020

19601978R00255